ARMY OF GOD

I0690199

DENNIS BAILEY

ARMY OF GOD By Dennis Bailey

ISBN: 978-0-692-14687-3

Copyright © 2017 by Dennis Bailey
Cover design by Darko Tomic
Interior design by Donato Toledo Jr.

Available in print and ebook from your local bookstore, online, or from the author at: www.dennisbaileyauthor.com

For more information on this book and the author, visit:
http://www.dennisbaileyauthor.com/

Library of Congress Cataloging-in-Publication Data
Bailey, Dennis
Army of God / Dennis Bailey

Printed in the United States of America

To Yahweh,

Who gave us His story, so I could tell mine.

GLOSSARY

Biblical and Talmudic units of measurement used in *Army of God*.

Measurements of Length

Finger	=	.75 inches
Handbreadth	=	3 inches
Span	=	9 inches
Cubit	=	18 inches
Furlong	=	220 yards

Measurements of Time

1 part	=	3.3 seconds
18 parts	=	1 minute
1080 parts	=	1 hour

PROLOGUE

"There it is!" Malluch pointed to an area of lush vegetation below, while inside, his heart pounded like a stallion in full gallop. Beside him, his longtime friend, Shechem, lifted off the saddle, craning his neck for a better look.

To the west, the Eden river exited the far side of the garden and stretched out in a four-fingered hand to form the great riverheads. He estimated the garden at about forty acres square, with the tributary running diagonally through the middle from southeast to northwest. At the center of the garden, in a clearing near the water's edge, two trees grew apart from the others. According to legend, to eat of the fruit of one of these trees meant eternal life.

Two furlongs separated Malluch and his companions, gathered on a sultry morning atop a Mesopotamian hill, from their prize. Malluch, along with his father, brother, and friend, led a party of twenty-five men from Eden. They were joined by another twenty-five from the far eastern city of Enoch.

But Shechem, wearing a sand-colored tunic and newly fashion sandals, appeared disinterested in the trees, gesturing instead to something in the foreground. "What about him?"

A man dressed all in white stood at the east end of the garden guarding the path leading from the entrance to the clearing. A gold band girded his chest, and the blade of a long sword extended from his grip.

A flaming sword.

Malluch's thick, wiry eyebrows dropped, and he scratched his short growth of beard. He drove his donkey to the edge of the hill, scanned the area below, and returned. "We'll stick with the diversion. But there are fifty of us. Against those odds, I wouldn't care if he had a sword of lightning. Everyone ready?"

Shechem and the others nodded, only to be distracted by the approach of a company of men on donkeys and camels riding up the rise behind them. In the lead, a man whose snow-streaked hair and mid-length beard Malluch recognized. He met Noah and twenty-one of the elders of Eden when they reached the summit. "You're a long way from the city, Preacher. Nobody for you to lecture out here."

"I have a message for the men of Eden from my father, the governor."

"Then by all means, deliver it and go."

"Lamech has learned of your scheme to pillage the garden and has sent with me the elders to turn back their sons from this evil."

He laughed. "Are these men not of age? Are they not free to make their own choices?"

The Preacher appeared to scan the faces of the men opposite him. "Age is no substitute for wisdom. And choosing to die is never a wise choice."

"We did not come here to die."

"No, you came here to steal."

Malluch narrowed his eyes.

"But you will die, all the same, if you continue upon this course."

"No Preacher. Each of these men will inherit the gift of immortality once they've tasted of the fruit of the tree of life." Excited murmurs rose from among his men.

"Do you not even fear God, seeing it was He who placed the angel to guard the entrance to the garden?"

VIII

"I don't believe in God or angels. What I see down there is a man. And a man, even a man with a sword of fire, can be defeated—or outwitted."

"Enough." One of the elders called his son's name and ordered him to leave the raiders. One by one, the remaining patriarchs called out their sons, and one by one they joined their fathers.

Malluch's jaw tightened.

When one son failed to move quickly enough, his father rode up beside him and kicked his mount in the right gaskin. The donkey bucked, unseating its rider, leaving his adult son sprawled in the dirt. The son got to his feet and staggered a few paces before joining his father. After this, the remaining sons of Eden were swift to comply with their fathers' orders.

By the time the parade of traitors finished cowering to their fathers, Malluch's anger had switched to contempt. He sneered at them. "Well, I guess I should thank you, Preacher. Thank you for helping to separate the wheat from the chaff. But the rest of these men are from Enoch. How shall you persuade them?"

"With the truth, I hope. Do they know you have brought them on a quest from which they may not return?"

He straightened in the saddle, lifting his chin. "I doubt that."

"Men of Enoch. I urge you in the name of YAH not to embark upon this path. It is folly to test an angel of God."

Some of the men whispered among themselves, but Malluch quickly intervened to reinforce their backbones, his voice rising. "There are still nearly thirty of us."

"Thirty or three hundred thirty. Would God have placed the man there alone were he not able to defend himself against an army?"

Shechem's face grew pallid, beads of sweat formed above his top lip.

"Remember the plan," Malluch said. "Angel, man, or demon, he can't be in two places at once."

Malluch's father raised his arm. "My son is right, men. The Preacher's just trying to frighten you with superstitious fables. That creature's no match for us."

The Preacher, seeming to recognize Shechem's fear, focused his gaze directly on him. "You all will be destroyed."

Malluch stepped between them. "You said that."

"Then let me say it another way. Should you succeed in reaching the tree of life, you may or may not obtain a chance at immortality. No one knows for certain. Greater is the certainty you will likely all perish in the attempt. Go back. Return to your homes to enjoy the lives you've been given."

"If it's the sight of blood that bothers you, no one's asking you to stay and watch." The mood among the Enochites lightened, some even snickering. He crossed his arms across an expanded chest. "Thanks for the admonition, Preacher. Now take it, and these cowards, back with you to Eden."

The Preacher shook his head as he, the elders, and their sons turned their mounts and headed east.

* * *

Shortly after the sun moved past its zenith, Malluch slipped into the water with Shechem and three Enochites 220 cubits east of the river access to the garden. They intended to remain low in the water, allowing the river bank and surrounding terrain to conceal them from the angel's line of sight.

To their south, near the terrestrial entry, his father, brother, and the other members of the raiding party had organized a distraction. Close enough to draw the angel's attention, but not so close as to trigger an attack. By the time the swimmers reached within fifty cubits of the entrance, the faint sound of musical instruments and singing voices told him all was proceeding according to plan.

Ten cubits past the edge of the garden, he stopped in the water and faced his companions. "Hear that?" The swimmers treading and the ambient sounds of nature around them provided the only noise discernible.

"What?" Shechem leaned in.

"The music. It stopped."

Violent yelling, followed by loud cursing and horrific screaming coming from the south drove the men out of the river. Malluch's co-conspirators looked to him for direction. "Go." He pointed to the water. "Stick to the plan. Get to the tree." He and his friend scurried up the bank of the river toward the sound of the commotion, leaving the men from Enoch to continue upstream.

They ran past the entrance and continued south. Just ahead, the angel clashed swords with three other figures while twenty-one bodies, charred black, lay smoldering on the ground around them. The two men froze in horror. The angel deflected a thrust from the last Enochite, tapping him on the arm with the fiery sword and completely engulfing him in flames. The man screamed and fell to the ground, writhing in agony. Shechem gasped.

Fending off another blow, the angel touched Malluch's brother on the side with the point of the blade, incinerating him. Malluch felt the blood drain from his head, and he reached for his sword. But his hand fell on an empty sheath, his weapon lost in their haste to get out of the river. Instead, he bent to pick one up from among the charred bodies, only to drop it when the steaming handle seared his palm and fingers. He cried out his brother's name.

Enraged, Malluch's father lifted his sword above his head with both arms and charged the angel while blaspheming the name of the Lord.

"Father. No."

But it was too late.

The two blades clanged, and fire from the angel's sword crossed over to his father's. He attempted to drop the sword, but the flame jumped the handle igniting his arm and covering his body.

"Father!" Malluch searched frantically for another weapon. Unable to find one, he charged the angel.

Shechem tackled him, and the two wrestled among the smoking corpses before his friend subdued him in an arm lock. "They're dead. And there's nothing you can do — except to die with them."

"Shechem, as my friend, I'm begging you. Let me go now." He struggled violently once more to try to free himself from the hold.

"The angel is gone." Shechem helped him to his feet. "And I don't mean he just ran away. He vanished." The two brushed the soot from their clothes. They pivoted to the sound of more high-pitched screams coming from the northwest. "The three Enochites." He hurried to the diversion point and returned with two donkeys. "Let's get out of here before he comes back."

The bodies of Malluch's father and brother lay at his feet. "I can't leave them like this."

His companion grabbed and shook him. "We're unarmed. And that thing just wiped out our whole party. The angel and the tree will still be there. But we need to leave."

Malluch looked behind him at the bodies, eyes tearing.

"Now."

The two climbed the rise with the screams of agonized men still fresh in their ears. Nearing the top, Shechem glanced over his shoulder. "I wonder if they ever made it to the tree."

"What difference does it make?" Malluch said. "They're dead now." He swore and muttered a threat against the Preacher under his breath.

"What did you say?"

"Nothing."

Chapter 1

Noah had managed to live 499 years without giving much thought to his own mortality. But as he searched the faces of the crowd just ahead, he calculated his chances of being stoned to death by day's end were pretty good.

Raucous voices dropped to a whisper when he entered the city gate. Two hundred of his countrymen gathered at midday to meet the trade caravans returning from the east.

"With what words do you seek to reproach us today, Preacher?" came a loud voice from the far end of the crowd that silenced the murmurs.

All eyes turned to Malluch, a person of medium height clothed in a dark gray robe, a man Noah knew intimately. Twenty years earlier, he'd lost his father and brother at the Garden of Eden. Since then, he'd become the leader of a group of men intent on deposing the city's governorship. He was flanked by his two lieutenants, Shechem and Bohar.

Clean-shaven, with lightly salted acorn hair, Shechem stood a bit taller than Malluch. He presented a stark contrast to the slovenly appearance of Bohar standing next to him, whose outer garment was so filthy it masked its true color. His oily hair and scraggly

1

beard added to the look of a man indifferent to the importance of personal hygiene.

Most kept their distance from Bohar and deliberately maneuvered to stake positions upwind of him. Others simply wrinkled their noses or twisted their faces.

Noah moved toward the trio, and the crowd gave way. Behind them, twenty-four donkey- and camel-drawn carts loaded with goods from Enoch filled one corner of the square. Men from the crowd hurried to help forty young women dressed in silk disembark the last four carts.

As Noah approached, the foul stench of a body that hadn't been washed in countless days assaulted his senses. Malluch anchored his hands on his hips. "Well, Preach—" but Noah brushed past him to the carts and a woman wearing a gold scarf.

She lowered her head, but he lifted her chin to meet his gaze. "Daughter, why do you journey so far?"

"My Lord, there are many women in Enoch and not so many men. They said we might find husbands in Eden."

Despite her attire, up close she appeared much younger than he first suspected, perhaps fourteen. Her green irises sparkled like emeralds through which starlight had passed. Not wishing to embarrass her, and with all the concern of a father, he reached to lift her scarf. "And why do you cover such beauty with jewels and silken robes? Do all the women of Enoch hide themselves in this way?"

In the manner of a child awaiting an expected gift, the woman's face beamed. "We were told the men of Eden have a great appreciation for women with finely braided hair and luxurious dress. Is this not so?"

The truth lodged in his throat, one befallen by hundreds before her. The girl had not been brought here to find a husband, but to become the paid object of men's lusts. And to put money into the pockets of her procurers. Shame for his countrymen besieged him, surpassed only by grief at the prospect of the girl's lost innocence.

"Perhaps for some." He dropped her scarf, smiled, and returned to where Malluch and his men held court.

Facing the assembly, Noah assumed a position that allowed him to keep an eye on the challenger and his men. "Sons of Seth, take heed to the words of my mouth. For I do not come to you today with a reproach but with a prophecy. Beware the descendants of Cain." This drew murmurs from some in the crowd. "Have we not lived in this land of our fathers for more than 1500 years in peace and prosperity according to the richness of the blessings of YAH? Has not this soil brought forth sufficient food to nourish? Or has there been even a single year when your flocks and herds have not seen increase? Why then is it the desire of your heart to travel to Enoch where the descendants of Cain continue his murderous legacy?"

Others in the gathering hunched over or turned away.

"Is it that you seek to forsake the birthright secured for you by your ancestors and exchange it for one under a curse?" He gestured to the carts. "Have you not been warned numerous times of the dangers of dealing with the Enochites? Yet you barter and trade with them. You give your daughters as wives and accept their sons as husbands, so that the righteous seed is mixed with the unrighteous."

Malluch laughed. "You cling too tightly to the traditions of the fathers, Preacher. Are we to remain farmers while the rest of the world prospers? Many cities trade with Enoch. Are we not destined to till the same ground as those descendants of Cain you speak of? Why should we not reap the same rewards?"

Several men in the crowd cried out their agreement.

Noah raised a finger toward him. "You would do well to heed those traditions, Malluch."

"Why? Our fathers toiled in the sun all their lives and had nothing to show for it except broken backs and gnarled hands." He walked to one of the carts and reached in. "But in Enoch, there are incomparable riches and wonders to delight the senses." He raised his arm holding a large wineskin. "Acres of vineyards to produce the world's finest wines."

This drew cheers from some of the crowd. He placed the wineskin back in the cart and moved to another, pulling out a bronze sword. "Artisans, who beat and temper hot iron and bronze into the finest tools and weapons."

He returned the sword and continued his litany. "Musicians, who play the harp and the flute to the dancing of the world's most beautiful women."

More cheers and clapping erupted.

Noah approached him and took from the cart the sword brandished by his rival. He scanned the weapon. "Malluch, you boast of the prowess of the metal artisans of Enoch, and indeed, you boast rightly, for their skill in fashioning with the hammer is without equal. And it cannot be denied their weapons are of the highest caliber. But for what purpose are they crafted? So the men of Enoch can arm themselves for an attack on their neighbors? Was it not the Enochites who carried out a raid just last year on one of the northern villages?"

"I heard that was no raid, but retribution for a wrong committed by one of the villagers against a Lord of Enoch," Shechem said.

Noah slammed the sword back into the cart. "And what wrong committed by one man against another could justify the destruction of an entire village?"

By now, some in the crowd fidgeted as if being bitten by fleas. Others gathered their supplies and left the square. Bohar signaled to his cohorts, who furtively reached to the ground for stones. He backed into the crowd and circled outside of Noah's view.

"Were you there?' Malluch said. "Did you see what happened?"

Noah moved forward but remained silent.

"These seven generations, you and our fathers have taught us to fear a God who hasn't revealed Himself since the time of Adam. If the Enochites felt the need to defend themselves, who are we to judge?"

4

"You do not have to be a judge to recognize the injustice of punishing many for the sins of one." He motioned toward the caravans. "And what about these women? Do they know why they were brought here?"

"To find husbands."

"Whose husbands? Do you mean the husbands of Eden who frequent the tents encamped just outside the city?"

Malluch glared, and Noah caught sight of Bohar attempting to flank him between two of the carts. Inching closer, the man whose reputation with a knife was well known, appeared to conceal something beneath his tunic.

Japheth, one of Noah's sons, stopped Bohar's advance by grabbing him from behind and immobilizing the hidden forearm with a strong squeezing grip. The would-be assailant twisted to see the huge man wearing a brown chagowr and sling towering over him by nearly half a cubit, but otherwise couldn't move. Noah exhaled in relief and threw an approving nod to the son whose power and strength he'd come to depend on but never took for granted.

At the same time, Noah's younger son, Shem, passed through the crowd and stood beside his father. "It's time to leave," he whispered.

"Would you have me leave before my message is complete? Can truth be deferred until tomorrow?"

Shem examined Noah through deep-set cocoa eyes fixed above a softly-chiseled, tanned face. "Father, we need to go ... Now."

He furrowed his brow. "Son, why do you show such disrespect for me in public?"

"Father, please. Look in their hands."

Roughly one hundred-twenty men remained in the city gate following the others' departure. Most, including Malluch, had withdrawn from the center of the square leaving Noah and his son alone.

Bohar's allies appeared to look to him for a signal, but he remained locked in Japheth's grasp. He walked him to join his father and Shem. Together the four exited the square and moved along a side street lined with flat-roofed houses of stone and mortar. Once out of sight of the crowd, they stopped, and Japheth pulled Bohar's hand — and the span-length knife it held — from beneath his tunic.

He sneered, exposing a mouthful of green-encrusted teeth. "You know, one day I'm going to be the one coming up behind you."

"Maybe." Japheth said. "If you tread lightly enough and the wind is right?" He squeezed his wrist until the knife dropped, then retrieved it and slowly turned it over in his palm. Dried blood stained both sides of the blade.

Bohar's eyelids froze and he slowly backed away toward the city gate, as though fearful Japheth might use the knife on him.

Noah thanked his son for the timely intervention but mourned his inability to reach his countrymen. Many in the crowd had been loyal to his father, Lamech, until deceived by the riches of Enoch. It was probably his final opportunity to reach those whose hearts were being led away from God. He feared the beginning of the end of a culture dating back to the creation.

"Did you see how red Malluch's face got back there?" Shem said. "Father, I'm afraid this will only make him more determined to have you killed."

"It seems twenty years has done nothing to temper his desire for revenge." News of the slaughter at the garden had traveled through Eden like the wind. Malluch made no attempt to conceal his feelings, vowing on his father's and brother's graves to repay Lamech and his son for their betrayal. Soon thereafter, he traveled to the land of Nod, allegedly to lay blame against them for the death of the sons of Enoch. For his part, Noah took no satisfaction in having been proven right. He and his family mourned the loss of life but, of course, could do nothing else to lessen his foe's suffering. He'd been warned.

"So, what do we do?"

6

"Well, the fact he tried to have Bohar's men stone me in the open means he's afraid to get his own hands bloody. And that could work to our advantage." At the top of the street, thirty to forty supporters gathered round an animated Bohar, who kept pointing to the four men. "But for now, we should get off the street."

As the four men moved between the houses, rocks fell around them, one glancing off Shem's left leg. The large group of men charged toward them. Shem and Japheth drew their swords, but their father touched them both on the shoulder. "Wait."

He reached for a palm-size rock, one hurled by their attackers. He threw it, striking Bohar in the center of his forehead and knocking him backwards off his feet. When the others saw their companion felled, they stopped and surrounded his unmoving body.

"Now we can *walk* home," he said.

CHAPTER 2

Noah stood next to Miryam at a table in the food preparation area of their home hoping to distract her. The aroma of fresh-baked bread filled the room. Four and a half centuries of marriage hadn't tempered his affection for her, and with good reason. Except for a few gray hairs, she hadn't aged, her thin lips soft and moist, her olive skin still smooth and without flaw. He wrapped an arm around the waist of her maroon tunic and drew himself in, burying his nose in her hair. The smell of lilac mixed with the yeast made for an enticing fragrance.

"Trouble in the square today?" Miryam batted his hand away from the bread.

"What makes you think that?"

She looked up from the table where she pitted some dates. "Those two."

Across the room, Shem stared out the window of their home just outside the city, while Japheth paced the room.

"Some men wanted to stone me."

"Oh, is that all?" Miryam smirked and raised her eyebrows before returning her attention to the dates.

8

He understood his wife well enough to recognize her attempt to make light of it was just a masquerade. She'd be worried, especially if she knew how close he'd come to really being stoned.

Japheth joined Shem at the window. "What are you watching for? If they were coming, they'd have been here by now."

"Your brother's right, son." Noah joined them. "Malluch is no fool. He knows it would be unwise to molest us so soon after the incident at the square today."

Inside, he agreed with his second born about their opponent's failure to incite the crowd against them. Malluch had his sight fixed on the governorship and wasn't about to allow today's setback to interfere with his plans. With Lamech aging, Noah remained the only thing standing in the way of his rise to power in Eden.

"That's what bothers me," Shem said. "What his next move is going to be."

For twenty years, they'd expected an attempt on their father's life, for Malluch wasn't the type of man to threaten idly. But being the son of the governor still afforded the heir a certain degree of authority and respect. Until today.

Miryam's penetrating chestnut brown eyes told him she knew his thoughts exactly. "Are the three of you going to stand there looking out the window all night? Husband, sons. Come and eat."

With his family seated on the floor around an area where they gathered for meals, Noah bowed his head. "Blessed be the Lord our God, who brings forth this bread from the earth—"

A light knocking interrupted the prayer. Shem started to stand but Noah grabbed an arm to restrain him. "Malluch's men wouldn't knock." He regarded Japheth's wife, Elisheva, a beauty of medium height whose face featured full lips and an even fuller set of eyebrows. "See who it is, daughter."

She rose to open the door, her thick and wavy dark brown hair swinging as she walked. "Father, it's a young woman—and a beautiful one at that."

9

* * *

Four hours of darkness had covered the land by the time Shechem arrived at the city gate to meet Malluch, Bohar, and twenty of their followers. Lamps long extinguished cooled inside the surrounding houses, while outside the moon offered just enough light to see without torches. "Lamech isn't going to like this," Shechem said. "Killing his heir."

"And which of you is going to tell him?" Malluch strained to make out the faces of the men gathered in front of him.

"No one is going to have to tell him. When Noah and his family turn up dead, Lamech will be suspicious. He may be old, but he's not senile. He knows what happened at the square today."

"Turn up dead, you said."

"Right."

"Suppose they don't turn up at all."

"That will make him even more suspicious."

"Will it? After today, he'll simply figure the Preacher took his family and fled the city rather than risk being stoned."

Bohar pulled out another knife. "Malluch, why don't you just let me sneak in there and slit their throats? It's my specialty."

"They'd smell you before you got halfway through the door," Shechem said. Muffled laughter erupted from the raiding party. In the subdued lighting, Bohar shot him a scowl. "And if you get caught, Japheth will do more than take your knife away this time. He'll stick it in a place where sitting becomes a problem."

Bohar manipulated the knife through his fingers. "We'll see."

"Forget this wrangling." Malluch waved a dismissive hand in front of them. "I didn't bring all these men so you could slit a few throats. Didn't I just say I didn't want them to turn up at all?" He glared at his two subordinates. "Which means they have to disappear. Without evidence of their bodies, it will be much easier for Lamech to accept they chose to flee the city on their own. Especially when a few of you witnessed it." Several men

10

nodded. "But no one's going to believe they fled on their own if you transform their home into a sacrificial altar."

Shechem stepped forward "All right, what's *your* plan?"

"We've got twenty-three men here, right?" And there are only three of them, not including the women." More heads bobbed. "Well, with those odds, if we can't move in and subdue six sleeping people, maybe I should have recruited some real soldiers. Like maybe half a dozen children." Some of the men scoffed.

"What about Japheth? He's a powerful man."

"I thought about that. Bohar, this is where you come in. Somebody get a torch lit the moment you've laid hands on the Preacher's family. Then you and three others put knives to the women's throats fast. The men will be less likely to resist if they see their women vulnerable."

"Then what?" Shechem said out of more than mere skepticism. Many years before, he'd confided to him his childhood love for Elisheva, Japheth's wife, a decision he hoped he wouldn't now come to regret.

"We bound and gag them, load them into carts, and transport them out of town along with some of their livestock so it appears they left on their own." Malluch eyed Shechem. "Then we take them to a remote location, burn them, and bury their bodies in a place where they will never be found.

"Burn them?" His heart melted, and he hoped the darkness concealed the shock on his face. Not Elisheva.

"Yes, burn them. Any questions?" No one responded. As they departed, Malluch turned to Bohar. "Remember what I said. Don't get overzealous with that knife now. If you don't mess this up, I may let you use it later. I may even let you have one of the women. I know about that specialty too."

Bohar's scowl morphed into a broad grin.

* * *

11

Twenty-three figures crept from the roadway leading two furlongs north to Eden and the modest stone house where Noah and his family lived. During their approach, Shechem's long-held opinion — that it wasn't much of a house for the son of a governor — confounded him again. Only now, he had more important things to focus on than the size and opulence of his enemy's home, chief of these being Japheth's might. Provoked, he possessed the strength to take half their company by himself. And what about Elisheva? Would he be able to stand by and let the love of his youth be murdered?

The three-quarter moon painted the slight rise of grass leading from the road to the house in a grayish-blue tint. Stone fencing built to contain livestock ran perpendicular to the left side of the house, while the sound of lowing cattle came from pastures in the rear. To the right grew vegetables and herbs cultivated in expansive gardens.

Halfway to the house, the sound of horses coming from the south prompted Malluch to raise his hand. "Get down."

Everyone dove to the ground, burying their faces in the grass while trying to remain motionless. On the road below, six horses and riders slowed to a stop. Why pause here at this time of night?

Two men dismounted and surveyed the area. Shechem slowly reached for the hilt of his sword. If detected, they'd have to kill the men. Worse, any commotion would surely arouse Noah's family, forcing him and the others to dispose of them immediately in opposition to Malluch's strategy.

"Can't it wait?" one of the men on horseback said. "We're almost to Eden."

One of the two men cursed, then he and the other man stood on the far side of the road relieving themselves.

The high-pitched whine of a blood fly buzzed in Shechem's ear. He tried to repel it by gently wiping the side of his head in the grass but only succeeded in driving the pest to the other ear. Other members of their party quietly attempted to fend off the swarming insects targeting their head and feet.

"Don't move," Malluch whispered, his voice low and threatening.

Shechem used every bit of strength to keep from slapping at the two flies feeding simultaneously from his neck and left ear, but he was weakening.

On the far side of the road, the two men continued to water the grass. They either had iron bladders or were returning from a long night of drinking.

When they finished, the men mounted their horses. Just as they hit the saddle, a smacking sound came from a few cubits to the right where Malluch and Bohar lay side by side.

"What was that?" one of the riders said, the six of them looking toward the house.

Even in the moonlight, the tall grass should've been enough to conceal them. But Malluch wasn't taking any chances. He drew his sword and slid it along the ground, laying it across Bohar's neck.

"Forget it," another rider's voice said. Let's go." The men turned their horses north and galloped off toward the city.

Following their departure, Shechem joined the others in a collective sigh and the furious scratching of skin. Their leader removed his sword from Bohar's neck, who tried hiding his face from the others.

Malluch used the interruption to issue a final admonition. "The souls of my father and brother cry out for vengeance. Tonight, I will silence them. Don't forget what I said about securing the women first. It will make handling Japheth much easier. Most of all, not a drop of blood spilt here."

Once the raiders reached the perimeter, he gestured for half the men to move to the rear of the house. The remaining members pressed themselves against the stone wall on either side of the front door. Blackness stared back at the group of intruders from the few window openings located in the walls. Not even a night lamp burned inside.

Shechem readied his team for entry, and hoped his loyalty and friendship to Malluch might later serve as a bargaining chip to

13

spare Elisheva. He cared little what happened to the Preacher or the rest of his family, even less for Japheth, whom he fully intended to kill himself. But for now, he only wanted to control him, to keep from being pushed into a fight that forced them to kill Noah's family tonight. Everything had to take place according to the plan if he was to have the time needed to plead for his friend's life.

Lookouts at the corners of the house signaled the readiness of the two teams. With a whistle, the assassins entered the front and rear doors.

CHAPTER 3

Despite traveling at night, Noah and his family had put six hours between themselves and the southern bank of the Eden River. He and Miryam steered one of three carts loaded with the family's belongings and food. Shem and Japheth, mounted on donkeys, drove the cattle. A dry summer had sapped the river of both power and depth, nullifying their father's concern about having to cross it.

"Father, I still don't understand why we didn't stay and fight," Japheth said. "Shem and I could have easily rounded up enough men loyal to you and Grandfather."

"You saw the size of that crowd this afternoon. Even if Malluch had managed to recruit only half of them, would you have been able to marshal a hundred men before sunset?"

Shem pulled ahead of his brother. "We don't even know if this woman is telling the truth."

Noah watched his youngest eyeing the beautiful stranger with the gold scarf sitting next to his mother. Just hours earlier, she arrived in Eden with the hopes of finding a husband, naïve to the fact she'd be forced into a life of harlotry. But her destiny changed when she overheard a group of Malluch's men planning to murder their family later tonight. Alone in a strange city, she managed to slip away from her procurers, locate their home, and warn them. Now, she found herself as they did, a fugitive fleeing for her life.

"For all we know, she's part of a ruse to get you out of the way so Malluch can take control of the city," Shem said.

"Tell me, why would someone, part of a ruse, alert our family to a plot to kill us, then insist on coming along?" Shem raised an eyebrow but remained silent. "After barely escaping with our lives today, do you really find her story that hard to believe?"

Shem's wife, Ariel, glared at the woman who'd identified herself as Shiphrah. Shem's wife wasn't as soft looking as Elisheva and a bit on the thin side, but she had strong features set in a nicely rounded face. "Father, this woman is from Enoch, brought here as concubine for the men of Eden. Have you not warned us repeatedly of the treachery of the Enochites? Who is she that we should trust her?"

"Perhaps the person who saved your life."

"Humph." Ariel returned to driving the oxen.

"Do you not think Shiphrah deserves, at least, our gratitude?" Noah wasn't really expecting an answer. He nodded at Miryam, who took Shiphrah's hand and thanked her.

Shiphrah forced a shaky smile.

Japheth brought his donkey alongside the cart driven by his father. "What about Grandfather? And Great-grandfather?"

Noah had expected questions from his family about those they'd left behind, especially from his firstborn, who'd enjoyed a special relationship with his grandfather. Elisheva was an orphan, and Ariel's parents died of a fever forty years ago. But Shiphrah's warning about the murder plot sent him rushing out to try and persuade Lamech to come with them.

"I am sorry, son, I could do nothing to compel them to come with us."

"But with us gone, what's left for them?"

"Their birthright. Your grandfather is the ninth in the line of Adam. Your great-grandfather has lived in Eden for almost nine

16

hundred years. YAH took his father before him alive to heaven from a field behind your grandfather's house. He said it was a legacy neither of them could leave."

"And Malluch? His hatred and desire for vengeance against Grandfather is as strong as it is for you."

"Your grandfather is still the governor. He has many old and influential friends. And if I know Malluch, he craves power more than he craves vengeance. He knows it would not be politically expedient to eliminate him. Not now." Several sheep and goats wandered off the roadway to graze. "Better tend your sheep, son." Japheth veered his donkey away.

Now, with the river behind them, Noah welcomed the quiet. They continued south, with the deadness of night marred only by the rhythmic squeaking of wooden wheels and the impact of cloven hooves upon the dirt road.

Despite their good fortune, he couldn't help questioning what the future held. Was their escape short-lived? And if not, how far would they have to travel to stay out of their enemy's grasp? What of Shiphrah? Shem and Ariel already held a deep suspicion of her. Most worrisome of all was the welfare of his father and grandfather. Japheth had been right: Malluch's vow of vengeance included both Lamech and Noah. With him gone, would his adversary become emboldened enough to have his father eliminated?

* * *

"Where are they?" Shechem cried out.

Confusion reigned inside before the two teams of assassins met in the center of the house, furiously aware something had gone wrong. "Somebody, light a torch," Malluch said. Light filled the room to him pounding his fist in his palm.

Several men searching other parts of the house joined them. One confirmed what everyone already suspected. "They're gone."

17

The lump in Shechem's throat subsided and relief washed over him. But he stifled his emotions. "A couple of you search outside," he said, then pointed to several others. "You three, check to see if any of the livestock have been moved."

Even in the reduced lighting of the torches, signs of a hasty departure abounded. A few small plates, a chalice of fine metal, and a broken piece of pottery littered the floor.

"Clothes in the other rooms?" he said. "Any food?"

Another member of the search team arrived. "Not a crumb. And it looks like the water buckets are gone too."

Bohar picked up the chalice and placed it inside his tunic.

Malluch frowned at him. "Put it back! I told you, nothing disturbed." Bohar dropped the chalice to the floor. The leader turned to Shechem. "I think the Preacher just made our job easier."

Two men outside called for Malluch and indicated they'd found something. He and his lieutenants hurried to where the men stooped beside the pathway. Torches illuminated disturbances in the soil. Tracks. Lots of them. Human, animal, and wheel ruts—all leading south away from the city.

Malluch stood and faced the livestock pastures. "Have the men bridle some of the donkeys and make it fast."

"We're going to follow them?" Shechem said. "The river is only twelve furlongs away."

"I know, but we don't know how long they've been gone, and they can't travel fast driving cattle and pulling loaded carts."

Five hundred forty parts later, the nearly two dozen raiders pursued their quarry south. Inside, Shechem waffled. Duty required his loyalty, even if he didn't agree with his friend's methods. On the other hand, he wasn't sorry Elisheva had escaped, fleeting though it may be.

* * *

18

A cacophony of croaks and whistles from the bulrushes greeted the search party when they arrived at the northern bank of the Eden River. They knelt at the water's edge next to tracks leading into the water. "You think they made it?" Shechem said.

"At this time of year—absolutely." Malluch grabbed the torch from him and waded into the river to his waist, about thirty-five cubits from the bank. He set his feet along the silt of the riverbed and raised the torch above his head, peering out over the water. "Current's not too strong."

"Well then what are we wasting time for." Bohar rubbed his hands together briskly. "Let's get after them."

"You still want to track them across the river in the dark?" Shechem said.

Malluch's head snapped around. "Any reason why we shouldn't, other than that heartache you've got for Japheth's wife?"

Bohar grunted and smirked, while several others laughed.

Shechem bristled. "You said it yourself. We don't know how long they've been gone. But if it's anything over eight hours, they'll have traveled a good ways, even driving cattle. Besides, isn't this just what you wanted—the Preacher to disappear?"

Malluch made his way to shore. "What I said is I wanted it to look like he'd disappeared. And knowing his charred body was rotting away in the earth somewhere would in no way conflict with that want." He sloshed up the bank to join them, pausing to turn back to the river. He pulled the torch in so that the flame's reflection danced on his face.

"Are we going, or not?" Bohar said.

Malluch brought the torch closer, turning it slowly in his fist. "No. Let them go."

"What!"

"Shechem's right. Even driving a small herd, they could be 150 furlongs away by now." He lifted his gaze skyward. "And this moonlight's not bright enough to track that distance." He leaned in so only the two of them could hear. "There are twenty chances for something to go wrong. The way things are, Lamech will figure the Preacher and his family fled a stoning. But all we need is for one of these simpletons to let a word slip, get drunk and start boasting, talk in his sleep, whatever, and I'll have more than Lamech to deal with."

"There's a solution to that problem too," Bohar whispered, smiling.

"Thanks, my friend. But I'm going to need every available man to help launch this overthrow."

While the posse mounted their donkeys, a brisk rustling came from the grasses to their right. Bohar grabbed a torch to investigate. A fox subduing a young rabbit proved to be the source of the commotion, but the predator remained too fixated on its meal to notice his advance. He drew his knife and threw it, impaling the fox just behind the left shoulder, drawing a sharp yelp. The fox attempted to crawl away—the rabbit still in its mouth. Bohar stomped on the fox's head, crushing its skull. He pulled the knife from the animal, not bothering to wipe the blood from the blade before climbing onto his donkey.

"Nice," Shechem said.

"At least the night wasn't a total loss."

CHAPTER 4

Six months had passed since Noah and his family completed an eight-day journey to settle in an area they deemed fertile to raise cattle and crops. To the southwest, a huge forest loomed as a living wall to defend them from the hot winds that blew across the Mesopotamian plain. The first lambs had been born to several of the ewes, and one of the heifers was gestating. Water flowed liberally from the well he and his sons had dug. Still, he worried each time they entered the local village for supplies. Today was no exception.

Two soldiers watering their horses stared at them loading provisions into a cart. The two men looked familiar, but with Eder having no army, they were unlikely to be acquaintances.

Shem moved in close to his father while lifting a bag of grain. "What do you think they're looking at?"

"It's not the what that concerns me, but the why. Keep loading, and don't look them in the eye." Noah walked to the other side of the cart to get Japheth's attention. "When we're done, I'll take the donkey, you two drive the cart." Both sons nodded.

The three men headed out of town en route to their new home. One hundred eighty parts into their journey, they noticed the two soldiers following at about a two-furlong distance. The trio increased their pace, but another 270 parts did nothing to increase their distance from the soldiers.

Just ahead, the road cut through a small forest. Noah slowed his donkey to allow his sons to pull next to him. "When you reach the trees, drive the ox as fast as he will go." He smacked his donkey on the rump and kicked at its sides.

"Where's he going?" Shem said as the animal pulled away. "Father!"

He entered the woods and glanced over his shoulder in time to catch Japheth slap the reins against the oxen's back.

Fifty-four parts later, Japheth and Shem passed by where Noah crouched at the base of a tree peering through the brush. They were followed by the sound of horse hooves pounding the road. He pulled taut the rope stretched across the roadway between two trees. When the horse's legs hit the rope, it slipped, burning and cutting his palms.

Horses and men tumbled, crying out on their way to the ground. Noah drew his sword and raced to the closest man, thrusting the weapon through his back. He checked the second man, who lay motionless, the skin of his neck distended by bulging vertebrae. The horses—to his relief—appeared to suffer no injury.

Shem jumped out and joined him. "You do nice work, Father."

Noah frowned. "There is no satisfaction in the taking of a life. But I couldn't risk their reporting us to their command."

"No argument here. I doubt they were following us to make our acquaintance." Shem kneeled to examine the dead man's clothing. "They're not from Enoch."

"No, they're not."

"Hey," Japheth said, climbing down from the cart to examine the bodies. "I think I know these men."

"I thought so," Noah said. "Can you place them?"

"They're two of Shechem's men."

"I was afraid of that."

"Afraid." Shem's head snapped up. "Why?"

22

"Because it can only mean one thing—Eden has its own army now."

Japheth nodded slowly. "Which means Malluch has seized control of the city."

"Probably," Noah said.

"Great. What do we do with the bodies?"

"There's a shovel in the cart. We should get them off the road and into the woods now."

While Shem and Japheth moved the bodies, Noah examined the rope burns on his palms and popped back into place the dislocated fifth finger on his right hand. His relief at having escaped detection or capture conflicted with the reality they were still fugitives. They'd traveled nearly thirteen hundred furlongs from Eden, yet he'd still been forced to kill to protect their secrecy. They were lucky only two soldiers were in the village today. When they didn't return to their command, more were sure to follow.

CHAPTER 5

A half year following Noah's disappearance, Shechem rode his horse north out of the city to a tent encampment where harlots entertained the men of Eden. To the northwest, the first courses of a stone wall rose from the ground surrounding rows of barrack-like structures. The early evening ride gave him an opportunity to reflect on one of the choices he'd made.

He had married who many considered the most beautiful woman in all of Eden. Taller than the average woman, Claudia's bearing drew immediate attention from anyone passing her on the street, man or woman. Flowing dark hair to her waist and high cheek bones added to her stately appearance. With such beauty, he often questioned why she'd consented to marry him, seeing she could have had her choice of suitors.

Yet all that beauty and grace had come at a price. Claudia was not only vain, but also expensive to maintain. Even after over 170 years of marriage, he found himself having to spend vast sums of gold to keep her in the finest things. He often wondered how different life would have been if he'd married someone less self-absorbed. Like Elisheva. *Was Elisheva alive? If so, where was she? Did she ever think of him?*

He located Bohar's horse outside one of the tents. Even if he hadn't recognized the animal, Shechem could have found it blindfolded. He waved the odor away before alighting his own mount, giving the horse a wide berth when approaching the tent. "Bohar, you in there?"

"What do you want?"

"Malluch wants to see us."

"Now?"

"Now."

"Give me a few parts." A smacking sound, followed by a quickly muffled cry reverberated from inside the tent. Eighteen parts later, Bohar exited the shelter. "How did you find me?"

"It wasn't difficult. You and your horse have a lot in common."

"What's that mean?" Bohar scowled.

"You know, if you'd bathe once in a while, you might find yourself a woman you didn't have to pay for."

"I didn't pay for this one."

"And how did you manage that?"

"I simply told her I wouldn't disembowel her if she were nice to me."

"You'd better hope she doesn't tell her handler."

"She won't."

"Why not?"

"Because I told her I'd come back and cut her tongue out if she did."

"You're going to ruin a good thing if you keep this up."

The two men mounted their horses and headed to Eden, passing by several construction sites of walls being erected around the city. Near the center, they entered a large two-story house built largely of marble. Men armed with swords and spears stood guard on either side of an ornately carved door post and lintel.

"Come in, my friends." Malluch smiled broadly and strode with open arms across the marble floor. "I hope I haven't inconvenienced you by summoning you at this late hour."

"No inconvenience." Shechem answered for both of them. Bohar twisted his mouth and raised an eyebrow.

"Good." Because tonight is a night for celebration." Malluch poured wine into three chalices and handed one to each man. He raised his arm holding the third. "Gentlemen, the city is ours. I must admit, I anticipated a great deal more resistance." He took a long drink. "But since the Preacher graced us with his departure, Lamech has become all but impotent."

"He doesn't even come out in public anymore," Shechem said.

"And many of his allies have either joined us or left the city. Congratulations."

The three men drank again.

"Never underestimate the power of a grieving heart to sap the fortitude of one who is weak. I take it you've seen the progress being made on the fortifications?"

"It's hard not to." Shechem swept the arm holding the chalice around the room. "They're everywhere."

"And so the reason I summoned you—besides this toast, of course. I would like you to personally oversee the construction. As it stands, there is no coordination between the various projects, and they are commencing far too slowly. If we are to match the formidable defenses of Enoch, there needs to be more centralized control."

"Coordination isn't the problem. We need more men."

"Then get them."

"Nearly all the men of Eden are working on the walls now."

"Then get some men outside of Eden."

"It's going to take a lot of resources to hire enough men to complete a project this size."

"I don't believe I mentioned the word 'hire.'"

26

Shechem turned to Bohar, then back to Malluch, who were wearing identical smirks. "The construction to the northwest? A slave camp?"

"I'm placing you in command of our new army as well. The men of Eden have been training for months, going out on short patrols. Time to put them to the test. And take Bohar with you. I'm sure his special talents will prove invaluable."

Bohar flashed his trademark moss-colored smile.

Shechem's stomach tightened at the sight of that grin, for he knew all too well its implication. Bohar wasn't excited at the prospect of going on a raid, of the spoils he might acquire, or even for another opportunity to use his knife. He was excited about the women. For him, it was always about the women.

The father of two daughters, Shechem had an aversion to rape. The killing of one's enemies was one thing—even women in battle—so long as it was swift and merciful. But he found the prolonged torture of rape unnecessary, committed only by the most loathsome of animals. A title Bohar wore proudly.

As the new commander, he couldn't even bask in the glory of his dual promotion, not with the prospect of having to tolerate his companion's perversions. Thoughts of pity entered his mind, compassion for a village full of women he hadn't even seen. He tried to drown them out by thinking again of Elisheva.

CHAPTER 6

Shechem entered his house a month later in the afternoon to find his two daughters, Channah and Naomi, conversing with their mother in the main living area. Channah, the older, was the exact likeness of her mother, but Naomi had her father's aquiline nose, mouth, and a head of curly hair. They ran to greet him, just as they'd done every day when they were children, leaning into his arms and kissing him on either cheek.

"What brings you by?" he said.

"Just picking up a few things we left stored here all these years," Naomi said.

"Do you need some help?"

"No, thank you. We have everything packed on camels outside."

His daughters had married twin brothers sixteen and eleven years ago, living with them at their parents' house on the east side of the city. But the men had recently inherited a large section of land 160 furlongs south of the Eden River and were preparing to move their families there. "So, I guess this is it, huh?" Shechem said. "Ready to make your fortunes raising livestock?"

"Or crops," Channah said.

"Well, from what I've seen of that piece of land you're getting, you could do either. Or both."

"Who knows, we may even plant a vineyard."

Shechem smacked his lips. "Do that, and you can expect regular visits from me."

Both girls smiled, but Claudia just rolled her eyes.

"Oh, I almost forgot. Congratulations on your promotion, Father," Naomi said. "I understand you'll be leaving soon on your first campaign."

"First thing tomorrow," he said.

"How exciting," Channah said, the hazel beneath her eyelids glistening. "Part of me is sorry we won't be here to see the walls go up. They should be magnificent."

"They will if I can get the men I need to help build them."

Channah reached for his hand. "You will, Father. I have faith in you."

"Me, too," Naomi said.

He hugged and kissed his daughters again before they departed then took a seat next to a window in their dining area.

"How long will you be gone?" Claudia said, placing a plate of bread, cucumbers, and corn before him.

He wished she'd asked out of a legitimate concern for him, but he suspected a more selfish reason. "It depends. Malluch wants a thousand more men to put to work on the walls. Three to five days, I suspect. Maybe a week."

"Please tell me you're taking that malodorous pervert with you?"

"Bohar?"

"Who else?"

"You have nothing to fear from Bohar."

She crossed her arms and pursed her lips, her shoulders shivering. "He's forever leering at me."

"He leers at every woman. But in your case, I imagine it's because of your exquisite beauty."

"That's not much consolation for being eyed like you're some animal's next meal."

"An interesting comparison, my dear, and not the least bit inaccurate. Bohar is an animal. But as I said, you have nothing to fear. I am second to Malluch in authority and Commander of the Army." Claudia uncrossed her arms while Shechem paused to pour a cup of wine. "An animal? Yes. But an animal that knows its place."

"I hope so."

"To answer your question: Yes, Bohar is going with us."

"Good." Without another word, Claudia walked to another part of the house, leaving him alone with his thoughts.

His attention was drawn to the window, where outside a boy and a girl about ten years old chased each other in the street. He left his plate to watch the children. In a moment, his mind returned to a place two hundred years ago.

"All right, Elisheva, I give up. Where are you?" Shechem had said.

He and Elisheva had been playing a game of fox and rabbit by the river when she managed to disappear. Elisheva was fast for a girl of ten, faster than many of the boys her age. But so was he, and it puzzled him how she managed to elude him. He searched nearly one hundred cubits up and down the river bank, along with two adjacent fields and several patches of brush and trees. "Elisheva. Come on. It's my turn to be the rabbit."

As he continued along the bank, she popped up from behind an outcropping of rocks at the river's edge. "Hey, fox, over here!" she said, just before slipping and dropping out of sight behind the rock to the sound of splashing water.

When she appeared from behind the rocks, arms flailing against a current dragging her downstream fed by three days of hard rains, his surprise turned to horror.

But Shechem was not only a fast runner, he was also a good swimmer. He bolted along the river's edge as fast as he could, passing Elisheva in the water.

30

He knew better than to try to swim against the current. When he reached a sufficient distance past her position, he waded into the river, but stayed out of the water's main flow until she was upon him. When she passed, he dove into the torrent, reaching the place where she should have been in three strong swimming strokes. He raised his head to locate her, but she'd disappeared.

He treaded water in the middle of the river for what seemed a long time, scanning in front and behind for signs of her. He wheeled to the sound of splashing and a cry for help downstream. Elisheva could barely keep her head above water, thrashing her arms twenty cubits in front of him. He swam hard for her, arriving within two cubits in a matter of moments.

When he reached for her, she dropped out of sight into the rushing water.

He dove beneath the murky waters, but he couldn't see a handbreadth in front of him. He swung his arms wildly in the blind hope of locating some part of her to grab. When he couldn't find her, he returned to the surface.

He rode the current downstream, but he hadn't seen Elisheva in nearly eighteen parts. He didn't know how long she could stay under. Just before diving below again, he caught sight of three small fingers breaking the surface off to his right. Alarm raced through him.

Dead ahead, a small island of rocks jutted out of the river. Only she wouldn't be able to see them from underwater, and she was headed straight for them.

Nearing exhaustion, Shechem pumped his arms against the water with all he had left in pursuit of the floating hand. Two parts later, Elisheva's body brushed beneath him and he reached to pull her head above the surface. She grabbed him around his neck, coughing and spitting water in his face. "Where did you come from?" Before he could answer, her eyes grew wide. "Look out!"

He snapped around in time to deflect them both safely around the rocks.

"Put your arms around my neck." Shechem swam with the current while angling toward the river bank. Eighteen parts later, they reached the shore, coughing and gasping for air. His lungs ached from trying to get air back into them, and an uncomfortable fullness invaded his stomach from all the water he'd swallowed. When he finally caught his breath, he turned to Elisheva, whose chest continued to rise and fall like a stick bobbing in the water.

"You all right?" he said.

She continued to cough. "You saved me."

He spit a small splash of water. "I nearly got us both killed on that rock."

"I fell in. You jumped in after me. I call that saving."

"Well, maybe. I was just trying to help."

"No way. You saw me out there." Blood oozed from a scrape to his knuckles. "You've cut your hand."

It hurt bad, but he wasn't about to let her know it. "It's nothing. I just caught it out there on the rock."

With the panic of their ordeal subsiding, he had time to consider the consequences. "How about we don't tell our parents about this? I'll be punished for sure if they find out I let you fall in the river."

"But you didn't let me fall in. That was my own clumsiness."

"It won't make any difference. They'll blame me just the same."

"Agreed. I don't want to get into trouble either."

"One last thing."

"What's that?"

"Next time, it's my turn to be the rabbit."

Elisheva smiled, then leaned over and kissed him on the cheek.

Outside, a child's playful scream brought Shechem back to the present, his fingers touching the spot on his cheek where Elisheva had kissed him. He sensed his wife's presence directly behind him.

"Aren't you hungry?" she said.

"What?" He turned from the window. "Yes, I am." He reached to kiss her on the mouth, only to have her turn so his offer of warmth landed on her cheek. He returned to his plate, hoping for one last opportunity to engender her affections. "Join me?" he said, raising his wine cup toward her.

"Not tonight."

Not tonight. Not any night. He was glad he was leaving for the northern villages in the morning.

CHAPTER 7

Pride swelled in Shechem at the sights and sounds of his first conquest while surveying the devastation in the northwest city of Jared. Dozens of bodies dotted the streets, and the clanging of metal craftsman's hammers rose above the crackling fire of houses set ablaze. Eight hundred men stood waiting in line to be shackled, surrounded by the imposing presence of Eden's newborn cavalry. Malluch would be pleased.

Shechem regretted the loss of those who'd chosen death over enslavement—not out of any sense of compassion, but because their foolishness had denied Eden a valuable resource. He twisted atop his mount to the sound of a woman screaming inside a nearby house, then back to one of his soldiers. "Where's Bohar?"

"I believe he is at the far end of the city, sir," the soldier said.

Shechem rode away down the street, meandering around the bodies in his path. As he came to one house, a woman being chased by a soldier ran out the door in front of him, startling his horse. "Pardon me, sir." The soldier saluted and dragged the woman back inside by her hair. Seventy-five cubits farther, another soldier carried two hysterical women, one over each shoulder, into a nearby cornfield.

At a house near the end of the street, the deafening cries of a man and a woman told the commander he'd located his quarry. Bohar's snorting horse hitched to a rock outside confirmed it.

Inside, four soldiers restrained a large man bound with rope, forcing him to view the scene in front of him. In an opposite corner, Bohar ravaged the man's wife. Several cubits away, his two naked daughters lay unmoving on the floor, blood pooling from wounds to their throats. Each time the man tried to turn away, the soldiers took turns striking the man in the head and stomach.

Shechem swore. He pulled his sword and moved to the bound man. "Hold him up." The soldiers hoisted the man and he thrust him through the heart, silencing his cries.

He strode deliberately to the corner where the assault on the woman continued, struggling to push from his mind his first inclination—to take advantage of Bohar's exposed back. Instead, he pulled him off the woman, and plunged his sword into her torso.

"What are you doing?" he said. "I wasn't finished."

"We didn't come here for this."

"I did." Red marks modeled Bohar's throat.

"We're here to secure the men, not torment the women."

"What torment. She was in ecstasy."

"Yes, I could see that." Shechem stared at the marks on his neck. "What happened?"

"Ah, I was just being friendly to the man's daughter and he up and charges me. Lifted me off my feet. If it weren't for your men beating him off, I don't know what would've happened."

He would have wrung your worthless neck. Shechem fought to keep from smiling. "So why the show?"

"I decided to teach him a lesson."

"Some lesson. He's dead."

"You did that."

"Like he would have been much good to us after what you did to his family."

35

"What's that mean?"

It means we need men, strong men, to build the walls of Eden."

"Yes."

"Look at him." Blood seeped from the wound of the lifeless man with the barreled chest crumbled on the floor. "He's huge. He could've done the work of three men."

"So, I'll find you another three men."

Shechem knew better than to argue with that logic. But he wasn't about to allow Bohar's proclivities to interfere with their objective of acquiring a slave force either. "I'd be content just to get out of here with the ones we have." He looked at the bodies of the three naked women on the floor, then at Bohar. "So if you think you've satisfied your appetite for one day, maybe you'd like to give us a hand with the prisoners outside?"

As they headed out, Bohar stopped short of the doorway, wincing to touch the wound on his neck. He moved back into the room and loomed over the dead man's body. A deep rasping sound filled the room, and he reached deep to pull phlegm from the bowels of his injured throat. He spit on the man, then kicked him in the face.

Shechem shook his head "Feel better?"

"Better than him."

36

Chapter 8

In the 500th year of Noah . . .

A soft but steady breeze arose to accompany Noah while he walked among the sheep bleating in the fields at twilight. He loved this time of the year, as the hot southeast winds of summer gave way to more refreshing gusts from the north.

Over a year had passed since their flight from Eden, and other than their narrow escape six months ago, there'd been no further sign of Malluch's soldiers.

With the sun crawling below the horizon, he strained to make out a faint sound mingled with the wind rushing past his ears — a sound like many waters. For a moment, he thought he might be hallucinating. The air seemed to whisper his name.

"Noah."

He whirled around.

"Noah," the voice repeated stronger.

He'd spent too many years walking in the Spirit not to recognize the sound of his Master's voice. Dropping to his knees, he raised his face and arms to the sky. "Here, Lord."

"The end of all flesh has come before Me, for the earth is filled with violence through them; and behold, I will destroy them with the earth."

Tears welled his eyes. He bowed his head to the earth.

"Make yourself an ark of gopherwood; make rooms in the ark, and cover it inside and outside with pitch," the Lord said. "And this is how you shall make it: The length of the ark shall be three hundred cubits, its width fifty cubits, and its height thirty cubits. You shall make a window for the ark, and you shall finish it to a cubit from above; and set the door of the ark in its side. You shall make it with lower, second, and third decks. And behold, I Myself am bringing floodwaters on the earth, to destroy from under heaven all flesh in which is the breath of life; everything that is on the earth shall die. But I will establish My covenant with you."

Noah raised his head and gazed heavenward.

"And you shall go into the ark—you, your sons, your wife, and your sons' wives with you. And of every living thing of all flesh you shall bring two of every sort into the ark, to keep them alive with you; they shall be male and female. Of the birds after their kind, of animals after their kind, and of every creeping thing of the earth after its kind, two of every kind will come to you to keep them alive. And you shall take for yourself of all food that is eaten, and you shall gather it to yourself; and it shall be food for you and for them."

When the Lord finished speaking, the wind subsided to a great calm. In spite of the warm outside temperature, Noah's body shivered as if naked in the cold. His heart raced. He attempted to process the magnitude of the Lord's proclamation. While he'd seen the evil the Lord spoke of, he could not fathom the destruction of the earth. He fell prostrate on the ground, arms reaching above his head to pull grass in either hand. "Lord, is there nothing that can quench the fire of Your fierce anger?"

For the next hour, Noah wept bitterly—and prayed for all mankind. Though the Lord concealed the timing of the coming flood, He made known His intent to take Lamech beforehand. *Thank You, oh Lord, that in the midst of Your wrath, there is mercy for Your servant, my father.*

He remained on his face well into the darkness, the silence replaced by the sound of chirping crickets, until out of his own mouth—"Shiphrah!"

He rose quickly to his knees, recounting the Lord's words " — *you, your sons, your wife, and your sons' wives with you.*"

"Oh, Lord. Not Shiphrah. Woe is me that I should have to bear Your sentence upon her."

CHAPTER 9

Shechem ceased rubbing the small of his back when Enoch's fifteen-cubit-high walls came into view. For a moment, he even forgot how much his rear hurt at being stuck on the back of a camel the last ten days. He, Malluch, and Bohar had led a trade caravan on the long ride east from Eden, and the sight of those fortifications signaled more than an end to their journey. This was only his third visit to the great city, but he'd experienced enough to know what Malluch had said was true. Enoch was home to the world's finest wine, weapons, and women. And those walls . . . they served as an invitation to good times waiting within.

In the distance, wood, stone, and bronze images of beasts peered down at them from the highest hills lining either side of their approach route. A light wind brought the scent of a burning incense of galbanum and frankincense to the travelers' noses. Vineyards covered hillsides, outnumbering plantations of food crops ten to one.

Today's journey had a special purpose—above the mere acquisition of additional weapons needed to outfit Eden's newly formed army. Ramalech, a prince of Enoch, was holding a celebration in honor of Malluch's rise to power in Eden. Their alliance, formed many years before, resulted in the initiation of trade between the two cities. Now, as the caravans passed through the city's massive iron gates, Shechem could almost taste the wine that would soon cross his tongue.

* * *

Shechem sat in awe at the preparations provided for the more than one hundred elite guests gathered at the prince's palace shortly after dark. Sounds of the timbrel, harp, and lute filled the gathering hall. Servants with wineskins stood at the ready, eager to ensure no one's cup ran dry. A dozen women in transparent silks whirled and skipped before the prince and his guests in sync with the music.

Bohar lay alone in a corner on several pillows, eyes closed, mouth agape, wine staining his chin and the front of his tunic. Seated on a throne, Ramalech turned to Malluch and Shechem. "Your friend is quite the winebibber."

"Yes, he does just about everything with gusto," Malluch said.

Ramalech wrinkled his nose. "I couldn't help but notice bathing isn't one of them."

"No. But then a faithful dog that smells is worth more than an unfaithful one that doesn't, don't you think?"

"Well put." Ramalech rose from his throne and raised a chalice. "Men and women of Enoch—a toast to our friends from Eden. May this mark the beginning of increased trade and prosperity for both cities." Cheers and clapping erupted from the gathering, and those with goblets drank at the prince's invitation.

"Thank you, prince," Malluch said, standing. "This is indeed an historic occasion. Enoch is renowned across the land of Nod. Eden shall carry Enoch's fame to the west and make her feared throughout the world." More cheers rose from the crowd.

As the ovation subsided, he moved to a nearby lampstand and stared into the flames. Ramalech addressed Shechem. "I see the fires still haunt him."

"Yes. It's been twenty years, but for him it is yesterday."

"To lose both a father and a brother in the same battle is — is, well — unthinkable."

"Vengeance is a strong comforter."

"Indeed. There are twenty-five families here who beseech me continually to avenge them for that day. I'm surprised Malluch allowed his adversary to escape."

"He would have preferred to see him dead, but to take his city proved a fitting consolation."

"Then he has given up his desire to return to the garden?"

Shechem shook his head. "It's stronger than ever. He still has a score to settle with the angel. And he craves the tree of life."

"Perhaps I can provide a bit of a distraction, if only for an evening." Ramalech spun back to him. "My friend." Malluch remained fixated on the lampstand for a moment longer before returning to the throne. "My friend," Ramalech said. "Tomorrow there is sport I think you and your men will find entertaining."

"Sport?" he said, a smile returning to his lips.

"Two slaves and a lion are placed in the arena with the promise of freedom to the one who survives. A fascinating dynamic unfolds as each man seeks to defend himself against the lion and his fellow slave. Quite the spectacle." Ramalech nodded to a servant across the room. "But now."

Nine parts later, the servant returned with two of the most beautiful women Shechem had ever seen, along with an incredibly handsome young man. The man's beauty may have exceeded that of the two women. Ramalech gestured to Malluch. "Your choice, my friend — or you may have all three."

"The prince is most generous." Malluch licked his lips.

Ramalech turned to Shechem. "And what about your friend here? Would he care to indulge?"

"A woman, I think." Given his wife's recent coldness, the prospect of knowing another woman didn't bother him much. What did surprise him was the twinge of guilt his conscience carried because of Elisheva. *Can't fool the heart.*

42

As they rose to leave, a soldier entered the hall carrying two medium-sized bags made of animal skins. When he reached the throne, he raised the distended bags to the prince.

"Are these the—" Ramalech said.

"Trophies, my lord."

"Yes. Very good, Commander. Place them here." The prince pointed to the right of his throne.

The bottom edges were darker than the upper portion of the two bags, as if a moist item or substance had settled there. The army commander confirmed Shechem's suspicions when he set them on the floor, their sloshing impact reminiscent of a man's foot stepping in wet mud.

Shechem waited for the prince's servant to return with his gift, a woman of near equal beauty to the two presented to Malluch. When she took him by the hand to lead him away, he turned for a last look at the two bags. Dark crimson seeped from the bottoms onto the floor next to the prince's throne.

Whatever was in those bags, they'd be missed by their owners.

* * *

Shechem made his way through the streets of Enoch in the early morning hours to a surprising level of activity. Eden would be dark by now. But here, burning torches on buildings gave light to the city's night denizens.

Voices of men cheering or arguing over games of chance rose and fell each time he passed by a window or the occasional open door. Sweet perfume hit him like he'd dove headlong into a lilac bush when he passed another. "Anyone out this late must be looking for company," a woman said, beckoning from the darkened doorway.

He paused at the sound of the woman's voice. "Not tonight."

"Some other night, perhaps?"

43

He gave the woman a noncommittal smile before continuing down the street.

"My name's Rachael. Remember this doorway."

How could he forget it? It would take another hour for the spikenard to clear his head.

Farther down the street, he propped one drunk against a wall and stepped over another. Down a side street, a group of adolescent young men beat and robbed some helpless fool. *Bohar? No such luck.*

Near the center of the city, an altar rose eight cubits high. Though he'd seen it before, he'd never given it much thought, other than a rumor about it having been built over the tomb of Cain. Except for its immense size, it appeared much the same as any other altar used by the people of Eden to offer their sacrifices. Staircases cut into the center of each of the four sides of the pyramid provided access to the top. He grabbed a torch from one of the buildings and climbed the staircase to examine the charred pyre.

Scattered bones and partial skeletons littered the pit, along with the pungent smell of old death. Nothing unusual there—he'd figured the altar for use in some sort of animal sacrifice. But these bones looked different, unlike any he'd seen before. He stooped to take a closer look, lowering the torch into the pit, but still he couldn't make out what kind of bones they were. Too small for oxen, sheep, or goat. Even the partial skulls scattered throughout the pit were too fragmented to identify. Some kind of smaller animal he deduced. Or—or. No, that's too sick to even think about.

He descended the stairs. Rachael had looked like a woman not easily dissuaded, so he chose to return to the palace up the opposite side of the street.

At the sound of running footsteps, he quickened his pace after crossing the intersection. A sharp pain at the back of his head sent him tumbling to the ground. He struggled to push himself up, turning his head to see the sole of a sandal coming toward his face. Blackness filled his senses.

44

CHAPTER 10

Noah paused fifteen cubits from the front door. Burning lamps shining through a window provided the only contrast to the blackness surrounding him. Inside, Miryam helped Shiphrah and Elisheva wash and dry dishes. Outside his view, Ariel provided accompaniment to the women's labor with a song that would shame a mockingbird. He basked in the tranquility of the moment, hoping to brand forever in his mind the untainted view. The world had already changed for him. And he loathed the responsibility of having to change it for his family . . . and for one member in particular. He reached for the door, and his heart sank.

"Father," Japheth said, rising quickly from the floor.

Miryam dropped a plate she was drying and rushed to him. "What on earth has happened?" She brushed grass from his head and tunic while the rest of the family gathered around him.

"Look at his face," Ariel said. "He looks like he's seen the dead."

"Shem, bring your father a cup of water," Miryam said. "Come, husband, sit."

Japheth escorted him to his usual place of honor where the family shared their meals.

Shem handed him the cup, and he drank voraciously.

Ariel leaned into Elisheva. "He's so pale."

45

Miryam touched his arm. "What is it?"

He scanned the curious faces of his family, and words caught in his throat. Tears blurred his vision, signaling he had better speak or risk losing his composure. "The end of days is coming. And only this family shall be saved." Wide stares and slacked jaws answered him.

"The end of days?" Shem bent over Noah as if he hadn't heard him correctly.

"A great flood is coming upon the earth, to destroy everything, both man and beast." Noah's children and Shiphrah exchanged glances, but Miryam's gaze remained fixed on him.

"How—" Shem said.

"I was in the field when the Lord spoke to me out of the wind."

"Father, surely you were imagining. The wind often plays tricks on our ears."

Miryam's head snapped, eyes narrowing. "Better bridle that tongue."

"Mother, he's—" Shem said.

"He's your father and the master of this house."

Shem softened his brow. "Father. I've seen 329 years in this house, and I know you to be a righteous man led by the Spirit of God. But haven't you told us many times, YAH hasn't spoken to man since the time Cain slew Abel? That's over 1500 years."

"I'm not learned enough to discern the Lord's timetable," Noah said. "As for His choosing to break His silence, could it be it is only now the arrogance of man rises to heaven?"

"But why you?"

"Why He chose to spare this family, I cannot say. I only know He said He would establish His covenant with me. Tell me, is it not enough for you to know you have been set apart for salvation?"

"But it's so incredible."

"Wait, Shem," Japheth said. "Father, you said only this family will be saved. How is it we will escape the coming floodwaters?"

46

"The Lord commanded that I should build an ark — an ark large enough to hold two of every kind of animal on the earth, male and female — and that we and the animals should go into the ark to keep us alive."

The furrow returned to Shem's brow. "An ark. Animals. Mother, is he feverish?"

"Shem!" Miryam said.

Noah covered her hand with his. "His question is understandable. It is not every day one is confronted with such news. Had I not heard it from YAH Himself, I, too, would have been skeptical." He rose to address his younger son. "Place your hand here."

Shem reached to touch his father's neck.

"Fever?"

Shem shook his head.

"I assure you, neither am I mad or drunk."

"And Grandfather?" Japheth said.

"Your grandfather will be gathered to his fathers before the flood."

Japheth gritted his teeth, and his cheeks flushed. "That's why he refused to come with us, isn't it?"

"It's possible —"

"He knew, didn't he?"

Noah ached for his eldest son. "It's possible your grandfather had been granted some insight into the plans the Lord has for him. Who can say?"

"He knew," Japheth whispered.

A few moments later, everyone turned to Elisheva, who with a whimper struggled to speak. "But why? Why does the Lord want to destroy the earth?"

This is what Noah had feared most waiting outside their door to bring them the news — Elisheva's reaction. Of all his children, she was far and away the most tenderhearted. Not that she was weak by any means, but she had an inherent sweetness and humility rare among women. Perhaps it was related to her being an orphan and having to depend on people other than her natural parents growing up. He understood early on what had drawn Japheth to her. While her unadorned, natural beauty may have captured his attention, it was her loving spirit that captured his heart.

"Because of the violence of man," he said. "Surely, daughter, you bear witness to the wickedness of your own countrymen, of how they have turned their backs on the God of their fathers. Were we not forced to flee for our lives and dwell in this strange land because of them?"

"But the whole earth?"

"Long ago, when Cain fled to the land of Nod after killing his brother, our fathers hoped the evil he'd done had fled with him. A righteous heir had been born in his stead, and for hundreds of years the sons of Seth kept themselves unblemished from the sin of that one lawless act."

"So what happened?"

"Our fathers were naïve to think evil could be contained by a mere expanse of desert or a range of mountains. Since then, the seed of Cain's nature has spread back across the land like a miasma, touching—yes, daughter—every corner of the earth."

Ariel scowled and raised an arm to her adopted sister. "Shiphrah is from that land. Isn't she a descendant of those who brought this curse upon us?"

Shiphrah ran out the door into the darkness. Noah went after her, stopping in the doorway. "Ariel, none of us is without sin. And lest you need reminding, Shiphrah saved our lives." More than a year later, Ariel still hadn't warmed to Shiphrah. Elisheva at least treated her civilly. Moreover, he was certain Ariel's animus toward Shiphrah was due more to envy over the young woman's beauty than her lineage.

Even in the dark, Shiphrah's sobs guided him to a location fifty cubits from the house. He stood beside her. "I know this is difficult, but try to overlook Ariel's ignorance."

She caught her breath. "She's right. I am an Enochite."

48

"Which makes you no more guilty than a citizen of Eden. Adam's sin was passed down to all men, not just to the descendants of Cain. Was it not with your own ears you heard the men of Eden plotting against us?"

"Yes, but—"

"The Lord pronounced judgment on the whole earth."

"But you said only this family shall be saved. Doesn't that mean I also am condemned?"

Noah turned Shiphrah toward him. "Child, hear me now and do not doubt. No daughter of my body could have a more secure place in this family. In the year you have been with us, have you not proven your worth many times over?"

"But what if God—"

"Shiphrah, do you not know the hand of the Almighty is already upon you, that He has chosen you for His service?"

"What do you mean?"

"Did God not work through you to save us?"

"I don't—"

"Think back a year ago. Why did you warn us?"

"You were kind to me. When I heard what the men of Eden were planning, I had to do something."

"Were you frightened?"

"Terrified."

"Yet you warned us nonetheless, knowing if you were caught you would probably be killed along with us. I tell you the Spirit of the Living God gave you the boldness to do what you did—to risk your life to save ours."

"Still, I fear—"

"This judgment may seem harsh to you, but believe me when I tell you our God is a just God. Would He allow to perish the one He used to save us from the wrath of Malluch? As He did not command me to exclude you, I think not." She buried her face in Noah's bosom and cried. He didn't know if his assertion of God's

49

intention would come to pass. He only knew the ark wasn't going to be built tomorrow. Each day would be another opportunity for him to make supplication to the Lord on Shiphrah's behalf. "Come back inside. I fear this will be a long evening."

Noah and Shiphrah walked through the door to the quieting of the other's voices. Shem stepped forward. "Father, I still say the whole thing sounds crazy, and why the animals?"

"Without knowing the mind of the Lord, I would say His purpose is clear. He wishes to preserve a remnant to replenish the earth."

Japheth placed a huge arm around Elisheva. "Father, an ark large enough to hold two of every animal on the earth would have to be — would have to be — "

"Three hundred cubits long, fifty cubits wide, and thirty cubits high."

Shem slapped the heel of a palm against his forehead. "Father! "Three hundred cubits? The three of us? It'll take forever to build. When is this great flood coming?

"The Lord did not say. But I trust it will not be until the ark is complete." He understood full well the reason for the Lord's silence here. Not knowing the time of the flood would serve as motivation for him and his sons to remain vigilant in the ark's construction.

Shem paced the room, stopping to lean against a window opening. "Where will we get the plans for this ark?"

"He has written the plans on my mind." Noah said. "Are there not three men in this family sufficiently skilled in the carpentries to undertake such a challenge?"

Shem swept his arm around the room. "Erecting this house is one thing. But none of us has ever built so much as a raft to go on the water. Where will we obtain the skills needed to construct such an enormous craft, or more importantly, to make it seaworthy?"

"The Lord will teach us."

"Father, what about the cattle and sheep?" Ariel said. "Who is going to tend them and cultivate the fields while you are building the ark?"

"We are," Miryam said, the conviction in her voice drawing everyone's attention. "There are four strong women in this house capable of caring for livestock or driving a plow."

Pride swelled in Noah's chest at his wife's boldness.

Noah's prediction to Shiphrah had been correct. The evening extended well past midnight. Raised voices, accusations, and sporadic tearful outbursts marked the discussion. Except for Miryam and Elisheva, the other members of the family remained doubtful, but agreed to obey their father. Construction of the ark would begin in the morning.

With the house dark and Miryam lying next to him, he prepared to go to his God. "Worried about Shiphrah?" Miryam said.

"Four hundred sixty years and still you know my thoughts."

"I imagine it's because of the 460 years, not in spite of them."

"I told her the Lord would spare her."

"And so He may."

For the first time in more than a year, Malluch wouldn't be the last thing on Noah's mind before falling asleep. Escaping with their lives seemed easy compared to the responsibility of carrying on the human race. And an ark that size was going to draw a lot of attention, even in the remotest of locations. How long would it be before word of the ark reached Eden?

Yet even the danger of discovery didn't concern him like the wave of doubt washing over him. Out in the field, he'd been so awed by the voice of the Lord that he hadn't had time to think. But now, in the quiet of his bed, the magnitude of the task he'd been given confronted him. Sure, he'd said what was necessary tonight to motivate his family, but in truth he was as skeptical as they. Not of the certainty of God's pronouncement, but rather of his ability to complete the task given him. Shem was right. This was a massive undertaking, and none of them knew a thing about marine construction. If they failed, would his family be made to suffer because of it? He closed his eyes. *Why me, Lord?*

CHAPTER 11

"That's an impressive lump you have there," Ramalech said.

Shechem looked up through bleary eyes at the prince and Malluch standing over him. "Ugh." He labored to raise his pounding head from the pillow enough to recognize a chamber within the palace.

"Good thing two of our guests recognized you from the celebration. Generally, we don't interfere with the affairs of men on the streets. As in nature, the strong prey on the weak and a man lies where he falls."

Irritated, Shechem forced a weak smile to keep from revealing it in his expression. *Now that's something that would have been nice to know ahead of time.* In spite of his injury, he knew he had nobody to blame but himself. Served him right for leaving the warm embrace of Ramalech's gift to go out roaming the streets alone.

"Those killed or wounded on the street at night are buried in the morning."

Shechem's curiosity was aroused at this practice, and he figured he could attribute his ignorance to his head injury. Malluch had been coming here for years, but there was still much for Shechem to learn about the culture. He blinked several times and reached to rub his forehead. "The wounded are buried?"

"Oh, yes. Our physicians are not wasted on those preyed upon in the street. Anyone still breathing at dawn is quickly dispatched and buried with the rest. Truly, a merciful exercise." Ramalech paused to allow the sternness in his countenance to relax. "But on the other hand, we take care of our friends."

"My clothes?" He peered below his waist at the small white cloth covering his groin.

"Picked clean. I'm afraid the robbers here put the buzzards to shame. Not to worry though, Enoch is home to the finest seamstresses in the world." Ramalech pointed to a gray tunic with gold embroidered around the neck, sleeves, and bottom lying on a chair a few cubits away. "You're lucky all they took was your money and your clothes."

"What do you mean?"

"Well, let's just say there aren't any virgins in Enoch, not above the age of eight anyway. And strangers." Ramalech shook his head. "Male or female, they're considered a carnal delicacy."

Shechem peeked under the cloth, then reached to touch his behind, still slightly tender from the long ride. Other than that, he'd sustained no additional injury.

"Feel like you could eat something?" Malluch said.

"Yes. There's nothing wrong with my stomach." He pressed his palms against his throbbing temples.

"Excellent," Ramalech said. "A good meal will bring you around. Then after midday, the entertainment I promised you."

* * *

Shechem squinted at the sun climbing high over the circular stadium filled with several thousand spectators located at the city's east end. He, Malluch, and Bohar occupied seats next to Ramalech's throne on a second story viewing stand overlooking the floor of the arena.

"There's been a slight change in the program I think your friend with the headache will find interesting," Ramalech said, turning to Malluch.

Ramalech signaled to a guard who yelled down to the floor for the prisoners to be brought out. An iron gate creaked open. Three adolescent boys were pushed out into the arena directly below, and the gate locked behind them.

Shechem leaned forward. Blood dripped from the hands of the three boys. One teen had his smallest finger severed while the other two were missing a pair of fingers each. In his opposite hand, each teen brandished a sword. "Hey, I've seen those boys before," he said, unable to recall just where or when.

"From a prone position, no doubt," Ramalech said.

Truth was, Shechem hadn't seen who'd assaulted him, but the prince's statement jarred his memory. The boys he'd seen robbing the drunk last night. "How did you identify them?"

"That was easy. They confessed."

"Confessed?"

"Yes. That boy there with the one missing finger. He broke easily. The other two were tougher. Of course, we didn't want them to be totally defenseless and unable to hold a sword. What sport would that be?"

A gate on the opposite side opened, sending three lions into the arena. Bohar moved to the half-wall of the viewing stand.

The teens, eyes wide and lips quivering, conversed briefly, then stood with their backs to one another, swords extended. Only the lions didn't rush them as expected, choosing instead to slowly stalk the boys in a predator's circle. Periodically, one of the lions would crouch, move in, and take a swipe at one of them, only to retreat at the point of a sword. The crowd roared with each unsuccessful attack.

During one exchange, a well-placed paw sliced open the thigh of one of the boys, dropping him to one knee. When the boy reached to cover the gaping wound, the lion rushed in and bowled him over, overpowering him with a savage flailing of claws and teeth and blood. As the lion ripped the boy apart, cheering spectators drowned his screams.

Shechem tried to hide his lack of experience with such matters by keeping his attention focused on the action below. But he discovered he was able to carry the façade only so far. He couldn't bring himself to cheer.

The second teen fell when he lunged too far with his sword, giving his adversary an opening to jump on his back and drive him to the ground. The boy attempted to crawl away, but the lion broke his arm, then pulled huge chunks of flesh from his back and side. Again, the crowd erupted while the boy, still moving, succumbed to being eaten alive.

Down in front, Bohar went wild, cheering and waving his arms.

While the two lions fed, the third teen backed against a wall to keep from being flanked by the last lion. The tactic proved successful for a while, with the boy managing to keep his attacker at bay for fifty-four parts. But the crowd grew impatient, booing and throwing things from the stands to distract him. A stone cup striking him in the head sent him to the ground, his last cries garbled by the lion's jaws closing around his throat.

Bohar turned to the throne. "That was incredible! That last one put up a good fight."

"It's not over." Ramalech smiled and nodded to several disturbances breaking out in the stands. "The citizens of Enoch are avid gamblers."

Bohar returned his attention to the arena.

"And sore losers," Ramalech said.

Directly across from them, a soldier threw a man with graying hair over the wall into the arena. Off to the right, spectators struck the hands of a second man in a dark tunic trying to pull himself back over the wall, dropping him to the ground. The first man appeared uninjured in the fall, but the second got up limping. When the men raised their hands and cried out for help, they were pelted with shouts of scorn and laughter from the crowd.

Both men tried climbing the wall, but the man in the dark tunic was forced to give up after the first attempt. This proved an advantage, for the moment. While he remained frozen, the gray-haired man continued to try to scale the wall, drawing the attention of one of the feeding lions. With his back to the arena, the man failed to perceive the lion's charge and was pulled down and smothered.

Shechem and those on the viewing stand looked to their right where a smacking sound, followed by a woman's cry, grasped their attention. "Worthless whore!" A balding, middle-aged man struck a woman across the mouth. She tried to get away, but he threw her over his shoulder and carried her screaming down to the wall.

He lifted the woman over his head with the ease of a pillow, but hesitated before throwing her down, as if changing his mind. Instead, he lowered her body, grabbed her by the arms, then leaned over the wall as far as he could before releasing her to the floor below. "No Abidan, No!" she said. "I'm sorry."

"A jealous husband," Ramalech said.

"What a waste," Bohar said. "She's a fine-looking woman."

"Ah, have we a chivalrous man among us?" Ramalech said.

Shechem knew better. Bohar was only thinking of his own libido.

"By all means, feel free to rescue her if you like" Ramalech gestured to the arena.

Bohar shook his head.

"Not that chivalrous, I guess," Ramalech said.

Malluch and Shechem joined him in a chuckle.

On the arena floor, the woman continued to scream her husband's name until one of the lions looked up from feeding and moved toward her. As the lion approached, the woman stopped screaming and, unmoving, leaned against the base of the wall in an apparent attempt to play dead. At first the lion seemed uninterested, seemingly content to sniff at her garment, before starting to walk away. A look of relief in the woman's eyes disappeared quickly when the lion turned back and tackled her, ripping into her neck and scapula.

Meanwhile, the injured man used the distraction to make his way to the abandoned boy's body and retrieve his sword. He stopped to take a deep breath.

The gate raised and two more lions entered the arena.

All color drained from the man's face.

He knelt, placing the handle of the sword in the dirt with the blade facing his heart. Leaning forward, he pushed his body onto the sword.

The crowd booed.

"Coward." Bohar said.

"I suppose you'd prefer to be eaten," Shechem said.

"No. But I sure wouldn't make it easy on the lion by falling on my sword either." Bohar pointed to the arena floor. "Look down there." The last lion chewed on a leg of the man who'd committed suicide.

"What would you do?"

"I'd make that lion regret eating me, that's what. I'd be kicking, and biting, and clawing all the way down its miserable throat."

"I don't think you ever have to worry about that."

"Why?"

"I don't believe lions eat skunk."

Bohar frowned.

Ramalech cackled. "I see that crack on the head hasn't affected your sense of humor."

"Nor my sense of gratitude, prince," Shechem said with a tip of his head. "My thanks for avenging me." He was compelled to show his appreciation, especially in front of Malluch, but inside, he took no satisfaction in the boys' death. He might have even been responsible. Had he not made himself a target by venturing out into the streets of Enoch, perhaps those boys would still be alive. Boys with their whole lives ahead of them. Now torn to shreds.

"I told you, we take care of our friends."

CHAPTER 12

In the 501st year of Noah . . .

Noah relished the pre-dawn quiet at the first hints of ashen appearing low in the eastern sky. In an hour the forest would be filled with the sounds of sawing wood and falling trees, but for now he had the morning to himself.

He and Shem made a good team anchoring opposite ends of a felling saw, but his oldest preferred to work alone with a chopping blade. And with good reason. Fast and precise, Japheth could take down by himself nearly as many trees as his father and brother working together. He often caught himself watching with pride at the way his eldest son swung an ax.

Selection and preparation of a building site and the harvesting of timber for the ark had not been without its challenges. Shem objected to the use of a nearby hill chosen for construction, complaining it was too far away from the forest. He also needed constant reminding to cut only gopherwood trees for use on the ark. "What difference does it make?" Shem had said. "Wood is wood." Noah might have agreed, but in his heart he knew the value of trusting God—including His selection of building materials.

Saying goodbye to the night, he knelt before his Creator. "God of Adam, God of Seth, give ear to Your humble servant. Has it

59

not been eight months since my ears burned with the words of Your righteous judgment? And have I not heeded with zeal Your commandment to commence construction of this ark?" He bowed his head to the earth, pausing to listen for the Lord's voice. "If I have found the slightest favor in Your sight, tell me now, oh God, that Your mighty hand might yet be stayed."

He continued in prayer for the remainder of the hour, receiving from the Lord a sense of peace and strengthening in his spirit. But as he prepared to rise, the thing he desired most — next to a reprieve for mankind — eluded him. Concerning Shiphrah, the Lord continued to remain silent.

He found Japheth standing quietly a few cubits away, ax at his side. "Where's your brother?"

"The last time I saw him, he was making his third trip to the woods behind the house." A slight grin crept onto Japheth's lips while he toed the grass with his sandal. "One too many green tomatoes last night, I suspect."

"All right. You want to take his side of the two-man saw, or would you prefer your trusty ax?"

"I'll take Shem's place."

"Taking pity on an old man?" Noah smiled.

"Not at all, Father. I appreciate the chance to work together."

Japheth's answer was grounded in equal parts of kindness and sincerity. "Good. Seeing it would take me about as long to cut through one of these with an ax as it would a beaver with a toothache."

Japheth laughed deep in his belly.

Soon, the two were working their way through the base of an eighty cubit gopherwood tree, the blade chewing away in alternating strokes. Sweat poured from the men's faces with each push-pull manipulation of the saw.

Halfway through the trunk, Noah thought he heard a creaking sound and raised his hand to stop the cutting. "Did you hear that?"

"That creaking? Yes." Both men stepped back from the tree.

60

Noah circled halfway around the trunk to inspect the cut. "What do you think?"

"Let's keep going."

The two men continued. On their fourth alternating stroke, the saw blade bound on the senior man's end, followed by a return of the creaking sound. Only this time it was shriller. As the tree began to split at the base of the cut and move up the trunk, it grew even louder. "Look out!" Noah yelled, but it was too late.

By instinct, his son threw his arm up to protect his face from the splintering slab. The failing trunk caught him under the left forearm, throwing him into an adjacent tree stump ten cubits away. Japheth let out a piercing cry that accompanied the sound of snapping bone.

Noah rushed to his injured son who lay in a heap against the stump, unable to lift his left arm. Carefully, he righted him against the splintered trunk while fighting to conceal the concern in his eyes.

Japheth groaned. "I'm all right, Father."

Words came, but not without difficulty. "Guess that will teach you to get on the other end of a saw with me again," Noah said.

Japheth grimaced, struggling to speak through short breaths. "More like teach me to move faster when you yell, 'look out.'"

Noah took a knife and cut off a strip from the bottom of his garment, positioning it in a sling around Japheth's neck to support his broken arm. What would he do now? One son nursing a stomach ache, the other a broken arm. Not exactly the circumstance he had envisioned as an answer to this morning's prayer.

Even so, the Lord had given him a command, and he wasn't about to lose a full day due to injury or illness. Work on the ark must continue. Sick or not, Shem would have to take his place on the other end of the saw.

* * *

61

Noah and Shem entered the house just before sunset following a record-setting day of cutting. Despite the previous night's overindulgence, Shem proved more than up to the task. His father estimated the two of them had taken down and trimmed eighteen two-cubit trees, three more than their average per day. In fact, so impressed was he at his son's zeal for work, he secretly considered encouraging him to eat unripe tomatoes before bed every night.

Japheth met them at the door, the two wooden splints supporting his arm sticking out of the top of the sling. He winced while rotating the other arm from the shoulder in a big circle. "Father, I think I can still swing an ax with my good arm."

"I'm afraid you're going to have to rest that arm for more than a few days," Miryam said.

"With all the work there is to do?"

"God blessed this family with two strong sons. Surely, your father and brother can carry the load until your arm heals."

"What I really could use is another strong back." Noah said. A curious smirk appeared on Miryam's mouth while she continued to move plates onto a food preparation table. Shiphrah tried unsuccessfully to suppress a giggle while slicing a cucumber for the late meal. "Well, you two sure seem to take pleasure in my predicament." The two grinning woman glanced briefly at one another, but remained focused on their tasks. "What is it? What are you two up to?"

"Not a thing, my husband."

"I'm afraid your face betrays you. Your lips say to me, 'nothing,' but that smirk conveys a different message, does it not?" He was anxious, but too exhausted to take an exasperating tone. He returned the expression.

"My, you are the suspicious one."

His eyes shifted to Shiphrah. "It's hard not to be, what with Shiphrah wearing the same devious look?" The thought of the two women sharing a secret warmed his heart, for it signaled his wife had accepted Shiphrah as a member of the family. Gone were the girl's silken robes and jeweled accessories, replaced by

62

a more modest traditional wool tunic. And yet, no simplicity of dress could hide her physical beauty. Elisheva and Ariel were attractive enough. But by almost any measurement, Shiphrah, with her curved figure and fair complexion, was stunning, made more so by the astonishing tint of those green eyes.

"What do you think, Shiphrah? Should we tell him?"

"Please," she said, "before I burst with laughter."

"Husband, you said you could use another strong back," Miryam said.

"I did indeed."

Miryam's nose twitched, and the skin stretched tight across her cheeks by a smile that could no longer be contained. "Well, if you think you can wait another seven months, I just might be in a position to grant you your wish."

Though they hadn't had children for some time, Noah knew exactly what Miryam was alluding to. "Another son?"

"Well, I guess there's a chance it could be a girl, but given your natural proclivity for siring boys, I wouldn't say it was a good one."

Noah moved to embraced her. It was a tender moment marred only by the reality work on the ark would be greatly impacted by Japheth's injury. Shem was an incredible worker, but even he didn't possess the strength and endurance to fell trees by himself with the speed of his brother. Without Japheth, it meant the production of timber would be reduced by half, not one third. And what would the Lord think about that?

CHAPTER 13

In the 507th year of Noah . . .

Seven years into construction, Noah signaled from atop scaffolding supporting the thirty-cubit high stem post to his eldest son at the stern. Up close, Japheth's four cubit and a handbreadth height and 230 pounds cut an imposing presence. But down the length of five massive sixty cubit timbers joined end to end to form the ark's keel, he appeared an insect. He beckoned his son again with a wave to indicate an end to the day's labor before descending the scaffolding.

Below, Shem pounded the last few trenails into the scarf-joint connecting the stem post to the keel.

To his credit, Shem had really stepped to the fore following his brother's accident, often volunteering to work past daylight to compensate for the reduction in manpower. And though no one was to blame for his son's illness, Noah could see in his face the guilt he carried because of Japheth's injury. Fortunately, the other news from that fateful day had resulted in a much better outcome.

Five years ago, Miryam presented her husband with a strong, healthy son—whom they named Ham—an event for which Shiphrah had further proven her mettle by serving as midwife for the birth. But the delivery proved bittersweet, with Noah facing the likelihood Lamech would never see his third grandchild.

As a jogging Japheth reached them, Shem tossed his hammer, bouncing it off the keel. "How is it you have so much energy left?" Shem said, the distinctive sound of iron striking wood ringing in their ears.

"Just hungry, I guess."

"I think we've all earned a good meal today," Noah said. He and his sons wiped the sweat pouring from their bodies. When he was finished, Japheth let out a deep sigh and leaned against one of the support timbers.

Shem walked around the scaffolding and looked down the modest incline to the forest below. "Father, we're too far from the woods. And the more trees we take down, the farther away we get." He wiped his brow. "If we were building near the trees, we'd at least have some shade in the late afternoon."

"Father explained long ago why we needed to build here," Japheth said. "This was the highest grade in the area large enough to construct the ark, plus it required practically no clearing."

"Yes, but building up here is costing us time and resources. It takes forever to drag anything up that grade, and one of the oxen collapsed hauling up the last keel timber."

"Which is why we increased the team of oxen from four to six," Noah said. "But believe me when I tell you, son, you're not going to want the ark anywhere near those trees when the flood comes."

"Why not?"

"The floodwaters are going to uproot those trees like a sickle cutting through wheat. And if one of them should come crashing down on the ark, well — having had some shade to work in won't mean much then."

"Which brings up another thing. We're over eight hundred furlongs from the Eden River, and more than twice that from the Great Sea. Where will these floodwaters come from?"

"Do you doubt that with a word the Lord could cause the rivers or the seas to overflow? Or if He wishes, let loose the rains He restrains in the spring and at harvest?"

"Look around you." Shem moved his arm in an arc parallel to the horizon. "How will the Lord flood so great a plain? And what of the mountain ranges to the north and east? Can even He raise the seas to cover them?"

"And Who was it Who gave them their height? How can you have been my son all these years and still your faith is small? Indeed, they are thousands of cubits high. And if He pleases, will the Lord not be swift to level them, or, as He has promised, drown them?"

"I don't mean any disrespect, but I just can't accept it. I—"

Noah raised a hand to quiet his son, more out of caution than to keep from hearing his words. The sound of pack animals coming up the opposite side of the hill grasped his attention. He, Japheth, and Shem moved back to the east side of the scaffolding where two men—one old, one young—arrived mounted on donkeys.

"Greetings," the older man said, dismounting. "I have a farm about four furlongs on the other side of this hill. My son and I have heard your hammers and saws for some time, but seeing these timbers rise really piqued our curiosity."

"Welcome," Noah said.

"What are you building?"

"An ark."

"An ark. Isn't that like a boat or something?"

"Exactly."

While the younger man remained astride his animal, the older man moved to rest his hands on the scaffolding, looking down the length of the keel. "A boat, huh? Here on the plain?"

"Yes."

"Big boat. What's it for?"

"Are you a son of our father, Seth?"

"Yes, my family is descended from the line of Seth."

Noah glanced at Japheth, then at Shem, who shook his head. Several plausible explanations raced through his mind, but he realized the truth would become evident soon enough. "The God of Seth is bringing floodwaters upon the earth. We build this ark to save our family and a remnant of the earth's animals."

The older man remained still for three parts, like he didn't hear, then dropped his hands from the scaffolding and turned to Noah. "A flood, huh? Must be a deluge if you're building a ship this size." He smirked, as though wise to some prank being played upon him.

"It will cover the earth."

The man's focus moved in succession to Shem and Japheth, but the sternness in their faces only reflected the gravity of their father's declaration. The man backed away from the ark, his own smile fading. "Thanks for letting us take a look." The man swung onto his donkey.

"Friend, you should reconcile yourself to God and make preparations."

"Yes, well, thanks again." The man and his son started back down the hill, striking their donkeys' backsides to quicken their pace.

"See, Father? Even our neighbors think we're crazy," Shem said. "This is a waste of time. And we're all fools." He stomped away toward the house.

"Have patience with Shem, Father," Japheth said. "Five years away from Eden has been hard on him."

"So it has on us all." Noah understood full well his middle son's discontentment. Their family had been forced from a life of comfort, wealth, and respect in Eden, to one of hardship and loneliness here in the wilderness. Shem missed his friends, Japheth his grandfather. And Shiphrah. Her selfless act of warning them had changed the course of her life, one he hoped she wouldn't come to regret.

"But more so for my brother. Shem was always skeptical of things confronting him in the natural world, much less the supernatural."

"And you?"

"I admit, there are days when I question what we're doing out here. But then I have something Shem is struggling with right now:"

"What's that?"

"Faith."

"Faith in the Almighty?" Noah's voice boomed.

"Faith in you."

Noah lifted a brow.

"Faith that as our father you wouldn't ask us to do this thing unless you truly believed it was from God. And for me, that's good enough."

He took hold of his son's upper arm. "I'll tell you a truth I never even told your mother. When I first heard His voice, I thought I was hearing things. Shem was right. The wind does strange things to the ears."

"So what convinced you otherwise?"

He paused. "There was something else. Something in addition to the voice."

"What was it?"

"When YAH called my name, I not only heard it, I felt it." He touched his finger to the center of his chest. "In here."

"You felt it?"

"It's difficult to explain. But it was like the message was being written on my heart at the same time the Lord was speaking in my ear."

Japheth's eyes widened.

"Having heard it once, I remember every word as if I'd memorized it. Five years later, I still do."

"Without having written it down. How is that possible?"

"Because it's written here." He touched his breast again. "Not here." He touched his temple.

Japheth shook his head. "I don't understand."

"Son, you may find this hard to believe, but I don't either. In fact, there are many things in this world beyond human understanding. But if I've learned anything in this life, it's that we have to take some things, obedience to God for one, on—"

"Faith."

Noah smiled. "That's right."

They turned and walked down the hill together.

CHAPTER 14

Shem remained silent through the evening meal, but Noah knew his son well enough to know the discussion begun at the building site this afternoon wasn't over. He decided to lance the boil. "So, Shem, you think us fools?"

Shem looked up from a crust of barley and spelt bread and gazed into his father's eyes. "I do not wish to sound impudent, but yes, I do."

"Since I asked you to speak your mind, how could I consider your answer impudent?"

"All right. Five years, Father—five years we've wasted here when we could have used the time to recruit an army."

"An army? For what purpose?"

"To retake the city, of course."

"You think it possible to retake Eden?"

"Japheth said it the night we left. Grandfather had many allies in the city, men willing to stand with us and fight to defend his government."

"And what do you suppose has become of those men now?"

"Who knows? If they're not in hiding, they're probably scattered across the countryside."

"If they're fortunate. Those who couldn't be won over by Malluch are most likely dead or imprisoned."

Shem stood. "Father. These aren't strangers we're talking about. These are friends—some you've known for hundreds of years—being killed and imprisoned."

"Have you forgotten the Lord's commandment to your father?" Miryam said.

"No, Mother. I only wish he'd forget it."

"You don't mean that."

"Forgive me, Mother, but Father asked me to speak my mind. This is how I feel."

Noah rose to place his hands on Shem's shoulders, softening his expression before speaking. "I forgive you, because I understand your feelings for our countrymen. But there is a reality you must face: these friends, the city, everything you knew there, have all been condemned. When the time comes, they will be wiped from the earth along with everything else."

Shem's ears reddened. "How can you stand there and say that and not want to do something about it?"

"Do you think I don't pray night and day for the Lord to relent from His sentence upon the earth?"

"For all the good it will do." Shem broke free of his father's grasp. He took three steps before wheeling back around. "I still say our time would be better spent recruiting an army. It makes a lot more sense than building an ark in the middle of nowhere."

Ariel rose to stand next to her husband. "I agree."

"Suppose we did put together an army and succeeded in recapturing the city," Noah said. "Don't you see? It would all be for naught when the floodwaters come."

"If they come." Shem grabbed a full wineskin from a peg on the wall and marched out of the house.

"Father, you realize our neighbor out there today was only the beginning?" Japheth said. "There will be others."

"Most assuredly."

71

"You don't seem worried."

"I have no delusion about keeping the ark a secret, only this family's whereabouts from Malluch."

"Don't you think discovery of the one will lead to the other?"

To reduce the risk of detection following their confrontation with the two soldiers, Noah had begun sending the women into the village for supplies. On occasion, he or one of his sons would enter the village in disguise after dark to procure a special need. "Has it not been five years since we've seen soldiers?"

"We've been lucky."

"Or divinely protected," Miryam said through thin lips set beneath olive cheeks and bracketed by slowly graying hair.

Noah nodded.

"Father, five years it's taken us to fashion the keel alone," Japheth said. "Which at this rate means we have a long way to go."

A five-year old Ham rose from his seat next to Shiphrah, and joined his father. "When do I get to help with the ark?"

Noah placed a hand on top of his head. "Soon, my son." He turned back to Japheth. "So what's your fear?"

"Simply that the more time passes, and as the footprint of the ark increases upon the land, so too does our risk of being discovered."

"Granted, the scope of the task is likely to make it a local attraction. But that doesn't mean word of the construction will reach Eden."

Elisheva stared out the window, looking toward the building site. "But what if Malluch does find out?" Her voice quivered. "It's not as if we can just up and take the ark with us."

"He'll think the same thing our neighbor thought today," Noah said. "Some crazy family is building a boat in the middle of a plain. He'll scoff. Malluch wouldn't travel over a thousand furlongs unless he thought there was some profit in it."

"Or he knew you were still alive," Japheth said.

The paleness of Miryam's face confirmed her feelings about that supposition.

72

Noah often regretted they hadn't traveled farther from Eden before settling. But then what would it matter? Malluch would pursue them to the ends of the earth to keep his vow. "We'll just have to remain cautious and continue to rely on the Lord's providence."

"We wouldn't have to rely on providence if it weren't for her." Ariel motioned to Shiphrah. "Shem is right. We've wasted five years here, and why? But for the word of a stranger from that wicked city."

"Ariel!" Miryam put an arm around Shiphrah. "I know you're upset, but that doesn't give you cause to attack Shiphrah."

"My being upset has nothing to do with it. I'm sorry, Mother, but the only reason we're in this wasteland is because she showed up at our door one night with a story."

"It wasn't a story," Shiphrah said.

"Wasn't it? Father said she saved our lives, but can any of us truly be sure? What if there was no plot to murder us? Suppose Shem was right and she was sent to frighten us into leaving Eden."

Shiphrah lifted her trembling chin. "What I told you that night was the truth."

"I thought I had effectively dispelled Shem's theory the night we left, but possibly it bears repeating," Noah said. "Had she been part of a conspiracy to scare us into leaving Eden, she surely wouldn't have begged to come with us. She could have simply delivered the fraudulent threat and departed."

"Maybe she was sent to spy on us."

"I'm sure if Shiphrah were a spy, she would have stolen away a long time ago and made our whereabouts known to Malluch."

"All right then, answer me this." Ariel's voice rose. "How did those two soldiers find us after only six months?"

"They didn't find us. We were careless in allowing ourselves to be seen openly in the village."

"Yes, but why were they in that village to begin with?"

"Probably part of a larger contingent patrolling the area."

73

"She could have got word to them."

"And just how did she accomplish that, considering she's been with us every moment of the last five years?"

"She could have slipped out when we were all sleeping, gone to the village, and sent a message leading them right to us."

Through tearing eyes, even Shiphrah smirked at that one.

"I think you're reaching for pomegranates," Japheth said.

"What do you mean?"

"He means your enmity for Shiphrah is affecting your perception of reality," Noah said.

"But—"

"I think there have been enough hurt feelings to go around for one evening, don't you?"

Ariel bit her lip, but didn't speak.

"Besides." He put his arm around Ham. "In a couple more years, we'll have an extra pair of hands and another strong back to help us. Right, son?"

"Right, Father," Ham said with a wide grin.

Movement caught his attention, and he pointed to an insect crawling along the floor against the far wall. "Look, a locust."

Growing up, he'd played with all sorts of insects, including these brown grasshoppers, but from where Noah sat this one didn't resemble any locust he'd seen.

Ham scurried over and bent to pick up the insect.

"No, son!" Miryam screamed.

With Ham's fingers less than a handbreadth away, Japheth's huge foot came crashing down on the insect, crushing the scorpion under his sandal.

The child squealed in disappointment.

"Not that one, little brother," Japheth said. "Bad bug."

As Japheth reached to pick up the insect, Noah leaned back and allowed a smile to cross his lips, thankful his doubts had proven unfounded.

74

When Miryam first announced their third child, his second thought, after elation, was concern over Shem and Japheth's reaction to having a younger brother. A girl wouldn't have presented a problem, and he trusted his sons to be the first to want to spoil her. But he worried the arrival of another boy, one so distant in age from his brothers, might stir jealousy among them.

Japheth hoisted Ham onto his shoulders and the two ducked going through the doorway to dispose of the scorpion outside. *What a great father he will make someday.*

CHAPTER 15

Three and a half years following his first military victory, Shechem led his army into a large rundown village located far to the east of Eden. What struck him most wasn't the village's state of disrepair, but how little attention his army received marching in.

The villagers continued about their business, displaying indifference and ignoring them. Residents walked the streets, worked their fields, tended flocks, and drew water from a central well. Although most of them looked apprehensive, they did not panic. He had a theory why: these people had seen troops before.

The second thing he noticed was the quiet. None of the people engaged in conversation, only hand gestures. Even some children playing in front of a nearby house chased each other in total silence.

Bohar turned to him. "What is this? A village of mutes?"

A woman in tattered clothing carrying a basket walked up the street toward them. Shechem motioned to her. "Woman, come here."

She stopped and drew the basket to her chest. Her gaze darted left and right.

He dismounted. "Please. We're not going to hurt you."

The woman slowly approached him, bowing her head when she got within a few cubits.

"What's the name of this place?"

She raised her arm, sweeping it around the village, but uttered not a sound.

"Do you understand?"

The woman nodded.

"Can you speak?"

She shook her head.

"Is there anyone who can speak?"

Again, she shook her head.

"I was right," Bohar said. "It's a village of mutes."

Shechem knew it was more than that. Even mutes are capable of making sounds. This woman didn't even make an attempt.

He looked up to the sound of an old man cursing at the far end of the village. He was being dragged toward them by two of Eden's soldiers. "Well, here comes someone who isn't."

The soldiers brought the man to him. Burned skin surrounded the hollows of his eyes, the eyelids sinking in overtop empty sockets. The man struggled against the soldiers' grip. "Get your hands off me you lousy Enoch scum."

"We're not from Enoch," Shechem said.

The man stopped struggling. "You're not? Where are you from then?"

"Eden."

"What brings you this far east?"

"We were trying to obtain some information from this woman here, but she can't seem to speak."

"Nobody in this village can speak but me."

"What happened?"

"Bring the woman to me."

Another soldier guided the woman to the blind man, who reached for her arm. "It's all right," he said. "Show them."

The woman opened her mouth, revealing a severed stump where her tongue should be. Shechem grunted.

"Following a raid by Enoch's soldiers seven years ago, the head of the village called Ramalech a worthless dog," the blind man said. "So he had his soldiers cut out the tongues of everyone in the village, including the children."

"And you?"

"He wanted to leave one person who could tell what happened. So he put out my eyes instead."

"You mean none of the women in the village can talk?" Bohar said.

Shechem shot Bohar his disgust, knowing why he'd asked the question.

"No woman, no man, no child," the blind man said.

"Let him go," Shechem said.

While the woman led the blind man away, he climbed back on his horse and addressed the four captains nearest him. "Pass the word. We're leaving."

"Without taking any spoils or men?" Bohar said.

"Look at this place. The people. Their clothes. You'd be lucky to get a handful of coins from the lot of them."

"Surely the men are worth something. They may not be able to talk, but they can work, can't they?"

"We're not taking a bunch of mutes. There are plenty of other villages and cities where we can find able-bodied men."

Bohar watched two young women walking away from them on the opposite side of the road. "And the women?"

"What about them?"

"You're kidding, right? A city where the women can't scream. It's paradise."

Shechem shook his head. "Is there no low to which you won't sink? Like I said, we're leaving."

"What about leaving me behind for a couple of hours? I'll catch up."

78

"It's all right with me. Just be careful you don't run into any more irate husbands or fathers."

Shechem gave the order to march.

Bohar led the way out of the village.

CHAPTER 16

In the 515th year of Noah . . .

Shechem doubted whether this day would ever come. Even with three thousand slaves, the wall had taken longer to complete — fifteen years — than he envisioned. But the city was finally secure.

Malluch had called for a late morning gathering of the people at the south gate to mark the occasion and to honor his commander. In a rare public appearance, Claudia, dressed in a scarlet silk chiton, stood beside him on the right, opposite Channah and Naomi to his left. With the last arriving citizens packing the square, Claudia leaned in to whisper in his ear. "Look at him. I might as well be turning on a spit."

Shechem followed his wife's eyes. Bohar leaned against a wall a few cubits away, staring at her while picking his teeth with a long, dirty fingernail. It took all Shechem's willpower to contain his disgust in front of the crowd, biting the inside of his lip hard enough to taste blood.

Malluch addressed the gathering. "Citizens. Today, the future of your children, and your children's children, has been secured." Cheers rose from the crowd. "These stones represent more than a wall to protect the city. They stand as a symbol of the ingenuity and engineering greatness of the people of Eden." The cheering intensified.

Shechem took a moment to admire his handiwork, scanning along the top of the great structure while his friend continued to speak. Forty courses of limestone, rising twenty cubits above ground, stretched four hundred furlongs around the city. Two fifteen-cubit high bronze-plated iron gates, one at the north, and the other at the south end of the city, controlled access. Watchtowers flanked either side of the gates, and at every thousand cubits along the wall's perimeter, making an undetected approach impossible.

Malluch's touch upon his back and the sound of his name followed by cheers from the crowd brought him back from distraction.

"People of Eden, I present to you Shechem. Friend. Confidant. Commander of the Guard and overseer of the building of this magnificent wall."

Soldiers in attendance waved swords in support of their commander, who blushed at the adulation. He drew and raised his sword in response, which provoked an even louder display. Malluch lifted his hand — revealing the palm scarred with burnt flesh — to quiet the crowd. "This wall shall make us impervious to attack. Soon, we shall rival even the greatness of Enoch." The crowd roared. Malluch grabbed his elbow. "Come with me. I have something to show you."

Shechem and Claudia followed the governor and Bohar the twenty-five cubits from the south gate to where a cart and several horses awaited them. Shechem helped his wife into the cart, while the other two men mounted horses for the ride to the center of the city. One of Eden's finest soldiers manned the cart, and the sound of leather slapping horseback rose through the square upon their departure.

Nearing their destination, the majestic marble walls of the palace that had replaced Malluch's previous lodgings rose high into the air. The horses stopped and discharged the passengers, who exited and proceeded up the twenty-four steps leading into the palace. Once inside, Shechem expected they'd be taken to the great hall for a toast, but instead they were led to the rear and onto a terrace. Below them and to the right stood a large, two-story house of considerable opulence. He'd been unaware of its construction. "What's this?"

"This, my friend, is for you." The governor bowed to Claudia. "Forgive my manners. What I should have said is, this is for you and your wife."

Claudia nodded.

Shechem's jaw slacked, a reaction both to the magnitude of the gift, and the fact Malluch had thought him worthy of it. Yes, he'd worked hard and had spent countless nights away from home on expeditions to secure slaves for the building of the wall. Worse was putting up with Bohar's incessant lusts. But he never expected this. "For the first time in my life, words fail me."

"Thank you, Malluch." Claudia's eyes sparkled. "It is a most extravagant gift."

"Yes, thank you," Shechem said.

Malluch raised a finger. "Nobly earned. Indeed, some might think it a small reward for one who has shown such loyalty to Eden—and to me." He walked to the edge of the terrace and looked down on the house, then turned back to Shechem. "Besides, I can't have my second in command and his beautiful wife living in such, shall we say, modest accommodations."

"Again, thank—"

Two guards interrupted them. "Lord, the former governor and a large group of elders are at the front door demanding to see you," one of them said.

"Want me to get rid of them?" Bohar said.

"No," Malluch said. "They would only be back tomorrow, and the next day, and the next. Better to pull this weed now before it has time to grow."

"I meant for good."

"How many times do I have to tell you? The patriarchs are father to a great multitude who serve Eden. Do you think I want to destroy a third of the population putting down a revolt because we had some old men killed?"

"They could just disappear, like the Preacher."

Malluch addressed the guards. "Show them into the great hall. I will join them momentarily."

"Yes, my lord," the guards said in unison.

Malluch suggested to Claudia she take a look at their new home while he, Shechem, and Bohar met with the elders of Eden. He directed her to a nearby staircase leading to the back courtyard and the house. As she disappeared down the stairs, the three men proceeded to the great hall.

"Most honored fathers," he said with a broad smile, leading his two lieutenants through the door to address the thirty or so men gathered there. Well advanced in years, nearly all the men had graying or white hair and flowing beards. A few, including Methuselah, leaned against staffs. "To what do I owe the honor of a visit from the patriarchs of Eden? May I offer you some refreshment?" He gestured to a nearby servant. "Wine for our guests."

"We didn't come to drink," Lamech said. Noah's father appeared less feeble than the others. His bleached hair and beard were neatly trimmed, and he moved about easily without a staff.

Malluch gestured with a wave, belaying his last command. "Lamech, Lamech. Such a somber tone. And on such a perfect day. A day of celebration."

"Celebration. The city should be in mourning."

"After fifteen years of construction and the successful completion of a wall that will ensure the people's safety for generations to come? Why should they mourn?"

"Innocence lost. Fifteen years ago, Eden had no need of walls. Its people were simple farmers who wanted nothing more than to sow their crops, tend their herds, and raise their families. Today you make Eden a fortress."

"The world has become a dangerous place."

"It would seem more so for those outside of Eden. Would such safeguards be necessary were it not for the years of aggression Eden has waged against its neighbors? You fear retaliation, so the walls go up."

Malluch's eyelids narrowed. "What do you want, Lamech?"

"The slaves."

Malluch looked at Shechem, then Bohar. "What about them?"

"I appeal to you in the name of our fathers to set them free."

"And why would I do that?"

"Beyond a gesture of mercy—you simply don't need them anymore. As you pointed out, the walls of Eden are complete." Lamech lifted his chin to the hall's high ceiling, raising his arm above his head. "So, too, this palace."

"Set the slaves free—so they can organize revolt against me?"

"Against the army of Eden? I doubt even you believe them capable of that, Malluch. Let them return to their villages and towns, to their families. Have they not suffered long enough in bondage?"

"My dear former governor. Could it be age has shortened your eyesight? You look at these walls, this palace, and see an ending. But I tell you they are just the beginning."

Murmurs rose from among the elders.

"The beginning?" Lamech stiffened.

"If you would accompany me onto the portico." He and Shechem led the patriarchs from the great hall back out onto the palace's columned front porch. Bohar and several soldiers followed a few paces behind the elders, dogs watching for the sheep to stray from the herd. "Elders of Eden," Malluch said, "except for these walls, you see a city much as it was twenty years ago. A city built by farmers."

"And content to be so." Methuselah said.

"But so stunted." The governor extended his arm along the northern skyline. "Imagine for a moment the construction of ten, or even twenty additional winepresses, each with its own tower and vat."

The patriarchs continued to speak in whispers among themselves. Malluch pointed to the south. "A garrison to house and train Eden's army, with a prison to hold its enemies. And an arena to serve as a venue for sport."

Lamech crossed his arms in front of him. "Built on the backs of our neighbors, I suppose."

"Walls cannot rise without slaves to build them."

"God did not make men to be slaves to other men," Methuselah said.

"Oh, didn't He?" Malluch said. "You think nothing of bridling a donkey or yoking an ox to do your bidding. Why not a man, who is more intelligent and far easier to train?"

"Because man was made in the image of God," Lamech said.

Malluch laughed.

"You mock God, Malluch!" Methuselah raised his staff and shook it in his face.

"Proudly." He lifted a brow.

Some of the elders gasped.

"I'll mock anybody or anything that stands in the way of Eden becoming the greatest city on earth," he said. Several elders placed hands over their ears and shook their heads while walking away. "But I'll tell you what. As an alternative to freeing the slaves, how about I—"

"What?" Lamech said.

"How about I just have them all put to death?"

"Malluch, in the name of YAH."

"Today, the lives of the slaves are forfeit. On the day you trouble me again about them, I will surely have them all executed. Such is the vow I make to the patriarchs of Eden."

85

The elders left in silence. Trailing the group, Lamech whirled after two steps to confront him. "Winepresses? An arena? Soon there will be no need for you to travel to Enoch, will there?"

Malluch didn't speak, letting ivory teeth behind grinning lips serve as his answer.

* * *

The celebration in the palace had gone on long into the evening, reminding Shechem of one of their visits to Enoch. Food, wine, and music flowed freely throughout the night to the delight of the more than three hundred celebrants. Malluch had used the opportunity to lavish praise on his army commander, drawing repeated cheers from the dozens of soldiers in attendance.

Now back in the home the governor had built for them, he and his wife shared a last chalice of wine before preparing to retire. She'd even managed to show affection, touching his hand and arm several times while they spoke. Then without saying a word, she placed her cup on a table and headed for the bedroom, turning to give him a last alluring look. It was an expression he recognized from years past, one that said she wanted him. She disappeared around the corner.

After a day like today, he questioned whether his suspicions about her had been unfounded. She'd been the perfect wife: attentive, supportive, rarely straying from his side throughout the day as the accolades were heaped upon him. Though he'd long suspected, there had never been any proof of her unfaithfulness. More than once he'd chosen to come home unexpectedly. Each time she'd been there. And although their coming together had decreased in frequency, she'd been careful not to spurn him completely.

Maybe their relationship would return to normal now that they were in their new home. And if something was going on, maybe it would be curtailed with so many watchful eyes around the

86

palace. For the first time in years, he saw real hope for a renewal of their marriage.

He took a last drink of wine and set the cup on the table next to his wife's chalice. He called to her.

No answer.

He called a second time, again receiving no response. He walked into their bedroom. His wife was asleep on the bed, still in her celebration gown.

CHAPTER 17

Noah had a great vantage point to see the commotion racing toward them from their house below. He and Shem were standing on shores twenty-five cubits high, preparing to fasten a longitudinal segment of framing between two rib sections at the front of the ark. Shiphrah chased Ham up the hill, chalky clouds of dust billowing from her hair as she ran.

"Get back here, you little aardvark!" Shiphrah said.

Ham was filling out as a young man, and even though he was just fifteen, he was fast enough to stay several steps in front of his adopted sister. When he reached the top of the hill, he peered over his shoulder where Shiphrah was gaining on him, then bore down to reach the ark's skeleton.

Once inside the structure, Ham increased his lead, nimbly weaving in and out of the transverse ribs along the left side while Shiphrah struggled to keep up. Passing beneath Noah and Shem, Ham climbed through the timbers like a monkey in a tree. He stopped several cubits above Noah and Shem, huffing and puffing to catch his breath.

"Come down here," Shiphrah said.

"How about you come get me," Ham said in a slightly effeminate voice.

88

Shiphrah shook her fist "I'm going to pound you."

"Not from down there you're not."

"Father, make him come down."

"What happened, daughter?" Noah said.

"What happened? Look at my hair. Ham dumped a bowl of flour on my head."

Biting his lip to restrain a smile, he looked to Ham.

"I just wanted to see how she would look as an old woman," Ham said.

"That wasn't a nice thing to do, son. And it was a waste of food."

Shem and Ham snickered.

Shiphrah reached to her waist to grab a handful of hair, lifting it in the air. Flakes of flour fell to the ground. "How can you joke about it?" Shiphrah said.

Noah hadn't really meant to be humorous, even though it had come out that way. "It will come out." The men turned to the sound of Miryam's voice wafting up the hill, calling for Shiphrah. *Now there's an answer to unspoken prayer if ever there was one.* "Your mother is calling you."

"Good thing for him." Shiphrah pointed up at Ham. "Because I intended to wait right here until he came down." She exited the ark then bent to shake the flour from her dangling hair in front of an approaching Japheth.

"Trying for an older look, Shiphrah?" he said.

She swung her hair in his direction, showering him with flour. Japheth coughed and brushed himself with both hands. "No, I thought I'd use my hair to sift the flour we're using to make your meal." She peered at him through narrowed eyes, forcing from him a sheepish grin.

"Shiphrah," Miryam called again.

"Coming." She looked up at Ham. "But he still has a pounding coming." She headed down the hill.

As the top of her white-streaked head vanished from sight, Japheth continued to brush himself off. "I'd stay out of her way for a while if I were you, little brother."

"If you're through playing around," Shem said to Ham. "How about helping us set the other end of this section."

Ham climbed down next to Noah. "Father," Ham said. "Why does Shiphrah have no husband?"

He'd been expecting this question for a long time. Ham had grown up in a house where all the women were married. It only made sense he would eventually come to wonder about Shiphrah, more so now that he'd entered adolescence. "You remember the story I told you of how she came to us?"

Ham nodded.

"Shiphrah's warning made her a fugitive as well and sacrificed her chance for a husband."

"That's not fair." Ham's brow furrowed.

"We not only owe her our lives, but a whole lot more. You might want to remember that the next time you think about throwing flour in her hair."

Ham dipped his chin.

"Here they come," Shem said. Noah and his two other sons looked downhill to where a group of fourteen people approached along a road from the east. Eight were mounted on donkeys, with a half dozen more—two girls, four boys—riding in an ox-drawn cart. They stopped on the road along the base of the hill.

Noah's prediction about the ark becoming a local attraction had come to pass. Their visit from a neighbor ten years ago was just the beginning. Now he, and dozens of people from nearby farms and villages, made almost daily pilgrimages to the ark site. Some were merely passersby, curious types who altered their travel route to see the construction. Others brought a meal, sat down in the grass, and made a day of it. One industrious farmer even set up a stand to sell bread, fresh vegetables, and water. "Dependable as the sunrise."

90

A man he recognized as the neighbor who'd first visited the ark waved when he dismounted.

"You boys planning to work all day?" he said, looking to the sky. "I think we're going to get some rain."

The sky was nearly cloudless. Shem shook his head.

How many times had they heard the same chides? Over the years, their neighbor had become predictable to the point of boredom. If he only knew what was coming, he'd choose another subject to deride them about. Yet for all his ignorant jesting, at least this neighbor had remained good natured about it. Not so with so many of the others.

"As long as we have light to see," Noah said for the hundredth time.

A man driving the oxen stood up in the cart. "Shipbuilder. My wife did laundry this morning with no place to dry it. Mind if I hang it on some of your boat timbers?" The crowd burst into laughter.

"I wonder if he'd be laughing if I hung *him* from one of the timbers," Japheth said.

"Shipbuilder, I hear you're looking to put a bunch of animals aboard this boat. I'll give you a good deal on a couple of donkeys." More laughter from the onlookers.

"Only if they're better looking than you, donkey face," Ham hollered back. The four boys in the cart, who Noah suspected were sons of the driver, jumped out and searched along the ground for something.

"Ham!" His father was concerned about more than the propriety of his son's outburst. They had enough to worry about without antagonizing the onlookers into more than name-calling.

"But Father, how long must we take these insults?"

"Did his words hurt you?"

"Well, yes."

"Show me your bruises."

"Bruises?"

"Bruises, cuts, scrapes."

"Ham quickly scanned his torso and both sides of his hands. "I—"

"The only thing injured is your pride. And believe me, it will heal."

A loud cracking sound against the ark's frame drew their attention back down the hill. About halfway up the incline, the four boys threw rocks.

Japheth started toward them, but a rock glanced off one of the beams, striking Ham in the forehead and sending him backwards off the shoring. Noah ducked under a timber and dove to the edge of the support to catch Ham by the forearm.

His youngest hung suspended twenty-five cubits above the ground.

Shem rushed to help Noah, but his older son was quicker, scaling the ark's frame in a matter of parts. He came up beneath Ham and grabbed him about the waste with one arm, while holding onto a crossbeam with the other. "Got him."

Noah released his grip and Japheth started back down with his unconscious brother cradled against his hip. Meanwhile, at the base of the hill, the sounds of squeaking wheels and galloping feet hinted at what they would see. Dust hung in the air while his family's tormenters headed back up the road from which they came.

* * *

Noah stood watching over Ham until his eyelids began to flutter. Miryam pulled a cloth soaked in cool water from his forehead, revealing a nasty crease above his right eyebrow.

Relief washed over him upon his son's return to consciousness. "Welcome back, son."

"How do you feel?" Miryam said.

"Stupid," Ham said. "I heard the rocks hitting the ark and didn't do a thing to move out of the way."

"I mean how does your head feel?"

"It hurts."

"It will, for a while. But I want you to take it easy the rest of the day."

"And leave Japheth and Shem to carry my load? Not a chance."

Japheth touched Ham's shoulder. "It's all right, little brother. Shem and I have it." Ham turned to Shem, who winked and nodded.

Ariel and Elisheva leaned over to speak a word of comfort to Ham before departing to another part of the house. Shiphrah sat down beside him, her long hair brushing against his arm. Ham wove his fingers through the few remaining strands of bleached hair. "I still think you'll look good in your old age."

"Thanks," Shiphrah said. "Looks like you got yourself a reprieve from a beating."

"Believe it or not, I'd rather have taken the pounding."

The whole family laughed.

"Father."

"Yes, my son."

Ham reached up to the wound on his forehead. "This one hurts more."

"Hurts more than what?"

"A wound to my pride."

"Don't worry. It will heal just as quickly. Now get some rest."

As he turned to leave, Ham grabbed his arm. "Do you have to go just yet?"

"Not if you don't want me to." Noah nodded at Shiphrah, who resumed her chores. He sat on the other side of Ham. "What is it?"

"How about a story? Like the ones you used to tell me."

"A story, huh? Now let me see." He wrapped his fingers around his chin to give Ham the impression he was deep in thought. "I

93

think I've about exhausted my collection of — I've got it. Something different from all the others. This story is true."

"A true story?"

"Yes. Has anyone ever told you the story about your great-great-grandfather?"

"No, but I'm curious because I overheard Shem and Japheth talking about it over a year ago. But when I asked them, all they would tell me was he disappeared."

"He didn't disappear, son. He was taken."

"Who took him?"

"Did your brothers tell you his name?"

"Enoch. But that's the name of that wicked city to the northeast. Surely he wasn't named after it?"

"No. Cain's firstborn was also named Enoch. The city was built long before your great-great-grandfather was born."

"So who took him?"

"To my way of thinking, Enoch was the greatest of our fathers, a man so righteous in his ways it was said he walked with God. Enoch was also a mighty prophet. He was the first to warn that God would return one day to execute judgment on the wicked and on those who had spoken evil against Him. About 580 years ago, your great-grandfather and Enoch were out tending the fields together when they were surrounded by a great light radiating from heaven. So bright was this light that your great-grandfather could barely make out the form of Enoch standing only a few cubits away."

Ham blinked rapidly beneath ever-raising eyebrows.

"And your great-grandfather tried calling out to him. But his voice was restrained and no sound came forth from his mouth. So he tried moving toward Enoch, but his feet were as if set in stone. Then after fifty-four parts, the brilliance of the light began to fade, and with it the image of Enoch. And when the light was gone, Enoch was gone with it."

"Are you saying God took him?"

94

"Yes, son. Now rest."

"Incredible." Ham smiled before closing his eyes.

Noah watched him for a few dozen parts until he'd drifted off. They were lucky today. A split part later and Ham would have fallen to his death. But what about tomorrow? Surely these mockers, or others like them, would be back and then what? Would the ease with which they'd taken out Ham provoke them to even greater acts of violence? Moving to the higher levels of the ark's construction came with its own perils, ones made worse now that Noah and his sons had become targets.

Tomorrow, they would arm themselves.

CHAPTER 18

In the 525th year of Noah . . .

Shechem looked in awe upon Enoch from the safety of a second story balcony in the prince's palace. Below, a celebration akin to none he'd witnessed since his injury here twenty-five years ago spilled out into the streets with hundreds of people. Tomorrow, a sacrifice to the gods of this land would be offered, but tonight was a night for revelry.

The scene reminded him of the marketplace at nighttime, with vendors lining both sides of the street. Only these merchants weren't there to haggle over the price of a melon or a loaf of bread. He might as well have had a front row seat at the arena, watching while hapless victims scurry about trying to keep from being eaten alive.

From doorways and street corners, men and women offered themselves to the many intoxicated patrons staggering by. Even those declining service often found their purses lightened by an affectionate touch to distract them from the unseen fingers slipping into their pockets.

Dozens of young men banded together in packs of three or more to roam Enoch's avenues in search of victims. After a while, even the drunks learned to stay together to keep from being robbed.

Two women brawling in the dirt over a customer to the left of Shechem's balcony drew only passing attention.

One enterprising young woman overestimated her cleverness when she foolishly tried targeting one of Enoch's soldiers. It was a mistake that would cost her more than her virtue.

Pressing her mouth against her would-be victim's ear, she deftly located and removed the soldier's moneybag. Everything was going perfectly during the transfer until several coins fell out and clanged together on the ground. Alerted to the theft, the soldier grabbed her by the arm, drew his sword, and cut her hand off. With all the concern of someone reaching for a dropped scarf, he plucked the moneybag from the fingers of the severed appendage.

On another corner, a woman bartered with a man for her young child. Only the transaction took a deadly turn when the man, possibly upset over the asking price, pulled a knife and stabbed the woman in the chest. He then seized the boy by the arm and pulled him down the street, leaving his mother to bleed out on the ground.

For a moment, Shechem wanted to go to her aid. But the screams of a man being beaten and yanked down a side street awakened him to reality. For the next 180 parts, people walked around or over the woman's dying body. One man, who had stepped in her blood, stooped to wipe his sandal with the hem of her garment. When she reached to grab his arm, he dragged her several dozen cubits down the street. "Get off me!" he yelled, pulling free and running away.

As if by command, the screaming subsided and the gangs rushed to hide among the buildings. The sound of an approaching cart driven by a middle-aged couple garnered his attention. In the rear, two young women and a teenage boy sat on straw-covered floorboards. They seemed out of place when they stopped across from the balcony where Shechem watched.

"Hello there," the man called out to the flesh peddlers standing nearby. "Is there a place we can spend the night?" An eerie silence hung in the air, broken only by the cursing of the two harlots who continued to scrap in the street. "We've traveled far. Is there somewhere we can rest?"

Like wolves approaching from four directions, no fewer than twenty howling men descended upon the family, grabbing and pulling them from the cart. The pillagers ripped their clothes off even whilst they carried their screaming victims away, each in a different direction. Two other men climbed aboard the cart and drove it—and all evidence the family ever existed— away. It was over in less than eighteen parts.

Once the remaining revelers returned to the street, Shechem decided he'd seen enough and turned to the equally rowdy gathering taking place inside the palace. Before entering, his eyes were drawn one last time to the macabre image of a dead body on one corner and a severed hand on the other.

When he entered from the balcony, two men, an intoxicated guest, and a palace guard met him. He moved back to allow the drunk to stumble past down the hall. "Are you the Eden Army Commander?" the guard said.

"Yes, I'm Shechem."

"Malluch would like to see you."

He was just a bit surprised. The governor had bid goodnight several hours ago, meaning Shechem hadn't expected to see him again until morning.

He followed a pace behind the soldier down a long corridor to where a pair of double doors opened to a room on the right. As they approached, two naked men holding hands ran into the hallway, saw them, and scurried back into the room. Laughter and sighs of passion spilled out into the corridor from the entrance. The guard passed by without looking in, but Shechem couldn't control his curiosity.

Dozens of pillows scattered the floor of the room, where forty or more men and women came together in various acts of natural and unnatural carnal knowledge. He stood mesmerized, staring into the room where the Enochites played.

"Sir," the palace guard said.

He took a moment to imagine himself a participant. But he quickly dismissed it, rationalizing his brief desire a consequence of Claudia's recent coldness. "Lead on."

At the end of the corridor, the guard knocked on the first door.

"What is it?" Malluch said.

You sent for Shechem, my lord."

"Send him in."

Malluch sat with his head down and a towel wrapped around his waist. Fifteen cubits across the room, a man and a woman, both naked, slept on a bed.

"Trouble sleeping?" Shechem said.

Malluch sighed and nodded.

"Nightmares?" He hated that his friend was being tormented.

"Yes. Getting worse. They were gone for a while, but they've returned."

Malluch's dreams had begun to haunt him shortly after his father and brother were killed. His wife said he would often call out to them in his sleep. On other occasions he would wake up screaming, or smacking his body to extinguish flames that weren't there. "What's the prince say about a return to the garden?"

"He's still reluctant."

"Together, the armies of Enoch and Eden total more than twelve thousand men. What does he have to be reluctant about?"

"He fears the guardian may be invincible." Malluch had refused to refer to the angel of the garden by his heavenly title, choosing instead a more functional description.

"Against twenty-five maybe, but against twelve thousand?"

"I know. He never thinks about the reward, only the cost. And given you and I were there to see it, it's hard to argue with him."

"He doesn't care about immortality?"

Malluch shook his head. "Fortunately, we have allies here."

"Parents of those slain at the garden?"

"Exactly. Some wield a great deal of influence and are never far from the prince's ear. And their desire for vengeance is as strong as mine."

"You think he'll heed them?"

"Eventually. But it needs to be handled tactfully. Ramalech is not a man easily pushed. And immortality or not, he won't commit Enoch's army unless he's convinced they'll return victorious—and with a minimum of casualties."

"How do we accomplish such a feat?"

"I don't know yet. But the pressure from the families of the dead is nothing compared to what he'd face if he sacrificed another ten thousand men."

Shechem scratched his head. "I see what you mean."

"But know this, my friend. If Ramalech refuses to bind the army of Enoch, we will return to the garden alone."

"With twenty-five hundred?" He was fairly confident in his army's ability to handle the angel. But after the defeat at the garden, he preferred the numbers a joint campaign with the soldiers of Enoch would provide.

"With whatever we have."

"Then why not let me lead our own army back now?"

"You saw what I saw, how the guardian fended off every attack to slaughter everyone in our company. And although I'm reasonably certain he could not withstand twenty-five hundred, there is always a risk. Besides, were I to send you now and you were somehow defeated, Ramalech would never agree to send his army."

Shechem nodded.

"Better to wait a while longer," Malluch said. "Let his own citizens work on him, and hold out for an army no guardian can overcome."

Shechem grasped his friend's arm. "Why don't you try again to get some sleep."

"I would if I thought I could." Malluch glanced at the two sleeping bodies and smirked. "You go ahead. I'll find something to occupy my mind. Thanks for looking in."

Closing the door behind him, Shechem turned right to avoid the temptation of the goings on around the corner. Though it meant having to negotiate the palace's labyrinth passages back to his room, better to chance losing his way than his dignity.

He entered his room and lay on the bed without bothering to remove his clothes. As he often did when his mind was troubled, his thoughts reverted to a time and a person he found more comforting.

Similar to the same way other children had grown up in Eden, Shechem and Elisheva spent their younger days working on their family farms. There were always goats to milk, beans to plant, or wheat to cut. But when the day's chores were done, most young people enjoyed the company of friends. These two were no exception.

Often they'd spend time with other friends playing games, exploring a neighboring village, or racing down to the river for a swim. Shechem even taught Elisheva how to use a sling to defend herself against, as he put it, "any wild animal coming around the house." Other times they would sit alone and talk, sometimes for hours, about life, the future, all manner of subjects. No topic seemed to be off limits for two people who often seemed to read each other's thoughts.

One evening, when they were walking home, he intentionally brushed against her arm, a gesture Elisheva seemed to accept by closing her hand around his. Nothing monumental, just a touch, and something he would never dare do in front of their friends. But alone in the twilight, it was worth the risk. After that, he had to restrain himself from reaching for her every time they were together. He didn't want to seem pushy. And even on those occasions when they did hold hands, he could sense it meant more to him than it did her. But he could accept it, so long as they remained friends.

101

One day everything changed. Some tall, rugged-looking grandson of the governor started paying Elisheva court, and she no longer had much time for Shechem. Naturally she denied it, accusing him of being too sensitive of her desire to have more friends, but he knew in his heart he'd lost her. He tried to rationalize why he was even jealous, not that they'd ever been passionate. Other than the handholding and that kiss on the cheek she'd given him when they were ten, there had never been a hint of intimacy between them.

Even more maddening was the fact she continued in her own sweet way to treat him like the friend he'd always been. He found himself wishing she would spurn him outright so he could feel good about hating her. But he couldn't bring himself to do the same to her.

He remembered exactly where he was when he heard the news about Elisheva's betrothal. It sent him running out the back of his family's house and down to the river, to where he and Elisheva had spent innumerable days. He stood on the riverbank staring into the moving water. As children they'd been inseparable. Now it appeared he would never possess her. Why hadn't he ever expressed his true feelings?

He turned to see if anyone was around, climbed the same outcropping of rocks Elisheva had slipped from so many years before, sat, and wept.

Now, a burst of laughter from the hallway kept him from dozing off. He got up to remove his tunic, having every intention of returning to bed. Instead, he stared for a few moments at the empty bunk before walking out into the corridor. Nine parts later, he leaned against a doorway peering in on a mass of entwining flesh.

This time, he was successful in pushing Elisheva and all guilt from his mind before stepping into the room.

CHAPTER 19

Noah joined Japheth who stared out a north-facing window. He had barely said a word at the evening meal. "Is there something troubling you?"

Japheth's focus remained outside. "I was thinking about Grandfather. What he must be doing now. It's been what, twenty-five years?"

"Your grandfather is not only a strong leader, but a shrewd statesman as well. He will have found a way to adapt to the changes that took place in Eden."

"But what kind of life must it be for him? Surely Malluch must have seized power."

"Undoubtedly." His son's questions raised old fears. What would Noah do if he learned his rival *had* harmed his father? Would he abandon the work of God and return to Eden to seek revenge? Not wanting to consider the answer, he quickly pushed those thoughts from his mind.

"Then for all we know, he could have thrown Grandfather in prison. Or worse. After all, Malluch hated him as much as you for what happened at the garden."

103

"Your grandfather was still the governor when we left Eden. And what you once pointed out is true. He has many loyal allies there."

"But—"

"Even if Malluch has assumed control of the government, the patriarchs are still greatly revered by the majority of citizens in Eden. Given your grandfather's lineage, I doubt even he would be foolish enough to have him harmed. Better to wait until he dies naturally than to risk a revolt by the people."

Japheth nodded toward his youngest brother talking with Shem on the other side of the room. "And what about him?" He lowered his voice to a whisper. "Doesn't it bother you Ham has never seen his grandfather, or that Grandfather doesn't even know he has another grandson?"

His words cut Noah to the heart. His only hope since they'd left Eden, other than Shiphrah's salvation, was that somehow they should come face to face. "Terribly. What would you have me do? Risk all our lives in a return to Eden just so the two of them could meet?"

Japheth's arms dropped to his sides. "I guess not. I just wish I could know for certain he was well."

"I told you, God has a plan for your grandfather, a merciful one that will spare him the coming terror. Right now, our job is to remain obedient and complete the task the Lord has given us."

"That's not much comfort." Japheth remained at the window for another nine parts in silence before heading for the front door.

After he left, Ham approached his father carrying a wineskin in one fist and a cup in the other. "It's unlike Japheth not to say anything through the meal," Ham said. "Is he all right?"

"Your brother misses your grandfather. They were extremely close."

"He told me. He said Grandfather used to take him hunting for the jackals and hyenas that came in to attack the cattle."

104

"When he was fourteen, he taught your brother carpentry, how to forge weapons out of bronze and iron, even how to make wine."

Ham's eyebrows rose at the mention of strong drink. He filled his cup. "Sounds very instructive."

From the age of twenty, Ham had developed a taste for wine that exceeded each of his brothers. It was a penchant that seemed to increase steadily over the past five years, to the point now where it had become a concern. "Of course, he did a lot of those things with Shem as well, but with Japheth being firstborn, he was your grandfather's favorite."

"Why wouldn't he come with you the night you fled Eden?"

"Two reasons, I think. First, he was still the governor. Even though his rule was being threatened, I'm sure he felt an obligation to the citizens of Eden."

"And the second?"

"Your grandfather is a man proud of his heritage. He never expressed it in words, but I think it was important for him to die and be buried in the land of his fathers."

"I wish I could have met him."

Noah smiled softly, placing a hand to his son's chest. "Me too, son. Me too."

Ham filled his cup again.

* * *

Shechem awoke near midday to the sound of a loud, slowly beating metallic tone resonating throughout the palace. He'd returned to his room near dawn to grab a few hours of sleep following his night with the women of Enoch. But the ringing in his ears reminded him he was late for a ceremony. He rushed to dress, then moved quickly through the palace corridors before coming to a large open vestibule where Ramalech, a six-man entourage,

Malluch, and Bohar waited. "Commander," Ramalech said. "I trust you slept well?"

"Like a bear in winter."

"Please join us on the balcony for a ritual no one outside Enoch has ever witnessed." Ramalech led them onto an upper side balcony overlooking the center of the city and the altar Shechem had curiously viewed.

At one of the corners atop the altar, a man with a club struck a large convex-shaped bronze disk. He was joined at the pyramid by four men in purple tunics trimmed in gold. Each wore an elaborate headdress. *Priests.* One positioned himself at the top of each of the four staircases cut into the pyramid. Slaves threw wood into the center of the altar-pyre to feed an already raging fire burning in the pit.

What a stark contrast in scenes from the night before. A few hours ago, an unbridled populace roamed the streets like wild animals. Today all was calm and orderly. Hundreds of Enochites gathered quietly around the base of the altar, their children clinging tightly to their necks or against their thighs. Many more people streamed from their homes, the dirge of the gong drawing them toward the altar from every quarter of the city.

They all had one thing in common: Each family included at least one child.

Shechem stretched to peer over the edge of the balcony, then leaned in to Bohar's ear. "Where are the animals?"

Bohar snickered. "There are no animals. Watch."

As the last arriving families gathered around the altar, the beating stopped. Three of the priests joined the fourth at the top of the staircase closest to the balcony. The four men knelt in a circle, each pulling from inside his garment a medium sized cube. The cube's six faces bore some kind of markings, with each side also being colored either black or white. The four men cast their die, examined the results, then rose while returning the cubes to their pockets. One of the men stepped forward. "Males—age one to three."

106

Some in the crowd gasped, while others seemed relieved.

"What's it mean?" Shechem said.

"The honor of sacrifice has fallen on the male children of Enoch between the ages of one and three," Ramalech said.

So the rumors had been true. Now it became clear to him why he hadn't been able to identify the skulls he'd seen here twenty-five years ago. He'd been trying to figure out what kind of animals they were when they weren't animals at all. "Children? You mean this altar isn't for crops or livestock?"

"Come, come, Commander. The sacred bones of our father, Cain, lie beneath this altar. Would you presume to satisfy the gods of Enoch with a bushel of wheat or the flesh of an animal?"

What disgusted Shechem most was the way the crowd reacted to the pronouncement. After the initial shock, they grew strangely quiet. Faces grew long and mothers sobbed, but for the most part, the people seemed to accept the sentence. No demonstrations, no outcries for mercy. Some even made preparations, with parents passing their condemned sons into the arms of older siblings to say good-bye.

With a nod from one of the priests, the striking of the gong resumed. Women kissed their sons one last time before handing them over to their husbands. Fathers carrying their infant and toddler sons moved to the bottom of the four staircases to begin their ascent. One unlucky father carried twin sons, one in either arm. At the direction of the priests, the first in each line stopped one step from the top, their neighbors lining up single file behind them down the stairs.

Once more the thundering disk was silenced by a wave of the head priest. Those at the top of the staircases handed their sons over to the four priests. Three stood holding the children in their arms while the head priest raised an infant above his head. "Glory be to the god of the sun—to the god of the moon—and to the god of the stars," he said. "Accept these sons of Enoch, and continue to shower us with blessings."

He and the other priests turned and threw the children into the fire. Their young screams lasted but a few parts.

Shechem never considered himself squeamish, but he found this sickening. As a father, his feelings about the murder of children matched his views concerning the rape and torture of women. He considered both practices taboo.

Still, he didn't want to appear weak in front of the others and so forced himself to keep from turning away. He closed his eyes, reaching inside his tunic and clasping his hands together to quell the quiver moving down his spine. Once the cries faded, he mistakenly tried to peer through half-open slits, only to witness the priests pitching the next group of children into the fire. More screaming followed. This time he couldn't help himself, averting his look to what proved an equally revolting sight. Bohar's face contorted into a malevolent grin.

While the priests continued to feed the fire with the flesh of Enoch's children, Shechem again found himself appalled by the people's reaction. He'd fully expected the parents of the condemned to depart quickly once their sons had been sacrificed, only the opposite was true. Husbands surrendering their sons descended quickly to comfort their wives and remaining family members, but not a single Enochite left the altar site during the ceremony. They seemed to be bound by a sense of duty to watch the massacre of their own flesh.

Commotion on the left-side staircase drew the attention of everyone on the balcony. A woman screaming her son's name dashed up the pyramid two stairs at a time just as her husband was handing their child over. When she reached them, her husband tried to grab her, but she broke free and snatched the infant from the priest. He and the other priests moved toward her and the woman ran to the edge of the pit, flinging herself headlong into the fire.

"Foolish woman," Ramalech said to Malluch. "At her age, she could have had a dozen more sons. Who will bear them for her husband now?"

108

Malluch nodded.

Shechem wanted to cheer. The woman was a hero. The only one willing to stand up in this herd of sheep and defend their own child.

After an hour, the lines on the staircases grew shorter while the last of the condemned were cast into the flames. He estimated close to two hundred of Enoch's male children had been slaughtered. The smell of burning flesh hung heavy in the air around the balcony, leaving a putrid taste at the back of his throat.

"Who's hungry?" Ramalech said.

Shechem swallowed hard to push the acid back down to his stomach.

CHAPTER 20

In the 530th year of Noah . . .

Noah was relieved to finally have a barrier separating the spectators from his family. Completion of that side of the ark's hull not only protected them from flying debris, but did much to mute the flying insults as well, which had grown louder and more scornful.

More than a hundred people a day visited the ark now. A handful turned it into a rest spot, pitching tents and staying for several days. Sometimes, those spending the night let off steam by raising a wineskin before using the ark for target practice. Come first light, his family often found the outside of the hull splattered with eggs, tomatoes, or melons.

One morning they found dung.

Following an increase in vandalism, the men had begun sleeping inside the ark. Each man would take his turn standing guard outside while the others slept, but even this proved problematic because of the ark's enormous length. Soon the guard was increased to two, one stationed at the prow and the other at the stern to afford better security for both sides of the structure.

A small campfire was kept burning at either end a safe distance from the ark to provide light, warmth, and ignition for torches.

110

But vandalism wasn't the only thing plaguing construction. Ham's drinking had developed into bad habits. He missed at least one day every other week on a drunken binge. After one such episode, Noah's patience ran out.

Ham had remained in bed late into the morning after a previous night's indulgence. "Get up, Ham." When he didn't respond, his father grabbed his feet and pulled him out of the bed naked onto the floor of the ark.

With his knees scraping against the rough timbers, Ham cried out. "What are you doing?"

"Showing you the price of a drink."

"What?"

"Your brothers and I have been up working since dawn."

"So, what? I'm sick."

"You may not be feeling good, but you're hardly sick."

"What's that mean?"

"It means if you're man enough to drink wine, be man enough to accept the consequences. Being drunk isn't an excuse to get out of work."

After that, Ham didn't drink for a month. And even after he ended his self-imposed abstinence, he made sure he was the first one up the next morning.

One night, as Noah and Japheth slept inside near the prow, they awoke to the sound of Shem's screaming from the port side of the ark. "Fire!"

He and Japheth rushed through the open frame of that side and followed Shem toward the stern. Flames danced along the shoring timbers supporting the rear section of the ark. The three men quickened their pace, sprinting past the large door opening built halfway down the side of the ark.

The fire was confined to the lower ten cubits on the port side. Ham lay on the ground a few cubits away from the burning timbers, two empty wineskins within arm's length. "Drunken swine. Get up." Shem pulled his unconscious brother out of danger, then returned to scale the shoring a few cubits upwind of the flames.

Even before they'd taken to sleeping inside the ark, the family had made contingencies in the wake of the vandalism. Buckets of water and sand were kept at several locations inside the ark in case of fire. Now, while Japheth carried water up for Shem to douse the flames from above, Noah threw dirt on the blaze with a shovel from below. In approximately fifty-four parts, the fire was extinguished. Sounds of music and laughter resounded from several tents down the hill behind them.

He turned to Shem, knowing it was too dark and the distance too far for him to identify anyone. "Did you see anything?"

"Just the fire, Father. Then I took off running."

His brother stood over Ham, who was snoring loudly. "Ham."

He continued to snore.

Japheth knelt near his brother's head and slapped his cheeks. "Ham. Wake up, you filthy winebibber."

Ham rolled onto his side. "Leave me alone."

Noah tossed a bucket of water over Ham's head. He shot upright, swearing while he blew water from his mouth and nostrils. "What in the—" He caught himself, glaring first at his father and brother standing over him, then at the smoke rising from the blackened beams. "What happened?"

"We were hoping you could tell us." Noah shook from disgust.

"Last thing I remember was feeling really tired. So I sat down to rest against this beam. I guess I fell asleep."

The elder picked up one of the two wineskins. "You were supposed to be on guard. And there's nothing in these that would help you to stay awake."

"I fell asleep."

Japheth grabbed the wineskin from his father and shook it in his brother's face. "This put you to sleep. You lazy drunkard." Always a defender of his brother, he'd finally had enough. "And this time your drinking endangered both the ark and us."

112

"Why you—" Ham lunged at his brother's leg in an attempt to tackle him. With a single stride, Japheth's powerful legs broke free, dropping Ham nose down in the earth. He got up spitting dirt and threw a punch at his brother, who sidestepped him, the overswing sending Ham spiraling back to the ground. He crawled away before stumbling to his feet and into the darkness back toward the ark's prow.

Noah's anger at Ham was only surpassed by his disappointment. If Ham couldn't effectively stand his watch, someone would have to take his place. Which meant someone was going to go without sleep. Yet there was no point arguing about it now. Ham was too drunk to realize how close he'd come to being killed tonight, or how much he had endangered the others.

"Shouldn't one of us go after him?" Shem said.

"What for?" Japheth said.

"What if he falls down and hurts himself?"

"So what if he does?" He cupped his hand to the side of his mouth and shouted after Ham. "Might knock some sense into him."

Japheth lit a torch, and the three men examined the ground around the burnt shoring. Sets of fresh tracks led from the scaffolding to the starboard side of the ark. The tracks continued across the rise and down the hill to the tent encampment. They extinguished the torch and drew their swords before creeping toward the encampment.

Lamps from three tents backlit the movements of an unknown number of people inside. When the would-be avengers crept within fifty cubits of the closest tent, a man peered out of the flap and shouted to warn his companions. Five armed men charged out of the tents, two from the closest tent, two from the one to its left, and another from the tent behind.

In the darkness, Noah and his sons had the advantage over men whose eyes hadn't adjusted to the night. He moved left and quickly cut down the two coming from that direction, while Japheth engaged the pair in the center. Shem clanged swords with the one from the tent farthest away. Noah hurried behind his oldest

113

to assist Shem, but by the time he got there, his son's well-placed thrust through the last enemy's liver had ended the confrontation.

Women from all three tents rushed out and fell screaming onto the bodies of their fallen husbands and sons.

"I wish we hadn't had to do this," Shem said.

"I know," Noah said. "But we were lucky not to have lost your brother and the ark tonight. We couldn't take the chance on their returning tomorrow to finish the job."

"So what are we going to do now?" Still gripping the sword, Japheth gestured toward the women. "You know these men are going to have friends or relatives."

"For one thing, find a better way of protecting the ark."

* * *

The passing of sixty months had done nothing to silence the cries of the children of Enoch inside Shechem's head.

That day had changed him.

For the first time in his life, he feared the influence of Enoch upon the culture of Eden. Like most boys, he'd grown up listening to the teachings of the fathers handed down from generation to generation. Chief of these was that life was a gift from God and only He had the right to take it away.

The procurement of slaves was one thing. So, too, the building of fortifications. And the formation of an army. These were all positive things, indicators of progress and worthy of emulation in a changing world.

But not this. What he'd witnessed that day was not progress. It was savage. How long would it take for this malignant practice to reach Eden?

Tormented by their cries, he tried every way to silence them, including excusing himself from Ramalech's yearly invitation to attend the celebration. No doubt it would be interpreted as

114

weakness, but better that than to risk embarrassing Malluch by trying to hide his revulsion in front of the prince.

At the same time, he also felt foolish about his own naïveté. He'd been the only one on the balcony that day unaware of what was about to take place. The people of Eden had been bringing their offerings before God since the time of Cain and Abel. Crops. Livestock. Gifts of wine and oil. The only commandment the fathers had passed down was they be the first fruits. But never human sacrifices.

Now, entering his home at twilight, he wheeled around to the sound of a baby crying and the prickle of the hair on the back of his neck. A young woman carrying a child across the courtyard to the servant's quarters proved to be the source of the disturbance. He rubbed the chilling flesh from his arms and entered the house.

He walked into the bedroom and called to Claudia, just catching a glimpse of the bottom of her garment disappear into an adjoining dressing room. After a few parts, he called again. *Not this again.* It would be more than uncomfortable for her to fall asleep in there. He'd hoped she was changing, and in anticipation of the surprise poured them both a cup of wine. But when she failed to come out after about sixty parts, He grabbed a cup in each hand and entered the closet. "Not to be anxious, my dear—"

Except for clothing, the room was empty.

Thinking his wife was being playful, he looked around to make sure she wasn't hiding.

Nothing.

Had he really seen the bottom of her tunic? He passed it off as his imagination and couldn't wait for her to get home to tell her about it. She would find it curious, if not amusing.

Either way, he hoped she would return soon. He was leaving early in the morning to secure more slaves, replacements for the few who'd escaped, and for those killed trying to.

Now, if he could just find a way to leave Bohar behind.

CHAPTER 21

Shechem didn't know the name of the city. All he knew is they were about two hundred furlongs south of the Eden River. Whatever its name, the city was smaller than most, more the size of a town or village really. Still, they'd managed to secure another three hundred men for service to Eden.

Bohar had disappeared again, which could only mean one thing — someone was being raped or someone was being murdered. Maybe both.

"Watch out!" A soldier's voice rose above the din of the burning village. Across the roadway, a female lion charged a group of three soldiers walking near the wood line. She caught the closest, driving him to the ground and ripping into his side.

"Get her off me!" he cried repeatedly.

Shechem drew his sword and started across the road, while fifteen other soldiers raced to their comrade's defense. The soldiers surrounded the lion, partially blocking their commander's view. Falling swords and thrusting spears drew successive howls from the beast. He arrived to see the lion's chest rise and fall for the last time. A few cubits away, the wounded soldier continued to scream.

"Where did she come from?" Shechem said to no one in particular.

116

"Out of nowhere," the injured soldier said, wincing with each spoken word. He took a couple of deep breaths, a soft whimper accompanying each exhale before continuing through clenched teeth. "We were escorting some prisoners when she came charging out of the woods."

"Better get that wound cauterized fast to stop the bleeding."

"Yes, sir," the soldier treating the injured man said.

Across the road, Bohar paced back and forth outside a nearby house. With a blood-drenched knife in his hand, he appeared to be searching for something. "Don't be afraid," he said. "I'm not going to hurt you."

After eighteen parts of searching, he moved out of sight to the rear of the house. Six parts later, a young girl of about thirteen years sprinted from behind the house into the woods opposite the soldiers. She had big eyes, a womanly figure, and a full head of flowing dark hair that bounced off her back as she ran. Bohar trailed sixty cubits behind her.

Shechem did a double-take when the girl passed by, reminding him of one of his daughters when she was young. The thought of her being violated, especially by this pig, made his blood boil. He ran into the woods after them.

A hundred cubits in, he heard Bohar tramping through the trees just ahead, calling to the girl. "If you come out now, I promise I won't hurt you."

Don't do it, little girl. The girl's parents were most likely lying on the floor back at the house with their throats slit. He also knew the girl would suffer far worse if Bohar found her.

Fifty cubits farther, he caught up to him in a small opening in the forest. His smelly cohort moved along the perimeter of the clearing, crouching every few cubits to peer into the surrounding brush.

"Give up?" Shechem said.

Still breathing heavily, Bohar spun around to reveal a creased brow and gritting teeth. "Not a chance. I'll find the little tramp."

117

"Why don't you—"

"Ssh!" Bohar put a finger to his lips. A soft rustling and what sounded like the weak cry of a baby came from the opposite side of the clearing. The two men crept toward the sound in slow deliberate steps, coming upon some sort of nesting area. Inside, three lion cubs wrestled with each other.

They'd stumbled on the answer to the lion attack back in the village. Shechem scrutinized the area. Could the male be far off?

His partner moved in for a closer look and the three cubs stopped playing, their noses and whiskers twitching at the unfamiliar scent invading their space. Two of the cubs hissed. The third growled and raised a distinctive left front paw—the second and third toes birth-marked white—in defense.

Bohar fixed his gaze on the tip of a log sticking out into the clearing. He pulled from the woods a three-cubit long tree trunk—its bulbous ragged root still attached to the far end.

He returned to the nest, groaning while he lifted the menacing limb over his head with both hands.

"Are you crazy?" Shechem said. But before he could make a move to stop him, Bohar brought the club down with enough force to shake the ground.

He crushed the skulls of two of the cubs with the single blow. But his choice of weapon, although deadly, proved cumbersome. Straining to raise the log again, the third cub—the one with the white toes—scampered across the clearing. Bohar dragged the bloodied trunk along the ground after the cub.

"Bohar!" *You're not just coldhearted, you're heartless.*

Reaching the wood line, the cub darted into the underbrush.

"No, you don't." He swung the huge club over his shoulder, hurling it where the cub entered the trees. The log bounced off the ground and into the woods, striking an object lodged in the branches of a bush. He peered into the hole the club had made.

Shechem couldn't see much from his position across the clearing, but a faint buzzing sound met his ears.

118

Bohar flew backwards from the margin as if struck by a bolt of lightning, his piercing screams filling the air. He hit the ground with hundreds of hornets pouring from the hole in the bush, swarming his face and upper torso.

Shechem paused to wrestle with his conscience before rushing to help his confederate, who screamed and rolled violently in the grass. He tried to help remove his tunic, but Bohar bolted into the woods toward the village, two dozen hornets still clinging to his clothes.

"Get that tunic off!"

For his trouble, he received more than a few hornet stings of his own. No matter. At least the girl got away — and the lion cub.

* * *

The next morning, Shechem walked with Malluch down a palace corridor leading to Bohar's chamber. "And how did you fare against the hornets, Commander?"

He pointed to welts on his neck and right ear and several others on his hands. "Better than Bohar, I'm sure."

"I was told the physicians had to work through the night and still couldn't get the swelling down."

As the pair turned right at the end of the hallway, a feminine scream sounded through the first door on the right. The door flung open and a woman carrying a pitcher of water and some cloths ran out into the hallway. She slammed the door behind her. With vacant eyes, she stared at Malluch and Shechem. "His face," she said, twisting her own. The woman scurried down the corridor, sloshing water from the pitcher as she ran.

A long, pitiful moan came from the other side of the door. Shechem turned to Malluch, half hoping the governor would change his mind about wanting to see him. When his silence indicated otherwise, the commander reached for the door.

119

Bohar lay on a bed with his head and back propped up with pillows and his arms held away from his body. He did not move, even when his two allies approached, although he did acknowledge their presence with another moan.

Shechem understood now why the woman had fled. Huge welts covered his cheeks and forehead, his eyelids swollen shut. His lips, bloated three times their normal size, covered the bottom third of his jaw. He likened the color and lumpiness of his wounds to a large clump of misshapen grapes.

Bohar's hands didn't look much better. So savage had been the hornets' attack that his fingers had swelled together into two separate masses of flesh with barely any definition between digits. Until the swelling went down, they would prove little more than dead weights fixed to the end of his arms.

"Does that hurt as bad as it looks?" Shechem said.

Bohar whispered a curse through swollen lips.

"Easy, my friend," Malluch said. "I'm sure the commander's use of sarcasm was merely meant as a distraction to help take your mind off the pain."

No it wasn't. He waved at a fly buzzing around his head.

"Is there anything we can get for you?" Malluch said.

Bohar struggled to lift his left arm, pointing to a wineskin on a nearby table.

Shechem retrieved the wineskin and a small hollow reed sitting next to it. He leaned over to give it to him, but again heard the buzzing sound.

Their injured ally moaned loudly and began flailing his arms in front of his face, knocking the wineskin to the floor. Shechem grabbed his arms to restrain them. "Bohar. Calm down." He continued to struggle. "It's just a fly."

Bohar let his arms go limp, and Shechem returned them to his sides. He picked up the wineskin and placed it next to him, gently inserting the reed between his swollen lips.

He noticed the fly alighting on the wall next to the bed and reached over, smashing it with his hand. "A fly. I would think after all these years you'd be used to them buzzing around you." He winked at Malluch.

Bohar spit wine and cursed again.

CHAPTER 22

In the 540th year of Noah . . .

Noah paused for a moment, gratified at the sight of his whole family working together on the ark. Now that the major framing and sheathing had been completed, it was safe enough to allow the women to help with the construction of the lower deck.

Shiphrah first expressed an interest in having the women work on the ark, pointing out how much an additional four sets of hands would increase efficiency. The idea had drawn instant resistance from Ariel. "Maybe you're for ruining your hands with more calluses and splinters, but not me," she said.

Less than a day of being alone in the house had changed her mind. Shortly after midday, Ariel arrived at the ark site on the pretense of asking Miryam what to prepare for the evening meal. She never left. Once Shem showed her how to use some of the hand tools, she seemed to take to the work. And watching her try to manipulate the tools with her hands wrapped in cloth brought a sense of comic relief to the work site.

Elisheva had become an exceptional carpenter, learning to handle a saw, hammer, and chisel with near the deftness of the men. Her skills proved particularly beneficial on those days when

Ham was incapacitated, showing herself an adequate replacement for all but the most strenuous tasks.

Today it was warm, and the men were working without tunics. Noah caught Shiphrah looking at Ham, his arm and back muscles bulging while lifting a plank. Not that she didn't have good reason. Ham had completed his transition to manhood some time ago and by almost any standard would be considered handsome. He wasn't as tall or broad in the shoulders as Japheth, nor did he have Shem's haunting eyes. But he had a square jaw and a slight wave in his deep brown hair neither of his brothers possessed.

Ham glanced up to see Shiphrah on the other side of the deck near one of the water buckets. "Bring me some water, will you?" Ham said, his voice curt and demanding.

Noah chuckled, sensing more than a twinge of anger beneath Shiphrah's exterior.

She frowned and took the water to him. When Ham bent over to set the plank, she dipped a cup of water and poured it over his back.

He shot upright, arching his back at the shock of the cold water against his skin. He wheeled around. "What's that for?"

"For being rude."

"How is asking for a drink of water rude?"

"Bring . . . me . . . some . . . water!" Shiphrah lowered her voice and placed emphasis on each word to imitate Ham's insistent tone.

Shock faded into a smile, then a hearty laugh. "Not a bad imitation. Did I really sound that bad?"

A frown returned to Shiphrah's face. "You did."

"Then allow me to apologize, my lady." Ham placed his palm on his stomach and executed a short bow.

"Now you're patronizing me." She shook the last few drops of water onto his head and chest.

He raised a brow, then looked down at the water bucket.

She backed away. "Oh no."

He moved toward the bucket, and she turned and ran across the deck.

He picked up the bucket and raced after her, but she leapt onto a deck beam heading in the opposite direction. She probably figured he would have difficulty chasing her across the beams carrying a bucket of water. He did. She managed to increase her lead each time Ham crossed onto another beam until finally they were on opposite sides of the deck.

Staring at each other huffing and puffing, she put her hands on her hips. "What now, brother?"

He looked down at the bucket, then back up with a wide stare like an epiphany had come to him. He set the bucket down on the beam. "I just realized I've been going about this all wrong."

"Oh, really?"

"Instead of bringing the bucket to you, I should bring you to the bucket." He started back across the beam, and now it was Shiphrah's eyes that widened. Without the weight of the bucket to slow him, he'd easily catch up to her. She moved quickly along the hull toward the front of the ark while Ham skipped diagonally across the beams in an effort to catch up. Even so, Shiphrah still managed to reach the deck ahead of him.

His foot slipped on the last beam, and he teetered on the edge of the decking while fighting to right himself. Just before losing his balance, he lunged for Shiphrah's outstretched hands. She pulled hard. The weight of his body rocketed back over the edge, and the two tumbled onto the deck. Shiphrah ended up on top of Ham.

"Thanks," he said breathlessly.

"You should really be more careful."

"I'll try to remember that the next time I find myself chasing you across beams ten cubits off the ground."

"You were the one bent on giving me a bucket bath."

"I still can, you know." A few parts of uncomfortable quiet passed between them. "You want to get up now?"

"Oh—sorry." She stood and straightened her garment.

"Not that I minded. I've had less comfortable things land on me."

124

She blushed and didn't make eye contact with the other family members. "I'd better go and see about our meal." She headed for the house.

Miryam whispered to her husband. "Was that what I thought it was?"

"I hope so."

Once Shiphrah disappeared, Ariel stomped over to confront the two parents, head leaning forward. "Did you see what happened?"

"With all the commotion, it would have been hard not to," Noah said.

"And you're not going to do anything about it?"

Ariel had never hidden her mistrust of Shiphrah, but he wasn't about to allow her petty jealousies to interfere with a prospective romance so long in the making. "What would you have us do?"

"Well, put a stop to it, naturally. Do you really want Ham getting involved with an outcast from Enoch?"

"After forty years as a part of this family, I hardly think Shiphrah could be considered an outcast," Miryam said.

"Tell me, Ariel," Noah said. "After all this time, how is it you still show contempt for your sister? Can't you see something beautiful is blossoming between them?"

Ariel's head snapped back. "She's not my sister. And whatever may be blossoming between them could only serve to poison our bloodline. Or have you forgotten the warnings you yourself gave us concerning the Enochites, Father?"

"I haven't forgotten them. Shiphrah may have been born in Enoch, but she is hardly an Enochite any longer. Did she not spurn her own heritage when she left her homeland to seek a husband in Eden? And was her allegiance to a new race not demonstrated when she risked her life to warn us?"

"She will always be an Enochite in my eyes."

"Then my pity is for you, not her."

Ariel crossed her arms over her chest. "He's your son."

"Yes—he is," Miryam said behind a firmly set jaw.

CHAPTER 23

Noah rose on his elbows to the soft sound of feet shuffling inside the ark. In the darkness, his ears followed the rustling as it moved across the deck to where a female silhouette slipped out through one of the hull openings. Since the women had joined the men to work on the ark during the day, Miryam had suggested they sleep there during the night for safety. He lit a torch and went to investigate.

Outside, the glow from his lamp illuminated the figure scurrying along the hull toward the prow. Shiphrah turned to face the light. Seeing what looked like a roll of clothing under her arm, he made the assumption she wasn't answering a call of nature. "Late for a stroll, don't you think?" he said.

"Not a stroll, Father. A journey."

"A journey? At this hour? Pray tell child, wherever to?"

"Away."

His response caught in his throat. "You're leaving?"

"It's time for me to get out on my own. Maybe even find a husband. That is, after all, why I came to Eden forty years ago."

"Kind of sudden, isn't it?"

"Forty years is sudden?"

126

"Not the forty years, just that after all this time you chose to act upon it tonight."

"I've been thinking about it for a while. I'm not happy here."

"I don't think any of us can say we're happy to have been driven from our home to live in this wilderness."

"It's not even this place. It's the circumstances."

Noah raised the torch, prompting her to drop her gaze. "Shiphrah, I've never known you to be dishonest with me."

"And I'm not now. I am unhappy."

"Is it Ham?"

"Yes . . . No." She twisted away, the clothing dropping to the ground. "I don't know." Her voice cracked. "All I know is something's happening that shouldn't be happening."

"You're talking about this afternoon?"

"It's more than just this afternoon." She leaned against the ark and drew in a ragged breath. "But I don't know exactly how to tell you."

"I've always found it better to let go of a sneeze quickly, rather than try to hold it back."

"Lately, I've been thinking about Ham as—as—well, as someone other than a brother."

Her admission only confirmed what he and Miryam suspected this afternoon. "Is that what's bothering you?"

"Well of course it's bothering me. Shouldn't it?" She drew up sniffles.

"Not necessarily."

She spun back around. "He's my brother."

"He's your brother by circumstance, not blood."

"I'm having trouble seeing the distinction."

"Then maybe you should look harder."

"Don't you understand? I bathed him. I changed him. I fed him. How can I be anything other than a sister to him?"

"By not looking at him like a brother."

127

"I don't see how I can after forty years."

"That's your head talking. Try listening with your heart."

"My heart? How?"

"You did it this afternoon, for a moment, when you fell into his arms."

"Which is why I'm leaving."

"No, you're feeling guilt. And it's misplaced. Think about what you were feeling, deep inside, when you were looking into each other's eyes."

"It's not a sin?"

"Shiphrah, living together as brother and sister doesn't make you brother and sister. You are from Enoch. Ham is descended from the line of Seth. There is nothing incestuous in your relationship."

"Ariel says otherwise."

"What's she got to do with this?"

"She saw what everyone else did this afternoon. She said it was wrong."

"She only wanted to hurt you. Ariel is miserable inside, and she can't stand the thought of anyone else being happy, especially you. She's resentful and she's jealous. But you've been listening to her sniping for forty years. Why should you let it bother you now?"

"Because it's not only me she's talking about, it's Ham. She said I should leave before something sinful takes place between us—before we are overcome with lust."

"Nonsense. What's happening between you and Ham is completely natural."

"I know, but—"

"Why don't you just tell him how you feel?"

"That's the other reason I'm leaving. After today, I realized I wouldn't be able to hide my feelings any longer."

"Good. A little honesty is just what the two of you need."

"But suppose I reveal my feelings and Ham doesn't feel the same. It's not like I can say, 'Oh, I was just joking,' and go back to being his sister again."

"Daughter, the man I saw with you today isn't likely to rebuke you."

"I wish I could be as certain."

"I'll tell you what's certain. If you walk away now without knowing, you could be throwing away whatever chance the two of you have to be happy."

"Swear."

"What—"

"Swear an oath you won't tell Ham the truth about why I'm leaving—"

"Shiphrah."

"Or my feelings for him."

"I cannot."

"By the God of your fathers, swear." Shiphrah clasped her hands together over her chest. "Please."

They stood silent for a moment, tears welling again. "I will do as you ask."

"An oath."

Noah inhaled deeply, and let it out slowly. "As the Lord lives, Ham will not hear the truth."

He walked Shiphrah down the hill and put a blanket and bridle on a donkey for her to ride. "Are you sure you don't want to wait until morning?"

"I'm not afraid to travel at night," she said. "Besides, seeing Ham in the morning again would only make it more difficult to leave."

"Where will you go?"

"I'll start in the small village where we get supplies. From there I should be able to join a caravan traveling west toward the Great

Sea, or possibly an expedition headed south. Anything, so long as it's far away from Enoch."

He knew Shiphrah well enough to know what her response would be, but he had to make one last attempt to change her mind. "What about the Lord's judgment?"

She looked directly into his moistened eyes and smiled. "His pardon was never intended for me." He pursed his mouth to respond, but Shiphrah quickly put her finger to his lips. She reached up and kissed him on the cheek and embraced him tightly before allowing him to help her onto the donkey. "Good-bye, Father."

"YAH go with you," He watched until Shiphrah's donkey faded into the darkness.

What would he tell Ham in the morning?

CHAPTER 24

A banging on their door roused Shechem in the middle of the night. He threw on a robe and opened it to a distraught woman he recognized as the governor's wife. "Come quickly," she said. "Malluch's in trouble."

"Is he sick?" He slipped on sandals and closed the door behind him.

"It's more than that."

"Did you notify one of the palace physicians?"

"I didn't want anyone to see him like this."

The woman led Shechem through the rear of the palace, up a staircase, down a short corridor, and into their sleep chamber.

Malluch stood shivering with his face in a corner. He was wearing two layers of clothing. As Shechem approached, beads of sweat poured from his friend's head and neck. "Malluch." Within three cubits he could hear the sound of chattering teeth. "Malluch. It's Shechem."

Malluch spun around and grabbed him by the throat. "Burning," he whispered. "I was burning."

"It's all right now."

131

"No. I could really feel it this time—feel the fire burning my legs, my back." Shechem tried to pull away, but his friend jerked him back. "Don't go. Not yet."

"I'm right here."

"We're both here, my love," his wife said.

Malluch loosened the grip on Shechem's throat and stared at his own scarred palm. "The flames, they're alive."

"Alive?" Shechem said.

"Yes. They jumped from the guardian's sword to my father's, then from the handle onto his arm?"

Shechem nodded.

"They were alive," Malluch said.

Shechem glanced at Malluch's wife, who had both hands covering her mouth, then back to his friend. "They're not alive now."

The governor closed his eyes and bowed his head, as though in prayer. After a few moments of silence, a single tear fell from beneath his closed eyelid and streamed down his cheek. "We were—" He cleared his throat. "We were so close, my brother and I. Growing up, I mean."

"And your father?"

"Not when we were young. Our father spent a lot of time away in those years, and when he got home, he stayed drunk most of the time. Then after our mother died, the two of us joined together to help Father get over the loss. It drew us all closer."

"I'm sorry, my lord."

"It took our mother dying for us to have the kind of relationship the two of us had always wanted with our father. That's why it was so hard for me to watch them die."

"I understand."

"No, you don't. Not yet. You see, my brother and I had been in Enoch for a couple of weeks when our mother, who was sick, passed away. By the time we got home, she'd been buried three days, and we were spared the heartbreak of seeing her dead."

132

"Something you couldn't avoid at the garden with your father and brother."

"Exactly." Malluch released his remaining grip and brushed the wrinkles he'd made from the front of Shechem's robe. He drew up a sniffle. "You are, indeed, my good friend. You saved my life then, and here you are helping me face my demons now." He took a step back. "But I think . . . I think the time has come to exorcise those demons." He had that same calculating expression sixty years ago at the garden.

"How?" What was he up to? Surely he was scheming.

"I have a plan. It's risky, and it could damage me politically. But in the end, I think it will give me the peace I've been seeking to put an end to these nightmares."

"What can I do to help?"

Malluch shook his head. "No, my friend. What I have in mind is not for you. The commander of Eden's army must remain above the fray—and above suspicion. This calls for someone with a special talent."

* * *

Noah's shoulders drooped when looking to the empty space on the floor where Shiphrah usually sat. Behind him, Ariel hummed a soft melody while she, Miryam, and Elisheva served a meal of bread, cheese, and tomatoes to him and his sons. Although they'd taken up sleeping in the ark, Miryam insisted they return to the house for meals.

He bowed his head. "Blessed be the Lord our God, by Whose word this bread springs forth from the earth. May Your merciful hand guide and protect our daughter and sister on her journey to wherever You will lead."

No sooner had he finished praying, then Ariel resumed humming. It was a beautiful sound, however inappropriate to the morning's mood and circumstances. He found it difficult to fathom how someone with such a sour personality could possess such a beautiful voice.

"What are you so cheery about?" Ham said.

"No reason. Just looking forward to another day." She took a bite of bread and grinned at Shiphrah's vacant place.

Ham's nostrils flared. He glared at her through steely eyes. "Sure. And Shiphrah being gone has absolutely nothing to do with it?"

"Look, I wish her no ill will. But am I sorry she's gone? No. She was, after all, an outsider."

"How can you say that about someone you've lived with for forty years? Is she not as much a part of this family as you?" Ham looked to his father. "She didn't even say good-bye."

"See, that's what I mean," Ariel said. "We took her in and gave her a home, and she didn't say so much as a thank you. What an ingrate."

"Enough, Ariel," Japheth said. "You're probably the reason she left."

Her mouth dropped. She looked to Shem for support.

"Don't look for me to defend you. Japheth's right. You picked on the poor girl from the day she got here. I'm surprised she lasted this long."

"She didn't seem unhappy," Elisheva said.

Knowing that Shiphrah's leaving had nothing to do with Ariel, Noah came to her defense. "I doubt Shiphrah would have stayed as long as she did if she were feeling persecuted. Clearly, she had her own reasons for wanting to go."

"But what were they, Father?" Ham said. "And why now?"

"I don't know, son."

"You didn't try to talk her out of it?

"Vehemently. But she's her own woman, and it was clear she'd made up her mind. I'm afraid all we can do now is pray she finds happiness."

134

"We can do a whole lot more than pray. Somebody needs to go after her."

"It's what she wanted, son."

Ham leaned forward, a sparkle returning to his eyes. "I'll go."

"And what will you do if you find her, force her back against her will?"

"Maybe just tell her how much we all love her."

"She knows, son. She knows. Besides, with her gone, we need all hands working on the ark."

Ham slumped back against the pillow at his back.

"Well, whatever her reason, I wouldn't be so smug about it, Ariel," Miryam said. "Shiphrah was a hard worker, and it will take the three of us working together to make up for her loss."

Elisheva nodded, but Ariel frowned.

Following the meal, Ham passed by the food preparation table, pausing to dip his fingers in a small dusting of spilt flour. He smiled and manipulated the flour between his thumb and fingertips, then brushed his hands and headed out the door. Outside, he sprinted up the hill to the ark before disappearing inside.

"Ham seems anxious to get to work today," Elisheva said.

"I don't think that's it," Miryam said.

Ariel waited for the others to leave before approaching Noah and Miryam. "This may sound cruel, but you should be thankful she's gone, especially after what happened at the ark yesterday."

"And you should be thankful you're Shem's wife. Otherwise, Ham might have smacked you." *I was tempted.*

Ariel stormed away.

CHAPTER 25

Just past midday, Malluch, Shechem, and Bohar led a company of mounted soldiers through Eden's north gate. They were followed by more than five hundred citizens on foot. Shechem turned for a last look before entering the walls. On a hill in the distance stood a statue made of bronze, with the head of a lion and the body of a man.

Lamech and the elders of Eden observed the troops passing through the gate.

Malluch raised his arm to stop the procession. "Ah. Fathers of Eden. Your absence from the dedication ceremony this morning was deeply felt."

"By what right, Malluch, do you blaspheme the name of God by placing an idol outside our city?" Lamech said.

"Blasphemy? I hardly consider it blasphemy to erect a statue in his honor."

"He who existed before time began, the God of our fathers, the God of Adam, Abel, and Seth, He who they called YAH, was not made with human hands. He is spirit."

"By spirit, I take it you mean invisible? I prefer to worship a god I can see, one I can touch. But to your first question, 'What right have I?' By my right as ruler of this city."

136

"You may be the governor—"

"Prince. I have chosen to take the title of prince. It has a more regal sound to it, don't you think?"

"Prince or governor, it matters little what you call yourself. But you would do well to remember there are still a great many people here who remain loyal to the ways of the fathers."

"Yes, that is proving to be a bit of an inconvenience." Shechem, Bohar, and some of the soldiers within earshot chuckled. "But then time has a way of changing everything, doesn't it?" Malluch said.

Lamech pointed to the statue. "I see you're still determined to make Eden over in the image of Enoch."

"And why not? Enoch is the richest, most powerful city in the world. Her armies are feared from east to west. And she has the blessing and protection of the gods that look down from the hills surrounding her."

"Idols of wood, stone, and bronze have no power to bless or protect."

"Don't they? Since the time Cain first built her, has Enoch ever been defeated? Has she even been challenged in nearly sixteen centuries?"

Shechem didn't have any more faith in the god they'd just erected than the One his fathers worshipped. But being Malluch's right hand, he was obliged to act accordingly.

Methuselah stepped forward, shaking his staff. "Cain did evil in the sight of the Lord when he murdered his brother and carried that evil with him when he fled east. If there is a power that protects Enoch, it is the power of Satan."

"Then I will invoke *his* power."

Collective gasps poured from the patriarch's mouths. Methuselah raised his staff in front of his face, as if protecting himself from the man's words. "You invite the wrath of God."

"Invite it. I welcome it." Malluch pointed to the hill with the idol. "You see, I have more faith in that god than in the one your fathers followed."

137

Methuselah turned to walk away, but Lamech stopped him. "What about the killings?"

"Yes, what about them, Prince," an elder said, a mocking tenor in his voice pronouncing the title.

"Killings?" Malluch said.

"There have been three murders in the city in the last two weeks, two men, one woman," Lamech said. "All with their throats cut."

"Four," another elder said, his voice cracking. "My son was found at the base of the wall near the north gate last night."

"What do we know about this, Commander?"

News of the killings had come as a surprise. And while the number of murders committed each year had risen since Malluch assumed power, they'd never experienced a series of slayings of this magnitude. "Other than the manner of death, we didn't have any reason to suspect the killings were related," Shechem said. "The first two men were found at opposite ends of the city, while one of the women had recently been caught in an act of adultery. We suspect her husband, only he has since fled the city. A third man was found in the rear of a brothel, an apparent casualty of his own vices. But with the discovery of these last two, it looks like a pattern is developing."

"I should say so. I want this killer found, do you hear?"

"Yes, my lord," Shechem said.

"Believe me my friends, we will get to the bottom of it. We're not going to allow the citizens of Eden to be murdered indiscriminately in the streets. I want troops patrolling inside the city, along the outside perimeter, and on the north and south roads, starting immediately."

"Yes, my lord," Shechem said.

"And double the patrols at night."

"It will be done."

Malluch softened his gaze for the elder who'd lost a son. "Please accept my heartfelt sympathy for your loss. You have my solemn promise we will do everything possible to capture this madman and bring justice to the families of Eden."

The grieving elder did not answer, but Lamech snorted. "We shall see."

"You question my sincerity?"

"Until forty years ago, there hadn't been six people murdered in the more than seven hundred years I've lived here. Now it seems they've become all too commonplace, so commonplace, in fact, that it took an outbreak like this to merit the government's attention."

Malluch sneered. "I know there's a point in there somewhere, but I'm having difficulty grasping it."

Lamech gestured first to the wall, then to the mounted soldiers. "Tell me, Prince, in spite of all these measures, has Eden become a safer . . . or more dangerous place to live?"

The governor grit his teeth, slapped the reins, and drove his horse away. The other soldiers followed, forcing the elders out of the way to avoid being trampled.

Back at the palace, Malluch remained resolute. "Shechem, use every resource at your disposal to locate this killer. I don't want the people living in fear, or have that fear turn to panic. This kind of thing, if it gets out of hand, could stir an insurrection."

"Yes, my lord."

"Why all the concern?" Bohar said. "So a few chumps get their throats slit. And the fact that one of them was the son of an elder should be cause for celebration. Good riddance."

Shechem shook his head. *You wouldn't be so crass if you were the one lying there with your throat laid open.*

"Every life has value, my friend," Malluch said.

Shechem had to keep himself from laughing at the insincerity of that remark.

"Even if you don't recognize it," Malluch said. "Each of those six people contributed in some way to the delicate economic and social balance of Eden."

139

Bohar smirked.

If he hadn't known better, Shechem would have suspected Bohar. He'd seen his work. He was good with that knife. But four of the six victims had been men, and his pungent friend was too much a coward to test fate against more powerful adversaries. Sneaking up from behind was his only advantage, one easily countered by a target with sensitive ears. Or a sensitive nose. If he got caught, he'd be the one getting his throat slit—with his own knife. What's more, Bohar wouldn't do anything on his own to bring Malluch's rule under scrutiny. Otherwise, he might find himself on the lion's menu during their next visit to Enoch.

CHAPTER 26

Noah joined Japheth outside the house to enjoy the last glimpses of dusk, the sound of Ham's pounding mallet floating down from the ark. "Listen to him up there," Japheth said. "He's been working since dawn without a break. He won't quit."

"And when he does, he'll be up all night standing watch because he can't sleep."

"Isn't there something we can do to get him to eat? You could put your thumbs in the hollows of his cheeks."

"He snapped at your mother just for asking."

"Not eating. Irritable as a mad hornet. Standing watch outside the ark all night because he can't sleep. This is more than just a brother missing his sister. You want to tell me what's going on?"

"He loves her."

"Of course he loves her. We all do." Japheth humphed. "Except for Ariel."

"Not like we do. He's *in* love."

"Are you sure?"

"You've seen them together. Haven't you noticed anything different lately?"

"I thought that was just playful banter between siblings."

141

"Like the banter between you and Ariel, or Japheth and Elisheva?"

"That's different. We're married."

"And so, too, have they become—emotionally."

"I'm not sure I understand."

"You were their teachers. Growing up in a house of married couples, they learned not just sibling love, but spousal love as well. And now that they're coming of age, each yearns for a companion, the way you and your brother did when your time came."

"Well, what are you going to do? Shiphrah's only been gone a month, and look at him. He's a mess."

"I'll talk to him."

Japheth went back inside. Noah walked up the hill where he found Ham at the far end of the ark holding a leaf. He cocked his ear at the sound of his father's approach but remained with his back to him. "Did you ever notice, Father, how green Shiphrah's eyes are?" Ham twirled the leaf by its stem. "More brilliant than this leaf."

"I noticed."

"I love her, you know?"

"I know."

"Is it wrong for me to feel this way?"

"No."

Ham faced his father, the dark circles above his cheeks just visible in the fading light. "Even though I'm supposed to be her brother?"

"But you're not."

"We shouldn't have let her go."

"I could do nothing to stop her. She was determined to leave, although—"

"Although what?"

"I was wrong to have deterred you from going after her." Noah watched Ham's eyes fill. "But I made a vow."

142

"What vow?"

"It's not important now."

"What do you mean it's not important? We have to find her."

"I'll find her."

"I want to go with you."

"No, my son."

"Why not?"

"To begin with, you're much too weak to travel. Stay here and regain your strength. I have an idea of where she might be headed. And it will be less conspicuous for me to travel alone."

"But—"

Noah clasped Ham by the shoulder, searching his face. "There's another reason you must remain here. We can't afford to fall further behind by having two of us away and unavailable to work on the ark. We must all remain vigilant, for we know not the day or the hour of the coming judgment."

Ham let out a big sigh, threw the leaf down, and moved away to the edge of the hill.

"Ham."

He slowly spun around. "All right. I'll stay. But I don't know how you expect me to keep my mind on my work after being kicked in the stomach like this."

"You'll manage."

The next morning, Noah's eldest helped him pack a donkey with supplies. "Are you sure you don't want me to go with you?" Japheth said.

"To be honest, I'd prefer to have you along. But I need someone responsible to take charge of things around here."

Japheth nodded.

"Keep an eye on Ham. See that he eats. He's lost too much weight the past month, and I don't want him passing out and falling through a deck or something."

"I'll ask mother to make succotash. It's his favorite."

"You know your brother. Keep him away from the wine. He's depressed enough already, and drinking will only make it worse and give him an excuse to get out of working on the ark. Get Shem to help you if need be."

"We'll put pinholes in his wineskin."

* * *

Shechem grimaced at the sight of blood coagulating around the head of the ninth throat slashing victim. He'd been found on the floor of his bedroom. Shechem had seen men fall in battle, but something about the volume of blood here and the gaping neck wound turned his stomach. Not quite equal to the smell of a child's burning flesh, but disturbing still. In an opposite corner, family members attempted to comfort the man's sobbing widow.

Two soldiers entered the room and approached Shechem. "Sir," one of them said.

"Your report."

"No one saw a thing, Commander. Apparently, the man's wife had taken their two children to visit her mother in another part of the city early last evening. She found him like this when she returned."

"Did you find anything outside?"

"There are footprints outside the bedroom window, which would seem to indicate the killer may have entered there. But the footprints lead out to the main street, where they disappear amongst the hundreds of others."

Shechem lamented the five additional killings that had taken place in the last seventeen days, three women and two men, the last, the man at his feet. Since Malluch's pledge to catch the killer, the number of murders in and around Eden had risen. This latest killing had been committed in the heart of the city, in a house located in a densely populated area.

Lamech and the victim's father entered the room. "Well, Commander, anything to go on?" Lamech said. The young man's father knelt beside his son's body.

'There weren't any witnesses, if that's what you mean. And the footprints found outside the window could be anybody's."

"Anybody's, Commander? I doubt that. A somebody I would think. A somebody with a purpose as yet unknown to us, but a purpose nonetheless."

"What purpose has insanity?" Because of the random nature of the killings, Shechem was more inclined to adopt Malluch's theory of a madman killing without conscience or reason.

"You think your killer insane?"

There'd been no connection between any of the victims. Two were only remotely acquainted. None had been robbed of their person or, for those found inside, had anything taken from their homes. None of the women had been violated — which once again, ruled out Bohar. "What else?"

"Would you happen to know what part of the day these killings are taking place?"

"Only one victim, a woman, was found in the afternoon. The rest were all discovered in the late evening or early morning hours."

"How do you suppose, Commander, an increase in patrols has resulted in an increase in the murder rate?"

Shechem was stumped, but realized Lamech had posed a valid question. "That is puzzling."

"More than that, Commander. I suggest it as a possible indication you have more than a madman on your hands."

"What do you mean?"

"Anyone sophisticated enough to plan and execute nine murders successfully in defiance of such measures isn't insane. They're inspired."

Shechem was forced to consider every possibility now. If the killer was the resourceful plotter Lamech had suggested, then even tripling the patrols wouldn't do any good. And with no link between any of the victims, attempting to predict who the next victim might be would prove just as futile. Sooner or later the killer would make a mistake and be caught in the act or be seen leaving the scene of a murder. And then they would have him.

That, or the killer would turn out to be one of his own soldiers.

CHAPTER 27

As Noah approached the small village his family frequented for supplies, he questioned again his wisdom in having discouraged Ham from going after Shiphrah. His pursuit of her might not only have resulted in her return, but would have also served to dispel any doubts she had about his feelings for her.

Now, even the vow he'd taken seemed trivial compared to the task of finding her. A month was a long time. And a determined person could travel a long way during this time, especially one running away.

He'd chosen to start with the merchant from whom they'd routinely obtained provisions. If anyone would have noticed a stranger in the village, it would be him. Noah estimated the man to be about his own age, between 500 and 550 years. He wore a striped tunic, and his face was drawn and weathered by the sun. He snickered when the patriarch asked if he'd seen a young woman riding a donkey pass through the village in the last month. "Lots of them," he said. "Lots of men, too."

"This one was pretty," Noah said. "She had on a beige tunic trimmed in blue.

"I admit in this part of the country that narrows it down, but at my age a pretty face just doesn't stick in my head the way it used to." The man pointed up the street to where smoke rose from an outdoor furnace. "You might want to try the metal craftsman. He also happens to be a good farrier. There was a young woman, I think it was about a month ago, whose donkey had a problem with one of its feet."

Noah thanked the merchant and rode up the street to the metal craftsman. He, too, recalled a woman about thirty days ago asking to have a crack in her donkey's right front hoof repaired. He remembered she was pretty and had a nice shape. But so, too, did a number of his woman customers. In the end, he wasn't able to provide enough information to confirm that the woman whose donkey he'd serviced was Shiphrah.

He mounted his donkey and started to pull away, only to wrench around in the saddle to something spoken by the metal craftsman. "What was that?"

"Green eyes," the metal craftsman said.

"What about them?"

"I remember now, she had the most dazzling green eyes I'd ever seen."

The metal craftsman also recalled the woman was in a hurry, trying to catch up with a caravan that'd passed through the day before heading west. Noah paid the man a small gratuity, then headed out of the village along the road reportedly taken by the green-eyed woman. He didn't have much to go on.

A woman that may or may not be Shiphrah. Traveling on a road that led to any of a hundred destinations. She already had a thirty-day head start and time was a commodity he could not afford to lose.

Two hours later, he came to a fork in the road. He dismounted for a closer look even though any tracks belonging to Shiphrah or the caravan would have long since been obliterated. One road led about twenty degrees northwest of his current due west heading, the other ten degrees to the southwest. Both appeared equally well-traveled.

148

Which path should he take? Either path might lead to the Great Sea. Either path might prove to be a dead end. He picked up a handful of dirt, as if doing so might give him some clue about which path to take. No amount of logic or analysis could help him now. Choose wrong, and he might lose any chance to find Shiphrah.

He let the dirt strain through his fingers, climbed aboard his donkey, and took the right fork.

* * *

Shechem noticed a difference immediately when he entered the great hall to inform the governor of the latest on the killings. Malluch rose to greet him while Bohar remained seated at the table, a tomato in one hand and a full loaf of bread in the other.

"Good morning, Commander," Malluch said. "I trust you weren't out too late investigating this latest murder. He motioned to the table filled with bread, wine, and a variety of fruits and vegetables. "Something to eat? Some wine perhaps?"

Bohar stuffed his mouth with both hands, the juice from the tomato running down his chin. Although hungry, the thought of sitting down with this glutton destroyed Shechem's appetite. "Thank you, no."

"I understand our killer is becoming more brazen."

"Indeed. Last night's murder took place in the heart of the city, inside the man's own home."

"You've taken all the precautions we discussed?"

"Yes, my lord."

"Well then I would say it is only a matter of time before you catch him. Sooner or later he'll make a mistake. All madmen do."

"Yes, my lord. There's something else. Lamech showed up at the scene of the killing."

Malluch's eyes narrowed. "What did *he* want?"

149

"I believe he was acquainted with the family of the victim."

"Is that all?"

Shechem didn't dare tell him what Lamech's theory of the killings was, not with Malluch insisting it was a madman. "Yes."

"Let me be clear, Commander. I'll tolerate no interference with your investigation. Not even from an elder."

"Understood."

Bohar concurred with a loud belch.

"Enjoying your food, my friend?" Malluch said.

Watching him ram the remaining crust of bread into his ravenous maw, Shechem grasped what the peculiarity in the room was.

Bohar.

Standing fifteen cubits away, he realized for the first time ever he couldn't smell him—at least not the odor he was used to smelling. And his hair, although still scraggily and unkempt, appeared as if it had been cleansed of a good hin of its oil. Even his tunic looked new, marred only by the stream of fresh tomato juice staining the front.

"What's this, another bath?" he said. "That's two in a month, isn't it?"

Bohar didn't speak, reaching instead to his groin in a gesture of obscenity. Shechem and Malluch laughed.

With the air free of smells to ruin the taste, Shechem relented and reached for an apple.

He couldn't wait to inform Claudia about Bohar's sudden change in hygiene habits. She wouldn't believe it, but seeing the look on her face would make it worth the telling. What was Bohar up to? Had he finally found himself a woman, one he didn't have to take by force? Or had Malluch had enough of him stinking up the palace?

Regarding Claudia, Shechem had seen her in the market this morning talking to the son of one of the richest elders in Eden. It was all quite innocent, at least in appearance, with the two exchanging little more than a smile and some conversation. But then Claudia wasn't foolish enough to do anything publicly that would leave herself open to gossip. On the other hand, something had affected her attitude toward him, and he was determined to find out what it was.

* * *

Shechem watched from a shadow across the courtyard while Claudia, her head covered with a veil, closed the door to their home behind her. She paused for a moment to scan the square before walking briskly past the palace and turning right onto the street. He followed at a safe distance wearing a hooded tunic.

He was eager and saddened at the thought of catching his wife with the lover he'd long suspected. Tonight might be the night he'd prove his theory.

He'd told Claudia he wouldn't be home tonight, expecting, if not hoping, she would take the bait. Now, following her down the street, it only brought him heartache to think his suspicions about her over the years had been founded.

Last night, Eden suffered through its first multiple victim evening when two men were found with their throats slashed. One of the men had been a son to another of Eden's elders. Shechem tried to head off the additional scrutiny the killing would bring for Malluch by taking extra security measures.

Shortly before dark, he'd addressed one thousand of Eden's finest soldiers gathered below him in the garrison courtyard. Four companies of 250 men, one assigned to each of the four quadrants, would flood the city in an overwhelming show of force. His strategy wasn't designed so much to catch the killer as it was to deter him from striking again, at least for this one night.

While Claudia continued north along Eden's main street, Shechem managed to stay within two hundred cubits of her. Close enough not to lose her, but far enough away not to be detected.

And with soldiers on every corner, the streets were filled with an intrepid populace dense enough to provide him cover.

She slowed her pace, stopping before the next intersecting street to look behind. He backed into the alcove of a building. Her suspicions allayed, she turned right and disappeared around the corner. He moved quickly to regain sight of her.

Would she be brave enough to roam the streets if not for the presence of his soldiers? Was her lover, if more than a figment, worth the risk of getting her throat slit? Shechem had to laugh inwardly at the irony of the situation. It was his strategy to saturate the city with soldiers. But had that strategy also served as the catalyst to embolden his wife to go out tonight?

He rounded the corner in time to see her turn left at the next street. Knowing the streets in this area grew shorter the farther they were from the palace, he burst into a jog to keep from losing her. At the next intersection, he peered cautiously around the corner.

Claudia crossed the next street and headed into an area where the only light cast on the road emanated from the windows of houses. He scurried along, hugging the house walls to stay up with her. For a moment, he thought he'd lost her, until the light from a window caught her veil-covered head passing by.

When she entered the next intersection, a man looking over his shoulder bumped into her from the street on her left. The man, dressed in a dark cloak, stumbled past her up the street while Claudia quickly composed herself and continued east.

Shechem started across the same intersection, but his feet froze at the sound of a woman's terrifying scream coming from his left. He turned to the sound of the disturbance. A woman kneeled over the body of a young man lying in the street. Shechem looked back in time to see his wife's shadow disappear in the darkness.

For an instant, he wrestled with his decision. Continue following his wife to learn if his long-held suspicions were correct, or come to the aid of a possibly injured citizen. He surprised himself with the ease with which he made the choice and sprinted toward the woman.

152

The woman had her hand pressed against the young man's throat, blood pouring through her fingers from a severed artery. The commander estimated the boy to be no more than twelve years of age. His breathing was labored and irregular.

The woman looked at Shechem with pleading eyes. "Help him," she said. "He's my son. Please, help him."

He threw off his tunic, kneeled, and covered the boy's body from the neck down, then turned to several bystanders and pointed down the street. "Find soldiers. Tell them to come right away. If they hesitate, tell them Shechem commands it."

The bystanders, three men, ran down the street.

Blood continued to flow from the boy's neck. "Try not to worry, madam. Help will be here soon." He didn't like giving the woman false hope, but it was the only thing he could do. Even if a physician was around the corner, he doubted he could do anything to stop the bleeding in time to save the boy's life.

The bystanders returned shortly with four soldiers. Shechem pointed to the closest. "You, take these three men and find a physician. If you can't locate one, go to the palace and bring Malluch's physician."

"Malluch's physician, for a peasant boy?" the soldier said.

Shechem grabbed the soldier's shirt at the neck. "Do as I tell you." The soldier led the three men down the street. He moved out of earshot of the woman tending her son to speak to the remaining soldiers. "I think I may have seen our killer. He was wearing a dark cloak with a hood. Not too tall. I'd say about a handbreadth under four cubits. He ran up that way."

The three soldiers drew their swords and hustled up the street. Just as they disappeared from view, the boy went into convulsion, his pupils rolled up inside his eyelids and his body shook violently.

"No, no, no." His mother wept. The boy's body thrashed two more times before going still, while the blood pouring through the mother's fingers slowed to a trickle.

153

Shechem sensed that queasy feeling in the pit of his stomach, similar to what he'd experienced at Enoch. Eden's killer had sunk to a new low, his murderous rampage taking a sickening turn. Tonight, he'd added children to the list of those within reach of his blade.

He jumped up, drew his sword, and cursed into the darkness so loud his throat hurt. "You miserable coward! I'll cut your heart out." He cursed once more, this time impugning the existence of the killer's father.

CHAPTER 28

Noah didn't know the name of the city he'd entered, only that it was a full two days west of the last village he'd passed through. A merchant there remembered a woman fitting Shiphrah's description because of the attention she'd attracted—admiration from the men, envy from the women. According to the tradesman, the woman was still a half day's journey behind the caravan.

About half the size of Eden, the city had a vibrant trade, with patrons bustling about the marketplace near its center in the heat of the day. Once again, he chose the merchants there as the best prospects for a lead. He tied his donkey next to several others at a small post at the near end of the market and made his way up the street.

Five hundred forty parts and eight merchants later, no one could recall having seen a woman fitting Shiphrah's description. Not until reaching the far end of the marketplace did he receive a morsel of hope. "What about a caravan?" he said.

"Now *that* I remember," the merchant selling melons and cabbages said. "Just over a month ago. Six carts and around twenty to twenty-five people. Sold almost double that in melons to them. Don't remember seeing a woman with green eyes, though."

"Headed west?"

155

"Yes. Said they were journeying to the Great Sea." The merchant paused. "Wait a part. You said she was riding a donkey?"

"Yes."

"I did hear of a woman who passed through here shortly after the caravan. Never saw her myself, but I overheard some of the men talking about how attractive she was. I remember thinking how foolish it was for her to be on the road by herself. I hope she's all right."

"What—"

The sound of a large group of horses entering the square grasped Noah's attention and all those nearby. Fifty or more soldiers dismounted and made their way toward them. Some visited the vendors in the market, others entered buildings along either side of the roadway where liquid refreshment was offered for sale.

The merchant pulled as many melons and cabbages from his cart as he could and placed them in baskets behind him. He then covered the produce in the baskets with straw. "Soldiers from Eden." The merchant snarled and spat on the ground.

"What about them?"

"Soldiers take and do not pay."

Noah pulled the hood to his tunic over his head. Although he might draw suspicion in this heat, he couldn't chance being recognized. Either way, he had an even bigger problem. His donkey was at the far end of the street, tied to a post in the middle of fifty horses belonging to the soldiers of Eden. A small group of them milled about standing guard.

The merchant, noticing him cover his head, gave a nod and a grin, indicating he understood the situation. "Do you need a place to hide?"

He nodded.

"Don't speak, and do exactly as I tell you. Turn and walk swiftly, but don't run, up the street to the houses on the left. Go into the second door, through the large room and into a smaller room on the right. Climb out the window in the back, then run

156

across the melon field into the wooded area where you can hide until nightfall."

He nodded again.

"If you're spoken to, don't stop, don't turn, just act like you didn't hear. By tonight, these vermin will be so drunk you could march your donkey right over their sleeping carcasses. Now go."

He did as the merchant instructed. A hundred cubits from the merchant's cart, a voice called out. "Hey you!" He didn't respond to the one calling him, but assumed it was a soldier. "Hey you, get back here. What are you hiding under that hood?"

"He can't hear you," the merchant said. "He's a deaf mute."

"Stop!" the voice said. "By order of the soldiers of Eden."

"I told you he's deaf!"

Once Noah hit the door, he sprinted through the house, out the window, and across three hundred cubits of melon field before reaching the woods. There, cloaked by the foliage, he kneeled several cubits from the margin, watching while several soldiers poked their heads out the window.

After seventy-two parts, eight soldiers brought the merchant around to the rear of the house for a search of the area. Though unable to hear what was being said, Noah grew concerned for the merchant when his discussion with the soldiers grew heated. At one point, a soldier shook a knife under the merchant's nose just before they all returned to the street side. Whatever the merchant said must have satisfied them, because fifty-four parts later he appeared at the window and threw a wave to Noah across the field.

With several hours of daylight remaining, he was anxious to move on. Instead he settled for the stout trunk of a tamarisk tree to lean against. Just before dark, he ventured into the field to retrieve a melon but returned to cover before cracking it. The melon was warm, but refreshing.

Once the moon crested the horizon, Noah walked back across the field. Since his face hadn't been seen, and because the soldiers were seeking someone with his head covered, he removed the hood. He would count on the darkness to keep from being recognized as Lamech's son, aided by the soldiers' expected level of intoxication. Judging from the noise coming from the square, it appeared they were well on their way.

He exited a side street onto the main road, where several vendors remained open for business. His benefactor, the melon merchant, was not one of them. He was sorry he didn't have an opportunity to thank him, or to speak to the men who'd seen the woman following the caravan.

He peered down the well-lit street to where the fifty horses, and he hoped his donkey, remained tied. In between, nearly four hundred cubits of ground had to be crossed without being recognized. About a dozen people occupied the street, five of whom were soldiers. He moved down the right side close to the buildings, the side where only two soldiers barred his way.

The first soldier was in the middle of the street talking with a vendor, a good forty-five cubits away, but glanced at him as he passed. He fought the urge to look away, instead he peered directly into the soldier's eyes and nodded in respect, a gesture returned by the soldier. Noah let out a deep breath.

The second soldier stood directly in his path, conversing with a young woman in provocative dress. Noah considered moving farther out into the street, but decided against it fearing the move might draw more attention.

It proved to be the correct one. The soldier was so busy negotiating the price of flesh, he didn't even bother to look at him passing within arm's length.

One hundred and fifty cubits to go.

He relaxed a bit when he cleared the near end of the marketplace. He quickened his pace and set his sights on where his donkey had waited for more than eight hours.

He stepped to move away from the building when a door swung open and three soldiers poured into the street. He stopped short to avoid running into them, but not far enough to keep from smelling them. Stumbling and slurring his words, one of them grabbed him and drew him in close. "Hey, I know you. You're—you're." The soldier gestured to his companions. "Who is he?"

"Are you kidding? I can't remember what my own father looks like right now." The second soldier chuckled.

"Leave him alone," said the third. "It's getting late, and I still need a woman."

"I got it," the first one said. "You know who you look like?"

Noah's heart raced within his chest, but said nothing.

"You look just like the son of our former governor." He again looked to his cohorts "What was his name? Noga? Boah? Nohar?"

"Noah," the second said.

"That's it! You look just like Noah. Did anyone ever tell you that?"

"Nah," the third said. He can't be. Noah died thirty or forty years ago."

"Really? Well he sure does look like him."

The second and third soldiers grabbed the one holding Noah and pulled him away. "Let's go." The three of them moved past him up the street.

He wiped the sweat and drunken soldier's spittle from his face and pressed on toward the horses. When he arrived, anger and exasperation seized him. He looked back up the street in awe of the obstacle he'd just negotiated, then to the empty post in front of him.

His donkey was gone.

And so were all the others.

What now? Even if he had the time, he wouldn't know where to begin to search for him.

"Psst," a voice said.

159

He spun around, unable to locate the source. "Psst. Over here," came the voice from a figure motioning to him from within a group of horses across the street.

He moved toward the man, but for the shadows didn't recognize his being a soldier of Eden until he was nearly upon him. Noah felt beneath his tunic for the hilt of his sword. "I wonder, sir, if I could impose upon you for about ninety parts?" the soldier said.

Do I have a choice? "How can I be of service?" Noah said.

"I drew the short straw and got stuck guarding the horses while my friends are stuffing their gullets with wine and food. Would you be kind enough to watch the horses for a short time while I get something to eat?"

Noah didn't want to appear too eager. "Will you be long?"

"Oh, no. I'll be right back."

The soldier raised his hand and walked away. Noah returned the wave. He moved to a group of horses furthest from the square, untied the last one, and quietly walked it out of town on the main road.

He rode all night to put as much distance as possible between him and the soldiers. Though he'd been unable to confirm her identity, someone matching Shiphrah's description remained in pursuit of the caravan.

He continued west.

CHAPTER 29

Shechem was grateful for the first real break in solving the murders. It'd come at the expense of the lives of twelve citizens of Eden, but his theory had been correct. The killer had finally been seen. No longer an invisible force or shapeless monster, the murderer now had a form. And it was the form of a man.

Even more gratifying was the fact he'd been one of the witnesses to see him. Another, the young boy's mother, confirmed she'd stepped outside in time to see her son's body fall from the grasp of the dark-cloaked man.

There'd been a third witness, but it was one he was loath to divulge lest he be forced to reveal he'd followed Claudia. Besides, he doubted his wife would be any help in identifying the killer anyhow, whose face, like hers, had been shrouded.

Still, his progress in the case was dampened by the reality the killer had escaped, despite an overabundance of troops in the area. The soldiers sent to pursue the killer immediately following the boy's murder had turned up nothing. And he and his men had spent the rest of the evening running to the sound of every disturbance or woman's scream.

This morning, Bohar provided an unfitting end to the previous night's frustration by razzing him about the low body count.

161

"Congratulations. I heard you only had a half person killed last night."

"A half person?" Shechem said. "What's that?"

"Wasn't it a child?"

"A boy. Twelve years old."

"A half person."

Shechem shook his head. "Bohar."

"Yes."

"Your sense of compassion amazes me."

Bohar nodded while displaying a wide grin. "Me too."

Shechem couldn't afford to be so droll. The death of a child would bring a new level of interest, and pressure, from the elders to apprehend the murderer. Being the official in charge of the investigation, the brunt of that pressure would fall on him. Only he didn't need any additional motivation. Being a father was motivation enough. That and never wanting to look into another grieving mother's eyes was all he needed to keep him focused on finding the killer.

* * *

Six days west of the city, Noah had his horse in a full gallop. He'd pressed the animal since their escape, pushing him to the limits of his endurance each day. Though largely constrained to navigating by intuition, if he maintained his present course he would eventually reach the waters of the Great Sea. Only one thing worried him, a fear intensified with each pause for rest or sleep. Would he be too late?

The Great Sea was home to half a dozen ports along its eastern border, each providing service to a great many ships. Were Shiphrah to secure passage aboard one of them, he might never see her again. Moreover, as a beautiful woman traveling alone, she might easily fall prey to any number of scoundrels along the road.

162

His best chance of finding her in time to avoid either calamity rested with the possibility Shiphrah had caught up to the caravan. Those were often slowed by the pace of the large number of travelers and animal-driven carts that defined them. They also tended to make more stops than riders journeying alone, increasing the possibility he might still be able to overtake them.

Rounding a soft curve, the familiar pattern of a blanket's weave caught Noah's eye, prompting him to yank back the reins. Off to the right, an animal carcass the size of a pack animal lie at the bottom of a gully, its flesh picket clean. He descended the hill to investigate.

Had he been ignorant of the possible injury to Shiphrah's donkey, he might have ignored the familiar sight of a dead animal beside the road. Now, negotiating the steep incline, his feelings of apprehension increased with each step, until . . .

Miryam's handiwork rested partly beneath the skeleton of a donkey.

Blood spotted the blanket.

He inspected the dead animal's legs, a lump filling his throat at the sight of a rawhide patch fastened around the right front hoof. He tried to swallow it away, but the scene of dozens of footprints, animal and human, surrounding the carcass made the lump grow larger. A collection of footprints, still viewable in the copper clay of the culvert, could mean only one thing.

Marauders.

He searched for other clues. The absence of a saddle or bridle only reinforced his suspicion about the origin of the tracks. Marauders would never leave such valuable commodities behind. As for the blood on the blanket. Was it the donkey's? Or Shiphrah's?

Perhaps it was better if she'd perished in the fall. For if she'd been taken by Marauders, she might now be wishing the same thing.

* * *

163

Shechem stood a few cubits behind Claudia while she brushed the sleep tangles from her hair. And with each downward stroke, his attention paused to focus on the soft, white skin of her neck.

Why had the killer passed her by? If the murders in Eden were just about a body count, it would have taken only a moment to rip the knife through her throat. He considered Lamech's theory, that indeed some method to the killings existed.

Did his wife know how lucky she was to be alive, or did she even suspect it was the killer who'd bumped into her? Part of him longed to tell her, to chastise her for being so foolish. But then he would have to admit he'd followed her.

Who was so important to her she would risk her life to see him? The silk merchant who made her clothes? He was handsome. The elder's son with over a thousand sheep and cattle? Not as handsome as the silk merchant, but he was rich. Dozens of men came in and out of the palace every day. And they all seemed to have eyes for Claudia. The question was, which of them did *she* have eyes for?

Without proof of an affair, confronting her would only serve to increase the schism between them. It would also alert her to his suspicions and cause her to become doubly careful about being secretive. No, if she had a lover, and he was to have any chance of catching her with him, he would have to remain patient.

Besides, he still cared for her. In spite of her vanity, coldness, and late-night odysseys to secret destinations, he couldn't bring himself to reject her. Not without solid proof. She was the mother of his daughters, and he would need more than supposition and coincidence for that.

He decided to test her instead. "You remember the young boy I told you about last week?"

"The one who was killed? Yes. What his mother must be going through."

"Well, I don't know if I told you, but he was attacked just outside his front door."

Claudia shivered. "How ghastly!"

"I wanted to remind you, even though we're within the palace grounds, to be careful."

She stopped brushing her hair and turned to him. "You know I don't go out alone at night."

There it was.

The lie.

Surely not the first, but the first he'd caught her in and another brick added to his wall of suspicion.

* * *

Noah continued west after observing tracks that appeared to both enter and leave the gully from the same direction. Based on the number of imprints found near the skeleton, he estimated the Marauder party to number around forty. He also knew they wouldn't remain on the main road for long and risk running into a patrol of soldiers. This meant hoping to find the place where they'd turned off, if such a trail were still visible after more than thirty days.

But even while he earnestly pursued them, he found himself wanting to lose them. Marauders were feared throughout the land of Eden.

These descendants of Cain had left Enoch centuries ago, banding together to roam the land in groups of forty to fifty wayfaring plunderers. Known for their skill with the sword and merciless savagery in battle, they were capable of defeating enemies more than twice their number. Yet, despite this ferocity, they tended to shun the major cities, choosing instead to prey upon the smaller villages and towns.

Fifty-five years earlier, Noah had witnessed firsthand the results of their ruthlessness when he passed through a village where every home had been burned and every man and woman killed.

165

Strangely enough, evidence indicated they'd taken the children of the village alive.

He briefly considered returning home for help but quickly dismissed the thought, realizing he would never be able to locate the Marauder's trail again. Then again, what would he do if he found it? Even if Shiphrah were still alive and being held inside their camp, how would he get her out? Still, he owed it to Ham, and to himself, to verify her fate.

He crested the rise in the road and was surprised by a group of fifteen soldiers approaching from the east. *Too late to run now.* Given their heading, he was fairly certain they constituted a separate company from the one he'd left behind. He just hoped they wouldn't recognize the horse. Noah quickly pulled up the hood of his tunic, but his eye was drawn to a familiar face, one that likewise studied his when they passed.

He knew better than to look back, although he could practically feel the fifteen sets of eyes piercing his back like darts. He pulled the slack out of the reins to keep his horse from increasing its gait and alerting the soldiers. Eighteen parts later the sound of their horses faded in the distance and he breathed easy — for a moment.

He turned to the sound of horses returning, their hooves lifting clumps of dirt from the road as they thundered toward him. The soldiers surrounded him, the one he'd recognized pulled alongside and leaned to see past his hood. "Where did you get that horse, old man?" he said, eyeing Noah's saddle. By his tenor, the man appeared to be in command of the group.

The soldier's saddle and the one his detainee sat on were identically fashioned. He gestured behind him. "In the city just ahead."

"Is that so?"

"Yes, I exchanged my donkey for it."

"Who are you, old man?" the soldier said, stiffening. "Your face looks familiar."

"Just a simple farmer. One not worthy to warrant the attention of the soldiers of Eden."

166

Noah gently kicked at his horse's sides, but the commander grabbed the reins from his hands. "What's your hurry?"

"Only the business to which I now find myself delayed."

The commander pulled the hood from his head and grinned. "It's been a long time, Preacher."

"Do I know you?"

"Not by name, but we encountered one another some forty years ago at Eden's city gate. I worked for Bohar then. And you—well—you were about to be stoned." The commander's smile broadened.

"Fortunately, that was not in God's plan."

"You mean fortunately your sons showed up to save you."

"As I said."

"Just where are those two cowards?"

He wasn't about to let these killers anywhere near his family. "It may please you and Malluch to know I lost my wife and youngest son crossing the river the night we left Eden. Japheth died eight years ago of a fever."

"That's too bad. I know Bohar was looking forward to seeing *him* again." Several soldiers joined their leader in laughter.

Noah didn't know whether the commander truly believed him or not.

"Bind him!" the commander said.

Four soldiers dismounted and yanked him from his horse.

"Gently, men," their leader said with a sneer. "Gently. This is the son of a governor of Eden. He should be treated with respect."

Noah's wrists were bound with shackles.

CHAPTER 30

Tethered by a chain drawn behind a soldier's horse, Noah accompanied his captors east along the road leading back to the city he'd escaped from. For three days, he'd gone without food or water. Twice today he'd fallen. Twice he'd been dragged. Cuts and contusions marked his wrists, and the heaviness in his legs made it difficult to walk. Had he the strength, he'd have been tempted to fight back, but the lack of nourishment had sapped his vigor.

How could he have managed to elude a whole company of soldiers, only to find himself captured by this small patrol? And what of Shiphrah? Who was going to find her now? His only hope was she'd already joined the caravan, and the dead donkey was just a coincidence. Not likely, but possible.

Yesterday, as they stopped to rest the horses, a soldier brought to his commander's attention the obvious. "Begging your pardon, Commander, but aren't we still a good ways from Eden."

"About ten days."

"With all due respect, sir, if you want to get him back alive, don't you think we should at least give him some water?"

"Maybe you're right." The commander pointed to a skin containing water on the soldier's horse, then followed him over to where Noah slumped in the dirt. The soldier held out the skin

168

to his outstretched hands, but the commander ripped it away. "I said to give him some water. Not the whole skin."

The commander opened the skin before his prisoner's cupped palms, then poured the water onto the ground just out of his reach. He shook the last few drops into his hands, which he lapped up ravenously.

"If it were up to me, I would have killed you back there and been done with it. But apparently Malluch has something special in store for you. Something to do with fire."

Now, with the sun beating down on him with the heat of a furnace, Noah's tongue felt like the clay of a dried riverbed. A lack of saliva made it difficult to peel from the roof of his mouth or to lick his cracked lips. And his head pounded in sync with the clanging of his shackles.

When his legs cramped, he feared he might fall and not be able to get up again. He battled the spasm for several more paces before dropping to one knee, then was dragged for the third time today.

Arms stretched taught, he tried to keep his head out of the dirt, letting his chest and knees absorb the punishment of the road. "Get up!" came the bark of the horseman's voice above him, followed by a barrage of cursing and vile names. His inability to rise the way he had earlier only seemed to increase the soldier's anger, who continued to drag him along the path.

Noah guessed he'd been towed over 350 cubits when, weakened by the journey and a lack of nourishment, he began to lose consciousness. Would they continue to drag him once they saw he was passed out? Using his last bit of strength to spare his face, he turned onto his left shoulder. Then all light disappeared.

Noah was convinced he was dreaming. What else would account for the cool, wet drops pelting his head and back? Surely not compassion from the commander of the soldiers. Only a rumble of thunder confirmed he was awake. With arms still stretched above his head, he rolled over onto his back and let the rain fall into his mouth.

How long had he been out? 270 parts? 540? When he was nearing unconsciousness, he remembered there'd been a few clouds in the sky, but the sun was still pounding him. Could a storm have developed that quickly?

He lifted his head to the sound of a horse's footsteps next to him. "Well, Preacher, this is disappointing. But I guess there's no accounting for the weather, is there?" The commander extended his palm to catch the rain. "On the other hand, don't think you can use this storm as an excuse for rest. On your feet."

He pushed himself to a sitting position when the commander started away, who then whirled his horse around. "Unless you'd rather be dragged through the mud."

CHAPTER 31

Noah's first experience of trying to sleep outside in a rainstorm was all he thought it would be—a soggy nightmare. While the soldiers warmed themselves in their tents, their water-soaked captive lay shivering in the night air shackled to a rock. Even with the hood to his tunic up, the constant pounding of the rain prevented him from ever fully drifting off. Being forced to stay awake did provide one benefit though. It gave him more time to plan his escape.

As had been their custom since his arrest, his captors drank heavily before going to sleep, a practice which served to loosen their tongues. This evening he found them particularly verbose, and when the subject of their conversation turned to him, he listened.

"This is a load of dung," a voice inside one the two tents said. "Why are we wasting time playing nursemaid to this cur, someone Malluch wants dead anyhow?"

"He's right," another said. "Good times await us in Cainan, and we're having to take time out to transport one lousy prisoner."

Cainan. So that's the name of the city he was in. He leaned forward, drawing all slack out of the chain.

"There's not much we can do about it," a third said.

"Oh, yes there is," the first said. "If we could somehow dispose of him, we could—"

"Dispose of him," the second said. "I doubt if the captain would go for that."

"I wasn't thinking of asking his permission."

"Pass me the skin." The shadow of someone backlit by a lamp raised a wineskin to his mouth, then passed it to another. "You're going to defy orders?"

"We won't have to. What if we all woke up in the morning to find the Preacher dead?"

"A nice idea, but just how do you plan on pulling it off?"

"It'll be easy. The Preacher's been getting weaker by the day, right? When the captain finds him in the morning, he'll figure he died from exhaustion and lack of nourishment."

"I don't know," a forth added. "The captain was adamant about wanting him brought back alive. If we get caught, he's liable to have us all executed."

"Do you want to spend the next four days dragging the Preacher back to Eden when we could be enjoying the wine and women of Cainan?" the first said.

Several others agreed.

"I guess not. Who's going to do it?"

"I will."

"I'll go with you," the second said. "How about it?"

"I'm in," the third said.

"One thing," the forth said. "How are you going to arrange to have him simply die?"

"We'll use this," the first said.

The silhouette of a raised arm holding a pillow shone through the tent.

"We'll move out as soon as the captain is asleep. In the meantime, toss me that wine."

With little time to waste, Noah inspected his shackles and the chain binding him. One by one, he ran each link through his

172

fingers, from the connection at his wrists to the end where the chain anchored. None had any defect.

On most nights since his capture, the soldiers had chained him to a tree. But tonight, because they'd chosen to camp closer to the road, they tied him to a rock. They'd looped the chain around an indentation about half way up the large, irregularly shaped stone.

Noah sought to test it, pulling on the loop to see if there was any slack. Although the chain rotated freely around the indentation, two protrusions above and the rock's wider circumference below secured it against the structure.

He used the flanges of his shackles for a chisel to chip away at the projections of rock, using short, precise strokes to limit the rattling of his chains. He hoped the rain, in addition to providing lubrication for chiseling, would help to obscure the sound produced by his labors. But his efforts were slowed by the rubbing of the shackles against his raw and bleeding wrists, which at times was excruciating. After 270 parts of work, he'd eroded enough of the first projection to move to the second.

A moment later, the light went out in the captain's tent. His executioners would be coming for him soon.

Noah increased his pace, and with it the noise being made by his chains. He didn't know how much time he had, but he was sure it wouldn't be another 270 parts. Ignoring the pain, he stabbed at the rock in an attempt to dislodge larger pieces. His wrists bled, dripping onto the stone before being washed away by the rain.

Two over-the-head downward stabs broke away a section of rock the size of his palm, but the shackles smacked against the bones in his wrists. His knees buckled slightly and he grit his teeth.

Movement and whispers from inside the tent drew his attention when the assassins extinguished the lamp.

He attempted to slide the chain past the chiseled areas, but had difficulty because of the rock's diameter. Each time he would get one side raised, it would slip back when he moved to the opposite side.

"Ready?" came a voice inside the soldiers' tent.

173

On his third attempt, Noah pulled all slack out of the chain while rotating it to the opposite side, inching it up and over the rock. He gathered the chain and headed for the forest ninety cubits away, the weight of indecision at his side. Should he continue running and hope the rattling chains didn't give his position away—or hide?

He dove into a dense thicket.

Eighteen parts later, he peered back through the shrubs to where three soldiers gathered around the rock that had once secured him. The one holding a torch cursed.

"What now?" another said.

"Keep your voice down," the first said.

"Why? Aren't we going to wake the captain and the others?"

"And blow our whole plan. Are you crazy? He couldn't have gotten far. Look." The soldier pointed toward the base of the rock.

"What?" the third said.

"The chain. It's gone. He won't be able to move fast lugging all that iron. Besides, orders or not, I'm sure the captain would prefer a dead prisoner over an escaped one."

The three soldiers laughed while the leader appeared to stare right at Noah. "He has to be in these woods somewhere. Get the others. And bring more torches."

Noah lowered himself to the ground, pulling the underbrush on top of him to further camouflage his body. Flickering lights and the sound of running feet in the wet grass warned of his captors' approach. He forced himself to remain motionless while his wrists continued to bleed and throb.

The soldiers marched past him and deep into the woods. A short time later, he heard voices in the distance, followed by the sound of the soldiers returning. On his way out, one of the soldiers brushed against the thicket he was lying under.

"This is getting us nowhere," said one. "The Preacher's gone."

"No, he isn't," the leader said. "He's hiding around here somewhere. We just have to keep looking."

174

"And if he is gone, he's getting farther away every part we waste here. I say we wake the captain and the others."

Noah had second thoughts about his choice to hide. He'd have been better off running deep into the woods and putting some distance between himself and the soldiers. Even if he'd gotten lost, he could have waited for daylight to make his way out. But if they woke the captain and the others, it would only be a matter of time before they located him.

The pressure against his wrists from the shackles was unbearable. In a slow and near imperceptible movement, he twisted his hands away from the side of the shackle. A few chain links clanked against each other.

"Did you hear that?" the leader said.

"Hear what?" another said.

"That clanking."

"I didn't hear anything."

"Well I did," a third said. "It sounded like it came from over there."

Noah buried his head in the ground beneath the hood of his tunic to make his profile as low as possible. Tramping feet marched around him. The underbrush on his back lifted away, and two soldiers dragged him into the clearing, rolling him onto his back.

While two of them held him down, the leader kneeled with his legs on either side of his head, pressing a pillow over his face. "Sorry Preacher, but taking you back to Eden just isn't in our plans."

He struggled against the soldiers restraining him and fought to draw a breath—a breath that would not come. Darkness swirled around him. Could Japheth lead the family to complete the task of building the ark according to God's commandment?

Just before losing consciousness, Noah heard running footsteps followed by a thump that relieved the pressure covering his nose and mouth. The pillow was pulled away, and the captain stood over him with a drawn sword. He kicked one of the two soldiers

175

still holding him. "I said let go of him!" He turned to the other soldier, but he'd already moved away.

Noah sat up and gasped for air while the captain and the remainder of the patrol looked on. Behind him lay the unconscious group leader, blood dripping from a deep laceration to his forehead.

The captain motioned to the leader's two companions. "Get him back to his tent. When he wakes up, tell him I said if he tries anything like this again, I'll put *him* in chains." The captain confronted the others. "And that goes for the rest of you. Malluch wants this man alive. If he doesn't make it alive, I'll see every one of you takes his place for whatever Malluch has in store for him."

He wheeled to address Noah. "Have you ever seen a horse hamstrung?"

"No, but I'm familiar with the practice."

"You try running again, and that's just what I'll do to you."

* * *

After three days of torrent rains, Noah was happy to see the stars again. Not that he hadn't appreciated the shower. It had come just in time to save him from the brink of exhaustion. Yet even with his thirst quenched, being towed behind a horse through a downpour had been a challenge.

By the second day, the road had become a sloppy mess, forcing the soldiers to slow their pace. He'd fallen repeatedly, but being dragged through the mud proved much easier on his body. He managed to return to his feet each time and continue the march.

Strange noises appeared to follow them the past two evenings. After they'd bedded down, the sound of something running in the forest next to where they'd camped drew his attention. But he couldn't tell if it were an animal or just the heavier rainfall striking the trees at the time.

176

Just before nightfall, the rain had stopped, and tonight only the stars were his companions. And the sound of a few frogs singing from a nearby pond or stream.

He lay back on dry grass for the first time in four days, hoping for a much needed night of rest. A soft breeze blew across the land. If it weren't for his stomach cramping from hunger, it would have been a perfect night. He tried to take his mind off it by thinking of Miryam and his family and started to doze.

There it was again.

A rustling of leaves in the forest next to them brought his head off the ground. He peered into the black abyss of dense foliage waiting for the next sound of movement.

Nothing.

Probably the wind.

CHAPTER 32

Thirteen days and no killings.

Shechem should have been elated. Instead, he questioned why the murders had stopped and when they would start again. Between that and worrying about the identity of his wife's lover, he'd barely slept.

He speculated the killer was just lying low after having been seen. Surely nothing else had deterred him. Shechem had flooded the city with soldiers, alternating their location, number, and schedule and still the bloodletting continued. He likened it to a mouse finding its way into a granary. Despite being surrounded by cats, each night the mouse had managed to find that one hole to sneak through to earn its prize.

Now, having just risen from another night of insomnia, what news would the dawn bring?

He didn't have to wait long.

A knock came at his front door. Two soldiers, Lamech, and another man stood on the other side. "Forgive the early morning intrusion, Commander," one of the soldiers said. "But this elder said it was urgent."

"That's all right, soldier," Shechem said, "I wasn't asleep. You're dismissed." He invited Lamech and the other man inside, squinting as he put fingers and thumb to the bridge of his nose.

"Headache, Commander?" Lamech said.

Shechem nodded. "Lots of them since these murders started."

"Maybe I can give you something for it. This is Babel. He thinks he may have seen your killers last week."

"Killers?"

"I'm a merchant," Babel said. "Someone's been stealing from me at night, so I came back late one evening hoping to catch whoever it was. The streets were nearly empty, except for three men I saw running away from a cart two stands down from mine. When I crept closer, I saw a dark liquid dripping from the bottom of the cart. I pulled back the canvas covering it and found one of my fellow merchants, Damascus, I think that was his name, with his throat cut.

"*Three* men? Are you sure there were three?"

"Yes."

"Did you see what they looked like?"

"Just three men wearing hoods all dressed in dark clothing. Two were larger, about four cubits high. The third one was smaller."

"Which way were they running?"

"Toward the south gate."

"How many does that make now, Commander?" Lamech said.

"Twelve, I think."

"Yes, it must be difficult to keep track."

If it weren't so depressing, he would have laughed at Lamech's response. Instead, he thanked him for bringing Babel and showed them out. Before departing, Lamech had offered to recruit men to serve as watchmen during the nighttime hours. But Shechem didn't want any other civilians on the streets after dark, only his soldiers. "They'd make better targets than lookouts," he'd said, shaking his head.

He teetered in the middle of the room trying to reconcile this new information with what he'd witnessed himself. He'd observed a single killer. Now it appeared three stalked the city. Could the one he'd spotted been the shorter of the three men seen by the merchant, or was there a fourth killer out there somewhere?

His temples throbbed.

* * *

An hour before sunset, Noah entered the city of Cainan, only this time neither alone nor of his own volition. Despite the approaching twilight, the marketplace remained busy, providing him hope he would see his melon merchant friend. Or be seen by him.

It appeared the larger contingent of soldiers had moved on. This provided ample room for the patrol to tie their horses — and Noah — at the near end of the market. How ironic to find himself lashed to the same post where he'd tied his donkey thirteen days before.

While the soldiers milled about waiting for direction from their commander, an old woman crossing the street fifteen cubits from the stock rails caught his attention. She hunched as she walked, her white hair peeking from beneath a veil covering her features. The commander called to her. "You there."

The woman continued on like she didn't hear.

"You there. Old woman."

She turned slowly to the sound of the commander's voice.

"Old woman. Bring this dog a drink of water."

She nodded and crossed the street into a tavern.

"And only a drink of water, do you hear?" The commander pointed to two of his soldiers. "You two stay here and keep watch. Don't let anyone near him except the old woman. I'll have some food and drink sent out to you."

"Yes, sir," the soldiers said.

180

While Noah waited for the old woman's return, he thought about the quirk of fate that had returned him to this place. Could he be as fortunate a second time? He craned his neck to the limit of his restraints but couldn't locate his merchant ally. Besides, he doubted whether the man would recognize him in his present condition.

"What are you doing, Preacher?" one of the soldiers left to guard him said. "Sit down."

He obeyed, then noticed the old woman shuffling toward them. He reached for the cup and drank, slowly this time to savor every swallow.

"Hurry up," the other soldier said.

He raised his shackled hands to the old woman, who leaned over to retrieve the cup. When she did, something fine and dry sprinkled onto his skin.

"Thank you for your kindness, sister," he said.

The woman nodded without speaking and walked away, disappearing up the street. Noah glanced at his shackles. Tiny flecks of a milky powder spotted his hands.

Several hours later, he tried to sleep over the sound of a growling stomach. How could he get word to the melon merchant? Would he see him in the morning?

* * *

Noah awoke to a soft thud against his side while he lay chained to the stock post. Dazed from sleep, it took him a few parts for his senses to arouse. The streets were empty, and most of the lights had been doused. Several soldiers snored around him, and he estimated it was well past midnight.

On the ground in front of his belly rested a fist-sized hunk of bread.

He grabbed it, but before he'd swallowed the first bite, another hunk of bread came flying through the darkness and landed at his knees. Then a third. He couldn't tell from what direction the bread had come, nor did he see anyone. Still, he looked around to make sure his captors remained asleep. Their snoring, and the song of the night's arthropods were all that disturbed the peace of early morning.

That, and the sound of teeth grinding bread inside his own head.

* * *

"I want these rebels caught and punished, do you hear?" Malluch said from the saddle of his horse, face red with rage.

He, Bohar, Shechem, and thirty soldiers gathered at the bottom of a hill just after sunrise, looking down at the broken remains of Eden's first idol. The cracked, bronze human body was partially embedded in the earth, the lion's head separated from the torso.

Shechem picked up a piece of shattered bronze. "Yes, my lord."

"How dare they profane a god of Eden? An attack on our god is an attack against this government."

"Blasphemous," Bohar said.

"And they need to be found and dealt with quickly, Commander."

Shechem nodded.

"To discourage this kind of behavior."

"Yes, my lord."

Malluch paused for a moment, as if changing thoughts. "There's been a lull in the killings?"

"Yes."

"Yes," Bohar said. "Our commander here hasn't allowed anyone to be killed in two weeks. We were thinking of giving him an award." He laughed.

"Good," Malluch said. "Then you can concentrate on finding these rebels. They shouldn't be hard to find. I'm sure they're

182

somehow acquainted with the elders of this city. Or at least sympathetic of their opposition to this government."

"And if they are?"

"Tell me, Commander. What do you think Ramalech would do to someone he caught defacing one of Enoch's gods?"

"Throw them to the lions?"

"And whatever was left in the fire. Find them, Commander, while there's a respite from these killings. And have the metal artisans get to work on repairing the statue."

"Immediately, my lord."

Just before pulling away, a slight breeze blowing from the direction of Bohar's horse brought a familiar odor to Shechem's nostrils. *So much for the baths.*

He feared the consequences of Malluch's order should he discover a link tying the patriarchs to the destruction of the idol. Lamech was no friend of the government that'd usurped him, but his willingness to assist in helping to find the killers had proven invaluable — at least in Shechem's eyes. Until now, the governor had shown a reluctance to take direct action against the patriarchs. But would their involvement in this vandalism give him a change of heart?

Chapter 33

A day's journey east of Cainan, Noah tried to conceal his increase in strength by allowing himself to be pulled occasionally. The coming of autumn and the coolness of evening aided his rejuvenation.

His shackles rattled when he stretched out on the grass to join the majority of sleeping soldiers. Sixty cubits away, a group of five squatted around a fire built in a small clearing a short distance from the road. Just beyond, their horses stood tied to trees at the wood's edge.

Something stirred in the trees, but Noah couldn't be sure what it was because of the voices of the soldiers talking around the fire. A few moments later, another rustling sound resonated from the woods. He lifted his head, but couldn't see anything. There it was again.

This time, one of the soldiers reacted, questioning his companions. "Did you hear that?"

"What?" another said.

"That rustling sound? In the trees?"

"Just some animal," a third said. "Probably attracted to the fire."

More movement in the trees, followed by the horses stirring and whinnying. At this, the soldiers around the fire rose to their feet and examined the woods.

"What is it?" the first soldier said.

"Shush!" the second said.

A twig snapped.

Then another.

Twenty-five to thirty men sprung from the woods, their heads and faces covered, charging into the encampment with raised swords. Several soldiers cried out to warn their companions, but they were quickly engaged by their attackers. Clanging swords filled the air. One of the soldiers, impaled by an attacker's sword, fell into the fire. Others were outnumbered two and sometimes three to one.

When the soldier guarding him rose to respond to the attack, Noah wrapped the chain of his shackle around the soldier's neck, choking him from behind. He grasped the man's sword and thrust him through the back, then killed another soldier nearby.

"Preacher!" the commander said rushing toward him with weapon in hand. Noah fended off the first few blows, but his shackles restrained him. The captain followed with five vicious overhead strikes, driving him to one knee. When the commander raised his sword again, a petite figure dashed across the clearing and ran him through from behind. He took one step and fell at his prisoner's feet.

The attack was over in thirty-six parts.

Noah examined the clearing. All fifteen soldiers lay dead on the ground, except for the one whose body smoldered in the fire. The thirty Marauders, their identities still masked, looked to the smallest among them for direction. The petite figure walked to the fire and motioned for two of them to pull the body from the flames and another two to fetch Noah. The leader whispered in the ear of one of the stoutest men, who retrieved a large flat rock and some tools.

How surprising to find so notorious a group of fighters being led by someone so slight of build. But after fifty parts of observing them, it was clear who was in charge.

185

The man with the tools told Noah to sit facing him next to the fire. While he worked pounding his shackles, the leader watched. Noah strained to see through the slight opening of his mask, hoping to gain some insight into what kind of man held his destiny. In the dark, the light of the fire offered only limited illumination, occasionally flickering off the whites of his eyes. Still, he found something familiar about them, about their shape, the way they were set in his face.

With a final strike of the hammer, the second shackle cuff fell from the captive's wrist. He thanked the man and rose to his feet, looking down at the leader.

Something about those eyes.

The leader took two paces back, turned his back to him, and unwrapped the scarf covering his head. He pulled off his hood, allowing a long mane of dark hair to tumble out.

A lump rose in his throat as Shiphrah turned, threw the hood to the ground, and hurried to embrace him. Together they cried.

"I found your donkey in the gully and feared the worst, child," he said, so relieved he wanted to laugh.

"It was all my fault," Shiphrah said. "I was pushing him to catch the caravan and got too close to the edge of the ravine. He lost his footing, and we both fell down. He must have broken a leg because he couldn't get up. I hurt my ankle in the fall and wasn't much better off."

"What happened?"

Shiphrah addressed the man who'd removed Noah's shackles, motioning for him to remove his hood. "Father, this is Rogan. He and his men found me."

"I'm grateful, Rogan."

"We are the grateful ones." Rogan drew his sword and motioned for the other Marauders to do likewise. Each took his sword by the blade, extending the handle toward the fire. Every sword had embedded in its hilt a single date-sized transparent green stone.

"Emeralds."

186

"Many years ago, we found a collection of these stones in the mountains east of Enoch. Since then, good fortune has followed us, and we have remained undefeated in battle."

"I see. But what does this have to do with my daughter?"

"As her father, I'm surprised you hadn't long ago taken notice."

Noah turned to Shiphrah, then back to Rogan. "You're talking about the color of her eyes."

"Does not the brilliance of these stones rest within them?"

Noah suspected he was in the presence of a vastly superstitious culture, but didn't want to risk offending them. "They do, indeed."

"Since the beginning, there has been not a son or daughter born to us with eyes such as hers. Neither have we seen such splendor in those of any of our enemies."

"So you believe they portend of some divine nature?"

"Why else would the gods have caused her donkey to go lame where and when it did, that we might come upon her? Could it be they have chosen her to lead our people?"

Noah studied Shiphrah, who shrugged. He worked to suppress a smile, realizing he had to come up with an effective challenge and quickly. Perhaps he could use to his advantage the Marauders' sense of duty and order. He also hoped Shiphrah would follow his lead. "Rogan, suppose your gods had another reason for crippling her donkey?"

"What could that be?"

"To stop her from running away?"

Rogan glanced at Shiphrah then her adopted father.

"Ah, I see she didn't tell you," Noah said. "I didn't think she would. At home, my daughter was a rebellious young woman. She would often sneak away, unchaperoned, to see a young man in the village of whom her mother and I did not approve. Eventually, she chose to run away."

Rogan stared at Shiphrah wide-eyed, in apparent disbelief. "Is this true?"

Shiphrah dropped her chin but did not answer.

"So, I believe your gods simply chose to intervene because of her disobedience," Noah said.

Several groups of three and four Marauders standing around the fire mumbled among themselves.

"Hmm." Rogan rubbed his chin while pacing in front of the fire. "If this woman has been chosen to lead us, do we not curse ourselves by sending her away? But if, as this man says, the gods have intervened on her parents' behalf, would we not be foolish to oppose them?"

"You still have the stones." Noah scanned the fifteen bodies littering the clearing. "And by the look of things, they still maintain their power." Rogan and many of the Marauders nodded. "I have but one daughter. Until a few moments ago, I feared her dead. But her mother mourns her. Would you save my life, only to have me return without her?"

Rogan moved several paces away, motioning for his companions to gather around. They spoke for over eighteen parts in hushed whispers before Rogan returned. "You must go with your father."

"Do I have to?" Shiphrah said, lifting those pleading emerald jewels.

"A woman not bound to a husband must remain obedient to her father."

"I understand." She reached up to Rogan's shoulder. "I will miss you, my friend."

"And we, you."

One hundred eighty parts later, Noah and Shiphrah finished packing two fresh horses with provisions for the journey home. When they turned around, thirty men, Rogan included, kneeled before them in the light of the campfire. "What's this?" Shiphrah said.

"May the gods watch over the green-eyed princess as she returns to the land of her fathers," Rogan said.

Noah faced him. "For my daughter's life, I am in your debt."

Rogan offered a slight bow.

188

Noah helped Shiphrah onto her horse, then climbed aboard his own.

"You would do well to stay off the main roads, at least during the day," Rogan said.

"We will," Noah said.

Heading down the road, he joined Shiphrah for a last look back.

In an apparent show of respect, the complete company of Marauders had moved from the camp out onto the roadway to watch their departure.

CHAPTER 34

When Noah and Shiphrah arrived within forty furlongs of home, excitement filled his heart. It meant in less than an hour the nightmare of the last seven weeks would be over.

They'd spent the last four days consoling each other and recounting the details of their own personal trials. Shiphrah recalled how the fear and pain of the accident quickly turned to terror when she found herself surrounded by Marauders. "I was helpless. My ankle was swollen like a grapefruit, and there was no way I could walk on it, much less run."

"So, what did they do?"

"For some reason they seemed fascinated by my eyes. First Rogan, then the others, in groups of two and three, came to stare at me before moving away to speak in whispers. The next thing I know, Rogan is picking me up and putting me on a horse for the ride back to their camp. One of their women mixed a poultice of herbs, spread it on my ankle, and wrapped it in some kind of tree bark. A week later, I was walking."

"Why did they make you their leader?"

"I don't think that was ever made clear to me. Something to do with my eyes and the fact I told them I was born in Enoch. All I know is one day they all started bowing and addressing

190

me as princess. Given the circumstances, I didn't want to argue the point."

"A wise choice. This Rogan, did he teach you how to use a sword?"

"Oh, yes." Shiphrah seemed excited to discuss her training. "He spent hours with me every day, not only teaching me how to block and thrust, but also proper footwork."

"So I observed." He chuckled. "An incredible warrior, no doubt."

"They all are. In spite of their primitive culture, they employ some surprisingly sophisticated training techniques that emphasize speed and quickness over power and strength. As you know, I'm pretty quick on my feet."

"Yes, I saw the way you sprinted across that clearing. Lucky for me."

"They had this obstacle course set up next to their camp in the woods. Once my ankle healed, I started running it every day. Lots of trees to negotiate, rocks to climb, and holes to jump over. I bet my calves grew a finger in diameter while I was gone."

Noah nodded while thanking God for providing for her during her ordeal.

"They taught me to use my quickness to advantage. You see, I could never be expected to pit my strength blade to blade against a man in a sword fight. So for a woman, it's all about dexterity. It's about constantly moving your feet to cause your opponent to reposition his stance in answer to your movements, then waiting for the right opening to strike."

"Fascinating."

"Of course, they had to make some adjustments for me being a woman." Shiphrah pulled out her sword and handed it to Noah. "They made me a specially designed sword, lighter and thinner than the men carry. But I trained with a heavier sword, which allows me to wield this one with aplomb. And I can handle it proficiently in either hand."

191

Noah told her about his miraculous escape from Cainan, followed by his carelessness on the road that had led to his capture.

"Was that you, the old woman in the city?" he said.

"You knew?"

"Not until I saw the specks of flour on my wrists."

"Good disguise, huh?"

"You took a big gamble one of those soldiers didn't want to have a look under that veil."

"At an old woman like me?" Shiphrah used her best graveled voice impersonation.

"Ham was right years ago when he said you'd make a good old woman."

Her playful look disappeared. "How is he?"

He didn't want to embarrass Ham by telling her he'd been sick with grief. Instead, he sought to put to rest any doubts she had about his feelings for her. "That fear you had about Ham not feeling the same?"

"Yes."

"You needn't hold onto it any longer."

She smiled, but was interrupted by her next thought. "You didn't tell him?"

"Child, did I not take an oath?"

"Then how do you know? Did he say something?"

"Let's just say from his behavior while you were gone, there's no doubt his heart belongs to you."

She allowed the smile to creep back and take over her whole face. It was a perfect complement to the blush rising in her cheeks.

Now, riding together side by side, the corners of his own mouth rose in anticipation of seeing his family again. But as they crested a rise in the road, his eyes grew wide and the excitement faded. The distinctive shape of the prow of the ark they expected to see rising above the trees in the distance wasn't there. He and Shiphrah goaded their horses to a gallop.

192

Passing by the house, they continued up the hill to the ark site. When they arrived, neither seemed capable of dismounting. Instead, they sat silently in their saddles, staring at the scene stretching four hundred cubits before them.

Every hull plank, rib frame, deck, and beam had been torn away and thrown down. Only the massive posts, positioned at the stem and stern, remained upright, still fastened to the keel now buried beneath tons of fallen timber.

CHAPTER 35

Noah slipped from his horse and onto his knees, his forehead touching the ground. Although he could hear the sound of his family gathering a few cubits away, he was too deep in prayer to allow himself to be distracted.

"Father," Japheth said. "Are you all right?"

"Ssh," Miryam said.

Fifty-four parts later, Noah rose to face Ham and Shiphrah, who were standing side by side with their arms around each other.

"I'm sorry, daughter, that the occasion of your reunion had to be spoiled by the sight of such malice. But I see you found the answer to your question."

"All of them," Shiphrah said, pulling herself into Ham's chest.

He turned to his oldest son, whose upper lip was split and his forehead bruised. "Japheth. What happened?"

"About a week after you left to find Shiphrah, all of the onlookers disappeared."

"Disappeared?"

"Yes. One morning we came out here, and they were gone. We thought maybe they'd gotten bored not having anything to see since we started working inside. A week later it rained for three days, heavy at times. During the storm, Ham checked on the stock and found all the sheep and goats missing from the pasture."

"How?"

"We're not sure. A good-sized section of the east wall had washed away. We figured they got out through there. Shem and Ham asked Mother, Elisheva, and Ariel to go with them to find the sheep, while I stayed behind to stand guard. Even with their help, it took more than a day to track them all down and round them up. And when they returned—"

"The ark was in ruins." His stomach tightened, an uncomfortable reminder of the hunger pangs he'd experienced during his ordeal with the soldiers. "And your face?"

"The rain was really coming down, and I guess I didn't hear the seven or eight men sent in to jump me. I put up a good fight, but they still managed to overpower me and tie me up."

Elisheva leaned forward. "You're lucky that's all they did."

Noah pointed to hundreds of animal hoof prints tracked along both sides of the hill. "Someone was using teams of oxen to pull down the ark."

Japheth picked up one of several waterlogged torches scattered among the debris. "The rains kept them from kindling a fire, so they decided to pull it down instead. I'm sorry, Father. I know you were counting on me to take care of things while you were gone."

He took the torch from his son's hand. "You should have sent the women to retrieve the herd while the three of you stayed here."

"That's not fair," Ham said.

Noah felt his cheeks flush. "Fair." He slammed the torch down against the closest beam. "I'll tell you what's not fair. This entire family working forty years on this ark, only to have it torn down in a day because you and your brothers got careless."

The mouths of his entire family, Miryam included, fell open. Ham threw his jaw forward. His eyes bulged. "Careless."

"Yes." His gaze moved from son to son.

195

"Father, it was pouring down rain," Shem said. "The six of us talked it over and made the decision to go after the sheep." He gestured toward the deconstructed ark. "Looking at the damage, it's easy to say now we were wrong. But we only did what we thought you'd do. Anyway, I don't see what difference it makes now. The ark is finished."

Noah scanned the wreckage. Whatever plans God had, some other force was working against them. Was this simply a test, or had the Lord changed His mind about sparing him and his family? Had he somehow displeased the Lord, prompting Him to revoke His covenant? Noah had been given no insight into the Lord's timetable for the coming flood. But if the sundial was already moving, they couldn't possibly complete the ark in time after this. "Perhaps you're right. It doesn't make any difference."

"So what are we going to do now?" Japheth said.

His father let out a huge sigh while the weight of depression settled on him like a yoke of bricks. "Nothing. What's done can't be undone."

"Father, you're not serious?" Elisheva said.

"Yes—I am. And I'm tired." He mounted his horse.

"Where are you going?"

"To have a drink that's long overdue."

* * *

After four days, Shechem hadn't made any progress in his investigation of the idol's destruction. As expected, there'd been no witnesses, and his usual sources of information, the harlots and street peddlers, had proven unreliable. He'd instructed the metal artisans to work extra hours to repair the idol, hoping to appease Malluch's fury.

Now, a few hours after sunrise, he watched from the rear balcony of the palace the handsome silk merchant knock upon

196

the door of his house. Claudia answered and invited him in, along with two servants, each loaded down with bundles of silk in a variety of scarlets, purples, and golds.

He couldn't help wondering about the silk merchant. With coal black hair, a straight nose, and full lips surrounded by a neatly-trimmed beard, he was a man of exceptional good looks. Shechem suspected a great many women had desired to be his consort.

But for now, he could do little more than speculate. Good looks alone weren't proof of anything. Even while his wife closed the door behind the merchant and his servants, there was little chance her fidelity would be tested. Not this morning. Not with spectators.

From behind, the sound of running footsteps distracted him when several soldiers rushed down the hall to the front of the palace. "Commander," one of them shouted. "You may want to see this."

He jogged through the palace and out onto the front porch. Below, more soldiers and several groups of citizens moved briskly through the streets. He stopped a soldier exiting the palace. "Bring my horse. Now!"

Shechem followed the line of onlookers through the city to a place just off the road 650 cubits outside the south gate. A group had gathered around an ox-driven cart while the animal, in utter indifference to the attention, continued to graze in an adjacent field.

In the road, a man in his early hundreds stretched face down, blood soaked into the dirt beneath his head and neck in a near perfect circle. Across from him in the field, his wife lay on her back, flies swarming the torn flesh of a yawning neck wound. But this sickening sight couldn't compare to what he and the others found inside the cart.

Two girls and a boy — the youngest, a girl no more than eight years — rested on a bed of straw cold and stiff, their throats slashed identical to their parents.

Seeing his own daughters in the death agonies of the young girls, he fought to remain composed.

197

"What on earth is going on, Commander?" a soldier on the ground said.

"I don't know. But I'd give a year's pay to find out." He searched the crowd. "Anyone know this family?"

"The father's name is Jachin, son of Azriel," a man in the crowd said.

"Azriel's son? Are you sure?"

"Oh yes."

Another son of an elder. I should have known the lull wouldn't last.

CHAPTER 36

Noah leaned against a collection of ark timbers that had come to rest in a perfect configuration for sitting, gazing up at the host of heaven. An hour ago, it was just a stagnant, jewel-encrusted black canvas covering the sky. Now that canvas and its collection of bright lights were spinning, He reached for another wineskin and took two big swallows.

A week after he and Shiphrah returned home, Noah was spending his sixth straight night mourning the loss of the ark. Unable to sleep that first evening, he decided to give nature a hand in making him drowsy. Each night, he grabbed two full wineskins and headed to the ark site where he would sit and drink himself to sleep. Sooner or later—he wasn't always sure when—Japheth and Shem would come and take him down to bed.

The light of a torch bouncing up the hill distracted his stargazing. *Here they come now.*

But when the flame drew near, even in his current state, he could tell it wasn't the reflection of a man who carried the torch. "You've not come up here to scold me, have you, Elisheva?" he said.

"Not at all." She set the handle of the torch between some planks and sat on a perch next to him.

199

"I was afraid your mother-in-law was using you as an emissary to get me to curtail my drinking."

"No. As a matter of fact, I thought I'd join you." She extended her arm.

He was stunned. Outside of a meal, he'd never seen her take a drink of wine. "Are you sure?"

"Of course, I'm sure." She opened and closed her forefingers in rapid succession.

"I'm sorry, but I don't have a cup for you." He was slurring his words.

"Who said I needed one?" Elisheva continued to manipulate her fingers until Noah handed her the wineskin. She turned it up to her lips and drank like a man.

"Better go easy with that. You're not used to it."

She pulled the skin away and used a finger to catch a drop of wine rolling down her chin. "What for? Who says you and Ham are the only ones in the family entitled to assault their senses?" She took another drink, only this time she leaned forward and spit some out.

Noah tried to stifle a laugh, but couldn't hold it when some of the wine ran out her nose. Elisheva coughed several times, and he slapped her gently on the back. "Are you all right? Here, you'd better let me have that." He took the wineskin.

"Sure, sure. I just wasn't ready for how fast it came out."

"Of course. Now do you want to tell me why you came up here—besides the drink?"

"I was hoping you might want to share with your favorite daughter-in-law what it is that's troubling you. Other than the ark being destroyed."

"You mean you were hoping I was drunk enough?"

"That, too."

"Good. I'm still sober enough to appreciate honesty. But who says anything else is troubling me?"

"I've been in this family for well over three hundred years, and this is the first time I've known you to have more than two cups of wine in a single day."

Noah sorted through the fog of drunkenness. For nearly forty years, he'd been unable to share his deepest fears concerning the Lord's proclamation with his own wife. Could he now disclose them to Elisheva? Something told him it was all right, that nothing he said would change her perception of him. He trusted her. "I never told this to your mother-in-law, and I don't imagine I'd be telling you were it not for the effects of the wine. But do you remember the night of the Lord's judgment?"

"How could any of us ever forget?"

"Believe it or not, I laid awake half the night thinking He'd made a mistake.

"Who? The Lord?"

"Yes. Even though I knew it would cost all our lives, I found myself wishing He had chosen someone else. Someone braver, wiser, or more noble. I'm a farmer not a builder."

"That's the wine controlling your tongue. You don't really mean that."

"Oh, but I do. Why should He choose me to be the one through which He'd save mankind? A man slow of wit and devoid of cleverness."

She placed an arm around him. "But rich in character."

Noah snorted. "Not that rich."

Elisheva twisted her mouth.

"I kept wondering why He hadn't chosen someone like my father." he said. "Here was a man who'd already proven himself a great leader, a man better suited to the task of guiding humanity in the new world."

"But a man also great in years. Could it be the Lord wanted someone young enough to be able to complete the long and arduous task of building the ark?"

"He didn't need to choose me for that."

"Oh, so now you're wanting to give advice to God?"

Noah took another drink and shook his head. "I'd never presume to be qualified to do that. But take the ark. Why didn't He pick someone with at least a fundamental understanding of shipbuilding? I mean, before it was destroyed, I had followed exactly the Lord's instructions regarding the construction. And yet, I had no idea whether the ark would even float, much less be able to withstand the rigors of a long sea voyage."

"I feel silly reminding *you* of this, but isn't that what you're always telling us faith is all about—trusting God to handle the unknown?"

He nodded. "You're right." Slowly, and with difficulty, he lifted himself from his seat and stood swaying in the night. She grabbed his arm to steady him. "Anyway," he said. "It doesn't matter anymore. The ark's gone."

"It may be down, but it's hardly gone."

"Unfortunately, my level of inebriation makes it difficult to discern the difference."

"Give it a few more days. You may come to see things in a different light."

Noah leaned his head back for another glimpse of the heavens. "Tell me, Elisheva. What do you think God sees when he looks down here?"

"Right now? A servant who's had too much to drink. Let's get you home."

She escorted Noah down the hill and into the house, where she and Japheth gently lowered him into a seated position on his bed. She kneeled to remove his sandals. "You're wrong, you know."

He lay on the bed. The room spun. "Wrong about what?"

She kissed him on the forehead. "God did make the right choice."

202

CHAPTER 37

Noah sat alone on the floor at his place in the dining area while his children tended to chores outside. In the next room, the sound of clanging plates pounded like a hammer on anvil inside his head. The wine had done its job in helping him to sleep each night, but it had come at the expense of a sixth consecutive morning headache. He massaged his temples.

"Does that help?" Miryam said, entering the room.

"Not much," Noah said.

"Then unless you can find a remedy that does, I'd give up the wine for a few days."

"It's the only thing that helps me to sleep."

"Strange. Until a week ago you didn't have any trouble."

He stared out the window. "A week ago, we had an ark standing out there on the hill."

She placed her hands on her hips. "How long are you going to feel sorry for yourself?"

"Who says I am?"

"Why else would you drink a half season's worth of wine if you weren't blaming yourself for the ark being destroyed? I bet you think if you hadn't gone after Shiphrah, none of this would have happened, right?"

"Something like that."

"You don't know, any more than you know your being here could have prevented the ark's destruction.

"But if I hadn't left—"

"If you hadn't left, Shiphrah would have been lost forever and Ham heartbroken beyond consoling. And from where I stand, no partially completed ark is worth that."

"So how do I overcome the guilt?"

"You act as if this is the first trial we've faced since we left Eden. Is this the same man who deferred the commandment of YAH Himself to go after Shiphrah? Or the man who was captured, tortured, and nearly killed by Malluch's soldiers? You didn't give up then. Why are you so eager to give up now?"

He slammed his fist on the floor, squinting when the shock of the blow shot pain through his temples. "Don't you understand? I can't do it." He took in a deep breath and exhaled slowly. "Not another forty years."

"That's the selfish part talking."

"What do you mean?"

"Do you still believe the Lord's proclamation?"

"Of course."

"So what you're saying is you're willing to give up, and in the process sacrifice all our lives, is that it?"

"That's not—"

"Don't you see? You're using the destruction of the ark as an excuse to shirk your responsibility to the Lord."

"I didn't ask to become the savior of the world."

"No, you didn't. God asked you. Or, rather, He commanded you. And in all our years together, I've never known you to disobey His will. So tell me, when did He release you from His decree to build the ark?"

204

Noah rubbed his temples again. "He didn't."

"Or when did He tell you He'd rescinded His promise to flood the earth?"

Noah had completely surrendered himself to doubt. He'd allowed it to cloud his reason and sap his will. Miryam was right. He was exploiting the tragedy to justify abdicating his responsibilities to God and to his family. He'd fallen into a mire of self-pity.

He clenched his jaw, forced himself to stand, and headed for the door.

"Where are you going?"

"To recruit some help."

Four hundred fifty parts later, Noah's family gathered around the stem post and fallen debris that once made up the prow of the ark. He circled behind each family member like an army commander inspecting his troops, but with an entirely different perspective than he had seven days ago. Despite the ruin at their feet, the reality was they'd been fortunate. Were it not for the rain, instead of a pile of broken timbers, they'd be looking at a mound of blackened ashes.

"So why are we meeting here?" Ham said when his father passed by. "I thought we were finished with the ark."

"We're going back to work."

"What?" Ham's voice rose. "Didn't you say just a week ago none of this could be undone?"

"The words of a man who'd given up, one who thought he could absolve himself of responsibility by using wine to numb his feelings. But since then I was reminded this isn't about me. It's not even about us as a family. It's about God's plan for the future of mankind on earth." Noah smiled at Miryam and Shiphrah.

"After what's happened, do you really think it's worth it?"

"Tell me, what has changed because of what was done here?"

"What has changed?" Ham climbed onto the heap. "Look at this!" He picked up a plank and threw it. "And this!" He tossed another, then kicked a larger beam causing it to tumble down the mound a few cubits. "And this!" He spread his hands. "Father, this pile of rubble represents forty years of work and you ask, 'What has changed!'"

Noah sympathized with his youngest son's frustration. And why not? Seven days ago, he shared it. "Forgive me. What I should have said is, 'What has changed from God's perspective?'"

"God's perspective?"

"Yes. Do you think because the ark has been torn down we have been released from His command to build it? Who told you He rescinded His promise to bring floodwaters upon the earth?"

Ham threw his hands into the air. "Father, I know you believe God called you to this task, and I respect you for it. But surely even you can see there are other forces at work here."

"If so, I don't know them. But the voice of YAH I do know, because I have heard it with my own ears."

"You don't seriously intend to rebuild?"

"Without further delay. As it is, we've lost a week because I was busy feeling sorry for myself."

"Japheth. Say something." Ham turned to his other brother. "Shem?" Both men remained silent. "Mother?"

"Son." Miryam pointed at the wreckage beneath Ham's feet. "You said this pile of rubble represents forty years of work."

"Yes."

"Forty years of rising early, laboring all day in the hot sun, soothing your aches and pains at night."

"Exactly."

"Forty years. That's a sizable investment."

"Wasted years."

"Only if you don't rebuild."

Ham shook his head. "What are you talking about, Mother?"

"Don't you understand? If you give up now, the investment is lost. You simply will have lived, and worked, and sweated for forty years and have nothing but a pile of timber to show for it. Only by rebuilding the ark can you recoup what you've already put into it."

Ham crouched on top of the pile for a closer inspection of the damage. "What do you think, Japheth?"

He reached down with one hand and picked up a hull plank, eyeing its length. "Oh, I don't know. My guess is a lot of this timber can be salvaged."

"Elisheva?" Ham said. "You're the second-best carpenter in the family."

"What Mother said makes sense to me," she said. "I'm for it."

"Well, I'm not for it," Ariel said. "Look at all that's gone wrong since we started building the thing. You killed an ox hauling logs up the hill. Japheth broke his arm. Ham nearly got killed falling off it, and someone tried to set it on fire. Now it's been demolished."

"She's right, Mother," Ham said. "The project does seem to have been cursed."

"Has it? For forty years you've enjoyed near perfect weather to build in. No long periods of rain or violent windstorms to contend with. And has the termite, bee, or ant so much as touched the ark? No, my son, the only thing cursed is the people who came here to destroy it."

Ham looked at his brothers, who nodded in succession. "I can't believe this. My whole family has gone crazy."

"Perhaps," Noah said. "But crazy or not, we must begin the task of cleaning up these ruins immediately. More than ever, we're going to need every able body working, especially since we know not the Lord's timetable for the coming flood."

"I'm sorry, Father." Ham stood. "But I can't see wasting another day on this thing. If that's not acceptable, Shiphrah and I can move on."

207

"Ham," Miryam said, frustration showing on her face. "You would leave your father and brothers to work on the ark alone?"

"What was it you said, Mother. 'Forty years of laboring all day in the hot sun.' If they're foolish enough to agree to do that again, well, I don't have any sympathy for them."

"Are you willing to stay and work the fields?" Noah said.

"Sure. I'll tend the herds and cultivate and pick all the crops you want. Only I'm not putting my hand to work again on that ridiculous ark."

"Very well."

"Come on, Ariel. As the only two rational ones left in this family, let's go make ourselves useful. I'll milk the goats while you pick some corn and cabbage for this evening's meal."

Noah had made the offer for Ham to work the fields to buy time, hoping his brothers would shame him into returning to work. If he didn't, it would be a long, slow rebuild. Over the years, Ham's maturity into manhood had increased their efficiency working on the ark significantly. It allowed the men to work together in pairs, which made the setting of beams and planks more productive. Now, their number of strong backs was back down to three.

CHAPTER 38

Shortly after sunrise, Shechem waited in the great hall with Lamech, Methuselah, and the other elders of Eden. He pitied the two who sat cross-legged on the floor, their heads bowed in grief while their friends tried to comfort them. Even the echoed clang of the two huge wooden doors being swung open into the hall failed to distract the mourners.

Bohar trailed Malluch as they entered the hall.

"Why all the somber faces?" Malluch said. "Have the patriarchs of Eden suffered some loss?"

"Two more of our sons have been murdered, Malluch," Lamech said. "Including Azriel's son, that's three in a week."

The governor bowed politely. "My condolences honored elders. It seems our killer has no respect for class or title."

Methuselah slammed the bottom of his staff on the floor. "These are our sons being murdered, Malluch! Not something to be made light of."

"And would you have me show less compassion for the other victims of this madman? For the women? For the children?" He turned to Shechem. "Commander, were there any other victims last night?"

"Two women. A mother of two and the daughter of a shepherd. She was twenty."

"How selfish of you not to mention *them,*" Malluch said.

"That's not what we meant, and you know it," Lamech said. "Our concern is for all the citizens of Eden."

"Of course. Please excuse my weak attempt to soften an otherwise grim circumstance. Clearly it was in poor taste. How can I help?"

"The murders. With all due respect to the best efforts of the Commander here, they're not stopping. If anything, they're increasing in frequency."

"Aren't we doing everything possible? Are there not soldiers on every street corner throughout the night?"

"Unfortunately, it's not enough."

"You are welcome to join our soldiers in keeping watch if you think it will help."

Shechem groaned at Malluch's offer. Having the elders on watch was the last thing he wanted, for it would require him to divert more resources just to protect *them.* "I've already discussed Lamech's offer, my lord, and we decided it wasn't a good idea."

"I doubt if a thousand more pairs of eyes would help," Lamech said. "What we need is information. And the best way I know of to obtain information is to pay for it."

"A reward," Malluch said. "Yes, that does sound practical. What do you think, Commander?"

"It couldn't hurt. I've tried everything I can think of."

"Very well, my friends, a reward it is. Shall we say fifty pieces of gold for information leading to the killer's arrest?"

"Thank you, Malluch," Lamech said. "You've been most gracious."

Several elders helped the two in mourning to their feet, and the group proceeded to the door until Malluch's voice halted their exit. "Ah, one more thing before you leave, please."

Lamech, Methuselah, and four or five others paused while the rest of the elders shuffled through the door. "Yes?" Lamech said.

"You wouldn't happen to know who vandalized Eden's god, would you?"

"No." Lamech raised his chin. "We wouldn't."

Shechem wasn't sure whether it was real or imagined, but the slightest smirk appeared at the corner of Lamech's mouth as he walked out.

* * *

"Japheth," Ham said with a loud voice.

Noah, tightening his sandal strap, saw a spear flying through the room and Shem enter from another wing of the house. Japheth snatched the lance out of the air with his massive paw. Ham continued across the room, tossing another spear to Shem before presenting one of two swords he was carrying to his father.

"What's this?" Noah said. "Hunting in the morning?"

"You're not going to believe it." Ham said. "There are two lions lying outside our front door."

"Lions." Ariel's voice trembled.

Noah's family gathered around a front-side window. A male and female lion lay next to each other thirty cubits from the house.

"What do we do, Father?" Shem said.

"I'll tell you what we do," Ham said. "We kill them before they kill us. You and I will go out the back and come up on the side of the house where they can't see us. Father and Japheth will go out the front door. When the lions move toward them, you and I should be able to flank them and get the first couple of thrusts in."

Ham's plan wasn't a sound one. Sneaking up on a pair of lions was problematic, whether distracted or not. Moreover, even with the element of surprise, Noah suspected the four of them would have their hands full with two lions fighting for their lives. One or more of his family might be seriously injured or worse. "That could be dangerous, son."

"Why don't we see if we can scare them away?" Elisheva said.

"That's a good idea," Ariel said. "We could make a lot of noise."

"I don't think that's going to work," Noah said.

"Well it can't hurt to try. Better than going out there to face the lions. Elisheva. Shiphrah. Give me a hand." The two women accompanied Ariel to the kitchen area of the house, returning with metal pots and wooden spoons for them and their husbands.

Ariel, Shem, and Elisheva joined the parents by the first window. The other three moved to another overlooking the front of the house. At Ariel's signal, the children leaned out the windows and began banging on the pots with the spoons.

After nine parts, the clanging stopped. Neither lion had moved, except to turn its head slowly toward the sound of the clamor.

"Again," Ham said.

The banging resumed, only this time they added their voices to the acoustic display, yelling and screaming as loud as they could. They stopped after another nine parts.

The lions just stared at them.

Noah tried to suppress a wry grin. Miryam bit her lip while chuckling softly in her throat.

"What now?" Japheth said.

"I say we try my plan," Ham said.

Noah moved to the center of the room to address his family. "I think you all are forgetting about the Lord's covenant. I don't believe these lions showed up by accident but are a part of the Divine appointment."

Ham frowned. "So."

"So—I doubt the Lord would send lions or any animal He has chosen for salvation, to harm us."

"But how do you know these are the chosen lions?"

"I shall go out there and find out."

Elisheva gasped.

"No, Father," Ariel said. "You can't."

212

"Father, these are lions we're talking about, not sheep or goats," Ham said. "You can't just go out there and shake hands with them."

"Possibly not. But you are welcome to come with me."

"We'll all come with you." Japheth nodded at Shem and Ham. "The women will stay inside."

Noah placed his sword against the wall beneath the window and walked to the door. His gut told him the lions were harmless, but his head held onto a pinch of doubt.

Ariel picked up the weapon and turned to him, arms outstretched. "Father, please. Just in case."

"No, daughter," he said. "After forty years of building the ark, am I not willing to trust God for the next sixty parts?"

As he and his sons walked out the door, Ariel reached to touch Shem's chin and shook her head.

"It's all right," Shem said, patting her forearm.

"Stay here." In slow steps, Noah moved toward the lions. When he was within ten cubits, the male lion rose on all fours, but made no move to signal aggression.

"Father, stop," Japheth whispered.

Concerned etched the faces of Noah's sons and they readied their weapons.

But their look turned to one of puzzlement when he smiled and pointed to the side of the house. His sons moved to where they could get a better look. Two gazelle grazed next to the house fifty cubits from the lions. He raised his arm in affirmation to indicate all was well, and they should remain calm.

He continued walking. At five cubits, the lioness moved to meet him, sniffing his extended palm. "Nothing to fear here, girl." He stroked her head and scratched behind her ears. The lioness pressed her shoulders against his legs. The male lion moved closer. "Not you, big fella." Noah leaned over the female to stroke the mane of her companion.

He ignored his sons' gaping jaws and motioned for them to join him. Shem and Japheth dropped their weapons and moved toward their father, but Ham stopped a few cubits short, sword at the ready. "What's the matter, brother?" Japheth stroked the lioness on the back. "Don't you believe your eyes?"

The front door opened and the women exited to mingle with their husbands and the new arrivals. Continuing their passive nature, the lions allowed themselves to be caressed by each family member. Even Ham relented, caressing the female on the back with one hand while holding the sword in the other. Ariel stayed close beside her husband.

The male lion seemed to take a special interest in Miryam, returning several times to her massaging touch. "Looks like you've made a friend," Noah said.

"Yes, well, I always had a way with men." Miryam and the family laughed.

"Shall we eat the meal our visitors interrupted?" Noah said. "We still have a full day ahead of us."

They moved back into the house, followed by the two lions.

"Oh, no, you don't." Miryam grabbed the male lion by the mane. "I've never had a dog in the house, and I'm not about to have a cat—especially one your size."

She escorted the lion outside, followed by her husband leading the lioness. They hurried back into the house, slamming the door behind them.

Once the family sat down to eat, an occasional soft growl accompanied the sound of the lions pacing outside. "You think they'll get tired and go away?" Shiphrah said.

They startled at the sound of the lioness bounding through the window opening, followed by the male. Both looked at the family and circled twice around the living area before laying on the floor ten cubits from the window.

"What was that you said, Shiphrah?" Noah said.

He and his family burst into laughter again.

Given their reputation for fierceness, Noah wasn't surprised God had chosen lions as the first arrivals to the ark site. More telling was that He'd chosen to send the gazelle with them, a clear message to his family they had nothing to fear from the predators.

CHAPTER 39

The sun had been up an hour when Noah walked the port side of the ark, the female lion trailing a few paces behind. Since returning to work three weeks ago, he and his sons had barely made a dent in the pile of wood that once stood as the ark. Even with the oxen, the process of dismantling the tangled mass had been a slow one. It had also proved dangerous. Several times, he and his sons were required to negotiate unsure footholds or dash out of the way of slipping sections of lumber to avoid injury. At least they didn't have to worry about spectators to the building site any longer.

At first, the sight of the ark lying in ruins seemed to attract a whole new set of onlookers. But one look at the lions prowling the perimeter or stopping to growl in their direction had quickly sent them on their way. Only the most curious bothered to visit now, and even those just long enough to catch a glimpse and move on.

Clearly, God had sent the lions to be more than future passengers on the ark. And although the male appeared content to keep Miryam within earshot, the lioness followed Noah around like a duckling trailing its mother.

One day Shem asked him about it. "Father, does she follow you everywhere?"

"Pretty much."

"What about your privacy? I mean, what happens when you have to, you know?"

"I talk to her."

"What?"

"She'll lie down if I tell her to. But if she doesn't see or hear me in around thirty-six parts, she gets up to look for me. I found that if I keep talking to her, she'll stay put and give me time to attend to my needs."

"I think I'd rather forgo the protection."

"I agree. Only she hasn't shown a desire to make that an option."

For Miryam, the lions, although protective, had proven to be a challenge, vowing from the first day to keep them out of the house. Each night she would put the cats out, and each morning she would find them on the floor in the main living area. She'd tried everything, including hanging blankets over the open windows, but they'd always found their way back inside. Except for one evening just over a week ago.

Right before going to bed, Noah noticed the male lion seemed to have disappeared. Miryam had entered the door from putting the female out. "Did you see her mate?" he said.

"No, but I'm sure he'll return by morning."

Fifty-five parts later, the two walked into their sleeping area to find the male lion sprawled on their bed. "Out!" Miryam pointed a finger away from the bed. She reached for a leather thong used to tie the waist of her husband's tunic. The lion hopped out of the bed and darted into the other room with Miryam hot on its tail. This time, he didn't wait for her to open the door, leaping directly out the window.

But at dawn, both lions appeared again on the floor beneath it.

This morning, the whole of Noah's family returned to work on the ark, including Ham. He didn't offer any explanation why he was breaking his vow, and his father didn't ask for any. The men labored to remove some of the larger sections, while the women carried away the lighter boards, separating the usable from the

217

unusable. Noah stopped to help Shem, who was driving a team of four oxen pulling away a large section of framing. When he did, the lioness lay on the ground about sixty cubits away.

"Come on, ox!" Shem said. "Get up there." He slapped the reins against the backs of the animals, their feet slipping against the strain of the load. At last, the section gave way, slowly moving the pile. Two thirds of the way down, it struck a pocket in the rubble, causing its weight to shift in the opposite direction. With their legs and backs buckling, the oxen cried out.

"Cut the ropes!" Noah yelled. "Quickly! Before their backs break!" Shem and he pulled knives and cut the tow lines. The structure tumbled away, crashing apart when it hit the ground.

"So much for the salvage," Shem said. "At this rate, we'll need to harvest all new timbers."

"We need something stronger than the oxen."

"Stronger? What would that be?"

"I don't—"

"Father, look." From his perch on a heap ninety cubits toward the stern, Ham pointed across the plain to where two elephants slowly made their way toward the ark. "How about these?"

Shem's jaw fell open. "Father, I know the Lord said only two of every animal for the ark, but do you think He might lend us a few more to help build it?"

"It sure wouldn't hurt to ask."

"Sooner, rather than later, would be nice."

"I'll see what I can do." Noah used his knife to point toward Ham. "Just as soon as we get your brother there married off tomorrow."

Ham fumbled the plank he was lifting, dropping it back onto the pile. When he turned, his father, Japheth, and Shem were staring at him. "What?" Ham said, his eyes blinking rapidly.

His father and brothers chuckled loudly.

218

Ariel's fidgeting throughout the late meal told Noah she had something on her mind. Afterwards, when the others went for a walk, she declined the invitation and approached him and Miryam. "I can't believe you're going to allow your son to marry a woman from Enoch."

"It's not our choice," Noah said. "It's Ham's. Just as it was Shem's choice to marry you."

A frown crossed her brow. "You could forbid it. Ham might not like it, but I'm sure he wouldn't disobey you."

"Why would we forbid it? You've seen them since Shiphrah's return. They're in love."

"Doesn't it bother anyone you may be giving your son to a woman who isn't pure?"

"Who told you she wasn't pure?" Miryam snapped.

"No one had to. But it's fairly easy to figure out, isn't it? Remember why she was brought to Eden in the first place?"

"Of course," Noah said. "But seeing she escaped with us before the end of that first night, I hardly see how her virginity could be questioned."

"What about the Marauders? Do you really think she was able to maintain her virginity all that time in the company of those animals?"

"Well, you heard the story. And I think it would be an extreme contradiction for them to be bowing at her feet one moment, then defiling her the next."

"Tell me, Ariel," Miryam said. "Aren't you even the least bit pleased Shiphrah has returned home safely?"

"That she's safe, yes. That she returned, no." Ariel crossed her arms.

"And what about what Ham wants? Do you despise Shiphrah so much you would deny your brother-in-law a chance to be happy?"

Ariel's gaze dropped. "No. I guess not. I just wish he could have found a woman from Eden to marry."

219

"We'll settle for a woman he loves." Noah stepped closer. "And I'd keep that talk about her not being pure to yourself if you know what's good for you."

Ariel lowered her chin. "Yes, Father."

The last rays of sunlight bathed the grass and the backs of Noah's several hundred sheep. For reasons he couldn't explain, walking with them at this time of the day always brought him a sense of peace. It was a perception evidently shared by the sheep, for they paid little attention to the lioness at his side, nor did she show any interest in them. Behind him, the sounds of a wedding celebration drifted through the air from a window of their house. Ham sounded more than pleased to have the rest of the family join him in a recreational drink. Even Ariel seemed to enjoy herself.

Last night, after the rest of the family had retired, Noah, Miryam, Shem, and Japheth stole up to the ark site for a special project. The men constructed the frame for a makeshift shelter out of some shattered timbers and covered it with several tent canvases made of goat's hair. Miryam added blankets, pillows, lamps, and a few soft frills to make the place more appealing.

What followed today was an amazing display of creativity while the family struggled to keep Ham and Shiphrah away from their wedding nest. Noah found it particularly amusing.

First, Ham spent half the morning looking for his sandals, which Shem had hidden. Then, when Ham went to dress, he found Miryam had given Elisheva all of his clothes to wash. Ham made quite the picture standing in the middle of the room, naked from the waist up and complaining to his mother. "You picked today to wash *all* my garments? What am I supposed to get married in?"

Later, when a nervous Shiphrah announced she was going outside for some air, Elisheva unexplainably sliced through her finger with a knife just as her sister reached the door. This prompted Shiphrah to help administer first aid, after which Miryam asked her to take Elisheva's place in kneading bread.

Now, walking the pasture, Noah was reminded of a conversation he had here forty years ago and dropped to the ground in gratitude.

'God of our fathers. Who am I that I should be blessed this day to see the marriage of my third son? And that through this joining You have revealed Your will for this woman, who You predestined for salvation and protection from the floodwaters to come. Thank You for Your mercy and for giving ear to the pleas of Your servant."

In his customary manner, he remained with his face on the ground for some time after making his supplication, waiting to hear from the Lord. Tonight, He was silent.

Noah rose for another glimpse of the mountain of wood covering the hill. How long before word of the rebuilding project would reach those who had failed to thoroughly destroy the ark the first time? And how swift and formidable would their response be? Would he and his sons alone be able to repel another assault? And even if they could, how much would it cost them? God never promised there wouldn't be casualties among them.

CHAPTER 40

In the 542nd year of Noah . . .

Two years later, Shechem squatted for a closer look at the 111th, 112th, and 113th throat-slashing victims of Eden's self-appointed executioner. A year ago, he'd stopped showing up at the murder scenes discovered during the night, preferring to wait until morning to be notified. But last night, unable to sleep because of his recurring insomnia, he chose to respond after overhearing two guards discussing the discovery of the bodies. He arrived two hours before sunrise.

He was glad he did.

All three men had been found on their stomachs together in the rear of a brothel in the city's north end. He rolled the first man over for a look at his face. *I know this man.* He then rolled the second and third men onto their backs, recognizing them as well.

He quickly scanned the murder scene. In just a few parts, everything he'd seen and heard over the past two years concerning the murders coalesced in his mind. He let out a huge sigh that sputtered across his lips in a horse's snort.

Intuition or insight, he had a feeling these three would be the last victims of Eden's slasher. He replayed the events that'd brought him here.

222

Malluch's offer of gold two years ago hadn't generated the information they were hoping for. The killings continued unabated. If anything, the killers had become more resourceful.

One evening, someone set fire to a grain storage facility located in the western end of the city. Shechem redirected over two hundred soldiers from the east to assist with the fire suppression effort. It had taken most of the night to get it under control. In the morning, six people were found murdered in the area left unguarded by the diversion of troops.

On another occasion, a woman who'd discovered a male murder victim said she saw a man dressed in black riding hard out the south gate. Shechem immediately dispatched more than a hundred soldiers to pursue the alleged assailant. When they returned in the morning, the woman who'd reported it and four others were found with their throats slit.

Fortunately, such diversionary plots were rare, and he learned to be more circumspect about committing his forces. There'd been additional pauses in the killings, but often these were followed by multiple victims in a single night. Overall, the killers had remained consistent, averaging just over a murder a week over the two-year period.

At the patriarchs' request, Malluch had increased the reward from fifty to a hundred, and finally to two hundred pieces of gold. Still, no one came forward.

Shechem had mixed feelings following the unearthing of one victim. Six months ago, the rich elder's son—one of several candidates he'd suspected of being his wife's lover—was found murdered like the others. Upon hearing the news, it brought him more than a bit of satisfaction. But when he told his wife, her reaction wasn't what he'd expected.

"How awful," she'd said, but showed little more emotion, even after several days had passed. If the man had truly been her lover, he was convinced she would have been unable to conceal the shock so easily.

Even so, guilt bothered him at having wrongly suspected a man now dead.

The night before last, the thirty-first son of an elder and his wife were found murdered in their home. Their three young children, asleep in another part of the house, were unharmed.

Now, studying the evidence at his feet, suspicions Shechem had denied for months could be suppressed no longer.

All three men were dressed in dark clothing, hoods attached to their tunics. Two of the men were over four cubits tall, the third somewhat shorter. All three carried knives. Half a dozen empty wineskins littered the floor around the bodies. With no signs of a struggle, it appeared the men may have been asleep or passed out when attacked. He recognized the men as longtime associates of Bohar.

It was time to go see Malluch.

* * *

While Miryam and Ariel prepared the early meal, Noah stared with anticipation out the window at the ark. It had taken every day of the past two years to complete the demolition, reclamation of wood, and the harvesting and preparation of new timber. Today the rebuilding would begin, and the excitement of a small boy whose father had given him his first set of tools overcame him.

During the first of the two years, five more species of large cats had arrived: tigers and leopards in spring, jaguars and cheetahs during the summer, and two sleek charcoal panthers at the onset of fall. Noah was confident they'd been sent to provide additional protection for the ark, and their behavior confirmed that suspicion. As if by instinct, the new arrivals never strayed far from the area, with each species establishing its own nesting area within the construction site. Even when leaving to forage for food, they would return each evening before sunset. Much to Miryam's chagrin, the lions refused to join their kindred at the ark, and so remained unwelcomed house guests.

He turned from the window to the sound of a frustrated Miryam. "All right, where are they?"

"Where are what, my wife?"

"I put two bunches of bananas here on the table, and now they're gone."

He looked at Ariel, who spread her hands. "Are you sure you put them on the table?"

"Well of course, I'm sure." Miryam searched under the table and around the food preparation area. She pulled two more bunches off a larger cluster and placed them on the table. Ariel returned to kneading bread.

He swung back to the window. After a few moments, her agitated voice again seized his attention. "What's going on?"

"I'm afraid I don't understand, my dear."

"Look." Miryam pointed to the table where a single bunch of bananas lay. "You saw me put two bunches there. Now there's only one."

"Well, I sure didn't take them," Ariel said.

Noah searched the area, including under the table. He and the two women looked at each other and shook their heads. "I don't know what to — "

A long, gray snake-like body entered through the open kitchen window and snatched the bananas from the table, prompting Ariel's scream. Noah moved to the window, motioning for the women to join him. Outside, the two elephants feasted on the bananas, their mouths slowly munching on the yellow crescent fruit.

"I hope you both get bellyaches," Miryam said.

Later that night, Noah awoke to the sound of men screaming, their shrieks fading away in the distance. Although the ark's destruction had forced his family to move back into their house, the cats' presence obviated the need for them to stand guard. He

225

met his sons in the main living area of their home and the four men headed up to the construction site. They found donkey tracks and a single torch smoldering on the ground on the starboard side of the ark. "Shem, you and Ham take a look on the other side," Noah said.

A short time later, his sons came running up from the stern.

"Did you find anything?" Noah said.

"No tracks, if that's what you mean." Ham said. "And no torches."

"The tigers are gone," Shem said.

"The tigers?" Japheth said.

"Yes," Shem said. "All of the other cats were nested down in their usual spots, but the place near middle of the ark where the tigers have been staying was empty."

"Where do you suppose they went?" Japheth said.

Their father raised his torch and looked out toward the east. "Hunting."

The next morning, Noah and Japheth returned to the ark to find the tigers back in their improvised den, grooming themselves. "What do you think?" Japheth said. "Just bathing or—"

"Or what, son?"

He grimaced and swallowed hard. "Washing up after a meal?"

Watching both tigers carefully lick each paw, Noah had the same thought, even though there was no evidence to show their prey had been human. "I don't know, but whoever our visitors were last night, I hope they had fast mounts."

226

CHAPTER 41

Teeth clenched, Shechem stared at Malluch's outstretched arm. "Please, Commander, have a drink."

He reluctantly took the cup from his hand, drank its contents, then slammed it down on the table. "So it was you, all along?"

"Of course. Well, to be precise, it was Bohar."

Bohar sat at the table, again using a dirt encrusted fingernail to pick his teeth.

"And you let me run around for two years trying to find a murderer you were controlling?"

Malluch poured more wine into his cup. "Forgive me, my friend, for using you. But hard as this may be for you to understand, it was necessary. To protect you."

Shechem's eyes widened. "To protect *me*?"

"Yes. You remember that night in my bedroom I said you had to remain above suspicion? Well, keeping you in the dark was the only way to accomplish it."

"How did keeping me in the dark help me to remain anything but a fool?"

"Not a fool, my friend. Ignorant. Once I began to take my vengeance against the cowards of Eden, I knew there would be

227

inquiries from the patriarchs. I had to have someone to convince them we were doing everything possible to apprehend the killers."

"And you felt I couldn't be trusted with the truth?"

Malluch handed him the cup. "Believe me, it wasn't so much a matter of trust as it was strategy. I couldn't risk the patriarchs being able to see through the facade of your trying to cover for what I was doing. They had to have someone they could believe was telling them the truth about the investigation. And that is exactly what you told them — the truth — as you knew it."

Shechem couldn't believe it. His closest friend, a man he'd been loyal to all his life — a man he'd killed for — had manipulated him like a potter fashioning clay. For two years, he'd done little more than chase his own tail. But he didn't mind being branded a fool nearly so much as being branded a liar. Despite being tied to Malluch's government, his investigation into the murders had earned him the trust of the patriarchs, or at least Lamech. Now that trust would be destroyed, and his integrity along with it. And what about the more than one hundred innocent victims? Heat rose along both sides of his neck. He took another drink. "So you had over a hundred people killed to cover up the murder of twenty-one?"

"You saw me that night, Commander. Imagine having to endure that several times a month for the past sixty years. I would have killed a thousand to rid myself of that torment. Whether you believe it or not, I do regret the innocent were made to suffer in order to repay the guilty."

Bohar threw his feet on the table and his hands behind his head. "I don't."

Shechem nodded slowly as realization after realization swept over him. He gestured with a head tip toward him. "His bathing. Part of the ruse?"

"Excellent deduction, Commander," Malluch said. "I knew you would immediately recognize our friend's, shall we say, distinctive aroma, should you come across it in your investigation. So I asked him to bathe prior to each of his nighttime forays." He chuckled.

228

"Not that it was without protest. As you know, Bohar and water are only passing acquaintances."

Bohar snarled.

"But in the end, he agreed it was the best way for him to protect his identity."

"Spring's over, Commander," Bohar said. "Guess you'll have to get used to the old me again."

Cursing. I should have run you through years ago when I had the chance. Shechem was besieged by guilt. Could he have saved the lives of all those people had he acted upon his first instinct and killed Bohar years ago? It would have been so easy to accomplish under cover of one of their raids. Then on the other hand, maybe it wouldn't have made any difference at all. Malluch was right. The look in his eyes the night in his bedroom was the look of a man unwavering in his desire for vengeance. He would have simply gotten someone else to do it. "And the three we found last night?"

"I'm sure you surmised, two were friends of Bohar who assisted with the killings," Malluch said.

"Assisted?"

"Mostly in helping to restrain the men. Bohar insisted on handling the mechanics of the executions himself. He said he'd mastered the proficiency of a physician near the end, able to slice through the large vein in the throat without touching the windpipe."

"And the third?"

"Ah. Another acquaintance of Bohar's. A selfless man who agreed to stand-in for him. You see, three killers had been seen, so three bodies had to be found."

"Naturally."

"Such a brave soul. I was thinking of having a memorial erected in his honor."

"What about the reward?"

Malluch shook a finger in the air. "That, my friend, was a remarkable and totally unforeseen twist of fate. Were it possible, I would thank the elders for it. The reward was the perfect diversion, made more so by the fact it was their idea."

"So that's why you never hesitated to increase it."

"Why would I? It provided the perfect cover for what I was doing. Every twenty to twenty-five murders, the elders would come to me demanding I increase the reward. What they didn't know is I was more than happy to accede to their wishes. I would have offered ten talents of gold if asked."

"Seeing no one was ever going to collect it."

"Exactly."

"You know something?" Bohar said. "When you got to two hundred, I nearly turned myself in."

Malluch and Bohar laughed while Shechem — still furious over being deceived — could only grit his teeth. But he would still have to face the patriarchs. "What am I going to tell the elders?"

"Tell them nothing," Malluch said. "Right now the bodies are being burned, and no one else knows of their association with our friend here. Word is being spread these three fiends got what was coming to them. Some grieving father or husband executed justice in the name of the government. After a while, once everyone sees the killings have stopped, the questions will too.

"Not from Lamech, my lord. I know him. He always suspected the killings were more than the work of a madman. If anyone can make the connection between the betrayal at the garden and the murders, it will be him."

"Why do you think I had Bohar eliminate an additional ten elder's sons?"

"I'm telling you, he'll be able to see through it."

"He may suspect it. But without proof he wouldn't dare raise an accusation of a conspiracy targeting those twenty-one cowards, not with another ninety-some innocent people having been killed."

Shechem fought to keep from reacting to the irony of Malluch's use of the word "innocent," nor was he at all convinced. Having dealt directly with Lamech for two years regarding the murders, he'd come to respect him for his insight. And with good reason.

He'd been right.

CHAPTER 42

Noah and Shem were setting a beam amidship when they heard Elisheva screaming her husband's name. A moment later, Elisheva appeared around the corner of the stern. "Father—Shem—Ham. Hurry! Japheth's in trouble."

The two men grabbed swords and met an armed Ham running toward them from the prow before proceeding down the right side of the ark. When they rounded the corner of the stern, Japheth rolled on the ground with one of the jaguars, their limbs wrapped around each other.

Shem and Ham started toward their brother, but Noah held them back. "Wait a few moments."

"What?" Shem said. "He may not have a few moments."

"Look at your brother's arm."

His left forearm rested unscathed and unbloodied inside the jaguar's mouth. Neither did their brother cry out. Shem and Ham's jaws dangled.

Noah's first instinct had also been to rush to his son's aid, although even unarmed he believed Japheth capable of holding his own against the big cat. But his fear was quickly allayed by the animal's apparent gentleness in combat. "Just watch," Noah said.

With the jaguar on top, their brother drew his legs up under the cat's belly and with a loud grunt thrust him twenty cubits away.

The animal quickly recovered and bounded back, launching himself through the air with a growl. The elder son caught the jaguar by the shoulders, falling onto his back in a reverse summersault that sent the huge cat flying overhead.

This time, Japheth was first to his feet, jumping on the jaguar's back and putting him in a headlock. The cat bowed his head to the ground, alternating swipes with his paws trying to dislodge his rider. Although he struck him in the head several times, his claws never broke the skin.

When this tactic failed, the cat raced across the hill, stopping every few paces in an attempt to shake him off.

Ham was first to realize what was going on. "Ride him, big brother."

"Father, make them stop," Elisheva said.

On the next pass across the hill, the jaguar stopped abruptly, sending Japheth flying over his head. He bounced up and stood with his knees bent and arms extended, readying himself for another pass. Other than a few scrapes from the ground, he appeared uninjured.

"All right you two, that's enough for now," Noah said.

The jaguar started again for Japheth, who raised a single finger. "Ah, ah."

The animal halted, dipping his head in apparent disappointed.

Elisheva ran to embrace her husband, then pushed away his towering body. "What is wrong with you? Scaring me like that. I thought for sure he was going to eat you."

"I'm sorry, but he wanted to play. He kept swatting at me so I'd pay attention to him. I figured the only way I was going to get any work done was to tire him out."

Japheth approached the jaguar, reaching down to scratch behind his ears. The cat playfully bit his hand.

"Well, the next time you want to wrestle with a jaguar or put your head inside a crocodile's mouth, have the courtesy to tell someone first, will you?"

Japheth's face lit up like a little boy's, looking past his wife to his father and brothers. "Are the crocs here yet?"

"Very funny."

* * *

Shechem smiled, nodding to several of the merchants in the marketplace who waved when he led his soldiers back into the city from their latest campaign. Now that the murders had ended, he was relieved to have returned to his primary job of securing riches and slaves for Eden.

Six weeks following the last death, he'd returned with a fine load—one hundred fifty slaves and a half talent of gold wrested from the southwestern territories.

Inside, he fumed over Malluch's deception. He was the commander of Eden's army and, up until then, a trusted friend. It devastated him to learn that for two years he'd been relegated to the rank of patsy. How long had he been lied to about other matters?

Yet being used was only part of it. The wound to his ego, though crushing, could be expected to heal with the passage of time. More disconcerting was Malluch's callousness toward those innocents whose death he countenanced in the name of vengeance. Shechem had expected as much out of Bohar, but for his longtime benefactor to sanction mass murder against his own people amounted to the vilest form of corruption. It was a side of his old friend he'd never expected.

He made his way past the palace, through the north gate and west to the slave camp. He was surprised to find Lamech and a group of elders waiting for him. Malluch, in an effort to mollify the elders, had consented for them to bring gifts of fruit and medicine

234

to the slaves once a month. But this was the first time they'd ever been there when he returned with a load of prisoners.

"I see your hunting trip was a success, Commander," Lamech said, pointing to the long lines of men shackled together.

"Malluch still has plans for an arena and more winepresses."

"Can't you see how wrong this is, Commander?" Methuselah said. "To turn those made in the similitude of God into beasts of burden?"

"You heard what he said. Buildings won't rise by themselves."

"You could speak to him," Lamech said.

"Suppose I did. Have you forgotten Malluch's vow? Do you want to see all these men killed?"

Chains rattled and the heads of most of the prisoners within earshot snapped up. Some of the elders lowered their eyes.

"I didn't think so," Shechem said. Silently, the elders moved away, and he started for the camp entrance, relieved Lamech hadn't brought up the subject of the murders.

"I guess you're relieved the killings have stopped, aren't you Commander?" Lamech said.

The question seemed to pinch the nerve running from his spine to his feet, stopping him cold. He whirled around. "It's been a long two years."

"Yes. Still, it must have been disappointing to learn vigilantes had robbed you of the opportunity to interview the killers. Especially after all the effort you expended trying to catch them."

"It was."

"I think we all would have liked to know what motivated them."

"Yes. Like you, I never could accept the lone madman theory."

"Were you able to identify them?"

"Unfortunately, no. It looks like they were strangers to the city."

"There was a rumor they had their throats slit."

Shechem nodded. "A fitting end, wouldn't you say?"

"Tell me, Commander, how many people were killed before these three met their demise?"

"One hundred and thirteen, I believe."

"And of these, would you happen to know the number who were sons to the elders?"

He didn't know where Lamech was going with this, but he didn't want to be tripped up by a lie that would come back to bite him. "Exactly thirty-one."

"Did you know twenty-one of them had accompanied Malluch on a raid to the garden seventy years ago—a raid that left his father and brother dead?"

Lamech paused and Shechem felt the blood drain from his face.

"But of course you did," Lamech said. "Because you were there."

That's where he's going. But now was not the time for candor. Besides, he, too, had been ignorant of what Malluch was up to until the end. "In the midst of all the murders, I'm afraid I was too preoccupied to recognize the coincidence."

"Coincidence?"

"I don't see how you can call it anything more, not with another ten elders' sons and over eighty other citizens killed."

"Maybe not. But it would have been a good question to pose to the killers—how their random killing spree happened to include those twenty-one?"

Shechem nodded.

"Had they survived, of course," Lamech said.

The corners of Lamech's lips lifted slightly. It was the same look he'd seen when he denied knowledge about the destruction of Eden's god. Shechem took a step toward the gates of the camp.

"Bohar." Lamech called out.

Shechem spun back around. "What about him?"

"Isn't he supposed to be good with a knife?"

"Yes. I suppose he is."

236

CHAPTER 43

In the 552nd year of Noah . . .

Noah glanced briefly at the setting sun before returning his attention to the end of the main rail he and Shem held in place between two rib frames. Ham and Japheth held firm the other end

"All right, my daughters. Let's get this nailed while we still have the light." Shiphrah and Elisheva hammered in the last of the pegs securing the rail to the frame and joined the others in climbing down.

On the ground, they all stared up at the completed frame, smiling and congratulating each other. Even Ham seemed pleased to have finished this portion of the construction. It had taken them just over ten years to complete the skeleton a second time. During that time, they'd received assistance from pairs of arriving rhinoceroses, yaks, and large brown bears—brutes well suited for the tasks of pulling and lifting.

And yet, the project proved more than just a backbreaking exercise in ship construction. Often, it served as a source of entertainment for the builders and some of the site's first arrivals.

Each new section of framing drew an increasing level of interest from some of the large cats. More than once, Noah and his family found themselves marveling at the nimbleness with which they bounded up and down the structure. The jaguars, leopards, and panthers, in particular, had all but turned the ark's skeleton into their own piece of recreation equipment. He would miss their antics once they'd hulled over the frame.

The lions, though, always remained on guard at ground level.

While the women, Shem, and Ham continued their small celebration, no one seemed to notice Japheth had moved forty cubits away toward the ship's prow. Gazing north, he leaned against the ark with his right forearm. He'd grown curiously silent. "Thinking about your grandfather?" Noah said, coming up behind him.

"Today's his birthday."

"I know."

Japheth turned to Noah. "I remember one birthday when we were children, Grandfather took Shem and I with him to the hills of Havilah to search for gold."

Noah nodded in recollection.

"Each night we'd camp out under the stars, and Grandfather would keep us up all night telling scary stories. Of course, we never found any gold, just a few onyx stones. But Shem and I had the best time. Here it was his birthday, and he was treating us like it was ours."

"Having you two around was the best way he knew to celebrate it."

"I sure hope he's not spending this one in prison."

"I doubt your grandfather's in prison. Malluch may have control of the government. He may even have the army to back him up. But he's smart enough to know he needs at least compliance from the people if he wants his regime to survive. And that's something he'd never get if he imprisoned or executed one of the patriarchs."

"I wish I could be as confident as you." Japheth kicked a clod of dirt and started down the hill.

Noah signaled to the lioness lying thirty cubits away. "Come on, girl. That's it for today." When they reached the bottom, he

238

paused for a last look up the hill, the setting sun a brilliant garnet through the ark's skeleton. It reminded him of a great abandoned carcass, behemoth or leviathan, stripped of its meat.

Adding to the surreal scene, a lone leopard fearlessly traversed the port side top rail thirty cubits above the ground. It bowed its head while it walked, giving the appearance of searching for that last remaining morsel of flesh.

* * *

Shechem lay more than an arm's length away from the sleeping stranger that was his wife, her straight, dark hair draped across the curvature of her bosom. Since he didn't believe in counting sheep, he chose instead to count her breaths. In—out. In—out. In . . . For over 220 years, she'd fallen asleep in his arms. Now it seemed she couldn't find enough space between them.

He slid closer, slipping his arm beneath her and drawing her into his chest. She moaned softly.

His mind was a whirlwind of thoughts keeping him from sleep. The decade following the murders had marked a season of change, both for him and the citizens of Eden.

During that time, Eden's army had grown to its original projected strength of five thousand men. The additional manpower allowed him to split his forces and conduct simultaneous campaigns in separate regions of the territory, resulting in a marked increase in plunder and slave power secured for Eden.

Another change came with Malluch ordering the placement of additional gods—sacred pillars, wooden images, and incense altars. He'd convinced himself such worship places had increased the fortunes of Enoch and was determined to emulate them. Shechem had overseen the construction of ten of these so-called high places, five each along two separate ridges to the northwest and northeast of the city. As expected, their erection had not come without protest from the patriarchs.

239

Two things hadn't changed: Shechem still suspected his wife was having an affair, and he was determined to find out with whom. Not that their relationship at home provided any indication.

They rarely argued. In fact, they argued less now than they ever had. Whenever an issue arose where they seemed to disagree, Claudia quickly apologized, even over the most minor perceived slights. Too much harmony existed in the home, as though she was working hard to allay any suspicions. Except for the fact she rarely invited him to come in to her, everything was perfect. Maybe too perfect.

With the elder's son gone, the silk merchant had moved to the top of his list of suspects — and with good reason. He was handsome. He was attentive to Claudia. His trade provided him regular access to her. But most of all, Shechem had uncovered a secret about him dating back to the time of Eden's murders.

Because the young boy's murder had interrupted his surveillance the night he'd followed his wife, he never learned where she'd gone that night. All he knew was it had to be somewhere in the northeast section of the city, the last place he'd seen her before she'd disappeared. He had little reason to suspect the silk merchant then, knowing he resided on the opposite side of Eden with a wife and four children.

Then one day a rumor he was bringing women to a small cottage in the area where the boy had been killed led Shechem to investigate for himself. He'd followed the silk merchant there during the day, ducking around corners and into doorways whenever the man looked over his shoulder. He waited for over an hour for him to leave before entering through a rear window.

The cottage's single bed and sparse furnishings told him the abode had indeed been readied as a lover's hideaway. Yet, he could find no evidence of his wife ever having been there. No women's clothing. No lingering odor of perfume. Not even a strand of hair.

But his wife's coolness towards him and the existence of the cottage only increased his skepticism. He was convinced somebody

240

was being brought there, and judging from the silk merchant's furtive behavior doubted it was his own wife.

Time and again he tried to repeat the strategy he'd used the first time: assure Claudia of his required absence from home and conduct surveillance. He'd employed the tactic nearly forty times in the last ten years—both day and night—including less than two weeks ago. All with the same result. Other than to visit the palace or go to the marketplace, his wife never left the house.

Nor had anyone come to visit while Shechem was away. Too much chance they'd be spotted by someone.

After years of anxiety, the stress of not knowing started to wear on him. Frustrated by his inability to catch her, yet certain of her infidelity, he briefly pondered having the silk merchant murdered. He even considered using Bohar to carry out the execution. Ultimately, he decided against it, fearing word of another throat-slasher stalking the city would cause a panic. He also didn't want to repeat the mistake he'd made in wrongly suspecting the murdered elder's son.

He had to be patient. Sooner or later they would make a mistake, and when he caught them, he would kill them. He fantasized about finding them together, and with a single thrust skewering both bodies at once.

Tonight, he anticipated his fantasy coming true.

Malluch had thrown a celebration at the palace to commemorate his son's one hundredth birthday. Most of Eden's elites were in attendance. Shechem was standing a dozen cubits from Claudia, but with a full view of her face when the silk merchant first entered the hall. The commander watched his wife's head follow him making his way through the crowd. Other women did the same, for the silk merchant was a handsome man. But Claudia looked at him like she hadn't seen him in her house once every three months for the past thirty years.

She had the look of a hungry wolf. The only thing she hadn't done was lick her lips. But even that only slightly irritated him.

241

What concerned him most was how she so clumsily peeked behind to check on his whereabouts.

The silk merchant was more subtle, offering only a smile and a short bow when he arrived at Claudia and their eyes met.

"Commander," Malluch said, motioning for him to join him across the room. Following 270 parts of discussion with his son on topics ranging from the building of winepresses to military tactics, Shechem scanned the hall.

Claudia and the silk merchant had disappeared.

"Excuse me, my lord," he said.

He exited the hall and searched the palace and its grounds. He entered every unoccupied room, balcony, and storage area. He traversed every cubit of hallway on all three floors of the palace, including the courtyard.

Moving down one hallway, he came upon two women and a man coming toward him from the opposite direction. They hugged the walls while offering looks of bemusement when they passed. Confused by their reaction, he looked down to see a knife in his right hand that he had no memory of drawing. He hastily returned it to its sheath beneath his tunic.

Finally, he entered his own home. If they were together, he couldn't find them.

Half an hour later, he returned to the great hall. When he entered, Claudia and the silk merchant stood next to a table of food and drink, conversing together with Malluch and eight other guests.

Shechem doubted his senses, and for the first time feared the onset of paranoia. Had Claudia and the silk merchant really ever left, or had they simply been eclipsed by the more than five hundred guests that filled the hall? Was he so desperate to catch them together he'd imagined the whole thing?

He moved to the table, filled a chalice with wine and drank it down. He refilled it and drank another. Then a third.

242

Now, laying with Claudia's head nestled in the crook of his armpit, the tension of an ordeal fueled by a wild imagination subsided. He started to doze. Claudia moaned again, this time pushing herself away and rolling over. He looked across the bed at the coldness of her back mocking him, then dropped his head back on the pillow.

He closed his eyes, hoping Elisheva would come to him in his dreams.

CHAPTER 44

Noah hoped the passing of his father's birthday would allow Japheth to refocus his energies back to working on the ark.

It hadn't.

For the past several days he appeared edgy, distracted. Twice today, Noah had to call him back to work from a place at the prow where he sat alone staring into the wilderness. The second time, he swung around, face glaring. "All right. I'm coming."

One hundred eighty parts later, he stopped in the middle of trimming a board, threw his saw to the ground, and climbed down the ark.

"What's got him riled?" Shiphrah said as the two of them watched him march down the hill.

"Something other than what I'm thinking, I hope." Since Miryam had already gone to prepare the evening meal, he announced they were quitting for the day. He waved for Shem and Ham to join them from the stern.

When they reached the house, they paused just outside the door to the sound of Miryam's voice. "You can't go back. You'll be killed."

Noah and the others came through the door to find Japheth packing a bag. Elisheva scurried across the room to him. "What's this? Where are you going?"

Shoving a folded tunic into the bag, his fist hit the bottom with a thud. "We never should have left him."

"Who?"

"How could you have done it, Father?" Japheth said to him. "And lived with it all these years?" He shook his head. "I should have gone back to get him that night."

Noah's stomach tightened at having to hurt his oldest. "He wouldn't have come with you."

"Can you say for certain? Can anyone?"

"What I told you then was the truth. Your grandfather said he would never leave the land of his fathers, not even to save his own life."

Japheth walked into the other room and came back with two loaves of bread, the first which he stuffed into the bag. "Maybe it's time somebody tried to change his mind."

"Do you think you're the only one who's missed him? Who's lost sleep over him? Do you think my heart hasn't ached for him every day since we left Eden?"

"How about him?" Japheth used the other loaf to point to his youngest brother before thrusting it in the bag. "Can his heart ache for someone he's never met? How about it, little brother? Would you like to meet your grandfather?"

Ham glanced at his father then to his oldest brother.

"No," Miryam said. "I'm not risking both of you."

Miryam stared them both down.

"What brought this on?" Noah said.

"What? Missing Grandfather?"

"I meant what brought it on today?"

"There's no better time, Father. The ark's frame is complete. And Elisheva is more than skilled enough to take my place until

245

I can return with him." He picked up his sword and lay it on top of the packed bag.

"Japheth," Shem said. "You know I'd be the last one to argue with you about wanting to see Grandfather, but it's been more than fifty years. Who knows if he's even alive?"

"That's what I have to find out."

"And if he is and still refuses to come with you, what are you going to do, kidnap him?" Shem said.

Japheth planted his feet squarely. "I'll think of something."

"Suppose he's in prison," Shem said. "We know Eden has an army now. Do you really think you'd be able to recruit enough men to help break him out?"

"I thought you were on my side."

"I am. Look, I miss Grandfather too. I just want you to think with your head instead of your emotions."

"Son," Noah said to Japheth. "You're forgetting about the Lord's proclamation."

Moistness seeped into his son's eyes. "You mean the one that says I get to live and he has to die? Who am I that I should be chosen over a man like Grandfather, a man who feared God all his life?"

"I told you before, the Lord has promised to pardon him from the floodwaters He's sending upon the earth."

"Good. Then why shouldn't he spend whatever time he has left here with his family? He's as good a carpenter as any of us. He could help with the ark."

With a nod, Miryam confirmed to her husband what they both must be thinking. "You can't go back to Eden," Noah said.

"Why not?"

"If you're caught, Malluch would have you killed, or worse, torture you to find out where we are."

"It's not my plan to get caught."

246

"A strategy no doubt shared by thousands who have been." He forced a chuckle. "I didn't plan on getting caught either."

"I'll be careful."

"Will you stop thinking of yourself for a part!" Miryam said in an explosion of emotion rare for her. "Your father just said Malluch could find us by torturing you. Do you want to put this whole family at risk just to satisfy some selfish need of yours?"

"I was thinking about Grandfather."

"No, you weren't. How many times has your father told you? Your grandfather refused to come. Believe me, son, I understand your love for him. We all do. But this whole idea of wanting to bring him here is about what you want, not what he wants."

"How do you know his wishes?"

"Your grandfather would want you to be obedient to your father, just as your father was the night he had to accept leaving him behind in Eden."

Japheth shook his head. "I'm sorry, Mother, but I have to go." He picked up his sword and bag and headed for the door.

"Japheth," Elisheva said softly.

He stopped short of the door when she called his name.

"Did it ever occur to you your grandfather is exactly where the Lord wants him to be?" Her voice was calm, but resolute.

He wheeled around. "What do you mean?"

"Think about it. If God had wanted him here, isn't it more likely your grandfather would have accepted your father's invitation the night we fled Eden?"

"Maybe, but—"

"For all you know, the Lord may be using your grandfather right now to perform some service there. He may be the only one left with influence enough among the people to keep them united in opposition to Malluch's government."

He sighed, and his features softened. "I never thought about it that way."

"Of course you didn't. Otherwise, you wouldn't be so quick to go back there and get yourself killed. And what about your great-grandfather, Methuselah? Did you ever stop to consider your grandfather might be needed in Eden to help care for him in his last years?"

There was something soothing in her voice. Something melodic in its tone, almost hypnotic. Noah felt its disarming power. The more she spoke, the less agitated Japheth became. Soon, the redness in his glower drained away.

He moistened his lips. "All right. You win."

Elisheva hugged him tightly.

Japeth leaned his sword against the wall, then removed the bread and tunic from the bag and put them back.

* * *

Several hours past midnight, Noah returned to bed from his third check on Japheth.

"He still asleep?" Miryam said.

"Like a baby."

"I hope you're not planning to do this every night, seeing he's 342 years old."

"No, just for the next few nights until he's back to normal."

"Do you think he'll try to leave again?"

"I don't know, but if he does it will probably be in the middle of the night."

"Why do you say that?"

"So he doesn't have to face you."

Miryam elbowed him in the side. "What does that mean?"

"You did a good job of beating him over the head with the guilt stick."

"Yes, but it was Elisheva who got him to stay."

248

"It's a good thing, too. He blames me for leaving his grandfather, so I don't think anything I could have said tonight would have made a difference."

"You know, I always thought Ham would be the one to leave."

"As did I. But Ham's problem has always been one of attitude, stemming from a lack of faith and maturity. Japheth is driven by much deeper values. He was really hurt by the loss, as he sees it, of his grandfather. And it's been festering now for fifty years."

"There's nothing we can do but encourage him. Now please, try to get some sleep."

His answer was to kiss her on the cheek. Sleep would be difficult to come by this night. He had only confided to her half the reason he was grateful she'd confronted their firstborn. The other was he would have felt like a hypocrite trying to talk him out of something he'd thought about doing himself a hundred times.

He missed his father terribly. Japheth's rebellion tonight only served as a reminder, one that would keep Noah awake until dawn.

CHAPTER 45

In the 580th year of Noah . . .

From within a deep sleep, Shechem dreamed someone was banging on his front door and calling his name, "Commander! Commander!" His wife shook him. The pounding was real. Malluch again, he thought, throwing his legs over the side of the bed. But when he opened the front door, one of his captains met him. "Sorry to wake you, Commander. But there's fire in the high places outside the city."

"I want three hundred men assembled in the courtyard ready to leave in 270 parts."

"Yes, sir."

Shechem dressed and rushed to the garrison. Two fires burned to the northwest. The first illuminated the hill where Eden's first god had been restored, and the second, the location of one of several incense altars. Fire and smoke rose to light up the night, two flaming eyes staring at him from the distance.

He ordered his troops not to focus on the fires, but to keep watch for signs of movement leading away from the sites. He made arrangements for extra soldiers to cover both gates, and assigned another hundred to ride the perimeter. If whoever did this returned to Eden, he wanted his men waiting for them.

"Commander," one of his men said. "Look." Forty furlongs to the east, another small fire burned along the same elevation that hadn't been there a few parts before. Even in the dark, Shechem recognized it as a probable location of another of Eden's gods.

He addressed the captain he'd assigned to lead half the company. "Take half your men and send them to where the two fires are burning, and divide the rest to cover the three remaining hills along the western ridge."

"Yes, sir."

"The rest of us will head north, then east before turning south along the eastern range to try to head them off."

"There's another one," another soldier said. A second fire ignited along the eastern ridge north of the first.

"Better move."

Shechem ordered his men to extinguish their torches, even though it would slow their pace. The night's quarter moon provided barely enough light to see the edges of the road, but it was the only way for them to avoid detection. His plan was to head to the worship site two hills ahead of the last one being burned and wait.

When they arrived, he found a hill that'd been only partially cleared. Near the top stood a large wooden ox. This contrasted with most of the other barren locations and afforded him a perfect location to secrete a portion of his troops. He positioned twenty of them in the woods just back from the tree line and hid the rest at the bottom of the far side of the hill.

A short time later, another fire to their south became visible, boosting his confidence in his strategy. He addressed soldiers to either side of him. "They'll be here soon. Keep quiet and wait for my signal."

Three hundred sixty parts passed when the sound of approaching horses alerted him. Too far away to see, he and his men listened while the tramping herd came to a stop, then moved about on the road below. Based on their movements and the murmur of voices, he guessed four or five riders.

Then silence before the horses galloped away in the direction they'd come.

He gave the signal, leading his men from the woods, down the hill, and onto the road in pursuit. They were joined by the others rounding the hill. As they crested the southern rise, he expected to catch a glimpse of the vandals fleeing in the distance. Instead, an empty road stretched before them to the darkened horizon.

But their disappearance only fueled Shechem's desire to pursue them. Forty years earlier, he'd been so fixated on solving the murders, he had little time to devote to tracking the defilers of Eden's first god. Failure hung around his neck with the weight of an ox's yoke. Capturing these blasphemers would go a long way toward lifting the burden.

He drove his cavalry hard over the horizon, ignoring the danger of a full speed chase in the dark over uneven terrain. After several furlongs, they entered a series of winding turns through the foothills that added another element of danger to the hunt.

Rounding a sharp curve, he heard the cries of men behind him. He glanced over his right shoulder to see two horses and their riders fall near the road's edge, the second tripping over the first. "Two abreast!" he shouted.

The soldiers continued through the foothills until they came onto a long, straight stretch of road. Faint moonlight indicated four men on horseback crossing over a knoll. They were still at least two furlongs ahead of the pursuers.

"There they are!" He pointed and slapped the reins against his horse's neck. The animal's breathing had grown deep and rapid, with droplets of sweat from its nape spraying his hands and forearms. Behind him, the hooves of more than a hundred horses beat on the road like thunder moving across the plain.

Nearing the city, his excitement grew. The men he'd stationed outside the perimeter would be waiting, and all he had to do was to keep driving the vandals toward them. His men raced around a wide turn running parallel to a deep ravine on their right. By the time they exited, the walls of Eden would lay before them. He slapped the reins again.

Lights appeared in the distance, and Shechem's arm shot up to slow his charging cavalry. Ahead, the road continued on another four furlongs to the north gate. Soldiers on horseback patrolled quietly outside the walls.

But the four riders. They'd vanished.

He cursed when they came to a stop.

Horses panted and snorted all around him. "Where'd they go?" one of his soldiers said.

Shechem studied the darkened surroundings. "They dropped into that ravine back there. Take half the men and hurry back to the other end to keep them from doubling back. We'll send a patrol in from here with torches to smoke them out."

Eight hundred ten parts later, the patrol exited his end of the ravine with the four riders in custody. He didn't recognize any of them.

He led his soldiers back to the garrison, turned over the prisoners, then stabled his horse and walked across the courtyard. Few lights burned in the palace, and he suspected it was well past midnight. But Malluch would want to know immediately about the arrests, a point he confirmed with great exuberance upon hearing the news.

He and Bohar joined Shechem for the ride back to the garrison. When they arrived, the keeper of the prison came running out the door. "Commander! Something terrible has happened."

"What is it?" Malluch said.

The jailer bowed, his hands trembling. "I'm sorry, my lord, but the prisoners the Commander brought in tonight are dead."

Malluch's lips flattened. "How?"

"I don't know, my lord. They didn't respond when the guards called to them. Then when they entered the cells to check on them, three were already dead and the other barely breathing. The one

253

who was alive was paralyzed from the waist down. He died a few dozen parts ago."

"If you're lying, I'll have you flayed."

The jailer threw himself on the ground. "My lord. That's what happened, I swear."

"Take us to the bodies," Shechem said. Could he have had any worse luck? For four decades he'd sought these rebels. Now that they were within his grasp, it appeared he wouldn't even have the satisfaction of interrogating them.

The four prisoners were laid out side by side in a vestibule near the cells. He kneeled to examine them. "Other than their clothes, were they carrying anything?"

"Two of them had pouches," the jailer said.

"Bring them."

The jailer left briefly and returned, handing the two pouches to Shechem. He examined the first and tossed it aside. With the second, he reached in and pulled out a tiny white flower with five symmetrical petals.

"What's that?" Bohar said.

"I'm not sure yet. Let me have your knife."

Bohar handed it to him. He moved from man to man, prying open their mouths. On the third man, he stopped after looking inside before motioning for the jailer to bring over a torch hanging on the wall. "Down here." He reached into the man's mouth with the knife. When he pulled it out, a sprig of green plant material in the shape of a fan clung to the tip.

"Is that what I think it is?" Malluch said.

"Hemlock." Shechem raised the flower in his other hand. "The flower too."

"You knew?"

"Let's say I suspected when the jailer mentioned the paralysis."

"How did they get it in here?" Bohar said.

"I don't think they did," Shechem said. "They died too quickly. Besides, the guards seized the pouches before putting them in their

254

cells. They must have swallowed it before they got here, probably somewhere out on the road when we were closing in on them."

"So much for getting any information out of them."

Malluch's face grew red. "Jailer."

"Yes, my lord."

"These men weren't poisoned."

"They weren't?"

"No. They were hung after being subjected to extreme torture."

"What are you doing?" Bohar said.

"Trying to turn a crock of dung into a pot of gold," Malluch said.

"But they're already dead."

"The patriarchs and their sympathizers don't know that." He spun back to the jailer. "Take these bodies and hang them, one each on either side of the south gate and two on the north gate."

"As you wish, my lord."

"And do it quietly, right now, before the sun comes up. Hang a sign on each of their chests that reads 'Desecrater of Eden's Gods.'"

The jailer bowed and started down the vestibule.

"And, jailer," Malluch said. "Tell the guards to keep their mouths shut, or I'll have them hung out there right alongside of them."

"Do you think it will work?" Shechem said.

"I'd have preferred a confession I could have used against the elders. I'll settle for conveying a message."

CHAPTER 46

In the 595th year of Noah . . .

Shechem didn't know how Malluch had learned of a plot to free the slaves, but he hoped to talk him out of his promise to destroy them. The hangings on the city gates fifteen years ago had accomplished their purpose. There hadn't been a whisper of rebellion against his government or so much as a cross word spoken against any of Eden's gods. Until now.

"I say we take the army out to the camp and wipe them all out right now," Bohar said.

"Wipe out three thousand slaves?" Shechem said.

"Why not?" It's better than letting them escape."

"Do you know how much time and expense we've invested in obtaining all those slaves? And that doesn't include the value in manpower they represent to Eden."

"Yes, and if they escape, they'll be of no more value than if we kill them."

Malluch strode toward them from across the great hall. "My lord," Shechem said.

"I'm sorry, Commander, but I made a promise eighty years ago. I intend to keep it."

256

"But why? Now that we know what they're planning, why not let me increase the guard around the slave camp?"

"Increasing the guard won't help us to identify the conspirators behind it."

"Then why not set a trap to catch them?"

"I'm afraid that's not enough, Commander. The four cowards who attacked our high places took their own lives to keep me from obtaining the proof I needed to accuse the patriarchs. I'm not going to allow that to happen again."

Bohar placed his palms on the table and leaned forward. "I still say we should go ahead and kill them right now."

"And rob our conspirators of their opportunity to be caught in the act." Malluch said. "I wouldn't think of it."

"My lord," Shechem said. "The slaves provide an invaluable service. Eden wouldn't be the city it is today without them. If we kill them, where will we find the labor to repair our walls or build your new arena?"

"Why from new slaves, of course."

"And you don't think catching whoever is behind the plot is deterrent enough?"

"No, Commander," Malluch said. "Besides, it will teach these rebels the price of defiance."

"But—"

"I want you to put together a plan to intercept the slaves just outside the camp and have your men in position shortly after midnight ten days from now."

"Yes, my lord." Good. Shechem had another ten days to make his case for sparing the slaves.

* * *

Just before midnight, Shechem walked the halls of the palace, as he did so often when troubled. Maintaining a brisk pace helped

257

to clear his mind. Especially when preparing to take an action he found objectionable, yet duty bound to carry out. He'd been unable to sway Malluch, who was determined to sacrifice the slaves in retribution for the elders' opposition to his government.

He passed by the open terrace at the rear of the palace on his way up to the third story. Whispered voices from the outside stoked his curiosity, so he moved onto the porch.

Below him, two shaded figures stood together. Even in the dark, Bohar's outline could not be mistaken, but the second figure Shechem couldn't place. The man kept looking over his shoulder, only the light wasn't good enough to make an identification. He stopped when coins were dropped into his hand, the clinking sound of money hitting his palm commanding his full attention. A moment later he scurried off while Bohar entered the palace.

Shechem continued up the stairs to a room where Malluch waited. Bohar arrived nine parts later, and the three men stepped outside onto a balcony with a view to the north. In the distance, lights flickered from each of the four watchtowers atop the walls of the slave camp. "Are your troops in position, Commander?" Malluch said.

"Yes, my lord. For several hours now."

"And are they clear on their orders?"

"They're not to make a move until the last of the slaves are in the open."

"Excellent, Commander. Excellent."

"This is going to be like hunting a herd of blind three-legged sheep," Bohar said.

Shechem couldn't bring himself to think so callously. These weren't sheep. They were men and represented a near one-hundred-year investment of time and resources. "You never told me, my lord, how you learned of the plot."

"A ruler must have some secrets, my friend," Malluch said. "Even from his closest advisor. How many slaves?"

He sighed heavily. "Three thousand one hundred forty-six at last count." He reached to straighten the sheath around his waist before heading inside. "I'd better be getting out there."

"Commander."

Malluch's tone froze him in his sandals.

"Not a one of them."

"Understood, my lord."

* * *

Shechem had never feared the coming of dawn. Today, standing on a plain surrounded by death, he loathed it.

Being a military commander, he'd experienced the feeling of euphoria associated with victory on the battlefield. Here, all he felt was shame when the first glimpses of daylight brought the bodies closest to him into focus. Two thousand nine hundred ninety-eight corpses spread across a thirty-acre area of plain just north of the slave camp. Another one hundred forty-eight lay bunched together around a large bush camouflaging an escape hole cut through the north wall. Malluch had ordered the hole blocked from the inside so none of the slaves could get back in once they'd fled.

Not a one had escaped.

Lamech, the patriarchs, and dozens of their kin lined the edge of the plain with their heads down. Many cried, apparently overcome by the carnage splayed before them. Soldiers surrounded eight of the elders' sons, their hands and feet shackled. "I—I." Lamech shook his head. "I can't find the words, Malluch. Have you lost your soul?"

Malluch laughed. "My soul?"

"No one in their right mind would do something this cruel and senseless. But since I don't consider you crazy, my only conclusion is you've lost your soul."

259

"Cruel? Look around you. Do you see any signs these men suffered? Each was relieved of his life swiftly and efficiently. And in near total darkness I might add."

"Oh, yes, a model exercise in compassion," Methuselah said.

Lamech walked onto the plain where three bodies lay next to one another. He gestured across the field. "All this was unnecessary. It's obvious you had advanced warning of the escape, and yet did nothing to prevent it. Instead, you used it as an excuse to sanction this slaughter."

"Merely keeping a vow I made long ago concerning the slaves. Have you forgotten?"

"No, Malluch. We haven't forgotten. But I prayed every day *you* would."

Malluch smirked. "Not to that invisible God of yours?"

"You see how much good that did you," Bohar said.

"I prayed your heart would be softened, so when the time came you would choose mercy over the vow."

"Mercy? Do not eight of your sons caught in this treasonous plot stand alive before you? Would you prefer I have them executed as well?"

"No!" three elders in the crowd said together.

"Spare my son, please," said another.

Lamech bowed slightly toward the governor. "I beg your pardon. But surely you've seen enough killing for one night."

"Take them to the prison in the garrison," Malluch said. The soldiers surrounding the prisoners marched the elders' sons off toward the city.

As they started away, Lamech rushed up behind one of the last soldiers in the formation and snatched his sword from its sheath. He moved swiftly to the elders, where he sliced through the tunic of one of the younger men standing with them. A money bag dropped onto the ground, spilling its contents of gold coins.

Who was he? Something about him looked familiar, but . . . *The man he'd seen the previous evening talking to Bohar.*

260

An elder standing next to the young man stepped back, staring wide-eyed at the coins on the ground.

"Father, I can explain," the young man said.

The elder took the sword from Lamech's hand, pivoted quickly and thrust it through his son's abdomen. He gasped, looking in disbelief while his father gently lowered his body to the ground. "Forgive me, Father," the young man said before closing his eyes.

For the next 180 parts, the father knelt with his son in his arms, rocking and weeping.

Malluch stood over the boy's body and addressed Lamech. "It would appear neither of us is good at keeping a secret."

"It's too bad," Bohar said, crouching to retrieve the gold coins on the ground next to the body. "He was a good informer."

Malluch raised a look to the twenty-five to thirty buzzards circling overhead. "Commander."

"Yes, my lord."

"Better find some help and get these men in the ground before you have a real mess on your hands."

CHAPTER 47

It came as no surprise to Shechem when sleep failed him the next night. The screams of three thousand slaves still resonated in his ears. So, after 720 parts of tossing and turning, he got up and went for another walk, this time in the courtyard.

Not since witnessing the sacrifice of the children of Enoch had he been so conflicted. If that day had changed him, last night had cast it in iron. The savagery he'd once feared would reach Eden had arrived. And it had only taken seventy years to get here. Even the murders covering the elimination of the sons of the elders couldn't match this level of ruthlessness.

Like many a soldier, he'd taken his share of lives, but only in pursuit of the military objective. Those killed had died in battle with a weapon in their hand. And under his command, the torture or mistreatment of prisoners had been strictly forbidden—Bohar being the sole exception. His sadistic predilections had remained a constant source of angst for him.

But last night had amounted to nothing more than a government-sponsored mass execution. Bohar was right. It had been a slaughter of blind sheep, unarmed men fleeing straight into the blades of the soldiers who waited for them in ambush.

262

Most of all, he was disappointed his friendship with Malluch hadn't been enough to talk him out of the massacre.

The sun rising in the east told Shechem he'd been walking all night, although it wasn't the light that stirred his interest in the sky. Two large owls, flying side by side, headed toward him from northwest to southeast. He'd seen the occasional owl before, but never two flying together and never out in the open away from the cover of the forest. They passed overhead and continued until they were out of sight.

Since it was too late to return to bed, he grabbed something to eat, then stopped by the garrison before heading to the palace. Malluch and Bohar were conversing in the great hall when he arrived.

"I still don't understand why you didn't just have the traitors killed along with the others," Bohar said. "They were caught in the act of helping the slaves escape, and there was nothing the elders could do about it. Ten to one they're the same ones destroying our gods."

Malluch shook his finger. "You must learn to resist the desire for immediate gratification, my friend. Tempting as it was to have killed them, I think they will serve a much better purpose for us alive."

"How's that?"

"Dead men cease to have value. But alive, they offer a tangible asset we can use to bargain with against the elders. I suspect the vandalizing of our gods will diminish greatly with these eight in prison."

"Well, maybe. But I would have gladly sacrificed two or three for the sake of aggravation alone."

"Fear not, my friend. The day will come when they will have outlived their usefulness. Should you wish, on that day you may participate in their demise."

The door opened into the great hall and a guard peeking his head through interrupted their discussion. "What is it?" Malluch said.

"Forgive me, my lord, but I have news for you."

"Speak."

The guard stepped inside and closed the door behind him. "It's about one of the elders."

"Which one?"

"Lamech."

Malluch rolled his eyes. "What now?"

"He's dead."

The mouths of the three men dropped open. "What happened?" Shechem said.

"His servant told my captain he died in his sleep."

"Thank you guard," Malluch said. "You're dismissed."

He grabbed both men behind the neck and led them toward a table containing a pitcher and gold goblets. "I'm not usually one for wine this early in the morning, but this calls for a celebration."

"A big one," Bohar said.

Shechem wasn't so sure.

* * *

Three days later, Shechem and Bohar packed their horses outside the garrison along with twelve hundred foot soldiers and one hundred cavalrymen. Malluch hadn't wasted any time ordering the immediate securing of replacements for Eden's slain slave force. "Did you take my advice and satisfy your appetite for a woman last night?" Shechem said.

"Not to brag. But I had two. Why do you ask?"

"Because I don't want to have to remind you we're on a campaign to obtain slaves. You remember what happened before?"

Bohar twisted his mouth. "That was ages ago."

"Uh huh."

264

The attention of both men was drawn to a commotion coming toward them on the main street in front of the garrison. "Look out!" a man in shepherd's garb chasing two camels said. "Runaway camels."

The animals ran toward them traveling north to south, causing people to scatter from both sides of the street.

The commander, Bohar, and another thirty soldiers moved out to the street for a better look. In the distance, the shepherd stopped in the middle of the road to lean against his staff while his two camels raced through the south gate.

"What was that?" Bohar said.

"I don't know," Shechem said. "Something must have frightened them."

CHAPTER 48

In the 600th year of Noah . . .

Ham's heel struck a bucket of hot preservative while applying it to the inside of the hull on the middle deck. "Best be careful, son." Noah moved closer to where his son was working on scaffolding erected to access the higher sections of the ark's interior. "I doubt if the women below would appreciate a shower of pitch today."

Shiphrah and Ariel looked up from the deck directly beneath them. "No, we wouldn't," Shiphrah said.

After almost a hundred years, they were on the last leg of the ark's construction. But the harvesting of sap needed to cover inside and out a structure this size had proven a monumental task in itself. Thousands of trees had been required—mostly pine, birch, and spruce—from which sap was extracted and converted into the water-resistant protectant. He and his sons had hand forged out of bronze nearly a hundred utensils: ladles and buckets for collection, and pans for production and refinement.

They could not afford to spare a drop. So before returning to work, he slid Ham's bucket a half cubit closer to the hull. "I'm moving this away from the edge, son."

"All right, Father." Only Ham never took his eyes off the place where he'd been working. Nine parts later, he stepped back again,

266

only this time his heel struck the bucket with enough force to knock it over.

"Ariel!" Noah yelled.

Ariel stared directly up into the falling tar.

Shiphrah had already launched herself through the air, striking Ariel in the torso and driving her out of the way. Pitch splashed onto Shiphrah's left calf and she screamed.

The two men vaulted down the scaffolding to the two women sprawled on the deck safely out of the way of the pool of resin. Noah, uncertain of an injury to Ariel, reached her first. "Are you all right?"

Though still dazed, she managed a single nod of her head.

He moved to Shiphrah, taking her injured leg in his hands while Ham comforted her. She winced in pain. Though the splatter was considerable, it could have been much worse. "This will be a bit uncomfortable, but we've got to get it off before it hardens."

"Go ahead." Shiphrah sucked air through clenched teeth.

"Hold onto her," he said to Ham.

Noah reached for one of several cloths they had handy for spills and tore it in half. He wrapped the one just below the burn to her calf, then wiped the dark substance onto it with the other. The skin beneath shone bright vermillion, but some of the preservative remained. "I'm sorry, but we can't leave any of it on your leg."

"Just do it," Shiphrah said and buried her head into Ham's chest.

He made three more passes across the burn, the last prompting her to cry out. "That's it," he said. "Let's get you back to the house."

Ham lifted her into his arms and headed for the up ramp, while his father helped Ariel to her feet. "Why?" she yelled after them.

Ham spun around, and Shiphrah raised her head.

"You risked your life for *me*?" Ariel said.

Shiphrah just smiled before falling back against her husband, who carried her briskly up the ramp.

Ariel stood with her mouth agape and looked at Noah. "I don't understand."

He put his arm around her and led her away. "Do you really need to? Maybe you should consider the possibility you may have misjudged her all these years."

For the first time in a hundred years, he saw real hope for reconciliation between his two daughters-in-law. Ariel's attitude toward Shiphrah since her marriage to Ham, though less vocal, hadn't changed much. From Noah's perspective, there had remained a quiet resentment lurking beneath the surface. Could this near tragedy be the impetus to finally soften Ariel's heart? "Praise God, let it be so," he whispered.

"What was that?'

"Nothing, daughter. Just thinking out loud."

* * *

"How is she?" Noah said.

Six days after the accident, he and Miryam hovered over a bedridden Shiphrah. Despite applying a salve of oil, aloe leaves, and beeswax to the burn on her leg, it had become swollen and red. Miryam removed her hand from the girl's forehead. "Hot. Ham and Ariel better return soon."

Shiphrah's fever started two days following her injury, and she was unable to make it out of bed the next. When her temperature failed to respond to the application of cold, wet cloths to her forehead, wrists, and ankles, Miryam insisted on a physician. Ham volunteered to find one, but Ariel surprised everyone by demanding to go with him. Noah suggested they begin their search in the local village where they obtained supplies. That was three days ago, and still they hadn't returned.

"If they're not back by tonight—"

The door opened abruptly. Ham and Ariel entered the house followed by an elderly man with unkempt white hair and a scraggly beard. He wore a crimson tunic and hunched as he walked.

"Father," Ham said. "This is Jubal. He's—"

"Where's the girl?" Jubal's voice was raspy but strong.

Noah and Ham followed behind Miryam, who led the man to Shiphrah's room. Jubal stopped and pointed to Miryam. "Just you. The rest, out."

Two hundred seventy parts later, Miryam came out with a small leather pouch containing herbs from which she prepared a broth for Shiphrah. She rejoined the physician for another short period before the two came out together.

"What's wrong with her?" Ham said, his face drawn.

"She has an infection from that burn on her leg."

"Will she be all right?"

"I wish I could say. The infection is what's causing the fever."

"Isn't there anything you can do?"

"Only what I've already done, which isn't much. She'll live now or she'll die. It's up to her."

Ham took a step back. He pushed past his family and into his and Shiphrah's room.

"Continue to change the dressing on her leg at least once a day," Jubal said to Miryam. "More if there's a discharge. Keep applying the cold water cloths. And give her the herbal brew three times daily. It will help with the fever."

"Thank you, sir," Noah said. "My eldest here will escort you home."

"I've got a mule outside. I can find my way. And that ark you've built makes a good reference point. It's practically due north from where I live."

After Jubal left, Noah entered Ham and Shiphrah's room to find his son on his knees next to the bed with his forehead touching her arm. He sobbed.

"Son."

"You heard what the physician said, Father? She could live or die."

"I heard."

"I can't believe it. After what you went through to bring her back, to think I could lose her to something as simple as an infection."

"You're not going to lose her. You must have faith."

Ham drew up a sniffle. "Faith. What's it look like? Can you show it to me?"

Like his brothers before him, age had robbed Ham of the innocence of his childhood faith. He had exchanged his wide-eyed belief in the Almighty for a pragmatic skepticism of anything he couldn't experience with his senses. Now, when he needed a spiritual pillar to lean on, it wasn't there. *Can you show it to me?* Noah knelt beside his son to pray.

* * *

Noah's sleep was broken. Miryam had just returned to bed from changing Shiphrah's wet cloths, a task she shared throughout the night with Ariel and Elisheva.

"It will be light soon," he said. "Any change?"

"No. She's still sweltering."

The shadow of someone entering the room startled them both, something none of his sons would ever do without asking permission. Not until the figure reached their bed did he recognize his last born. "What is it?" Noah said.

"It's Shiphrah. She stopped breathing."

CHAPTER 49

Shechem watched the sunrise from the north bank of an unknown river south of Eden where he and his men had chosen to camp. Across from him, a scene played out that made him envious.

A woman washed clothes in the river while her toddler son played in the grass a few cubits behind her. The boy seemed fascinated with the small block of wood someone had fashioned into a small boat. It reminded Shechem of a time when he was a young father and his two daughters had to depend upon him.

He longed for those days.

It had been four years since Lamech died, two since they'd completed replacing all of the massacred slaves. After that, two things never happened again: the elders never mentioned the slaves, and Eden's gods were never vandalized. The second was undoubtedly a consequence of the elder's sons being imprisoned— Malluch had correctly predicted that one. But the first, Shechem was certain, resulted from Lamech's absence of leadership.

Of all the elders, Lamech had been the most annoying pebble in Malluch's sandal. He also happened to be the grandfather of the man who'd stolen his best friend's first love. Despite these shortcomings, Shechem couldn't bring himself to hate the man.

More than once during the murders, he'd offered to help and was the only one who seemed to know they weren't coincidental.

Lamech had not only served as the elders' spokesman, but was also the driving force behind the campaign to release the slaves. If Methuselah was the patriarchs' head, Lamech had been their heart.

Shechem's thoughts were interrupted when Bohar and two of his closest allies approached. "What are you doing down here, Commander?" Bohar said. "Going swimming?"

"I was enjoying a peaceful moment alone."

"Great. Looks like we're just in time to ruin it for you."

The commander chuckled and shook his head.

Across the river, the woman rung the water out of her clothes and placed them in a reed basket. She scanned the river again before moving up the bank, leaving her son to play in the grass. She headed for a cypress tree twenty cubits away near the crest of the bank where more clothes hung from its branches. Her steps appeared labored by the incline and the weight of the basket.

Movement in the water diverted Shechem's attention. A pair of eyes and a long, dark snout floated to the surface and moved with stealth toward the boy onshore. They were joined by a second pair of eyes, behind which thrashed great reptilian tails that propelled them both toward land.

On the river bank, the child remained fixated on the toy, oblivious to the impending danger.

"Hey, look at that," Bohar said to his two companions. "I'll take the one on the left. Five silver shekels he reaches the boy first."

"Reaches or eats?" said the first companion.

"Let's make it the first one to bite him, because after that they're going to fight each other ripping him apart."

"It's a bet. I'll take the one on the right."

"Me too," the second man said. "Five shekels on the one on the right."

Heartless. Shechem shouted at the woman, who turned in time to see the approaching predators.

272

"What are you doing?" Bohar said. "You'll spoil the wager."

Screaming her son's name, she dropped the basket and ran back to the bank, arriving just when the crocodiles broke from the water onto shore. They were five cubits from her when she kneeled to gather her son in her arms. She stood to run, but froze when she saw the crocodiles. The woman closed her eyes and pulled her son tight against her bosom.

"Same bet for the woman?" Bohar said.

Both companions nodded.

Shechem waded into the river, yelling at the reptiles and striking the water with his sword, but they continued toward the boy and his mother. In desperation, he threw his sword, which landed several cubits away from its intended targets.

When the pair of crocodiles got within a cubit of the woman's feet, they split, as if moved by an invisible divining rod. They passed on either side of her, continuing up the riverbank. The woman, still clutching the child to her chest, remained motionless so that the tail of the croc passing on her left brushed across the top of her foot and ankle.

The crocodiles crested the incline, continuing southeast and disappearing in the tall grass.

"Did you see that?" Bohar said.

"Yes," the second companion said while the first just shook his head, mouth ajar.

"They must not have been hungry."

"Or they had someplace to go," Shechem said.

"Someplace to go? Where outside of a river would two crocs go?"

Shechem didn't answer, but he'd seen and heard too much over the past few years to continue to accept it for coincidence. The owls. The camels. The stories told by a dozen others concerning the strange behavior of animals moving through the region. Always in pairs, and always moving toward the south.

Now these crocs.

"Too bad his mother got there in time," Bohar said. "Someplace to go or not, there's no way those crocs would have passed on that boy had he stayed within range."

* * *

Noah's family gathered around the bed where Shiphrah lay motionless. All attempts to revive her—calling out, shaking her body, slapping her face—had proven ineffective. Noah stooped for a closer look and placed his ear against her breast. It was silent. And yet, when he touched her arm it was still quite warm.

He gestured to Miryam. "Would you take everyone in the other room?"

"I'm staying," Ham said.

"Please," he said. "There's nothing more you can do."

Japheth put his arm around his brother. "Come on, Ham."

When the room cleared, Noah knelt beside Shiphrah and slowly scanned the length of her body. He slammed a clenched fist on the bed next to her. "Lord." Pushing the pronunciation through gritting teeth, he bit down on his tongue to keep from uttering his true feelings. The sorrow and confusion of the moment had been overshadowed by a much stronger emotion—anger. Anger at God. *After all You've done to protect her, how could You take her from us now?*

He took her hand in his, but couldn't bring himself to pray. Instead, he allowed his mind to wander, all the way back to their first meeting in Eden's square. Here was this naïve young woman dressed to look much older than she was, holding onto the false belief she'd been brought there to find a husband. Bereft of a daughter of his own, she'd stolen his heart immediately. Then later that evening, the knock at the door that had changed all their lives.

One by one, recollections of Shiphrah's life among them unfolded onto his consciousness like the images in a dream, images

274

of her beauty, kindness, and courage. As they played across his mind, he was reminded how blessed they were to have had her for the time they did. Gradually, his anger subsided, and with each successive memory subsided a little more. When the hint of a smile tugged at the corners of his mouth, he was ready to go to God.

Near the end of his petition, he asked the Lord to forgive his anger and to grant him the wisdom to understand His will. His last request was for the strength to comfort his family in light of Shiphrah's death. At that moment, a drop of moisture struck the heel of the hand holding hers. He opened his eyes to the morning's light reflecting off the other droplets spotting her arm.

He pushed her hair aside. Beads of sweat streamed from her forehead, down her cheeks, and onto her neck.

Slowly, her chest rose and fell.

"Ham," he shouted.

CHAPTER 50

Shechem and Bohar waited for the governor in the great hall. In usual fashion, Bohar helped himself to food set out on the table for their leader.

"Good morning, my friends," Malluch said, entering the hall. "I trust I didn't keep you waiting long."

"Interminably," Bohar said with bread crumbs flying out of his mouth.

Malluch laughed, but Shechem was surprised Bohar even knew the meaning of the word. "Such a sense of humor," he said. "How was your latest campaign?"

"Fine, except Shechem ruined my bet on the way back."

"And how did he do that?"

"Ah, he shouted at some woman to come save her child just as two crocs were about to eat him."

"Sounds thrilling."

"It could have been." Bohar scowled at Shechem.

"Perhaps next time. But onto more pressing matters. You're aware I just returned from Enoch last night?"

"Of course," Shechem said. "Were you able to win the prince over to your way of thinking?"

"I took with us a tribute of one hundred talents of gold, three hundred talents of silver, and two hundred horses."

Bohar's eyebrows raised. "That's some tribute."

"Unfortunately, it wasn't enough. He turned me down."

Eating a pear down to the core, Bohar spit a seed that bounced across the table onto the floor. "Really? I never thought he'd run scared."

"What about the families of those Enochites slain?" Shechem said. "Have they given up?"

"Not a mite's worth," Malluch said. "I know some who have hounded the prince every day for the past 120 years. But he won't budge."

"I don't know what all the fuss is about," Bohar said. "From what you've told me, it's just one man we're talking about, right?"

"Somewhat more than a man, I'd say," Shechem said. "By himself he managed to destroy our entire company."

"Of what, twenty-six, twenty-seven men? But against the combined armies of Enoch and Eden? No one man, or angel, or whatever he is could withstand a legion of twenty thousand men."

"My friends," Malluch said. "I'm afraid the prince's rejection of our request makes the point moot. It's clear he's unwilling to risk the welfare of his army, not even for the prospect of eternal life. It's time to move on."

"So what are we going to do?"

"Eden's army will go it alone."

Bohar threw both fists in the air. "Yes! Finally."

"Commander, I want you to draw up a battle plan for a campaign to the garden."

After 120 years of planning and waiting, Malluch's patience had run out. The time had come for him to complete his revenge. "For how many men?"

"The full contingent."

277

"Five thousand men? Surely, my lord, we can accomplish our objective without calling out our whole army."

"Perhaps, but I'm not taking any chances. Remember, we're going there not only seeking the tree of life, but to take vengeance on the creature who destroyed my family."

"All right. Do you have a timetable in mind?" Shechem's stomach tensed, part in anticipation, part in apprehension.

"Soon. But I'm far more interested in the details of your plan than in how quickly you can put one together. I've waited over a hundred years. I can wait a little longer."

Shechem nodded and walked toward the exit.

"Just don't make it too long," Malluch said.

* * *

Noah jogged down the left side of the ark to where Shem was applying pitch to the hull from scaffolding fifteen cubits above the ground. When he arrived, Shem wore the same expression he had as a child when he brought home his first firefly. Strange how after 429 years, the memory remained fresh in his mind. "Father, can you come up here? I want you to see this."

Shem swatted at something above his head, and continued flailing until his father reached him. "What are you waving at?"

"Bees. Hornets. I don't know, but they've been buzzing around here all morning."

Noah heard a buzzing in his left ear, and followed the sound around to his right.

"See, there it is again." Shem waved once more.

"Will you stop for a moment?"

"You don't want to get stung, do you?"

"They're not bees or hornets."

"What are they?"

278

"Well, if you stop waving for a part, we might be able to see them. Now be still."

The two men sat motionless on the scaffolding. When the buzzing returned, Noah nodded for Shem to look to his left. Two small green bodies about the size of locusts floated in the air in front of them, their wings a blur because they beat at such great speed. They had needle-like noses, and when one lifted its head while hovering, it exposed a bright ruby throat.

"I don't remember ever seeing one of these before." Shem moved closer to the hovering creatures. Or maybe I have and never paid attention to them. But you're right, Father. They're not bees. At least not any kind of bee I've ever seen."

"Hummingbirds."

"They're a bird?"

"I believe so."

"Small for a bird. But the name sure fits."

"Indeed. Now what did you summon me for?"

"Oh, yes. Right. Remember, Father, when the Lord told you to build the ark out of gopherwood? Only gopherwood? And how I groused about why it made any difference?

"Both events remain clear in my memory."

"Well, I think I know why. Watch this."

Shem dipped a pole with a sheepskin brush on the end into a bucket of hot pitch and slid it along the outside of the hull. Not a drop of pitch ran down the side but was absorbed immediately into the wood the way water sinks into sand.

He took the pole and touched the brush to a piece of scaffolding. This time the pitch adhered to the wood, but the excess dripped off the sides of the timber.

"Do you know why?" Noah bent to examine the hull.

"It's oak," Shem said, grinning. "We made the shoring out of ash and oak trees."

He slapped Shem on the back, only to have the joy of their discovery cut short by the women calling for help.

279

They hurried down the shoring to the other side of the ark. Ham and Japheth met them at the top of the hill and together the four men and the lioness ran to the house. When they arrived, Ariel, Shiphrah, and Elisheva, their faces pallid, pointed to the doorway where a man held a knife to Miryam's throat. "That's far enough," he said. "Unless you want me to start carving her head off right here."

Noah searched his daughters' faces.

"He came in through one of the back-bedroom windows," Elisheva said. "Before we knew what was happening, he grabbed mother and ordered us outside."

Noah eyed the lioness. *Where's your mate?* "What do you want?"

"Justice." The man holding Miryam, naked from the waist up, was deeply tanned and had a closely-trimmed, gray beard. "For my son."

"Who is your son?"

The man pointed the knife toward the ark. "He and four others died on the other side of that hill seventy years ago. At your hand."

Japheth had warned about the men they'd killed that night having relatives. And at least one of them had a good memory. "A long time ago."

"For my wife and me, it was yesterday."

"You said you wanted justice."

"Yes. These are your sons?"

"They are."

"Choose one."

"What for?"

"Like I said. Justice. A son of yours for one of mine. You're going to kill one of your sons right now or watch your wife die."

Miryam struggled, but the man maintained his grip.

"I'm responsible for your son's death," Noah said. "Let my wife go, and I'll surrender to you."

280

The man shook his head. "It won't go that easy for you. Your own death would be too quick. You and your wife are going to suffer the way we've suffered. For a lifetime. A bit more painful perhaps, because you killed him yourself, but a fair trade nonetheless."

"No, Father," Japheth said. He and his brothers drew their swords and moved toward the house.

The man dragged Miryam outside the door. "Take another step, and I'll slit her throat. Drop those swords."

They froze, but held onto their weapons.

"I mean it." The man pulled Miryam's head back and pushed the knife blade against the skin of her throat.

Three swords hit the ground.

"There, they just made it easy for you," the man said. "Pick up the sword next to the son you've chosen and run him through. I'll let your wife go."

"I'm going to kill you," Japheth said.

"Not if I get there first," Shem said.

"One of you may indeed kill me, but not before one of your brothers or your mother lies bleeding in the dirt." He addressed Noah. "You've got nine parts to pick up a sword and do as I told you or your wife dies."

Noah's attention was drawn to the male lion exiting the woods at the rear of the house and heading toward them. Should he say anything? If he did, what would the man do? Would he panic and hurt Miryam?

"There's a lion coming up the side of the house."

The man smiled. "You mean like the one standing next to you?"

"I should warn you, it's my wife's lion."

"Three parts."

When the lion rounded the corner, the man swung Miryam around to face him. Shiphrah grabbed one of the dropped swords and threw it, the blade plunging deep into the man's left thigh. In pain, he yelled out, releasing his hostage. The lion bolted toward him, and he tried to raise the knife to defend himself, but the cat

281

was already in the air. The man screamed again when the lion leveled him and ripped into his throat, the lioness bounding over to join her mate for the kill.

Meanwhile, the three brothers surrounded Shiphrah, congratulating her. "I know the Marauders taught you a few things, but that was amazing," Shem said. "Japheth. Have you ever seen anyone throw a sword like that?"

"I've never even *heard* of anyone throwing a sword like that."

Noah and Miryam pulled the lions off once they were sure the man was dead. "Where have you been?" he said to the lion.

"I think he was answering a call to nature," Elisheva said.

Several cats and some of the other carnivores wandered down the hill and took up positions near the body. The wolves moved to within seventy cubits, pacing and licking their lips. One of the crows flew in, landed on the man's shoulder, and cawed.

"We'd better bury him quickly before we have a riot on our hands," Japheth said.

"Why bother?" Shem said. "The wolves and jackals will just dig him up."

Japheth approached the two jaguars and smacked them each on the rump, chasing them back up the hill. "Go on. Get out of here."

"Shem, Ham," Noah said. "Wrap his body in canvas, load it on a cart, and take it at least eight furlongs from here before you bury it."

The two brothers picked up their swords and headed for the house. Meanwhile, two jackals joined the wolves in pacing.

"But just in case, better make sure your hole is at least four cubits deep," he said.

282

CHAPTER 51

The next morning, Shechem and his twenty captains sat around a table in the garrison to discuss plans for the campaign. A knock on the door was followed by a guard entering the room. "Excuse me, Commander."

"What is it?"

"One of the patriarchs has asked to see you."

"Show him in."

"I'm sorry, Commander. He asked that you come to his house."

"What for?"

"He's dying."

"Who?"

"Methuselah."

Shechem rode to Methuselah's house, located in the oldest section of the city just north of the palace. When he entered the room, the eldest of the patriarchs lay on a bed surrounded by his sons and daughters. At 969 years, he had a full head of white hair and a long matching beard that rested on top of the blanket covering him. But his face was gaunt, his eyes sunken. He looked tired.

Still, he had enough strength left to raise his hand and dismiss his children. He motioned for Shechem to come closer. "Commander," he said, his voice raspy and slow. "Soon, I go the way of my fathers." He coughed twice. "My son, Lamech, said you were a man of striking contradiction."

Shechem didn't know exactly what he meant by this or how to respond, so he simply nodded.

"He was convinced you had nothing to do with Malluch's ruse to cover the murders of our sons. He also said he respected you because you had opposed the massacre of the slaves."

This surprised Shechem, who because of his standing in the regime had assumed Lamech considered him complicit in the cover-up. How he knew of his opposition to the slaves being massacred, he had no idea. "Is that why you summoned me, to tell me this?"

"No." Methuselah coughed violently five times, wheezing to catch his breath. "There's a rumor Malluch is planning a return to the garden."

"We leave tomorrow."

"I advise you not to go, Commander. He who guards the entrance is not of this earth."

"I've met him."

"Yes, you have. And you know what happened to those who were with you."

"We were but twenty-five then. Now we are five thousand."

"Five thousand or fifty thousand won't make any difference against an angel of God."

"Malluch doesn't believe in angels."

"A skepticism that cost his father and brother their lives, along with all the others."

"What do you want from me?"

"To save your life. If only for a short while."

"If you're talking about the garden, save your brea—"

"You have two daughters?"

"Yes, but they moved with their husbands to villages south of the city years ago."

"Go to them. Take them and their families to the mountains to the north. Repent to the Lord and savor the time you have left with them."

Shechem had a lot to repent for, but it was too late for him. "Why?"

Methuselah lifted his arm and swept it across his body in an arc. "Three months from now, there won't be a dry stone onto which you may set your foot."

"A flood?"

Methuselah struggled to breathe. "More than a flood. A calamity."

This wasn't the first time Shechem had heard this. Years ago, a story had surfaced about a farmer in the south who'd predicted a great flood. But it was soon dismissed, like so many other fables. "Who told you this?"

"The Lord showed it to me in a dream."

Could the senility of old age and the nearness of death have affected Methuselah's mind? "I'm sorry, but I can't leave now." He gave him a final glance. "But I appreciate your concern."

"You know she's betrayed you."

The commander spun to find Methuselah straining to prop himself up on one elbow, his eyes set firmly beneath bushy silver eyebrows. Shechem knew exactly who he was referring to.

"With whom?"

Methuselah collapsed on the bed, fighting for each word. "You know him, but—" He let out a long, slow exhale. His chest did not rise again.

Shechem leaned over the expired patriarch. "Who?" He grabbed Methuselah by the shoulders, lifting him off the bed, only to have his head loll back against the pillow. "Who is it?"

285

Methuselah's family returned to the room. "He's gone, Commander," one of the sons said. "Please allow us to tend to our father's body."

He gently lowered Methuselah back onto the bed.

* * *

On the ride back to the garrison, Methuselah's last words tormented Shechem. If only the dying elder had fought for one more breath, he could have revealed the name of his wife's lover. A selfish thought, but it would have put an end to his lingering search.

No matter. Whatever insight into Claudia's infidelity the patriarch had been given, Shechem was convinced now more than ever her lover was the silk merchant. Methuselah had confirmed his betrayer was known to him. Who else but the silk merchant?

The only thing left to decipher from the old man's dying words was what the elder intended to communicate in the last part of the sentence. "You know him, but—" What did the "but" mean? Was there some warning about the person Methuselah felt compelled to share? Or maybe he meant to tell him not to look at someone so obvious. Could she have had more than one lover?

Whatever it was, he would take care of the man or men immediately upon his return from the campaign to the garden.

* * *

Gasping for air, Ariel pushed through Noah and Japheth standing in the doorway of the ark, ran down the ramp, and headed for the house. "Daughter," Noah said after her. A moment later, Shem charged up the ramp from the deck below to join his father and brother at the door.

"What's wrong with Ariel?" Japheth said.

"She says she can't breathe," Shem said.

His father and brother shared a dazed look. "Well, if she can't breathe, what's she running for?" Japheth said.

Shem pointed inside the ark. "She can't breathe in *there*."

"Do you know why?"

"She has this fear about being in enclosed areas. I learned about it years ago before we were married. One day we were walking in the hills and got caught in a thunderstorm. I found this cave, so we went in to wait out the storm. Well, we had barely gotten inside when Ariel panicked."

"What did she do?"

"She ran out of the cave and refused to go back in. I grabbed her and ushered her under a nearby tree until the storm passed."

"Father, this isn't good," Japheth said.

"What are you saying?" Shem said.

"I'm saying it could be dangerous having someone who's afraid of confined spaces on board the ark."

Shem grit his teeth, his nostrils flaring. "What do you suggest? Leave her behind?"

"We may have to."

Shem punched Japheth in the jaw, knocking him back a step onto the ramp, then tackled his brother so that the two rolled down the incline. When they reached the bottom, they continued to punch each other in the grass. Noah ran after them, calling their names and ordering them to stop, but the two brothers fought on.

Japheth gained the advantage over his smaller brother, resting on his rib cage while the two exchanged blows. Noah grabbed him with an arm around his neck. "All right, son. That's enough."

He shook Noah off, causing him to lose his balance and fall backwards, striking his back against the edge of the ramp. Shooting pain raced up his spine, and he cried out.

The two brothers rushed to aid their father. "Are you all right, Father?" Japheth said.

287

He found it difficult to speak through the excruciating pain. But what worried him more was the strange numbness in his legs. "I can't move."

Noah lay tied to a plank of wood next to his bed in the hopes immobilizing him would help reduce the inflammation in his back. It was an uncomfortable position that'd made it difficult to sleep, but it had relieved some of the pain. Three days had passed since his injury, and still he was unable to move his legs.

As they'd done for each morning of those three days, his sons entered the room to greet their father and receive his instruction for the day's work. Japheth had a swollen lip and Shem a black eye.

"Good morning, my sons."

Shem shot Japheth an accusatory glare.

"Is there anything we can get you today, Father?" Ham said.

"Thank you, but that won't be necessary. Your mother and your wives have pampered me like a newborn. How much of the ark is there left to pitch?"

"We're finished with the inside," Shem said. "And we probably have about a third of the outside remaining."

"Splendid," Noah said. "Sounds as if you've made excellent progress without me." Japheth shuffled his feet. "All right. No solemn faces. You three still have a lot of work to do. I'll be back to work before you know it." None of them looked up. "Get going now."

Shem and Ham walked out, but their brother stayed behind and kneeled next to the bed.

"Father, I—I—" Japheth had trouble swallowing. "I don't have the words to say how sorry I am."

Noah put a hand on his son's knee. "Don't you think I know that? It was an accident."

"Yes, but my fighting with Shem wasn't. I shouldn't have said what I did to rile him."

"Perhaps. But it's over now."

288

"What happened between Shem and I may be over, but the consequences aren't. You can't walk."

"I can't walk because I'm injured. When the injury heals, I'm sure I'll be fine."

"What if it doesn't?"

"If that's YAH's will for me, then when the ark is ready, you and your brothers can carry me onboard like one of the lambs."

Japheth tried to force a smile.

"Go on. Your brothers are waiting."

Noah had put on his best face for them, even though the way he felt now could mean he would never walk again. But even being a cripple wasn't the foremost thing on his mind. It was the implication of Shem's revelation concerning Ariel. Could she survive being trapped inside the ark for an indefinite period? She had escaped the fear of the cave, but only by fleeing from it. If she couldn't adapt to life inside the ark, there would be no place for her to run.

CHAPTER 52

"Ah, come in, Commander," Malluch said when Shechem entered the great hall, clasping him on the shoulder. "How are the preparations going?"

"Very well, my lord. My captains and I met for over six hours yesterday discussing strategies."

"Good, good. I wish there was a way to share with you my excitement. After 120 years."

"It's written on your face."

Bohar entered the room, eating an overripe banana. "Good morning, my lord. Commander. Did you hear a man was found drowned last night in one of the eastern winepress vats? If I had to drown, that'd be my beverage of choice."

Shechem shook his head, not in answer to Bohar's question, but in pity for the dead man.

"By the way, Commander," Malluch said. "Do you remember that story we heard some years ago, something about a man building a boat in the desert?"

"More than a boat. The story was this farmer and his three sons were building this massive ark on the plain. Somewhere in the south, wasn't it, Bohar?"

290

He laughed. "Yes. He said some great flood was coming to cover the earth."

"How long ago was that?" Malluch said.

"It's got to be close to a hundred years now." Shechem said. "Why?"

"Well, my wife said she overheard some of the women servants talking about it just yesterday. They'd heard it from some merchants who'd come from the south."

"Old news," Bohar said.

"Do you think there could be anything to it?" Malluch said.

"Anything to what? If there was a flood coming, it would have been here by now."

What a strange coincidence for them to be discussing the flood, especially since Methuselah mentioned it on his death bed only yesterday.

"Well, there must be something to a rumor that's lasted a hundred years," Malluch said.

"Just a bunch of old palace hens telling tales," Bohar said.

"Look into it, will you, Commander?"

Shechem and Bohar exchanged identical looks of surprise, but Malluch's stoic expression told them he was serious. "Very well, my lord. I'll take care of it as soon as we get back from the expedition to the garden."

"I would like you to leave today."

"Today?" Bohar said. "But what about our plans for the campaign?"

"I'm postponing the campaign until the commander completes this assignment."

"What—"

"That will be all, my friends."

Bohar, jaw hanging, clenched a fist but before he could say another word, Shechem grabbed him by the upper arm and pulled him toward the door. "Let's go."

The commander maintained a grip on the door handle after they exited the great hall, watching Bohar storm up the hallway toward his quarters. When he'd rounded the corner, Shechem re-entered the hall and approached the governor, who had his back to him. The two men stood in silence for what seemed a long time.

"My friend," Malluch said.

"Yes, my lord."

"How typical of you to return, even to defy my order dismissing you, because you perceive I am troubled."

"Yes, my lord."

"I suppose it's why you've remained my closest confidant all these years. Sometimes I don't even think my wife knows me as well." He paused. "I didn't want to say this in front of Bohar, but they've come back again."

"The nightmares?"

"Yes. Of my father and brother. And the fire. They were gone for the longest time. Sixty years. But in the past few months they've returned."

"I'm sorry, my lord."

"More than anyone else, you know what I've been through. You were there. You watched them die too." He paused again. "And now, you must be wondering what this has to do with a one hundred-year-old rumor."

"I was curious."

Malluch placed his finger on the table and scratched the wood with his fingernail. "It was a mistake to let him go, Commander."

"Let who go?"

"The Preacher."

Shechem was taken aback. Malluch hadn't mentioned the Preacher in decades. "It troubles you after all these years?"

He nodded without looking up. "I didn't realize at the time how important it was for me to see him dead."

292

'I'm afraid I don't understand. His leaving all but destroyed his father and opened the door for you to take control of Eden."

"I know. But eliminating him would have accomplished the same thing, and I might not now be suffering these nightmares."

"You don't know that."

"Don't I? Did they not disappear for the longest time after the destruction of the traitors? What possible explanation could there be for their return other than that my vengeance is incomplete?"

"We don't even know for sure the river didn't take him that night."

"Six people and who knows how many livestock drown in the river and not a single one of them washes ashore? I don't think so, Commander."

"So what's all this have to do with the man building the ark?"

"It's him."

"Who?"

"The Preacher."

"It's just a rumor, my lord."

"Is it? The Preacher fled south from Eden nearly a hundred years ago. And this story. Did it not originate in the south a short time following his disappearance?

"It's like Bohar said. Superstitious prattle from a flock of old women."

"I wonder."

"Forget for a moment he's a mortal enemy. You and I both know he's not the kind of man to do something crazy like building a ship in the middle of nowhere."

The color drained from Malluch's face. "It's him, Commander. Don't ask me how I know. I just feel it."

Sensing his conviction, Shechem resigned himself to the inevitable. "What can I do to help?"

"Find out, Commander. One way or the other."

"And if the story is true and it is him?"

293

"I want him alive. Take all the men you need to help deal with his sons, but bring the Preacher back alive."

Shechem headed out.

"A final thought, Commander. I know you think I send you on a fool's errand. But keep in mind that if you do find him, you'll find her."

Elisheva. Shechem smiled and offered a short bow of gratitude.

* * *

Shechem had trouble believing what his eyes were telling him. But there it was — a massive ship built atop a small hill in the middle of a plain. He and his squad of fifteen men had located the gigantic structure in the southern wilderness 1280 furlongs from Eden nine days after their departure. Now, using an adjacent forest for cover, they moved quietly up the wood line for a closer look.

Hundreds of animals surrounded the ark. Elephants, rhinoceroses, gazelle, wildebeests, and every kind of predator cat imaginable occupied the hill and nearby grassy areas. As did a considerable number of smaller mammals. Above him and his men, the trees teemed with more birds than he would ever have expected in an area of forest this size. *So this is where all those pairs of animals journeyed to. Why?*

Malluch's intuition had been correct. Shechem recognized the Preacher limping down the port side of the ark and a female lion walking several paces behind. Japheth, Shem, and a younger man entered and exited the ark via a ramp that stretched from the ground to the cargo door. Either the Preacher had sired another son since he'd been gone, or hired someone to help with the construction.

Shechem's attention shifted to a woman walking up the hill toward the ark, and his heart skipped a beat. If Elisheva had aged in the last century, he couldn't tell, at least not from this distance. She was just as lovely and shapely as he'd remembered. A sinking feeling swirled in the pit of his gut, the same one he had the first time he held her hand.

"What are we going to do, Commander?" one soldier said.

He pointed to where a pair of tigers and two brown bears passed each other going in opposite directions near the bottom of the hill. Closer to the ark, jaguars and hyenas did likewise. "What do you make of that, soldier?"

"Looks like their walking guard."

"I agree. Does anyone have a suggestion?"

"I have one, Commander," another soldier said. "Let's go home. We're going to need a whole lot more than the fifteen of us."

The remaining soldiers all nodded.

A part of Shechem wanted to stay in hopes he could devise a plan to get close enough to at least speak with Elisheva. But he estimated his chances of being torn to shreds by one or more of those predators were greater than getting anywhere near her.

CHAPTER 53

Striding toward the great hall, Shechem's thoughts were far away from the news he was about to report to Malluch. Instead, he was lost in a sentimental fog, thinking about his first sight of Elisheva in nearly a hundred years.

From that moment, he'd regressed to being a lovesick adolescent, unable to keep her out of his mind. All the way back to Eden, he fixated on her. At night, he dreamed about her. For the first time in his life, he even pondered the existence of the supernatural.

And why not? Finding Elisheva alive was the closest thing to a miracle he'd ever experienced. Someone who'd been dead to him for a hundred years had, in a moment of serendipity, been brought back to life.

"Good afternoon, Commander," Malluch said looking up from the long table where he was seated with Bohar. "Did you find him?"

"Yes, my lord."

"You're joking," Bohar said.

"And was it the Preacher?" Malluch said.

"Yes, my lord."

Malluch rose quickly from the table. "Well, where is he? Why haven't you brought him before me in chains?"

296

"We were unable to get close enough to capture him."

"Unable? What do you mean?"

"He was—uh—being protected."

"By who? Does he have his own army?"

"Of sorts." Shechem hesitated, unsure how to explain the animals.

"Well?"

"They're—they're beasts."

"Beasts?"

"Yes, my lord. The Preacher, his family, and the ark are surrounded by hundreds, maybe thousands, of beasts. Lions, bears, wolves, and every other kind of animal and bird you can think of. Even some I've never seen before."

"That's crazy," Bohar said.

"Yes, about as crazy as the story of a man building a boat in the desert."

"And you couldn't get near him?" Malluch said.

"Impossible. The beasts were everywhere. We saw pairs of tigers, jaguars, bears, even hyenas walking the perimeter, as though they were guarding the ark itself. And the Preacher had a lion that followed him wherever he limped."

"Limped?" Bohar said.

"Yes, he was hobbling along like he was eight hundred years old or something. And that lion was two paces behind."

Malluch paced the floor. When he stopped, he addressed Shechem directly. "Prepare your army, Commander. You leave for the southern territories tomorrow."

"South!" Bohar said. "What about the garden, the guardian, the tree of life?"

"They will be there waiting for us when you return. Remember what I said about the Preacher, Commander."

He nodded. "Alive. What do you want done with the ark?"

297

Malluch took a torch from the wall ten cubits from the table and stared into the flames. He grinned broadly before looking back to them. "It's made of wood, isn't it?"

* * *

Noah awoke to a dissonance of noise pouring in through their bedroom window. He rolled over to find Miryam lying on her back, eyes open. "Yes," she said. "I've been listening to that for about half an hour now."

"I heard it too, but thought it was part of a dream. What happened to the rooster?"

"I think he called in reinforcements."

He rose and walked to the window. In the forest next to them, thousands of birds in an array of colors flitted about the trees, each species singing its own song. In spite of the commotion, he was amazed by this display of beauty and song. God had filled His earth with an immeasurable variety of creatures, and now He was bringing them all together in one place.

He and Miryam met Ariel and Shiphrah in the main living area.

Shem studied the birds through the window. "Is it me, or did a whole lot more animals just arrive overnight?"

At least a half dozen new species of grazing animals fed in the fields and on the surrounding hills visible through the window. They were joined by an assortment of previously unseen small mammals. Even the creeping things appeared well represented, what with dozens of new breeds of serpents and other reptiles crawling along the ground. Animals that would normally prey on one another lay peacefully together only a few cubits apart.

Japheth walked into the room yawning, followed by Elisheva. "Do you hear the noise out there?" he said.

"You'd have to be deaf not to," Shem said.

"They're not going to make that racket in the ark, are they? If so, we'll never get any sleep."

"Not too many species sing at night." Noah said. "Some mockingbirds, whip-poor-wills, and owls. Maybe a few others. The rest should be fairly quiet."

Ham burst through the front door. "You should see it out there. They're everywhere."

"So your brother and I were just noticing."

"But you should really come take a look at some of these animals. I've never seen anything like them. There's this creature that resembles a spotted deer, only it's much larger and it has this really long neck. Taller than some of the trees out there."

"A giraffe, I think Adam called it."

"Then there are these two black and white striped horses."

"Zebra."

"Oh, and Japheth. Your crocs are here."

His brother turned to Elisheva. "Don't you dare," she said.

The men laughed.

"Father." Shem pointed to where five robins hopped along the ground looking for worms. "I thought there are only supposed to be two of every animal going into the ark."

"There are."

"Well, in addition to those five, I counted four pigeons and seven sparrows in the trees out back when I got up this morning."

"I can't explain it, son. Probably just coincidence."

"Who cares about the birds?" Ariel said. "What does all these animals showing up overnight mean?"

"I suspect it means we're running out of time," Noah said.

"What do we do?"

"We need to start gathering food for the ark. Today."

"All right, then," Japheth said. "Let's get to it." He opened the door and started to walk out.

"Watch it!" Elisheva said.

Japheth froze in mid-stride before his right foot came down on a pair of sand lizards crawling just outside the door.

"Careful, son," his father said. "From now on, we'll all need to watch where we step."

While Noah followed him out the door, questions about the sudden influx of animals danced in his head. When would the floodwaters come? This week? The next? If they came without warning, would there be time enough to get all the animals and his family on board the ark?

What if they came tonight?

CHAPTER 54

Shechem led his army to within a furlong of the ark, raising a hand to signal his captains of the command to halt. Fifty voices echoed across the plain, bringing to a stop five thousand foot soldiers and another three hundred men on horseback. Some of the men carried lighted torches.

He scanned the area, which seemed strangely quiet and devoid of all but a few grazing animals on the hill near the ark. Gone were the patrolling animals he'd seen only two weeks before. To the right of the ark, at the bottom of the hill, stood a large, yet modestly built stone house. Shechem faced his men. "Destroy the ark. Kill anyone or anything that tries to stop you. But bring the Preacher and the women to me alive."

Bohar's head snapped around. "Malluch didn't say anything about sparing the women, only the Preacher."

"I'm saying it. You have an objection?"

"It's your army, Commander. If you want to put their lives at risk to save a couple of women, that's your business."

"Yes. It is." Shechem whirled his horse around and lifted his arm to give the command to move. His captains cried out and the sound of marching feet filled the air in unison with the forward movement of the multitude.

* * *

Inside their house, the two lions paced back and forth beneath the living room window like a nervous father awaiting the arrival of his first child. Every few parts they let out a soft growl. Noah and his sons, armed with swords, stared out the window with the women behind.

"How many, you figure?" Japheth said.

"Five, maybe six thousand," Noah said.

"What do we do now?" Shem said.

"Maybe if we surrender, they'll spare our lives," Ariel said.

"Malluch didn't send five thousand men to take us captive," Miryam said. "No, they're here to destroy us and the ark."

"I'm afraid your mother is right," Noah said. "After waiting a hundred years, I doubt if Malluch's quest for vengeance could be placated by a plea for mercy now."

"What are we going to do?" Ariel said. "Surely, you don't expect to go out alone against five thousand?"

"We are not alone, my daughter. God Himself is the general Who will lead this battle."

"But how —"

Noah spoke with a forcefulness he had seldom used. "I tell you the truth. The sun will not set this day until Malluch's army is reduced to nothing."

Ariel's head snapped back at her father-in-law's words, but she remained silent.

Noah and his sons hugged their wives and started out the door, but had to wait when Ariel refused to let go of Shem. "Don't go." Her eyes filled with tears. He kissed her on the forehead and pulled himself away to join the others.

"Wait a part," Shiphrah said. Before anyone could say anything, she dashed into the other room and returned carrying a sword. "I'm going with you."

302

"Going with us, where?" Ham said. "Not out there, you're not."

"Look, this is no time for chivalry. You're going to need all the help you can get against that mob. I can handle myself." Shiphrah locked to Noah. "Father?"

'She's right son. She handles a sword like your brother does an ax. Remember the man seeking revenge?"

"All right, but stay close to me." Ham said.

"Right," Shiphrah said.

The female lion followed them out, but the male hesitated, stopping to look back at Miryam. "Go on," she said, shooing him with a backhand. "They need you more right now than I do." She closed the door behind him.

Noah, his sons, Shiphrah, and the two lions moved to a spot near the bottom of the rise leading up to the ark. There, they stood side by side to face the approaching army.

CHAPTER 55

Shechem watched Noah, his family, and the two lions take up a position between his army and the ark. Drawing ever closer, he considered the seven bodies lined up ahead. What was it that drove them to act so foolishly? A twinge of guilt at the prospect of having to crush their brave, but futile, gesture tugged at his heart.

Within a half furlong, he could make out the figure of a woman among the seven challengers. For a moment, his heart dropped at the possibility of it being Elisheva. Though he'd issued orders to the contrary, out here, in the uncertainty of open combat, he realized he might not be able to save her.

Two hundred cubits closer and still no movement from the seven creatures arrayed before them. Mystified, he raised his arm again to stop the march. What were they up to? Five people and two lions just standing there, ready to be mowed down. For a reason he didn't understand, a cold shiver raced down his back.

He detected movement on the ground and the rustling of grass as though blown by the wind.

Only the air was calm.

From a perimeter completely encircling his army, the grass parted in a pattern of hundreds of meandering lines headed directly for them.

304

The first outcry came from Shechem's left flank, from one of the outermost columns. "Ahh!" a soldier cursed.

Too far away to see for himself, he called to one of his captains. "What is it?"

"I think something bit him," the captain said. "He's on the ground, grabbing his ankle."

More cries followed, coming from every quadrant of the battalion while men fell and writhed in pain. Comrades rushed to their aid, only to find themselves victims of whatever is was striking at them from the ground.

Shechem wheeled in the saddle to his right at the sound of a soldier shrieking only a few cubits away, followed by another right next to him. Shechem's horse reared at the unmistakable sight of a cobra's hood rising above the grass in front of him.

"Whoa, boy." He patted his horse's neck and yanked the reins to back him out of range of the deadly serpent. He managed to regain control without falling, but across the plain, other horses — panicked by the movement at their feet — threw their riders to the ground and into the mouths of the swarming reptiles.

Panic wasn't limited to the cavalry. Many foot soldiers sought to defend themselves by hacking and slashing at any movement coming from the tall grass. It was a strategy that proved both futile and dangerous in the close quarters of a military formation. Frightened strikes and misguided aim resulted in several soldiers finding themselves with wounds to their legs and shins.

A soldier determined to kill the snake that had bitten him, chased after it wildly swinging his sword. On his third chop, another high-pitched scream joined those already piercing the air when he cut off four toes of a fellow soldier.

Shechem had to act quickly to save his army.

* * *

305

Noah touched the lioness on her back, restraining her from charging. "Hold on, girl. You'll get your chance."

"Somebody's anxious," Japheth said.

"What's happening?" Shem said.

"Serpents," Noah said.

"Shouldn't we go help them?"

"We will. After a bit more tenderizing."

Confusion continued to plague Malluch's army. Men raced back and forth across the formation, reduced to a herd of rabbits hopping about on hot coals to avoid being bitten. Dozens of riderless horses fled the brigade in every direction. Soon the shouts of men being attacked drowned out the commands of the captains attempting to restore order.

One soldier near the front rose from the ground, a viper attached to his hand. "Get it off me," he said. "Get it off me!" After several unsuccessful attempts to shake it free, the snake dropped off on its own and disappeared in the grass. The viper must have struck a vein because the man immediately fell back to the ground and started convulsing.

Another two soldiers broke from their ranks and ran toward Noah and his family, not to attack, but because they were being chased. Two black mambas—known for their aggressiveness and speed—floated along the top of the grass in pursuit. They quickly overcame the soldiers and delivered their poison before heading back to claim more victims.

Unlike the lioness and Shem, Noah was in no hurry to join the battle. He was content to allow the serpents to erode the better portion of Malluch's army, which already seemed overmatched. A part of him even felt sorry for them, not because of what the snakes were doing, but because this was only the beginning.

306

CHAPTER 56

"Head for the trees!" Shechem cried out to his captains. Although the trees wouldn't offer much protection, right now they were fighting an invisible enemy. The dark, grassless earth of the forest floor would at least make the snakes easier to see.

His army broke for the forest, driven by the sound of their captains' voices repeating the command to take cover. He rode his horse around the outside of the formation, galloping to the head of the new front line now parallel to the trees. Two hundred fifty cubits from the wood line, his internal alarm sounded again for a reason he couldn't fully grasp.

Something was moving in the trees ahead. But what?

His answer came when the shrill cry of a screech owl echoed from deep within the dark forest. He recoiled at the muffled sound of flapping wings when the owl's signal sent thousands of birds aloft from the treetops. He paused to admire the majesty of the bird-filled sky, only to jerk back to reality when they abruptly changed direction.

The birds descended on his army like a swarm of locusts, targeting the skin of exposed heads and hands. Hawks, owls, and other birds of prey swooped in to gouge with iron talons and rip apart with razor sharp beaks. Yet the smaller species proved just as savage, attacking in flocks of three and four per soldier by pecking away at their eyes, ears, and mouth.

In a matter of fifty to ninety parts, Shechem found himself surrounded by soldiers bleeding from their faces, their hands pressed tightly against cheeks of torn flesh. Cries of, "My eyes," and "I can't see," rained across the formation. When a raven flew by holding an eyeball and the torn retina of some unlucky soldier in its mouth, he cringed. What had caused this madness?

He recognized the deteriorating condition of the battlefield and that he had to act fast to save his army. The chaos on the ground had moved overhead with soldiers seeking to defend themselves from their avian antagonists. Swords flailed wildly, leading to a host of injuries and two near decapitations. Compounding the situation, the increased noise caused by the screams of the injured and dying made it impossible for him to issue commands.

Still, he realized more than ever the importance of making it to the forest. Out in the open, his army remained vulnerable to attack from above and below. But the trees would afford at least a measure of cover. Again, he tried to rally his forces. "Get to the trees!"

If they didn't secure safety soon, his men would all be dead.

* * *

Noah turned to the sound of thunder and the ground rumbling beneath his feet. From both sides of the ark, hundreds of animals hurtled down the hill. He, Shiphrah, and his sons joined the charge, sprinting to keep pace with their quadruped allies before wading into Malluch's wounded and confused army.

Most of the big cats arrived first, leaping onto groups of paralyzed soldiers, knocking them to the ground and scattering those around them. Two leopards, the panthers, and the male lion made short work of twelve men with well-placed rakes through muscle and crippling bites to their throats.

308

The two tigers proved even more formidable. Slower than the smaller felids, they used their immense size and strength to maim or kill fifteen soldiers in the first eighteen parts of the skirmish. For whatever reason, the cries of these men seemed to echo louder than any other on the plain.

Soon after, several of the larger creatures arrived to change the dynamics of the battle. Elephants and rhinos plowed into the army's ranks, tossing soldiers into the air with the ease of a farmer's winnowing fan. Large, ebony buffalos used their huge, winged horn caps to gore and fling. One hippopotamus carried a soldier's body around in its mouth impaled on its lower incisors, swinging it back and forth as a weapon. Had it not been so sickening, Noah would have found the image amusing.

For one group of soldiers, their encounter with a pair of giraffe proved anything but humorous. Noah watched six or seven soldiers largely ignore the approach of the two stately creatures. Maybe the soldiers were too distracted by the attacking birds or believed they could easily avoid the giraffes' lumbering gait. Five parts later, all seven soldiers lay injured and dying on the ground, felled by the snapping front kicks of the two giants.

To his left, ten soldiers made the mistake of taking on a pair of massive brown bears. None of the soldiers laid a sword on them, but with each powerful swipe of the bears' paw, another soldier went flying. And the sight of one of the bears closing its mouth over a soldier's face made him squeamish.

Shem stayed close to his father when engaging the enemy, although early on, Noah had no need for human supervision. Each time he would clang swords with an opponent, the lioness would rush in and overpower the enemy. Even in the midst of fighting another soldier, she would invariably break away and come to his aid whenever she perceived him in danger.

Ham and Shiphrah fought alongside a pair of wolves and two hyenas. Without a word between them, the six worked in concert to attack and defend each other with a skill that belied their never having fought together. In one instance, Ham ran through three soldiers that had cornered one of the wolves. A short time later, two soldiers converging on Shiphrah were disabled by the two hyenas biting them on the groin.

Time and again, Noah's attention was drawn to Shiphrah, not out of a sense of concern, but for admiration of her fighting style. Although Ham's strength and ferociousness allowed him to overpower his foes, Shiphrah rarely locked swords with anyone. Instead, she moved like a dancer, displaying the nimbleness of foot and skill with a sword she'd developed in training with the Marauders to outmaneuver her opponents. By Noah's count, Shiphrah had dispatched twice the number of soldiers as Ham.

While he marveled at Shiphrah's skill, he pitied the men in Japheth's path. Flanked by the two jaguars, Japheth stormed through the enemy, wielding his sword with the same vigor he used to swing an ax. In his first clash, his devastating power shattered three opponents' swords and cut off the arms of two others.

The jaguars proved equally efficient, dragging their victims to the ground and disabling them with a single ripping bite to the throat. At times, it appeared the three of them might have been engaged in a competition.

Shem was the first to notice the opposing army's change in direction. "Looks like they're heading for the trees."

"It won't help them," Noah said.

CHAPTER 57

Plagued by two blue jays and a mockingbird, Shechem swatted them away in time to see Noah's animal legion tear into his army's left flank. Watching his soldiers flung into the air only reinforced his conviction they needed to get off the plain. Only this time he didn't have to issue the order. His army was already in an all-out sprint for the woods.

He halted his horse at the wood's edge and raised his sword to signal his fleeing soldiers. "Get to cover."

Moments later, more screaming filled his ears, this time coming from the woods behind him. The soldiers who had gone in were headed back, and in a big hurry. They collided with their brethren going the other way. Many bled from wounds to their head and face.

He stopped one of the soldiers exiting the forest to ask what was happening. The man was missing his left ear.

"They're everywhere," the man said. "Apes. Baboons. Bobcats. Lynx. Even snakes. Dropping down on us from the trees. And on the ground, more snakes, giant lizards, and crocodiles."

Two more soldiers followed behind him. The first, covered by what looked to be no fewer than a dozen species of spider, fell to the ground thrashing in agony. The second, trying to remove a pair of scorpions from his neck, wasn't faring much better. Each time he tried to remove one of the arachnids, the second would sting his hand again.

A dozen cubits away, another soldier stumbled out of the woods screaming, a raccoon draped around his head. Cursing violently, the soldier flung the raccoon to the ground, which scurried into the woods. He threw his sword at the creature but missed badly, prompting him to curse again. When he went to retrieve the sword, a crocodile rushed out of the brush and grabbed hold of his arm. With two crunching chomps and three lateral shakes, the croc tore the soldier's arm away before disappearing back into the brush.

Angered and frustrated that he'd been outmaneuvered by a collection of animals, Shechem tried to think. He'd lost more than half his army without inflicting a single casualty on the enemy. Now his men lay trapped between an inhospitable forest and an untenable plain. Even if he issued the command to withdraw, he couldn't guarantee his forces would make it safely back across the savannah. Something supernatural was at work here.

By now, some of the larger animals had smashed their way through the ranks to reach the woods. Two hundred cubits up the tree line, a rhino trampled and gored three soldiers, then hurled the fourth against a tree, snapping his spine. The two tigers, their mouths and front paws stained with blood, disabled seven more men with powerful swipes that opened gaping head and belly wounds.

He swung his horse around to screams coming from the battlefield. A hundred cubits behind him, two elephants performed a dance routine across the chests of several fallen soldiers. Fortunately for them, their screaming didn't last long.

Fighting off a pair of seagulls, Bohar rode up with his two henchmen. "What do we do now, Commander? In case you hadn't noticed, we're getting slaughtered out here."

We've run out of room to maneuver. It may be time for a retreat."

Bohar's head jerked back. "Through that sea of serpents?"

312

"Look around you." Bohar's eyes followed Shechem's nod, first to his deteriorating left flank, then to where his soldiers were fleeing the forest behind him. "Which way would you choose?"

"I have a better idea." He huddled for a moment with his two subordinates, and the three of them rode away through the ranks of soldiers headed toward the woods.

Experience told Shechem exactly where Bohar was headed and what would happen if he got there. It was the reason he'd issued the command in front of his battalion to bring him the women — to deter his miscreant colleague from exercising his predilections. Now it appeared he was the only one who could stop him.

To avoid the larger predators, Bohar would have to ride east, circle around outside the field of battle, and approach the house from the side or the rear. Shechem pursued them, slowed by the sea of soldiers coming his way. It took him another sixty to seventy parts to reach the rearmost ranks of his fleeing army. The sound of beating wings spun him around in the saddle. He threw his arm up in time to deflect the talons of a diving eagle but was still driven off his horse.

He lay dazed on the ground trying to clear his head, hoping a serpent wouldn't find him.

* * *

Throughout the battle, Noah kept a close watch on his family while they continued their push toward the woods through the left flank of Malluch's army. Fighting to their father's right, Ham and Shiphrah momentarily disappeared behind a group of soldiers interposed between them. Noah backed away from the skirmish in front of him to locate them.

"Look out, Father!" Shem shouted.

He turned back in time to block the sword thrust of an attacking soldier but was knocked off balance and fell. The foe raised a sword to finish him, but a golden blur came flying through the air and

313

landed on his back, driving the soldier to the ground. The lioness neutralized him with a vicious throat attack.

Shem hurried to help his father up. "Are you hurt?"

"Only at the thought of my own imprudence. Thank you." He glanced to his right to see the last of the soldiers blocking his view fall to strikes from Shiphrah and Ham. Of the six soldiers slain, Shiphrah had killed four.

At the same time, Japheth continued to overwhelm the enemy, cutting a swathe of bodies and severed limbs twenty cubits on either side. By Noah's estimate, only the two tigers had inflicted more casualties. Near the forest, four soldiers foolishly tried to surround him. Japheth swept his sword at waist level, 180 degrees in front, then behind, sending all four to the ground holding their spilled entrails.

Noah and Shem reached the wood line at the same time the bodies of two soldiers came flying out of the forest a short distance away. Two gorillas bounded after them, pouncing on their chests and pummeling them with both fists. When another soldier attempted to come to their aid, one gorilla took the soldier's sword and broke it in half, then slammed his body against a tree.

Above them, hundreds of animals darted about the trees, a stark contrast to the battle taking place on the ground. In another venue, they might just have easily been at play. Closer to the ground, a man hung from a tree limb with a large python wrapped around his neck.

A gruesome reminder of reality.

Japheth and the jaguars joined Noah, Shem, and the two lions at the woods' edge. Fewer than a thousand soldiers remained on the battlefield, most of them still trying to fend off attacks from above and below.

"Have you seen Shechem?" Noah said.

"Not since the battle started," Japheth said. He rose on his toes for a better look. "I'm more concerned about Bohar's whereabouts."

314

Noah had expected the enemy commander to come looking for his oldest, to use the battle as a subterfuge to settle their rivalry over Elisheva. But he also understood why his son was more concerned about Bohar, whose reputation for the abuse of women made him equally dangerous.

* * *

Shechem arrived at the house still disoriented from the fall. It had taken him around fifty-four parts to gain his bearings and retrieve his horse before following Bohar's path around the battlefield. Exhausted and confused, he entered Noah's home.

Two soldiers held swords to the throats of Miryam and Ariel. One also held a lit torch. On the floor to the left, Bohar lay on top of a struggling Elisheva, trying to kiss her. Shechem put a sword to his throat and peered at him through burning eyes. "Get up."

Bohar tried to stand, but the blade cut deeper into his flesh, causing a trickle of blood to flow. "Shech — "

"Slowly. Unless you want me to cut an artery." Bohar lifted himself off of Elisheva while Shechem kept the sword pressed against his throat. "Over here." Using the sword against his neck like a bridle, he maneuvered him away from Elisheva and to the front door before pulling the blade away. "Now get out of here — before I change my mind and do what I should have done a long time ago."

Bohar backed out holding the bloody cut on his neck. When he did, Shechem grabbed the torch out of the soldier's hand.

"Bohar." He threw him the torch. "I don't expect any of us will make it out of here alive, but if you want to improve your station with Malluch, get to the ark."

He nodded and disappeared out the door.

"No!" Elisheva jumped to her feet. "Shechem, don't do this."

"Find something to tie and gag them with," he said to the soldiers.

"What are you doing?" Elisheva said.

"What I came here to do."

CHAPTER 58

Noah and his sons watched first one, then another of the captains on horseback issue the order to retreat. Malluch's remaining army turned and headed north across the plain, predators nipping at their heels.

From the ark, a new wave of animals charged down the hill. Wildebeests, bison, zebras, and dozens of other herding animals joined their larger brethren in a stampede that would soon overtake the fleeing soldiers.

If this weren't enough, above them, a cloud of birds followed the soldiers' withdrawal and continued to harass them.

Infantry in the rear ranks fell first, disappearing under the legs of the galloping eclectic herd that included horses, camels, and antelopes. Carnivores, large and small, stopped to finish off those unlucky enough to still be alive after being trampled.

In 180 parts, it was over. Five thousand men lay dead or dying on the plain, crushed under the heels of God's army. Other than the bodies, little evidence remained of a battle. Some of the animals had already returned to grazing.

Except for the birds. They'd descended from the air to enjoy their feast.

317

"Ouch. I wonder what that feels like," Shem said, gesturing to the birds gorging themselves on the flesh.

"Be thankful, my sons. For with a mighty hand the Lord has delivered us this day."

Out of the corner of his eye, he noticed Ham and Shiphrah running toward them. "Father!" Ham said, pointing. Someone's headed for the ark."

A man on horseback rode from the house up the hill carrying a lighted torch.

"It's Bohar," Japheth said. "If he gets inside the ark with that torch—"

Noah, his sons, Shiphrah, and the four big cats ran toward the ark. The jaguars and the male lion kept pace, but the female lion, seeming to sense the urgency, pulled out in front by a good fifty cubits.

Bohar reached the top of the hill and headed for the ramp.

The nine pursuers increased their pace, but were just reaching the bottom of the hill when their quarry turned his horse onto the ramp. The lioness was closer, but had still only made it halfway up the rise.

"She can't get there in time," Shem said.

Bohar pulled back on the reins just before reaching the door. He wildly swung the torch back and forth over his head, as if trying to defend himself from some kind of airborne attack. Meanwhile, his horse backed away from the doorway, heading for the left edge of the ramp.

Noah's family hurried up the hill. "What's he swinging at?" Ham said.

Bohar screamed, increasing the speed and intensity of his swings. His horse's left rear foot slipped off the edge of the ramp, dumping him out of the saddle and plummeting fifteen cubits to the ground below.

When Noah and the others arrived at the ark, he lay moaning beneath the ramp, his right leg broken. He tried to drag himself to retrieve his torch only a few cubits away. When he reached for it, the lioness slammed her right front paw down on the handle. Bohar yanked his hand away but remained focused on the paw with two white toes holding down the torch.

Bohar's body trembled when the lioness leaned down to smell him, her nose and whiskers twitching. She growled once, then with teeth tearing into his throat cut short his final terrified scream.

A few moments later, a buzzing sound behind him caught Noah's attention. Two hummingbirds hovered at eye level between him and Shem.

"You think they had something to do with this?" Shem said.

"With God anything is possible. We'd better return to the house and see about our wives."

They found Miryam and Ariel on the floor bound and gagged. Noah and Shem rushed to untie them.

"Where's Elisheva?" Japheth said, looking around the room.

His father removed the cloth covering Miryam's mouth. "She's gone."

* * *

Noah returned from the pasture leading two horses he'd recovered from the soldiers following the battle. Japheth paced back and forth outside their front door. "Father, where have you been? Let's go."

"Just a part, son."

"But Mother and Ariel said they've been gone nearly two hours now."

Miryam told them how after she and Ariel had been bound and gagged, Shechem ordered the other two soldiers back to the battle before he took Elisheva from the house. "We'll find them," Noah said.

"Shouldn't we go with you, Father?" Ham said.

319

"No. Japheth, the lioness, and I will bring Elisheva back. I need you and everyone else to start loading the animals on the ark."

"But why?"

"Just now, in the pasture, the Lord came to me in the wind again. In seven days, He will bring rains on the earth that will last forty days and forty nights. And every living thing on the earth will be destroyed."

He drew blank stares from each family member, except for Miryam, who looked at him with her soft, understanding eyes. "Seven days?" Ariel said.

"Yes." Noah said.

"And how do we get the animals to the ark?" Shem said. "Blow a horn?"

"The Lord will send them to you, just as He said, two of each, male and female. But for every clean animal and every bird, you shall take seven. All you need do is lead each kind to the pen or cage we constructed for them."

"Father, please," Japheth said. "Every moment we waste here increases the distance we have to travel to catch them."

"Don't worry. We'll catch them."

"Not if we don't leave now."

"Did I not say the Lord just gave me instruction? If you can't wait, you're free to go on ahead and we'll follow."

Japheth's face reddened. "All right." He tramped to his horse and mounted with such force he nearly slipped off the other side. "I'll wait for you at the bottom of the hill."

Noah pulled Shem aside, out of range of hearing of the others. "If we're not back in seven days and it starts to rain, move everyone inside the ark and close the door."

"And what about you, Japheth, and Elisheva?"

"It won't take long for people to figure out what's going on. Panic is sure to set in. Some may try to commandeer the ark. Do what you must to keep them out. Once you've closed the door, don't open it for anyone."

320

"But what if—"

"Even if you believe it's us."

"Mother's not going to let—"

"Not anyone. Do you understand?"

"Yes, Father."

He hugged and kissed Miryam, whispering in her ear. "Take a moment to enjoy the sunset the next few nights. They'll be the last ones you'll see for a while."

Miryam kissed him again.

When they reached the far end of the field of corpses, Noah swung in his saddle for a last look behind. Half a dozen pairs of animals, including the elephants, giraffes, elks, and buffalo had lined up near the bottom of the ramp. Another twenty species walked side by side with their mates back up the hill toward the ark. "Japheth."

"Amazing. *Now* can we get moving?"

CHAPTER 59

After four days, Shechem and Elisheva camped for the night on this side of a river, still a day's journey from Eden. Although they could have easily made it across, he chose not to chance it in the dark. They had one horse between them, and he didn't want to risk losing Elisheva to a fall should they encounter a problem in the water. Besides, he was convinced he'd outdistanced anyone who might be following them, so why rush to get home?

What bothered him more was what he was going to do with her now that he had her. It wasn't as if he could take her home. *I should have gotten rid of Claudia beforehand.* But he'd acted purely on impulse in taking Elisheva, a longing he'd carried with him for a hundred years.

He and Elisheva sat warming themselves around a fire. For the eleventh time since being taken, she tried to reason with him. "Shechem. This doesn't make any sense. We've known each other all our lives. Please, let me go back to my family."

He gazed into the fire, unable to look at her. "I can't."

"Why not?"

He didn't answer but peered at her across the dancing flames with moist eyes that said, "You know why."

322

'You were my best friend. Surely you don't believe I married someone else just to hurt you."

He jumped up and threw a handful of dirt into the fire. "But I loved you first."

Elisheva rose to face him. "We were children. I grew up. You grew up. You went on to marry the most beautiful woman in Eden." She stood directly behind him, but he kept his back to her, partly out of anger, but also to hide his tears. "Listen to me. Do you know what I did when I heard the news? I had Japheth pour us each a cup of wine in honor of you. We rejoiced, both of us, knowing you were finally going to be as happy as I was."

"Happy? Huh." He walked a dozen or so cubits to the river's edge. "This river reminds me of the Eden, that group of rocks over there the ones you slipped off of."

"A long time ago."

"I remember it like it was yesterday."

"Don't you understand? The fact is, it wasn't yesterday. And no matter how hard we try, we can't go back and live that part of our lives again."

"We could start a new life."

Elisheva placed her hand on his shoulder, turning him to her "But I don't want a new life," she said, her voice lowering. "I'm happy with the one I have." Her look seemed to bore directly into his soul. "And the man I have it with."

"I'm not."

Her brow furrowed. "Well there it is. You're not happy with your life, so you think you have the right to ruin mine. That's not love. That's selfishness."

"No, it's—"

"Sure, you can kidnap me. You can keep me locked up. You can even take me against my will. But it won't change what happened a lifetime ago." She softened her gaze. "All it will do is destroy that special relationship we enjoyed when we were young."

"But what about—"

"Didn't you hear what I just called you? My best friend. That's a memory lasting three hundred years. Let me keep it. Don't do something to make me regret you saved my life."

They turned to the sound of movement in the grass to the south and slipped back to the light of the campfire. The flames cast light reflecting off five approaching figures: Noah and Japheth leading their horses, and the lioness. They entered the camp.

Shechem reached for his sword, but the lioness let out a growl and started toward him, causing him to think better of it. He lowered his arm.

Japheth didn't hesitate. He charged his rival and lifted him off his feet by the throat. Elisheva grabbed his forearm. "Japheth, don't."

"What do you mean, don't? This murdering swine took you from me."

"He didn't harm me. Now let him down. Please."

Japheth glanced over at Noah, who nodded. His son lowered him to the ground and removed his sword.

Elisheva hugged her husband, then ran to her father-in-law. "Mother and Ariel. Are they all right?"

"Yes," Noah said.

"And the ark? Shechem sent Bohar to burn it down."

"He didn't make it." Noah reached to stroke the lioness. "Did he, girl?"

Japheth joined him and Elisheva, pointing at her abductor with the sword he'd taken. "What do you want to do with him?"

Noah paused to look down at Elisheva. "Let him go."

"Let him go? So he can run to Malluch and they send another army against us."

"Eden's army is destroyed. And in three days it won't matter."

At first, Shechem was thankful Elisheva had saved him from Japheth's wrath, until he realized he was about to lose her again. He briefly considered attacking him when his back was turned, but thought better of it. He wouldn't get two steps before the lion

324

would be all over him. And what did the Preacher mean by three days? "Is this the flood we heard you've been preaching about?" Shechem said.

"It is."

"Well, all I can say is if it does come, you've got the ship built for it."

"We have to go." Noah mounted his horse.

"For what it's worth, Preacher, you should know your father died in Eden five years ago—of natural causes."

Japheth's look told his father he had something to say, but remained silent. "I'll remember your kindness." Noah said.

His son lifted Elisheva onto the horse and climbed on behind her. He threw Shechem's sword at his feet.

Shechem watched the three of them and the lion disappear into the darkness. Loneliness descended over him like a bad omen.

* * *

The next day, Shechem arrived at his daughters' farm without a clue about what he was going to say to them. But he'd seen and heard enough in the past few weeks to justify paying them a visit on his way back to Eden. Methuselah had warned him of a coming flood, something the Preacher had confirmed would begin in another two days. And after what had just happened to his army, he wasn't nearly so skeptical about things beyond his understanding.

"What happened to you?" Naomi said when her father entered the house. She, Channah, and their husbands gathered around him, their eyes drawn to several blotches of dust and dirt that stained the front of his clothing.

Channah reached to gently touch several cuts on his face. "Who did this?"

"Believe it or not—birds."

325

She twisted her mouth. "What kind of birds?"

Shechem raised his arm to reveal the gouges inflicted by the eagle. "Ones with sharp beaks and claws."

"Whatever they were, those cuts need to be cleaned." Naomi said. "Come. Sit over here, Father." She led him to a place with cushions on the floor before disappearing into another room to retrieve some water and clean cloths. While she dressed his wounds, he told them the story of how his soldiers had been annihilated by the Preacher's army of animals. Several times during the telling, he noticed several raised eyebrows and a tightening of the lips on the men's faces. Naturally, he left out the part about Elisheva.

"That's quite a story," Channah said when he was done.

He surmised they hadn't believed a word he'd said, but out of respect for him as their father, they weren't about to challenge his story. "Unfortunately, it's true."

Naomi and Channah exchanged glances. "Father," Naomi said.

Shechem put his hand up. "I know, I know. It all sounds crazy. But the fact is, I didn't come here to tell you about the battle. I came here to warn you."

"Warn us about what?"

If they doubted his reason after hearing about the battle, what would they think when he told them about the flood? "Don't ask me how I know this, but there's a possibility this whole plain may soon be flooded."

"Fath—" Channah said.

"Two days from now."

"That fable's a hundred years old," Naomi's husband said. "It was started by some farmer to the south, right?"

"I thought so, too," Shechem said. "But now, I—I just don't know."

"Why two days from now?" Naomi said.

"I can't tell you. You'll just have to trust I know what I'm talking about."

326

"Say we do," Channah's husband said. "What do you expect us to do about it?"

'I don't know, exactly. Maybe take a trip to the mountains for a few days. Anything to get you off this plain until the threat is passed. Then, in about a week, if nothing happens, you can come back and make fun of your delusional father-in-law."

"We can't leave now. We have crops of peas and spinach that will spoil if we leave them in the ground another week."

"Then send my daughters—just for the week. Please."

Naomi's soft look of concern disappeared, replaced by a firmly set chin. "We're not leaving our husbands."

Channah shook her head.

"You know the closest river large enough to pose that kind of threat is the Eden?" Naomi's husband said. "One hundred sixty furlongs away. Where is this flood supposed to come from?"

"I don't know that either. But however it comes, whether by an overflow of rivers, an expulsion of groundwater, or rain falling from the sky, it'll be enough to wash this all away." He swept his arm in front of him.

"After such an ordeal, you must be hungry," Channah said.

That was his daughter's not-so-subtle way of changing the subject, which was probably a good thing since it was obvious he wasn't convincing any of them.

After the meal, while the women cleared and cleaned the dishes, Naomi's husband pulled him aside. "Forgetting about the flood for the moment, what about this battle?"

"What about it?"

"Well, it's obvious something attacked you. But from what I know of Malluch, you're going to have to come up with a better excuse for how you lost five thousand men."

"What would you suggest?"

"A huge party of Marauders. An earthquake swallowed them up. They drowned crossing the Eden. Anything but that story you told us."

327

Shechem wasn't offended by his son-in-law's skepticism. On the contrary, he appreciated the concern and his decision to voice his doubts privately. Moreover, what he said made sense. "You may be right."

An hour later, his family walked him outside, where he hugged and kissed his daughters and shook the hands of his sons-in-law. Just before riding away, he leaned over the front of his saddle. "Just promise me one thing. In two days, if it starts to rain and doesn't let up after five, or you see water accumulating in the valley, head for the mountains."

"Agreed," Naomi said.

* * *

Noah rose from sleep before dawn on the seventh day with a sense of urgency. They'd made good time the past two days, having ridden all through the first night and deep into the second with the aid of torches. But they'd been slowed by Japheth and Elisheva having to share a horse and still had a long way to travel to reach the ark.

Not wanting to worry them, he hadn't told them of the instructions he'd given Shem. And despite his history of recalcitrance, this was one time he had faith his son would obey him without reservation. Holding two pieces of bread, he kneeled to rouse his children. "Here, eat this. We need to get moving."

Noah packed his horse while the sun rose more clear and bright than he'd ever seen it. He remembered his words to Miryam a few nights ago and closed his eyes, letting the rays wash across his face.

He climbed aboard his horse, turning to his son and daughter-in-law mounted to his right. He looked past them. "What is it?" Japheth said.

To the west, storm clouds gathered.

CHAPTER 60

Shechem watched a red-faced Malluch stride up and down the great hall dressed in a purple tunic trimmed in gold. He hadn't seen him so angry in sixty years, not since the destruction of Eden's first idol. At that moment, he wished he'd taken his son-in-law's advice, instead of opting for the truth.

"Your whole army?" Malluch said in a low tone exuding rage. "Five thousand men wiped out by some animals and birds?" Cords popped out on his neck.

"More than some, my lord. A lot more."

Malluch stopped pacing to stare at him. "I don't care how many there were. They're just mindless animals? It's preposterous."

"And serpents."

"How many serpents?"

"Who knows? We couldn't see them all in the grass. Hundreds, maybe thousands."

Malluch moved in for a closer look at the wounds on Shechem's head, face, and neck. He lifted his arm, exposing the two talon marks. "Uh huh. And Bohar?"

Shechem wasn't about to tell him what he knew of Bohar's fate, or how he knew it. Better to let him think he died a hero. "The last I saw, he was heading for the ark with a torch."

"Good. If I know Bohar, he will have burned it down or died in the attempt."

Shechem nodded.

"But we must be sure. First thing in the morning, Commander, I want you to begin recruiting new soldiers for our replacement army. In the meantime, I'll travel to Enoch to try to get Ramalech to support us with his."

"What makes you think he'll agree this time?"

"Because I'm not asking him to accompany us to the garden."

"But—"

"Look, we know Ramalech fears the invincibility of the guardian. But he also knows the guardian poses no threat to Enoch while he remains posted as sentry at the garden."

"So what's your plan to convince him to join us now, another tribute?"

"Something simpler and more visceral than that. How do you think Ramalech would react if he knew the creatures that wiped out our army were headed for Enoch?"

"I see. An incentive."

"Exactly. It's easy to say no when there's no consequence for it. It's a different matter altogether when the threat is headed your way."

"Very shrewd, my lord."

"But for now, my son's getting married in a couple of hours, and I need to put this tragedy behind me. I don't want him to see fury in my eyes on his wedding day."

Neither did he.

* * *

Somewhere close to midday, Noah, Japheth, and Elisheva rode hard for home. Of course he couldn't be certain, not with dark clouds blocking the position of the sun, but he was fairly sure of the time of day. He was pleased with the progress they'd made, and that the lioness had been able to keep up with the horses.

Coming to a small stream, he raised his hand to slow them. "We should rest the horses a few hundred parts."

Japheth kneeled to fill a wineskin, while the horses and the lioness drank from the stream. Elisheva's long hair blew in a wind that had increased throughout the morning. With a look of concern, she approached Noah. "It's coming, isn't it? The rain?"

"Yes."

"Will we be able to make it home?"

Elisheva jumped when a flash of lightning lit up the sky in the distance, followed by a clap of thunder that sent the horses running off in opposite directions.

Japheth turned quickly to his wife, "Stay here!" and raced off after his horse.

Noah and the lion splashed through the stream chasing the other one. As he ran, doubt entered his mind for the first time that they'd make it home in time. He quickened his pace, running faster than he thought capable, but still the sight of his horse's backside grew smaller with each stride. "Go ahead girl," he said to the lion between panting breaths. "See if you can catch him."

Noah continued to run, but slowed to a jog while the lion sprinted ahead. Anxiety grabbed hold of him when his horse crested a small rise, receding on the other side. *Stay straight.* The lion vaulted over the rise after him.

Facing exhaustion, he stomped the last few strides to reach the top of the hill, bending over and placing his hands on his knees to catch his breath. Ahead lay a grassy plain, dotted here and there with small groups of trees, brush, and a small forest to the left.

He searched for signs of movement. Other than the grass and trees swaying in the blowing wind, the plain provided no trace. The lion and his horse had disappeared.

What now, Lord? He filled his lungs and started down the rise. At the bottom of the hill he lost his sightline, forcing him to rely more on his hearing. Every hundred cubits or so, he stopped to listen, hoping to pick up some cue that would direct him. But the wind buffeting his ears made it difficult to hear.

Five hundred cubits past the bottom of the hill, Noah lost sight of the tracks, the imprints in the grass erased by the breeze. He continued along the same heading until his attention was drawn to the soft growl of the lion off to his right. He stopped to listen. Again, the wind brought the lion's howl to his ears.

He moved to his right, toward and around a small crop of trees. On the other side, his horse trotted back and forth in short bursts, bobbing his head toward the ground and whinnying. He appeared skittish and ready to bolt at the next clap of thunder. But at his feet walked the lion, mirroring his gait in a herding maneuver intended to confine him to his present path.

He approached his horse slowly and took the reins. "Easy boy." He patted the side of his neck.

He slid onto the saddle and headed back to the stream where Elisheva waited. "You've been gone so long, I was beginning to worry."

"Japheth?"

Elisheva pointed west in the direction her husband had taken. "He hasn't returned yet."

"Daughter, stay here in case we miss him on his way back."

He and the lion headed along the path he'd last seen Japheth pursuing the other horse. After about a furlong and a half, he spotted him walking on the prairie. He returned his father's wave and jogged toward them.

"He get away?" Noah said as they met.

"It's been nearly an hour since I lost sight of him."

"Well, climb aboard. We need to pick up Elisheva and start for home."

332

"The three of us can't ride one horse. Shouldn't we use this one to help us find the other?"

A wicked crack of thunder followed another lightning strike that creased the southwest horizon. Noah's horse stirred beneath him, and he stroked his mane. "You just said you haven't seen him for an hour. Now maybe we could find him using this horse, and maybe not."

"But Father, one horse will slow us down. Even with Elisheva riding, it will still take us another three or four hours to make it back on foot."

"Take a look at those clouds, son." He and Japheth lifted their eyes to the thickening slate gray quilt covering the sky. "How long do you think they're going to hold off?"

"Which is exactly why we should go after the other horse."

"Suppose we found him right away, what then? We might be able to cut our time in half. But if we don't find him, all the time we spent looking will have been time we could have been on the road."

"It seems like a gamble either way."

"It is. But at least this one starts marking time with us headed in the right direction." Had God abandoned them? Under most circumstances, the loss of an hour during a long journey wouldn't make much of a difference. Only they hadn't just lost an hour, they'd lost a horse too, which would cost them more time. Getting Elisheva back from Shechem was supposed to be the hard part, not getting home. Now, even if they made it, would they arrive in time to make it into the ark?

CHAPTER 61

Noah raised his arm, turning to Elisheva in the saddle behind him and to Japheth and the lion running off their left quarter. "There she is!" he shouted above the pummeling wind. Five furlongs ahead and barely visible against the blackness of the southern sky, the tip of the ark's prow pierced the horizon.

Another clap of thunder and Elisheva tightened her grip around his waist. They'd traveled nearly three hours from the stream where they'd lost Japheth's horse. But the wind had only grown stronger, biting their faces and bending the trees above them like swaying wheat fields. Flashes of lightning and claps of thunder grew closer together, and Noah fought to maintain control of his horse. To their right, several trees crashed to the forest floor.

Up ahead, hundreds of birds swirled about, lifted by winds blowing from west to east before dropping back to the ground. At first glance, their flight appeared somewhat whimsical, until they rode close enough to see what it was. "Oh, what's that smell?" Elisheva said, burying her nose deep in his back.

Noah wrinkled his nose at the putrid odor, but recognized it immediately. "Death. Don't look."

As they came upon the battlefield, thousands of birds had gathered to feed on the rotting corpses of soldiers. Mostly vultures,

334

buzzards, and crows. They were joined by dozens of jackals and hyenas in harvesting the carrion. Not even the coming storm appeared to deter them.

Four hyenas dining closest to them raised their heads when they passed, blood and saliva dripping from their chomping snouts. Japheth reached for his sword. "No need, son. They won't bother us unless they perceive we're a threat to their food."

Directly in front, a tree bent over onto their path by the wind began to fall. Indecision seized him. Dare he pull back on the reins or continue forward? He shouted, slapping his horse's rear.

"Look out!" Japheth yelled.

Noah spun his horse to the sound of the tree striking the ground behind him. Japheth appeared uninjured on the far side of the great poplar, but the lioness had been trapped beneath several of its upper branches.

"What happened?" Noah said.

"She tried to follow you," Japheth said.

Father and son hurried to assist the distressed lioness, her howls barely audible above the roar of the wind. She'd been pinned by two branches, one pushing onto her hips, and another holding down her tail. Even with his son's great strength, the two men could not budge the massive trunk.

Two more flashes of lightning and their accompanying cracks of thunder preceded the first rain drops striking Noah's scalp and forehead. With them, he remembered his instructions to Ham. *Close the door.*

Japheth looked at the helpless lion, then reached across one of the branches to touch his father's forearm. "Father, I know how you feel, but we have to go."

He shook away the emotion thickening his throat and set his eyes. "We're not leaving her behind." At that, the heaven's opened. He turned to Elisheva. "Go to the house. Bring back the two-man saw."

With rain pouring down his face, Japheth held out his palms and gestured around him. "Father, we must get to the ark."

"Do you want me to bring back Shem and Ham?" Elisheva said.

"There isn't time. Just bring back the saw. Quickly, daughter."

Elisheva ran to mount the horse. "Bring my ax," Japheth said. She nodded and headed off, returning in less than 180 parts.

In the driving wind and rain, her husband moved about inside the tree top pruning away branches so he and Noah could have a clear cutting field. Again, Noah marveled at his son's power, which he used to cut away more than twenty quarter cubit branches in less than forty parts. Not one took more than a single stroke.

When he was finished, he moved to the other end of the saw over the lower branch securing the lion's tail. "Shouldn't we get that big one off her hips first?" Japheth said.

"When that one comes off, she's going to bolt. And if her tail is still trapped, she might really hurt herself."

His son nodded and they began to cut, slicing through the half cubit branch and freeing the lion's tail in under eighteen parts. Halfway through the larger branch, it started to bow downward at the cut, drawing a series of louder howls from the lion.

Japheth motioned for Elisheva to take his place on the saw. He positioned his shoulder beneath the branch on the lion's side of where they were cutting. With clenched teeth and a shout, he lifted the limb to straighten the bow while Noah and Elisheva continued cutting. Near the end, Japheth ripped through the last bit of tree flesh and bark with a final upward thrust of his legs.

The lion bounded from beneath the limb, soaked but uninjured. She took a moment to nuzzle her head against the legs of her three rescuers before joining them as they mounted the horse and dashed off for the ark.

With one hand holding the reins and another shielding his brow, Noah strained to see through the storm. Now less than 250 cubits away, he feared something was causing him to hallucinate. He'd looked at the ark several times during their final run for safety,

336

and each time his eyes had given him a different picture. Was the door to the ark open or closed?

Arriving at the base of the ramp, his fears dissipated at the sight of Miryam and his family rushing out to greet them. The patriarch slipped from the saddle, his heart heavy at the thought of what he was about to do. He smacked his horse on the rump, sending him running down the other side of the rise. "Wish we had room for you boy, but we're full."

Once they were inside, he and his sons pulled in the planks joining the edge of the ramp to the bottom of the door. "Close it." he said.

Ham and Japheth pushed against the huge access door, but it was ripped from their hands, slamming tight against the door frame.

"What was that?" Shem said. "The wind?"

"There's no wind in here," Ham said.

CHAPTER 62

Shechem stood alone on the covered terrace watching shards of water pelt the house Malluch had given him. Inside, the noise of a wedding festival filled the halls of the palace, vying with the whistling of the wind for his attention. He couldn't recall it ever having rained this hard. Could there be something to the Preacher's prophecy?

Footsteps approached from behind. "So this is where the commander of Eden's army is hiding," Malluch said. "What possessed you to come out here on such a wretched night?"

"Just getting some air. And giving my eardrums a rest."

"Ah, yes. Strange isn't it, how wine decreases men's inhibitions, yet increases the power of their vocal chords?"

"It is, my lord."

"I must admit I missed Bohar today. By now, I'm sure he would be passed out somewhere, or forcing himself on some unlucky woman. Odd as it sounds, it was his character flaws I found the most entertaining."

Shechem suffered no such feelings of nostalgia. He was thankful Bohar was gone. And the fact he may have ended up in the stomach of the Preacher's lion made it all the more satisfying. "I remember."

Malluch stepped beside him to peer out across the terrace, the wind billowing his purple tunic. "Quite the tempest, isn't it? Tell me, Commander, you're not thinking about that wild threat of the Preacher's, are you?"

"Given the power of this storm, it's hard not to at least think about it."

"I've seen a thousand storms like this. Tomorrow when the sun comes out, you'll feel silly you even considered it."

"I hope so."

"You will. Now that this wedding is over, we can concentrate on recruiting a new army, destroying the Preacher and his legion of beasts, and then—" He paused as though mulling the idea over in his mind.

"Then what, my lord?"

"Then we return to the garden as we planned."

"Without an army of our own, and without Ramalech's support?"

"Once his army succeeds in defeating the Preacher's, I think he'll be more agreeable to joining us for a return to the garden Out of gratitude alone."

Shechem nodded at his friend's logic.

"But even if he doesn't, we'll be going," Malluch said.

"What? When?"

"One hundred twenty years, Commander. All this time I've waited to take my revenge. I eliminated the twenty-one traitors who abandoned my father and brother, and soon the Preacher. That leaves just the guardian to close the circle of retribution."

"It's going to take time to replace our army."

"Which is why you must begin your recruitment effort in the morning. We must rebuild Eden's army to at least its former strength in the event we're forced to return to the garden alone."

"You think five thousand will be enough?"

"Years ago, you said you could do it with half that. Putting aside my personal reasons, don't forget our original purpose for going

339

there. If we're successful in obtaining fruit from the tree of life, no one on earth will dare oppose us—including Ramalech."

"When do you figure on traveling to Enoch?"

"Tomorrow or the next day." Malluch lifted his eyes to the falling torrent. "Just as soon as this rain lets up."

* * *

Seven days later, Shechem marched into the great hall where Malluch, his wife, son, and new daughter-in-law were seated around the dining table. "Commander, I see by the grim look on your face you're about to spoil a perfectly good meal."

"Forgive the intrusion, my lord, but might I have a word with you in private?"

Everyone in the room stopped to look up at the hall's vaulted ceiling, its acoustics magnifying the sound of the wind whistling outside. "If it's about the rain, I've already heard enough whining from the guards, priests, and servants."

"I really think I should speak to you alone."

"Nonsense. This is my family." Malluch waved his arm around the table. "Whatever you have to say to me affects them."

"Eden's river is overflowing."

"So? It's overflowed before during periods of hard rain."

"Not like this. The banks are gone and we estimate the river's width to have more than doubled. Dozens of homes and farms built near it have been washed away by raging waters that have made it impossible to cross."

"Commander, this city is surrounded by a wall twenty cubits high. You mean to tell me if we barricade the south gate, it won't provide protection against a river that's still ten, twelve furlongs away?"

"The walls are failing, my lord. The foundations have been weakened by the heavy rains, and the driving winds have caused sections to collapse all around the city. Even using the six hundred men I'd managed to recruit for our army hasn't enabled us to keep up with the repair efforts."

Malluch examined the dazed faces of his family.

"There's more, my lord." He paused and stared deeply into the governor's eyes, hoping he would take the cue.

Malluch stood and grabbed Shechem's upper arm, leading him away from the table. He lowered his voice. "More?"

"Water is pouring into the streets from the two wells dug at either end of the city. And we've received word from our sailors returning from the Great Sea of strange happenings there."

"What sort of happenings?"

"Violent eruptions along the sea floor have opened fissures, pumping out water that churns at the surface like a bubbling cauldron. Closer to shore, they spew as fountains rising fifteen cubits in the air."

Malluch's mouth fell open.

"The tide there rose eight cubits in one day. By the third day, the seaport was completely underwater. The sailors barely made it back to shore to escape and warn us."

"Your opinion, Commander?"

He knew exactly what was happening, only he dare not admit to him his belief the Preacher had been right all along. Better just to suggest a departure strategy. But before he could answer, Malluch's son rose from the table. "I'll give you an opinion, Father. We need to get out of here and make it to the high ground."

"Your son is wise," Shechem said. "Many of our citizens have already moved to the surrounding hills."

"Very well, Commander. We'll head for the northern mountains first thing in the morning."

"I'm afraid we don't have that much time."

Malluch glanced at his family, then back to his army's commander. "Are you saying we don't have a day?"

341

"I'm saying we may not have hours. The ground is saturated. There's just no place for the water to go. The streets are a muddy quagmire, trapping both man and animal. We have to leave now."

Malluch looked again to the pleading eyes of his wife and daughter-in-law before turning back to Shechem. "Give the order for everyone in the palace to be ready to leave in two hours."

"Yes, my lord."

CHAPTER 63

Noah's mind ran in half a dozen directions while he and Miryam added straw to the panther's pen just before midday. It had only been a week, and already he worried how he was going to keep his family together — and sane. Ariel wasn't the only one affected by the enclosed space, the smell of confinement with thousands of animals had been more than any of them expected.

He likened it to being in a cave, dark and damp, the window on the top deck providing the only aperture to the outside world. Lamps were kept burning throughout the vessel, which he had his sons reduce by half at dusk to simulate the passing of day into night.

For efficiency of movement about the ark, he and his family had located their quarters on the second deck near the ship's midsection. They shared the deck with the medium-sized animals and the cats. Below them, the largest land mammals were housed to assist in maintaining ballast. The top deck was reserved for the smaller creatures, the creeping things, and all the birds.

Despite having been provided bedding materials inside their pen, the lions insisted on sleeping on the deck outside he and Miryam's quarters. They'd spent their first night in the ark

343

growling their displeasure and keeping everyone awake until Miryam let them out.

Ariel had trouble sleeping and spent all day and sometimes half the night pacing up and down the deck's walkways. Most of the time, Shiphrah or Elisheva walked with her. When they weren't walking, they'd stand or sit near the window, cracking it just a bit against the wind to get a breath of fresh air.

Outside, the wind and rain lashed against the ship's roof and hull, instilling a sense of foreboding throughout the family. There had been a panic yesterday among the women when the ark shifted slightly in the softening earth. Noah grew concerned their fear would only increase once they began to ride upon the waters.

He dropped an armful of straw at the sound of Shem's voice resounding from below.

"Father, you'd better come down here."

With puzzled eyes, Miryam called to Japheth at the prow before joining Noah in hurrying down to the lower deck. The two lions followed. One hundred twenty-five cubits down the walkway, Shem waved to them from outside one of the pens.

"What is it?" Noah said.

"Listen," Shem said. He gestured across the pen to the inside of the hull.

Something struck against the outside of the ark. Japheth and the other family members arrived, their footsteps silenced by Noah's raised hand. Shem pushed against a bison partially blocking the pen entrance so his father could enter. Together the two men moved to the hull wall past the other bison lying on the floor.

"Let us in!" a voice called, barely audible through the hull and above the din of the storm.

"Help us," another said. From several places along the wall on either side of Noah and Shem, the pleas were repeated by other voices, along with more pounding.

"Japheth," Noah said. "You and Ham check the other side."

344

Elisheva walked through the pen to her father-in-law. "Father, can't we let them in? "Surely there's enough room in the ark, and we have plenty of food."

He'd expected this question for some time. And knowing Elisheva's character, he wasn't surprised it came from her. "I'm sorry, but those people are a part of a world the Lord passed sentence on over a hundred years ago. We couldn't help them now if we wanted to."

"Not even a few?"

"A few? And how would you choose who to let in and who to leave behind?"

Elisheva lowered her gaze. "It all just seems so cruel and tragic."

"It is. But how much more so for Him who created them. Must not the Lord's heart be breaking to have to destroy those He made in His own image?"

"Surrounded by people dying, it's hard to look at it from God's perspective."

"I don't know why we have to take all these smelly animals with us," Ariel said. She caught the male lion looking at her and quickly covered her mouth, as if trying to stop what had already come out

Noah resisted a smile, turning to the sound of his two sons returning.

"Same thing on that side, Father" Japheth said. "People banging on the hull, crying to be let in."

A man screamed from above, the cry growing louder the closer it traveled towards them, until it was silenced by a muffled splat in the mud outside. It was followed by another which seemed to come from an area farther up toward the prow.

"They're on the shoring." Japheth said.

He nodded. "A futile gesture."

For a moment, the wind outside appeared to let up, making it easier to hear the pounding against the hull. Noah's family grew silent the louder the reverberations grew.

345

Ariel covered her ears. "Make them stop." She buried her head into Shem's chest. "Make them stop."

"Take her above, son," Noah said. "Better yet, maybe we should all move to the upper decks."

A short time later, he and Miryam were in their quarters discussing ways to lessen the impact of the pounding when Ariel ran by outside on the walkway.

"Ariel," Shem said, chasing her. "Stop!"

She dashed up the ramp to the top deck.

Noah, Miryam, and the rest of the family gave chase. They arrived to find Ariel at the top of the stairs trying to climb out the window and Shem hanging onto her heel. "Let go of me." She tried shaking loose, but he stepped to where he could get an arm around her waist and pulled her from the window. She fell sobbing into his arms.

"What's your plan for dealing with this?" Japheth said to his father.

"Can't we put some kind of lock on the window?" Ham said.

Ariel's terror had been prompted by the banging outside the hull on the lower deck, something the rising waters would soon put an end to. "Let's make sure she stays on the upper decks. She'll be all right once the pounding stops."

CHAPTER 64

A thin stream of water trickled from the ceiling down a wall of Shechem's bedroom. It had been a good house, and eighty-five years ago Malluch had spared no expense in its construction. But then it had never been subjected to a storm of this ferocity.

Claudia waited for him in the palace while he made a final walk-through to ensure they hadn't left anything essential behind. He smiled examining a rock in the shape of a tortoise one of his daughters had once given him. He picked up a jewel encrusted chalice his other daughter presented him on the day of his promotion to Commander of the Army. He hoped both of them now had the good sense to move to higher ground.

He carefully placed the rock and the chalice back on the shelf of the alcove and moved into his wife's dressing room. *Not much chance of her leaving any clothes behind.* He scanned the empty space. In the far corner, another trickle of water seeped down the marble from the ceiling. Only the water wasn't pooling on the floor like in their bedroom. Shechem moved to the end of the room and squatted before the slightly less than three cubit wall to inspect the anomaly.

The water appeared to drain through a joint where the bottom of the wall met the floor. He ran his finger along the joint, confirming

347

by feel what his eyes were telling him, that the two surfaces weren't permanently joined. Shechem pushed on the wall but it didn't move. Standing, he pushed again near the right corner. Still, the wall wouldn't budge.

He moved to the opposite corner, this time throwing his shoulder against the wall. Hinged at the opposite end, the slab broke free, nearly sending him tumbling down a set of stone stairs leading into the darkness below.

He grabbed one of the two torches on the wall giving light to his wife's dressing room and started down. He descended in measured strides, the light from his torch illuminating stone walls on either side. By the sixth stair tread, he could feel the drop in temperature of being underground and caught a whiff of dankness from below. At the eighth stair he stopped and lowered his torch when his sandals splashed water. Before him stretched a flooded passageway, while at the far end the faintest shimmer of light fell from the ceiling. The distance was about 180 cubits.

He had no way of knowing how deep the water was, but his feet already told him it was cold. He took another step, shivering as the water reached the bottom of his calves. Two more treads and he reached the floor of the passageway. He raised the torch at the sound of water pouring from multiple cracks along both sides of the wall into the pool now covering his knees.

He paused, wanting to turn back. What purpose would it serve to go on, other than to satisfy his curiosity? He felt exactly the way he had years ago when he followed his wife — wanting to catch her in the act yet secretly hoping he was wrong. Would the answer make him feel better, or worse? No, he couldn't turn back now.

He moved forward down the passageway.

Two thirds of the way, a stone in the wall to the right above his head popped out, splashing in front of him. Water poured from the hole into the corridor, and Shechem realized he didn't have much time.

He reached an identical staircase at the opposite end and climbed toward the light above. At the top, a door stood slightly ajar. He peered through the crack.

Inside, torch light bathed a room adorned with opulent furnishings: a bed with pillows, silken bedding, and a table with pitchers and chalices made of gold. On an opposite wall, another table, where a censer for burning incense rested.

He waited fifty to sixty parts to make sure no one was returning before cautiously entering the room. Located at the opposite end of the chamber, another closed door. He moved to the bed in search of clues, moving pillows and turning down the bedding. He pushed his nose deep into the pillows, the faint scent of his wife's perfume filling his senses. Near the head of the bed on the far side, he found a blue and gold scarf on the floor he recognized as Claudia's. When he picked it up, the soft sound of voices coming from the other side of the closed door piqued his attention.

For a brief moment, he considered fleeing, but when the voices grew no louder, he investigated further. He cracked the door, but the light of the room illuminated only the first four or five steps of an otherwise darkened staircase leading up. This time he decided not to test fate. He placed his burning torch in one of the two wine pitchers, entered the staircase, and closed the door behind him.

In the pitch blackness, he mounted the stairs using his hands to feel his way along the walls. At the top, a thin sliver of light shone through the crack at the bottom of the door. Here, the voices were easier to make out, although he could tell they were coming from a distance farther away than the other side of the door.

"You don't need to take every garment you own," Malluch said.

"If I have to live in a tent for who knows how long, I'm going to be comfortable," his wife snapped back.

Shechem's knees buckled, and he fell against the wall of the staircase. How could it be? Negotiating the corridor, he'd figured early on the passage from his wife's dressing room was leading back to the palace. But Malluch? Shechem had been a loyal friend

349

and servant to him for over three hundred years. He'd saved his life at the garden. How could Malluch be the one to betray him?

He leaned against the wall, occasionally reaching to wipe mucus from his nose. Then, like a candle being blown out, his emotions turned. He felt his face flush and clamped his teeth together. He clenched his fists so tight, the fingernails dug into his palms.

He drew his sword and reached for the door, only the moisture on his hands caused the handle to slip through his fingers. It stopped him from acting on impulse and gave him a moment to think.

Were he to charge in now and kill him, he might not be able to convince his wife of her husband's treachery before she summoned the guards. And even if he did, what if she didn't care? In either case, he would be forced to silence her to protect himself, a decision he didn't want to make. She had, after all, been made to play the fool also.

Shechem wiped away a tear on his cheek. *The rising water!* He composed himself and started back down the stairs, bridling his impatience to keep from stumbling in the darkness. He grabbed his torch on the way through the secret room and descended the staircase on the other side. This time, his feet hit water on the third stair. He continued down until his chin touched the surface of the water, and still he hadn't reached the bottom of the corridor. He would have to swim back.

Struggling to tread water holding a torch or with a sword on his belt was near impossible. So he placed both on the stair nearest the corridor ceiling, hoping the torch would light at least part of the way for his return. With the sound of leaking water urging him on, he dove headfirst into the cold, wet abyss.

Thankfully, his swimming skills hadn't abandoned him after all these years. Despite the cold and the diminishing light behind him, he estimated he had reached the halfway point in less than eighteen parts. But when he brushed against the ceiling, he recognized the corridor was filling faster than he thought. He quickened his pace, shortening his stroke to keep from scraping his arm again.

350

Shechem's satisfaction with his progress evaporated when turbulence in the water pushed him off course, slamming his body against the left wall. Beneath the surface, rocks and dirt from the opposite side crashed into his legs. Fear embraced him watching the corridor disintegrate. His body floated to the ceiling, a buoy in the rising water. An instant later, it covered him.

Before going under, he managed to steal two things: a final gasp of air and a glimpse of light at the end of the passage. Now, he hoped he could hold onto both until he reached the staircase. The final leg of the journey he would have to navigate blind.

He fought to master his fear. Panic was his enemy, and it would cause him to expend at a greater rate the precious oxygen stored in his lungs. So instead of reaching and kicking for speed, Shechem pulled himself through the water in short, synchronized strokes. He groped the water in front with one hand, while pushing over and through the rocks and silt piling beneath him with the other. Was he headed in the right direction? Or had he been driven off course toward a dead-end void by the disturbance of the crumbling wall? He would need the answer soon because his lungs were about to burst.

With two more labored kicks, Shechem's fingertips touched something solid, a horizontal ninety-degree corner. He released the air from his lungs and mounted what he hoped was a staircase. If it wasn't, or if it had somehow become blocked above him, his next breath would be water.

His head breached the surface, and he continued up the staircase into his wife's dressing room. He ran to the far end and stopped, taking in huge gulps of air. All the while, water poured from the doorway into the room. He hurried out.

"What happened to you?" Claudia said when he approached her in a hallway of the palace.

"What do you mean?"

"It took you over an hour to check an empty house? And look at yourself. I know it's pouring outside, but really. You look like you bathed with your clothes on."

"I was outside longer than expected."

"What happened to your sword?"

His hand fell to his empty sheath, and he deliberately screwed on a puzzled look. "I fell on my way back to the palace when my foot stuck in the mud. I must have lost it then. I'll draw another from the armory." At that moment, he was thankful he'd left the sword behind. In his state of mind, he feared the temptation to use it on his wife would be too great.

CHAPTER 65

Two weeks had passed since the banging outside the ark had ceased, replaced by the sound of lapping water. Noah had noted its daily rise up the sides of the hull. It wouldn't be long before they'd be waterborne.

One evening at twilight, he and his family sat down to a meal on the second deck near their quarters. There was a shudder. The ark listed slowly left, then right, drawing gasps from the women and toppling two pitchers of water and all the cups. Everyone put their palms on the deck to steady themselves, and the sound of animals stumbling in their pens or crying out resounded from below.

"Is it an earthquake?" Ham said.

"No, son. We're being lifted by the water."

Timbers squeaked, and a scraping sound came from several places along both sides of the ark.

"What's that?" Ariel said, latching on to Shem's arm.

"The shoring rubbing against the hull as the ark is being raised. It will stop soon."

But after about seventy parts, the scraping continued. All heads followed the sound of the screeching planks. Except for Ariel. Her lip quivered and her eyes grew wider, so wide Noah feared they might burst from their sockets. She covered her ears.

A moment later, she pushed out of Shem's arms and ran across the room toward the exit. Noah grabbed her. "I've got to get out of here," she said. "Please, let me out."

"Where would you go?" he said.

"Father, I'm sorry, but I can't stay in here any longer. Please, let me go. I'd rather drown with the others than be locked in here."

Miryam came up from behind and put her arm around her. "You don't mean that, dear."

Ariel whirled sharply. "I do mean it, Mother. I'm suffocating in here. This is my last chance to escape."

"Being in here has been tough on all of us. But that's no reason for you to sacrifice yourself."

"Isn't it? I can't sleep. I can barely eat. I feel like I'm going crazy. Can death be any worse?"

Noah pulled Ariel back to him, fixing his gaze on hers. "You can't leave. And you mustn't die."

"Wh—"

"God chose you for salvation for a reason." He gently turned her to face the others, bending in close to her ear. "You three are the mothers of a civilization. You're the new Eve."

Tears stained the tops of Ariel's cheeks. "Let them be the new Eve. I don't want the honor."

Noah motioned for Elisheva and Shiphrah to join them. "Go with your mother and take Ariel to the window for some fresh air. At least until we've cleared the shoring." On their way out of the room, he pulled Shiphrah aside. "And keep a close watch on her. Make sure she doesn't try to climb out."

* * *

Shechem marched toward the top of a hill where Malluch gazed toward Eden some forty furlongs to the southwest. What he

354

must be thinking, standing there in the pouring rain watching floodwaters engulf his city.

Shechem was, of course, thinking of murder, and had been ever since finding his wife's secret room two weeks ago.

Should he do it now? He could get away with it. All the people were huddled safely inside their tents. He could clasp his hand over Malluch's mouth and run him through with a single thrust from behind. All that would be left would be to roll his body down the hill and allow the roar of the storm to cover any final death throes.

Instead, he came up beside him. He cringed watching the wall he'd labored over for fifteen years crumble into the waters like a dune disintegrating in the wind.

Pitched tents littered the hill, and across each of the higher ones on either side. Despite his personal woes, he was pleased so many of Eden's citizens had made it to safety. Until just a few days ago, they'd shared the hills with a variety of animals fleeing the same rising tide.

Now, only the horses and donkeys that'd carried them to safety remained. Malluch had ordered the destruction of all the wild animals in retaliation for losing his army. Shechem estimated his recruits had butchered thousands.

"There goes the palace," Shechem said. The spire to the magnificent structure toppled over, disappearing in the swirling flood.

Malluch stared at the city with arms folded, rain pouring off the end of his protruding jaw. "Commander."

"Yes, my lord." Though he'd given the response a thousand times, the title now burned on his tongue. He no more considered the man his lord than the hill they were standing on. And an expression he'd uttered out of respect for over a hundred years had overnight become profane.

"You think the Preacher is still alive?"

355

He paused to consider his response, careful again not to reveal too much of what he knew. "Probably. Even if Bohar succeeded in destroying the ark, the Preacher is smart enough to have made plans for an alternate escape."

"I hope he is."

"Why?"

Malluch's head swiveled to him. "Oh, I think you know, Commander. Twice now he's escaped me. And the nightmares. You remember. The ones that came back after having disappeared for all those years. They continue to haunt me. Will I ever truly know peace until I've looked upon his dead body?"

Shechem couldn't believe it. With the world drowning around them, his betrayer remained obsessed with his hatred. He decided to change the subject to something more pressing. "Tomorrow we should head for the mountains."

Malluch turned back toward Eden, sighing heavily. "If we must."

CHAPTER 66

A week later, Shechem stood outside Malluch's tents on the side of a mountain surrounded by his army watching the chaos below.

Hundreds fought in the pouring rain over diminishing numbers of supplies and positions of elevation along the hillside. Bodies littered the landscape or floated in the waters, most the result of these fracases, others dying at their own hands. For whatever time he had left, he was certain he would not forget the image of dozens of men on their knees, slumped over their swords. Some had the bodies of their slain families around them.

To his left, a man rolled down the hill in front of him and cried out. He was followed by a leather bag that broke when it struck the ground, scattering gold coins. It was a scene he'd seen repeated numerous times in recent days, with the rich attempting to buy food or a higher place on the mountain. Laughter greeted most of the attempts, but one arrogant and persistent barterer had his jaw forced open and the coins stuffed into his mouth.

"Try eating that," one of his tormenters had said.

Until a few days ago, Shechem's recruit army had been successful in quelling most of these disturbances. But after losing over sixty men to mobs swarming them for their weapons—weapons which they'd then turned on each other—he suspended

357

all policing operations. His soldiers' job now was to protect the governor and his family.

It was an order he had loathed to give, but did so out of a sense of duty more than anything else. He also couldn't take the chance Malluch would be killed accidentally in an uprising, robbing him of his opportunity for vengeance.

With the day's light fading, the violence below subsided. If it followed its usual pattern, the fighting would cease overnight and resume when daybreak revealed to those at the bottom the threat of encroaching waters.

A touch of a hand on his shoulder spun him around to face Malluch, cloaked beneath the hood of his tunic. "Let's take a walk, Commander." He led Shechem to a place overlooking the far side of their tents, away from the soldiers and other prying ears. "Tell me, how many people would you say are left on these mountains?"

He scanned the mountain range. "About eight thousand." When Malluch didn't respond immediately, Shechem saw the wheels turning in his head again. "You're not thinking of—"

"Look down there, Commander. What do you see? How long do you think it will be before they come to take *our* place on the mountain?"

"But they're our own people. Relatives. Friends."

"Not any more. Now they're just animals fighting for the right to survive."

"Surely, there must be another way, my lord."

"Each day the waters rise and the land shrinks." Malluch studied the mountain. "By the time we reach the top, there won't be room for all of us."

"But murdering our own citizens?"

"And how many men did you lose in the last few days in confrontations with those citizens?"

"More than sixty."

"Leaving you fewer than 540 to protect us."

"Yes, but they are armed."

358

"Armed." Malluch snorted. "Commander, what do you think would happen if those eight thousand people decided to rush us right now?"

"We'd probably be overrun."

"Exactly. And what do you think the men below are thinking right now?"

"I don't know."

"Sure you do. They've lost more than three quarter their number on the journey from Eden. You and your men represent the last guardians of civil authority on earth. If I were them, I'd be thinking of ways to overpower you while they still maintain an advantage in numbers."

"But we don't know for sure."

"Don't we? Think about it, Commander. And be honest with yourself. We need to act. Now."

Once again, Shechem found himself conflicted by a decision he could neither avoid nor escape. This wasn't the massacre of three thousand slaves or the even the ritual sacrifice of two hundred children. This was the murder of eight thousand of his fellow countryman and the thought left a rancid taste in his mouth.

But what could he do? If he refused, the governor would simply give the order to one of his captains, bypassing him completely. Maybe even have him eliminated.

He could kill Malluch right there and hope his men held a stronger allegiance to their commander than to him. But then killing him wouldn't change the reality of what was transpiring below. Unless the rains stopped, his men would eventually be forced to kill to protect themselves or be overrun by the mobs. With a deep sense of regret, he conceded the inevitable. "What's your plan?"

"Five hundred forty soldiers and eight thousand people. That's roughly fifteen people per man, give or take. Can your men handle that number?"

He wanted desperately to say, "No," that the odds were too extreme, his soldiers too green, or their chances of being detected too great. Anything to put a stop to this madness. But it wouldn't do any good. "They can handle it."

"Of course, a good number of these are going to be women and children."

Shechem cleared his throat, straining to keep his emotions in check.

"You'll want to wait until well after midnight and the camp is asleep. Night and the drumming of the rains will provide cover for your men to sneak into the tents. Be sure your soldiers target the men of each family first. A firm pass across the front of the throat with a knife or sword will discourage screaming." Malluch lifted his chin as though searching the heavens. "Oh, how I wish Bohar was here."

"You want them to kill *all* the women and children?"

"Commander, I've known plenty of women able to wield a sword or a young man a knife. But for now, in addition to their own families, have your soldiers spare any children under the age of six along with their mothers. Kill the rest."

Shechem couldn't maintain his composure any longer. He shook his head.

"Unthinkable?" Malluch said. "Not really. In fact, it might be a more compassionate fate than awaits the rest of us."

"How's that?"

"Two weeks from now, we may all find ourselves at the top of this mountain with the waters swirling around our feet. At that moment, I suspect the mothers of those spared will wish their children had perished quickly with the others."

"Then why bother to spare any of them?"

"There's always the possibility the rains could stop. If so, we'll need at least some women and children to seed the new world."

Shechem went off to meet with his commanders and plan another slaughter, after which he spent the remainder of the

360

evening alone in quiet contemplation. But he couldn't get the governor's last words out of his head. *Compassionate? Wonder how compassionate he'd find the firm pass of a sword across his throat.*

For the first time, he even considered ending his own life in addition to Malluch's. Leave the problem of dealing with the end of the world to one of his captains. What kept him from doing it? Was his sense of self-preservation that strong? Or was he simply a coward? Three times during the evening and early morning he got out of bed to summon his commanders to cancel the order, only to back out each time.

By the time he got up a fourth time, it was too late.

Two hours past midnight, his men snuck out to do the unthinkable.

* * *

The next night, Shechem awoke to a waterlogged back and the sound of his wife and every other woman in camp screaming. He scampered to the entrance to their tent, to where water dribbled in from the outside. "Gather our things. I'll be back shortly." He threw on his tunic and walked out.

In the darkness and pouring rain, women and soldiers ran back and forth across the plateau, their feet splashing in water up to their ankles. He could barely see, but the thunder of the waves striking just below told him what was feeding the shallow lake they walked in.

He stopped four soldiers passing by in opposite directions. "Find your captains. Tell them to meet me here in front of my tent immediately. We need to get ahead of this panic."

"Yes sir." They hurried away.

Shechem headed for Malluch's tent directly behind him, but was interrupted by a woman's scream coming from his left. He wheeled to find her seated in the water a short distance away with

361

the corpse of a man lying across her lap. "Get it off," she said. "Get it off me." He charged over and dragged the body off, then helped the woman up. She ran off crying in the dark, careful to avoid the other bodies floating in her path.

"What's happened, Commander?" Malluch said, splashing toward him. "Where's all this water coming from?"

He pointed to where white waves continued to beat against the edge of the grade. "I knew we should have broken camp after last night's—" he fumbled for a suitable word. "Last night's exercise. But my men were exhausted, and your advisors assured us we'd be safe here for another night. Looks like they miscalculated."

"And the bodies? I thought your men were supposed to dispose of them in the sea."

"And so they did, my lord. But with nearly eight thousand of them, some were bound to float."

"When we make it out of here, my advisors will wish they were among them. What's your plan, Commander?"

"My captains are meeting me here." He pointed up to several passes leading up the mountain. "As soon as the tents are down, we'll begin moving everyone up to higher ground."

"Good. My guards are—"

Shechem shot his hand up. "Do you hear that?"

Both men whirled around to the rushing sound behind them. They were bowled over by a wave of water and corpses washing across the plateau. The torrent flattened most of the tents, including all in Malluch's party. Shechem screamed, adding his voice to all the others being carried away by the wave passing through the camp.

362

CHAPTER 67

Noah didn't know why he was awake. It had been a long day, and he was tired. Since they'd been launched upon the waters, most nights the billows rocked him to sleep the way his mother used to. Not so tonight.

Earlier, he'd heard Ariel and Shiphrah walking the decks. He decided to get up and join them.

On his way toward the rear of the ark, he and the lioness peeked into Shem and Ariel's quarters. Shem lay alone on the floor, snoring louder than the elephants below. *Poor girl. No wonder she's up walking half the night.*

Nearing the stern, he caught sight of a single figure in the reduced lighting coming toward him. "Out by yourself this evening, daughter?"

"Ariel said she was tired and going to bed," Shiphrah said. "I was just saying goodnight to some of our passengers."

"How long ago did Ariel leave you?"

"About half an hour."

"Well, I just checked on her quarters, and she wasn't there. We'd better try to find her. Why don't you check below and I'll look on the top deck?"

"Yes, Father."

363

The three walked briskly together toward the front of the ship, parting at the landing where the ramps lead up and down. Noah headed directly for the stairs that provided access to the window, but finding it secured, he moved on to search the remainder of the top deck. Shiphrah's cry sent him and the lioness running for the down ramp on the opposite side. "Ariel, No!"

He reached the bottom of the ramp to find Ariel standing on the far side of the access door trying to pry it open with a lance. Behind her, Shiphrah ran toward her along the walkway.

Ariel glanced behind at her charging sister-in-law, then back to him. She threw all her weight against the shaft of the spear, breaking the seal. The door burst open just as Shiphrah reached her, the rushing waters knocking the two women off their feet and sending them sprawling across the deck. Noah yelled for help when the force of the flailing door struck him, pushing him against the inside hull.

It took about nine parts for Shem, Ham, Miryam, and the male lion to arrive. Noah's family took a position against the door beside him and together the four managed to push it about halfway closed. Standing off to the side, the two lions watched the wind and water continue to pour in through the gaping entrance. "Where's your brother?" Noah groaned.

"He was down below." Ham said.

"Japheth! Get up here. Hurry!"

Japheth and Elisheva appeared on the walkway opposite them through the translucent spray washing in.

"Son, you have to go around."

"There isn't time." He motioned for Elisheva to go around, then backed up a dozen paces. He ran toward the doorway and attempted to leap across the threshold. Just then another wave poured water in through the door, catching his body in midair and driving it across the deck. He was stopped when his head struck the bottom of one of the stanchions.

Shiphrah and Ariel scrambled to their feet and, with an arriving Elisheva, fought against the flow of rushing water to reach Japheth. Elisheva kneeled and raised her husband's head onto her lap.

"How is he?" Noah said.

"Unconscious," Elisheva said.

The rest of the family was losing ground, the force of the water inching the door back against them. "Father," Shem said, straining. "If we don't get this door closed in a hurry, the ark is going to flood."

"You have to rouse him," Noah said.

Elisheva slapped his face, gently at first, then harder. "Japheth. Wake up. You've got to wake up."

"Put some water in his nose."

Elisheva's eyes widened in disbelief "What!"

"Put some water in your hand and drip it down into his nose."

"Are you sure?"

"Quickly!"

Elisheva reached for the water and followed Noah's instructions. At once, Japheth gagged and coughed.

"That's enough. Now turn his head to the side so he can get the water out."

Elisheva turned his face into her lap, and he continued to cough. After a few parts, he lifted his head and gasped heavily, trying to gain his bearings. Seeing his father and the others, he stumbled to the opposite walkway out of sight.

A moment later, he came up behind them. "Excuse me, Mother." He gently moved her out of the way to take her place on the door.

His height allowed him to throw his shoulder against the highest part of the door, while his father and siblings assumed positions beside and beneath him. Slowly the door closed, choking off the flow of incoming water. The four let out a collective grunt, slamming the door and securing it against the far doorpost.

Shem and Ham comforted their wives, while Japheth touched the back of his head impacted by the stanchion. A small amount of blood stained his fingers. "What happened?"

He and the rest of the family looked to Noah, Shiphrah, and Ariel for an answer, but no one spoke. Ariel sobbed into her hands.

"Well?" Japheth said.

Ariel mumbled something unintelligible through her fingers.

"What did she say?" he said to Shiphrah standing next to her.

"It was me," Ariel said. "I opened the door."

The two brothers descended upon her. "What?" Japheth said. He towered over her, hands on hips.

"Are you crazy?" Ham said.

Miryam eyed her youngest sharply. "Ham."

"But Mother. She could have killed us all."

Miryam spun to her husband seeking support.

"Unfortunately, he's not wrong," Noah said. "This could have been a disaster."

"I tried to tell you," Ariel said. "For weeks I tried. I told you I was going crazy in here and begged you to let me go. But you wouldn't listen. I couldn't take it anymore."

Red-faced with anger, Japheth took two steps toward her before turning back to Noah. "Let her go, Father."

Miryam grabbed her son by the upper arm. "Japheth, no!"

Shem started toward him, but was restrained by Ariel. Japheth pivoted to his brother. "I'm sorry Shem, but maybe Ariel's right. We should have listened to her."

"That's your brother's wife you're talking about," Miryam said.

"Yes, Mother. But being our brother's wife doesn't absolve her of responsibility for the rest of us. Next time we might not be so lucky. What if she sneaks up here again?"

Shiphrah rose up like the female bear in the hold below, pushing her chest into Japheth's stomach, neck craned back to address him. "Who are you to say 'let her go'?" She began poking her finger into

366

his sternum, pushing him back a little with each poke. "Have you no compassion? You've seen what Ariel has been through since we've been locked in here. How would you feel if someone said to let Elisheva go?" She glared at Ham. "Or me?"

When she was done, Shiphrah had backed Japheth halfway across the deck. His mouth hung open, and the redness of anger had been replaced by a blush of shame. "Well, I don't know what else to do." His voice roared. "We can't watch her every hour of the day."

"Can't we?" Miryam said. "We can do what you men did when the ark was being vandalized. Shiphrah, Elisheva, and I will take turns standing watch at night. If Ariel gets anxious and feels the need for a walk after dark, one of us will be there to go with her. Just like Shiphrah's been doing during the day."

"Father?" Japheth said.

"I think your mother has the ideal solution," Noah said.

Japheth winced and reached to touch the back of his head again. "What now?"

"I'd say we'd better see how much water we've got to bail out of here."

"Somebody want to take a look at this first and tell me how bad it is?"

Elisheva and Shiphrah turned their backs to join the rest of the family moving toward the down ramp, leaving Ham alone to examine his brother's head wound. "All right, so I'm a scoundrel," Japheth hollered after them.

CHAPTER 68

So this is what it's like to be on an island. Shechem trembled in the frigid altitude and rain from one of the last visible mountaintops on earth. He estimated no more than a hundred cubits separated the top of the roughly twenty-acre peak from the rising waters below.

After thirty-five days, he, Claudia, Malluch, and another man with a wife and two sons had ended up on the same piece of limestone. Other refugees from Eden populated similar summits across the mountain range.

The flood in the camp had scattered both the living and the dead across the plateau. He and Malluch had been swept to one end of the elevation, and his betrayer's family to the other. During his search for Claudia, he caught sight of Malluch's son leading his wife and mother to safety up one of the other passes.

The majority of his army had suffered the same fate as the people they'd murdered. Those that hadn't been washed away by the flood turned their swords on each other when quarrels erupted over space on the mountain. Even Shechem was forced to kill some of his own men in self-defense.

Of the more than forty thousand people left in Eden at the time of their departure, he guessed fewer than two hundred had survived to reach the peaks.

Now these few vestiges of rock were all that was left for any of them.

And the birds. Thousands of birds.

Though the last of the terrestrial animals had perished more than a week ago, the gift of flight had granted the birds a reprieve. Now they covered the mountains and filled the skies above them. So dense was their number on land, he and his party could barely take a step without displacing one of them.

But he wasn't focused on either the birds or the sea. The only thing he cared about now was how much time he had left to exact his revenge. Any previous notion he might have been mistaken about his wife and Malluch had been dispelled during the last few weeks. The looks he'd seen them exchange when they thought he wasn't watching said it all. If the Preacher's God was truly behind the flood, He would have to wait His turn.

Windswept waves crashed against the bottom of the mountaintop, splashing his feet and the hem of his tunic. He signaled to his wife beside him and to Malluch a few cubits above. "Time to move again."

The father of the family examined the surface of the cliff. "Too steep. We'll try the other side."

Shechem nodded, watching until they disappeared around the edge of the peak. He, Claudia, and Malluch started up the irregular surface of the crag. Although sharp, the slope offered numerous spurs and clefts to cling to. The governor would negotiate a half dozen cubits, then wait for him and Claudia. Despite the driving rain and ubiquitous birds, they succeeded in climbing two thirds of the rock face in less than 270 parts.

Nearing the top, Malluch brushed aside a seagull on a small ledge above him and kicked away a pair of crows occupying his next foothold. He went to pull himself up to the next rock but failed to notice the returning gull, which landed on his wrist and began biting his hand.

He attempted to shake off the bird but lost his footing and started sliding down the peak. He and Claudia screamed, but

Shechem took a long stride to his right and lunged to catch him. Their right hands slapped against each other's forearm before locking grips, the scarred flesh of Malluch's fingers closing around his wrist. His betrayer hung suspended in midair, kicking to gain a foothold against the slippery precipice.

At that instant, Shechem realized this was the moment he'd waited for—the time providence had reserved just for him. He entered a dream world. His hearing faded, so that he could barely hear the storm or Claudia's repeated refrain of, "Pull him up! Pull him up!" What he could hear was the sound of his own beating heart. But instead of it racing at the excitement of the moment, his heartbeat slowed and calmness overtook him.

He glared into Malluch's bulging eyeballs and ashen grimace, then turned to Claudia. Her eyes held the same panicked expression.

Without looking back at him, Shechem let go.

Claudia's shriek brought him out of the trance. "Malluch! No!" She screamed and reached after his falling body.

Shechem moved toward her along the rocks, grabbed her by the back of the neck, and drew her in close. "Harlot!" He forced her to look at the body floating face down in the water. "Your lover awaits."

He pushed her off the mount, her scream fading as she plummeted to the sea.

He stood there for eighteen parts, surprised at how close his wife's body floated next to Malluch's. Over and over, the waves slammed their limp corpses against the rocky base of the mountain.

He scaled the remaining distance to the top, then marched through a blanket of birds to the other side to search for the others. The father had been right: The slope on that side of the mountain was less steep. He and his family had made it up about two thirds of the way. Shechem waited to help them up the last few cubits. When he stepped onto the crest, the father scanned the summit. "Where's Malluch?" he said. "And your wife?"

In a faux display of sorrow, Shechem dropped his head. "You were right. It *was* too steep."

The father placed his hand on his shoulder. "I'm sorry, Commander."

He nodded slowly, biting his tongue to keep a smile from appearing.

With daylight fading, he, the family, and about ten thousand birds huddled together under the pounding rains to batten down for the night. Between the five of them, he estimated they had food enough to last for another week.

But he doubted they would have need of it.

* * *

Sometime after noon on the third day, Shechem sat by himself on a ledge staring into the deep. It was a sea he could almost touch, and when the waves hit just right against the rocks, the water touched him. It reminded him of the speed and power of the Eden River and a time when he'd gone there to cry Elisheva out of his system. How ironic to have once risked his life in those waters, only to be trapped by these.

Surely by now, she would be safe inside the ark. It was the only thing left that brought him any sense of comfort. That, and the knowledge she would remember him the way they'd been in their youth. In a moment of desperate romanticism, he dreamed of catching a glimpse of the ark passing by that he might wave good-bye.

Yesterday, he and his companions awoke to less than ten cubits separating them from the waters below. Meanwhile, the last of the bird population was being decimated. Unable either to remain aloft or to find a place to roost on the shrinking mountaintops, they crashed, exhausted, into the sea.

371

But the rising waters and expiring bird numbers only portended of things to come. The mount they were on had become unstable, shaking violently several times over the past three days. They didn't have much time left before the sea would rise or the mountain would fall.

Shechem rose to his feet on the ledge for a better look at an image appearing in the distance. He shielded his brow from the rain while straining to make out what he hoped might be the ark. After a few moments he laughed out loud, realizing it was just the shape of a dark cloud on the horizon.

He stared at the last representatives of humanity dotting mountaintops to the north and south. He comforted himself with the thought his daughters might be among them.

Then the ground began to shake.

At the other end of the summit, the man's wife screamed while the family struggled to cling together against the power of the quake. The ground broke apart beneath his feet, followed by a wave that lifted him up and sideways before pushing him under the water.

He let the wave take him to its chosen depth before beginning his kick back to the surface, which took him longer than he expected. When he arrived, the family and the mountaintop were gone.

He inhaled deeply, forcing air back into his lungs, all the while pulling with his arms and legs against the rolling of the sea. In the distance, maybe eight furlongs from where he floated, the first of three mountaintops remained visible above the surface. Even in these rough waters, he felt confident he could make it to one of them. He set out for the closest mountain.

He swam to within three hundred cubits of safety when he stopped to drift again on top of the waters. He wasn't tired. In fact, he was surprised at how much energy he still had left.

But something inside was telling him it was time to quit. In spite of his hopes, his daughters were in all likelihood gone already, or soon would be. So what was the purpose? Somehow, in the face of their loss and the destruction of the world, his instinct for survival just wasn't that strong. And even if they were alive, he could never look them in the eyes and tell them about their mother.

His mind raced, making it difficult for him to focus on one thing. *This is what happens to you when you're about to die.* He had time to think about the things he'd done wrong in his life. And the things he'd done right. His greatest regret was he hadn't had the courage to kill his betrayer before the slaughter of the remnants of Eden on the mountainside. But then again, perhaps Malluch was right. It was better for them to have died by the edge of the sword than to have to endure this slow, inexorable death. Especially the children.

Thinking of them took him back to his own childhood, to a time when most of the citizens of Eden still believed in the God of Adam. And so had he. But he'd abandoned his faith as he got older, and completely renounced it when he became friends with Malluch. One of the elder's teachings he remembered vividly was that God was slow to anger and eager to forgive. Could Shechem possibly be forgiven now, after all he'd done? Would his confession seem hollow because he was on the brink of death?

He cleared his mind of every thought and—for the first time since he was a young man—went to God.

When he finished praying, a sense of peace he hadn't expected overcame him. Not like the peace he experienced when he was about to drop Malluch. This one seemed to envelop his whole body, as though the temperature of the sea surrounding him had risen. He treaded water for a few dozen parts before resigning himself to the inevitable. He was within reach of land when he cried out in a loud voice to all that was left of humanity. "Elisheva!"

He stopped struggling and allowed the waters to swallow him.

373

CHAPTER 69

Noah had kept an accurate count of the days, placing marks on a beam in his quarters: one hundred and ninety-seven days on the waters. Nearly seven months — six since Ariel had opened the ark to the sea — without another incident. Miryam's plan had worked, she and the other wives rotated shifts to ensure Ariel was never left to walk the decks alone, day or night.

Although sheltered inside the ark, he and his family were keenly aware of events taking place on the outside. Forty days ago, the Lord had caused the rains to cease upon the earth. On the forty-first day, they all gathered at the window in the morning to fully open it for the first time since being shut in.

"What's that yellow thing up there?" Ham said.

The whole family burst into laughter, except for Ariel. She stood with her head pressed against the left frame, letting the sun's rays wash her face. Even when the others had returned to their chores, Shiphrah remained behind with Ariel so she could savor her first taste of freedom.

Noah's family fasted the rest of the day until sunset, then held a feast to commemorate the Lord fulfilling His promise.

For the next one hundred and ten days, the ark floated upon the waters over mostly calm seas. It was a smooth ride compared

374

to the first forty, when the wind and rains had churned the waters into thrashing swells.

On the one hundred and eleventh day, the wind returned, only it wasn't the driving, destructive wind of before. This wind was brisk, but steady, and appeared to blow in a single direction, a condition that did not escape Noah's attention. Whereas during the storm, the ark had been tossed about in an aimless manner, this wind seemed to be pushing the ark in a specific direction. North.

Where was the Lord taking them? And when would they arrive? Once again he dared to ask himself if today would be the day they would receive an answer.

He'd just finished marking the day on the beam when a vibration reverberated through the deck in his quarters. It was joined by a screeching sound coming from below that started at the prow and ran all the way to the stern. With startled faces, he and his family met on the deck outside their quarters.

"What in heaven's name is that?" Elisheva said.

"Let's find out." Noah and the eight of them, along with the two lions, ran for the ramp leading down. When they reached the bottom, another loud screech came toward them from the prow. The deck beneath them trembled, increasing in intensity as the screeching drew closer, then decreasing after it passed.

"Something's scraping against the keel," Japheth said.

His father nodded.

"But what?" Ham said.

An elephant's cry echoed throughout the lower deck, and the sound of the two hippos banging against their pen added to the tension.

"Like them, let's hope it's land." Whatever it was, Noah could tell it had slowed the ark's forward movement, leaving them to bob up and down in the water.

Following 180 parts of silence, together the family started up the ramp. Halfway there, the whole ark shuddered before striking something solid. The jolt sent everyone, including the two lions, toppling onto the ramp. The ark teetered a bit before settling down in a near upright position.

Dazed from the fall, Noah and his family rested in different states of recline along the ramp. Japheth broke the silence. "We've run aground."

Expressions of shock turned to smiles and cheers rang out all around. After the men helped their wives regain footage, they all exchanged hugs and congratulated one another. Ham even hugged the lions. He was also the first to call for a celebration. "How about it, father? Some wine tonight?"

Miryam nodded.

"Why not?" he said. "But first, a word of thanks to He who delivered us."

They joined hands and bowed their heads.

* * *

Noah sat with Shiphrah in the window of the ark near evening four months after striking land. "It's getting dark," she said. "You think she'll be back?"

He peered out over the waters. A week ago he'd sent out a raven after the waters had receded to reveal the tops of the mountains. When the raven didn't return, he sent out a dove, but the dove returned in only a short time. After seven days, he sent the dove out again and here he was waiting for her. He pointed to something flying toward them. "There's your answer."

Shiphrah leaned out the window for a better look. "It's the dove."

Noah stretched out his arm and the dove flew to his hand. He drew her in through the window.

"What's that in her mouth?" Shiphrah said.

376

He removed a green leaf from her mouth, examining it in his palm. "An olive leaf." He broke the leaf in half, exposing the vein. "Fresh."

They embraced before running to tell the others.

CHAPTER 70

In the 601st year of Noah, in the seventh month, the twenty-seventh day of the month . . .

Two months later, Noah and his three sons remained kneeling with their faces to the ground long after the Lord had finished speaking. Before them, smoke rose from a burning altar upon which were laid the quartered pieces of a goat and a split turtle dove. Beyond that, the ark rested five hundred cubits up the mountain.

When the men rose to their feet, the women were leading the last of the large animals—the elephants, hippos, and rhinoceroses—down the ramp. At the bottom, the women stopped and pointed to the sky, then ran toward the altar.

In the clouds above, a ribbon of colors arched across the heavens in a bow that stretched from one horizon to the other.

Elisheva arrived out of breath, just ahead of the others. "What does it mean, Father?"

"A promise," he said.

"What kind of promise?"

"A promise from God to never again use the waters to destroy the earth."

378

Noah's family watched the sky for a few moments before Miryam broke the silence. "Did He say anything else?"

"To be fruitful and multiply," Japheth said.

"You heard it?"

"We all heard it, Mother," Ham said. He moved to his father, bowing his head. "Father, can you forgive my unbelief?"

"There's nothing to forgive. I rejoice the Lord has opened your heart to the truth and that your doubt has left you."

Ham gestured to the two lions standing beside them. "I stopped doubting the day these two showed up and didn't try to eat me." Everyone laughed, but quickly grew silent when Ham's face became set. "But to have heard with my own ears the voice of YAH— speaking to me—" His voice cracked, and he couldn't continue.

Noah pulled Ham to him and the two shared a long embrace.

It was Miryam who lightened the mood. "Be fruitful and multiply. Well, Shem, apparently you take well the Lord's instruction." Miryam reached over and touched Ariel's rounded belly, proudly displaying a five-month pregnancy. Everyone laughed again but Elisheva and Shiphrah, who each put a hand to her own abdomen.

"Worry not, daughters" their father-in-law said. "The Lord will open your wombs soon enough."

Miryam, who without moving her head, rolled her eyes to the corners looking down on the lions. Noah pivoted away from the altar to where the animals from the ark were descending along three separate passes two by two according to their kind.

Inside, he ached at the thought of what he had to do. He nodded to Miryam. She reached down and grabbed the male lion's mane, but quickly let go. "I can't do it. Son, would you take him for me?" she said to Japheth.

"Of course, Mother." He took the lion's mane and led him away toward the passes. When they got within a hundred cubits, he released his mane, turned and headed back. The lion appeared to understand his future and watched the animals move down the passage. He laid down where Japheth had released him to wait for his mate.

It wouldn't be so easy for Noah. He and the lioness had been through too much. He walked the same path toward the passes, his feline shadow at his heels. When they reached the male lion, he stroked her head a final time. "Time for you to go as well, girl." The lioness seemed to bore right through him.

He attempted to walk away, but the lioness stayed right with him. He pointed back to the male. "Go ahead. He's waiting." She stared at him again, but continued to follow when he tried once more to leave.

Noah dropped to one knee, taking the lioness's head in his hands. "Look girl. You can't stay here. You have a responsibility waiting for you out there, just like the rest of us." The lioness pushed her head through his hands, rubbing it and the rest of her body against his chest. He stood and raised his arm toward the passes again. "Go on, girl." The lioness slowly moved away with her head down.

Please, don't look back. She did, pausing once more to look over her shoulder before continuing on. His eyes filled.

When she reached her mate, the two entered the flow of animals moving downhill.

Noah walked back blinking to clear his vision. He joined Miryam, who wiped her own tears and greeted him with a hug. "Are you all right, husband?"

His attention was drawn to where the rainbow continued to adorn the sky. "On a day like today, how could I not be?"

Man had been given another chance. The sinfulness that had begun with Adam and Eve's disobedience in the garden had been washed away by a cleansing flood. Or had it? Noah and his family still carried the stain of that first sin. Would things be any different in another sixteen hundred years? Or five thousand? Would man choose the ways of God over the pleasures of sin? And what would God do if they didn't, given the promise He had made? As Noah considered the beauty of the rainbow and what it represented, he pondered all these things in his heart.

380

EPILOGUE

But as the days of Noah were, so also will the coming of the Son of Man be.

For as in the days before the flood, they were eating and drinking, marrying and giving in marriage, until the day that Noah entered the ark.

And did not know until the flood came and took them all away, so also will the coming of the Son of Man be.

Matthew 24:37-39

God's Animal Army

For years I dreamed of telling a tale about the animals of Noah's time rising up to defend the ark against an invading enemy. But it wasn't until after I'd begun writing *Army of God* that I learned there existed in the archives of rabbinical literature a basis to support the theme of my story.

Several ancient Hebrew texts reference a confrontation where a group of people trying to break into the ark "were destroyed by the lions and other wild animals which also surrounded it."[1] And while the details of such a struggle are not recorded as part of the Biblical record, the Scriptures are rife with examples of how God called to service members of His animal kingdom. Students of the Bible will remember how He commanded armies of frogs, lice, and flies to afflict the Egyptians preceding the Exodus, shut the mouths of lions to spare His servant Daniel, and sent the great fish to keep Jonah from fleeing to Tarshish.

Now if the Lord could use those creatures, I didn't consider it heresy to suggest that the animals identified in Genesis 6 could have been organized to form an army capable of protecting the ark.

Of course, all this is mere conjecture, offered as background to support the premise of a fictional story. On the other hand, I hope you will allow your imagination to consider the possibilities this story proposes, recognizing the awesome power of God and His ability to use the whole of His creation to help exercise His will.

Blessings,
Dennis

---

1 JewishEncyclopedia.com (Tanhuma, Noah, 10; Genesis Raba xxxii. 14; "Sefer ha-Yashar," *l.c.*)

ABOUT THE AUTHOR

Dennis Bailey is a retired police detective, sex crimes investigator, and devoted researcher of the Word of God. His experience in the criminal justice system gives him a unique insight into the workings of the perverse criminal mind. Combined with his investigative and analytical skills, he uses this knowledge to search the Scriptures for personalities from which to create unforgettable characters and story lines.